HAMMER OF THE SCOTS

JEAN PLAIDY

FAWCETT CREST • NEW YORK

A Fawcett Crest Book
Published by Ballantine Books
Copyright © 1979 by Jean Plaidy

Library of Congress Catalog Card Number: 81-13789

ISBN 0-449-20046-9

This edition published by arrangement with G. P. Putnam's Sons

Manufactured in the United States of America

First Ballantine Books Edition: July 1983

Edward received the Welsh chieftains who had come to Caernarvon to pay homage to him.

"My lord," said their leader, "there will be no peace in this land until we have a prince of our own—a prince who is beyond reproach, one who can speak neither French nor English."

"And if I do will you promise me peace in Wales?"

"My lord, we promise it."

"Wait here awhile. I shall not be long."

The chieftains looked at each other in astonishment. It was victory beyond their expectations. The King was agreeing to their request. A Welsh Prince for Wales!

The King returned. They stared at him in astonishment for in his arms he carried a baby, his infant son.

"You asked me for a Prince of Wales," he cried. "Here he is. I give him to you. He has been born in your country. His character is beyond reproach. He cannot speak either French or English, and if you wish it, the first words he shall speak shall be in Welsh."

Contents

The King Comes Home	1
Exit Henry Enter Alfonso	29
The Welsh Prince and the Demoiselle	63
The Return of Joanna	97
The Sicilian Vespers	113
The Prince of Wales	133
Joanna's Marriage	145
Exodus	177
The Queen's Crosses	185
Joanna Defiant	197
The King's Bride	229
The Adventures of William Wallace	245
Betrayal	291
The Death of the King	315

THE PLANTAGENETS

HENRY II _m_ Eleanor of Aquitaine

William   Henry   Matilda   **RICHARD**   Geoffrey   Eleanor   Joanna   **JOHN** — _m.1_ Hadwisa
(died young)   _m._   _m.2_
         Berengaria   Isabella of Angoulême

HENRY III   Richard   Joan   Isabella   Eleanor
    _m._   _m._
Eleanor of Provence   Simon de Montfort

                        Henry   Simon   Guy   Almeric

EDWARD   Margaret   Beatrice   Edmund   Katharine   Eleanor
                                                      _m._
                                               Llewellyn
_m.1_ Eleanor of Castile   _m.2_ Marguerite of France   Prince of Wales

Eleanor   Joanna   Margaret   Mary   Elizabeth   **EDWARD**   Thomas   Edmund   Eleanor
   _m._   _m._   _m._   (went   _m._
                        into   1 John of Holland
Duke of   Duke of   convent)   2 Humphrey de Bohun
Bar-le-Duc   Brabant

          1 Earl of Gloucester
          2 Ralph de Monthermer

The King
Comes Home

Although the King had been dead for more than a year, the Queen still mourned him. Somewhere across the sea was her son, the new King, who must now return to claim his crown. The Queen, who had so long ruled her husband, and therefore the Court, had been prostrate with grief. She could think of nothing but that he had gone for ever—that dear kind husband who had adored her from the day she had been presented to him as his bride.

She often smiled to recall how, when their marriage had been negotiated, he had haggled over the paucity of her dowry and there had been a time when it had seemed that because of her father's poverty there would be no marriage. Yet, as soon as he had set eyes on her, such a consideration had been of no importance whatsoever, and from that moment and throughout his life he had made no secret of the fact that he considered himself the most fortunate of monarchs to have secured as his wife this dowerless daughter of an impoverished Count. It was love at first sight and had continued throughout their lives. She had ruled him and that had made for connubial bliss such as was rarely experienced in royal households. That she had attempted to rule England at the same time had brought about less happy results.

And now he was dead, and she lay alone on this magnificent royal bed in the Palace of Westminster in this splendid chamber which was the wonder of all who beheld it. The King was responsible for its beauty. Henry had loved art, literature, music and architecture. Often he had said he wished he could escape the trials of monarchy and follow those pursuits at which he would have excelled. Some of the barons had exchanged covert looks at such times implying that it would have been a good thing for the country if he had. The barons could be insolent. They had had too much power since Henry's father John had been forced to put his signature to that Magna Carta document which had thrown a shadow over their lives.

She liked to lie in bed and survey this room and recall how they had planned it together. The murals were exquisite. Henry had been a deeply religious man and had ordered that angels be painted on the ceiling. "One could lie in bed and believe one was in heaven," she had said. And, always the ardent lover, Henry had replied that when she was with him he was.

"Oh God," she said aloud, "why did You have to take him. There could have been many years left to us."

She remembered how they had come here often to watch the workmen. "It must be finished before the summer is over," Henry had said. "If you have to hire a thousand workmen a day I will have it done." "The cost, my lord..." they had whined. How impatient Henry grew at this continual harping on money! He had shrugged aside such excuses. The people would pay. Why not. The London merchants were rich and there were always the Jews. "People have no souls," he had said to her. "They are always worrying about money."

Oh yes, a good and religious man Henry had been. There was evidence of his piety in this room. Even on the window jambs texts from the Bible had been carved. Scenes from the life of Edward the Confessor were painted on the walls to bear out the fact that Henry had admired the Confessor far more than he had any of his warlike ancestors. "A noble King," he had said. "I would I could be like him." She had challenged him. She hoped, she had said, he would not have preferred to live like a monk and he did not regret his life with her which had produced their lovely children. How he had soothed her, reassured her! In his family circle he was the happiest man alive. It was only the barons who had tormented him because they were always trying to rule him, and the merchants of London who would not give of their wealth for the improvement of the country. People should pay for their privileges. His favorite motto was actually engraved on one of the gables of this room. "He who does not give what he holds, does not receive what he wishes." There was a warning to his rapacious subjects who made such a fuss about paying their taxes.

She must stop brooding on the past. The future had to be considered. But what future was there for a dowager Queen? Most of them went into convents, to live the last years of their lives in pious solitude that they might be forgiven those acts which worldly needs had imposed on them.

That was not the life for Eleanor of Provence. She was a born ruler and she would not easily relinquish her rôle.

Edward would soon be returning to claim the crown. Her beloved first son—that son of whom she and Henry had been so proud. In the meantime she was still the Queen, and she would allow no one to forget it.

When her women came in for the dressing ceremony the Queen's first question was: "How are the children?"

They knew that she would ask and they were ready, having ascertained that all was well in the royal nursery before coming to her. Her grandchildren were now her greatest concern and since the death of little Prince John she had made a point before rising of assuring herself that there was no cause for anxiety.

The children were well, she was assured.

"And Prince Henry has had a good night?"

"He said it was so, my lady."

She smiled and took the shift which was offered to her.

When she had completed her toilette and taken a little ale with oaten bread, one of the men at arms came in to tell her that there was a messenger without who wished to see her.

She received him immediately, and even as he knelt before her and she bade him rise she guessed that he came from her son Edward. She was right.

"My lady," said the messenger, "the King has sent me to

you with all speed. He is on his way to England and if the wind is fair should be with you within the next few days."

She nodded. She had been expecting such a message for many months.

As soon as she had dismissed the messenger she went to the nursery. She had insisted that while their parents were absent the children should be under her care. They alone could relieve the gloom which descended on her when she thought of her late husband. They had brought great anxieties of course. The death of little John had been an agony but then Henry had been there to help her bear it.

How they had wept and stormed at the physicians who could not save that young life. How they had clung together and comforted each other. Henry had said, "Edward is young yet. He will have many children. And thank God we have little Henry."

It had been painful to have to send the news to Edward and his wife Eleanor of the death of their son: and that it should follow almost immediately by news of that of his father was heartbreaking. Small wonder that those two who remained in the nursery were her special care, that she should ask every morning after the health of young Henry who was too frail for her comfort.

So she was now turning to the children for solace, and because she loved them so devotedly, following in the family tradition they adored her.

Her spirits were lifted when she heard their cries of joy as she entered the schoolroom. Precious children! Not only because their father was a king but because they were her grandchildren.

They were seated at the table—eight-year-old Princess Eleanor and her brother Henry who was a year younger. The Queen Mother could not look at them without overpowering emotion—half pain half pleasure. She could not forget little John—who would have been the eldest of the three. Everything had been done to keep him alive but the saints when appealed to had been cruelly deaf to royal pleas; the physicians had advised and had failed to save him. There was not a known remedy in the kingdom which had not been tried—yet John had died. It was an ill-fated name, some said. How could they have expected a child named John to prosper. All the devils in hell had been waiting to receive the child's great-grandfather who, some said, was the devil himself come back to earth for a brief spell. They had ignored such folly, but they would not give another child a name to which so much ill repute still clung.

The Princess Eleanor flung back her long yellow hair and ran to her grandmother, flinging her arms about her.

The Queen stroked the child's hair. Of course she should have demanded the respect due to her but she would rather have this spontaneous show of affection from them than cold ceremony any day. Although there was no one who demanded the respect due to her rank more strongly than she did in public, in her family circle there was nothing but softness.

She held out a hand to Henry who was coming to her more slowly than his sister.

"And how are my darlings today?"

"I am well, my lady, but Henry has been sick," said the Princess.

Quivers of alarm beset the Queen.

"Henry, my darling child . . ."

"Henry is *always* sick," said the Princess Eleanor somewhat disparagingly.

The little boy looked up at his grandmother appealingly. "I cannot help it, my lady. I try not to be."

She picked him up and held him against her. How frail he was! This was how John went. What was wrong that a man like Edward could not get healthy boys? She and Henry had produced Edward—and surely a finer specimen of manhood did not exist.

She kissed the child. "I am going to make you well," she promised.

He put his arms about her neck and returned her kiss. "Then I shall run faster than anyone. I shall hunt and take my falcon into the forest."

"Yes, my love, so you shall, and when your father comes home he will find you grown into a tall and handsome prince."

"When is he coming home?" asked the Princess.

"Now that is what I have come to tell you. He is on his way. Very soon your father and mother will be here."

The children looked very solemn. They had vague memories

of a handsome golden man, the biggest man in the world, a giant. He had been strong and put them on his shoulders and carried them around the room. Henry had been a little frightened of him. Then there was his mother—memories of a soft voice, gentle hands. Henry had cried a good deal when she went away.

"When, when . . . ?" demanded the Princess and Henry waited breathlessly for the answer.

The Queen Mother sat down and took Henry on her lap while Eleanor took a stool at grandmother's feet.

"Will our grandfather come back with him?" asked Henry.

"Of course he won't," cried the Princess scornfully. "He has gone to Heaven, hasn't he, my lady? He went up to be with our brother John. People don't come back from Heaven do they, my lady?"

"Why don't they?" asked Henry.

"Because it's so much better there of course," retorted the knowledgeable Eleanor.

"I think my grandfather would come back to see me if he knew how much I ask him to."

The Queen felt she must stop their innocent chatter or she would be unable to hold back her tears.

"Now," she said, "you must prepare yourself for the return of the King and Queen."

She told them as she had told them before—but they never tired of hearing it—how their father had gone to the Holy Land to fight for God and the Cross and their mother had gone with him and how, when he returned, because their dear grandfather was in Heaven, the people wanted to put the crown on his head.

"And you, my little love, are heir to the throne so we have to build you up to be King."

Henry looked alarmed. "When shall *I* have to be King?"

"Not until you are a man and praise God not until a long time after that. But you must be ready when the time comes. You will learn to do everything better than anyone else can . . . as your father does. You will learn to be exactly like him."

Henry remained puzzled and his grandmother kissed his forehead.

"Don't be alarmed, little one. I shall be there to show you."

"I'll show him too," said the Princess nestling close to her grandmother.

How adorable they were! And how alarmed was the Queen as she held the too-small body protectively in her arms.

"Now," she said, "we must be ready to greet the King. We shall go to Dover to meet his ship for the first thing he will wish to see when he steps on to the English soil will be his family. Oh, you are going to have a wonderful time. There will be a coronation . . . which neither of you have ever seen. Oh, I promise you life will be wonderful when King Edward comes home."

Queen Eleanor stood beside Edward her husband as the ship brought them nearer and nearer to the coast. The white cliffs were visible now and Edward was obviously clearly moved by the sight of them.

He put his arm about her and said, "Soon you will see the castle. The key to England they call it. And you'll understand why. There it stands . . . offering a menace to our enemies but a welcome to us. It is time we came home."

She agreed. She always agreed with Edward. Taller than most men so that the majority of them came only to his shoulders, with his thatch of bright fair hair which was growing a little darker as he grew older, but which when she first knew him had been almost white, with his long legs and arms and magnificent physique inherited from his Norman ancestors, and which had earned him the name of Longshanks, he was godlike. The fact that one eye drooped a little—as his father's had done, although this was not so noticeable in Edward as it had been in King Henry—gave him a slightly sinister look which she believed had stood him in good stead when he was dealing with his enemies. When Edward stood among other men he could be selected without question as the King and the leader. Edward was magnificent and she often wondered how she—little Eleanor of Castile—should have come to be the wife of such a glorious creature.

From the moment she had seen him she had been struck with wonder. Edward had been only fifteen years old then and she nearly five years younger. Much too young for marriage but royal princes and princesses were often betrothed at an early age. That was why very often the marriages did not take place. She knew that her family had not expected the English King—Edward's father—to honor his pledges. Strangely enough her mother had been betrothed to Edward's father but he had set her aside in order to marry Eleanor of Provence— now her formidable mother-in-law—and her grandmother was that Alice of France who had been sent to England to marry Richard Coeur de Lion, and about whom there had been a great scandal because when she was only a child Henry II had seduced her and kept her as his mistress for years so that she never married Coeur de Lion after all. So the English royal family had not a very good reputation for honoring its pledges. However, she was told that if the marriage did take place it would be a very grand one. She was after all only the half-sister of the King of Castile. Her father Ferdinand, the King of that country, had been old when he married her mother— who had been kept dangling with hopes of Henry of England— and he already had a son Alfonso, so the marriage with England was highly desirable.

Joanna, her mother, was determined that her daughter should not share her fate and between them she and Alfonso had arranged that the betrothal should take place at Burgos and had declared that if Edward was not at Burgos to receive the hand of his bride by a certain date the contract should be set aside.

Somewhat to the astonishment of the Castilians Edward was there at the appointed time and the youthful Eleanor, on seeing her prospective bridegroom, was so overcome with admiration that she determined to grow up quickly, and learn all she could to be worthy of him.

What festivities there had been. Surely no Infanta had ever been so fêted; and of course it was all due to the importance of the union. She had sat beside Edward and marvelled at his splendid appearance. Moreover he had been so kind to her, so tender. He explained to her that she would have to go away to complete her education and as soon as she was ready he would come to claim her.

She had been terrified of her mother-in-law—one of the handsomest women she had ever seen—and her fear had not been calmed by her mother's obvious animosity towards that lady. It was understandable, for the stately Queen from Provence had been the one who had supplanted Joanna in Henry's

affections and news of his uxurious attitude towards his Queen
had spread even to Castile.

But the young girl had immediately loved her father-in-law,
Henry King of England, who had received her so warmly and
had kept her at his side during the sumptuous feast he had
ordered should be prepared to honor her. "You are now a
member of our family," he had told her; and she had learned
that that was a privilege, not so much because it was the royal
family of England, but because there could not have been a
more loving and devoted one in the whole of the world.

The late King of England and his Queen may not have been
the wisest of rulers, but they certainly had a talent for family
life.

In her brother's court of Castile it had been pleasant enough,
but it was not until she came to England that she realized what
a warm and comforting thing family life could be. All she had
to do was obey her husband and her mother-in-law; if she did
this she would have their unbounded love.

It had been a wonderful day when she had joined her knightly
husband. So kind, so loving and oddly enough so faithful had
he been, though she soon heard rumors that while he had been
waiting for her to be old enough he had had adventures and
that many ladies of the court were only too willing to surrender
to him. Fortunately she only heard these rumors after her marriage, and then only because those who told her were struck
by his conversion to a model husband.

So she had much to be thankful for, and the only time she
had really asserted herself was when he had decided to go to
the Holy Land. By that time she had shown herself to be a
fertile wife—to the delight of the family—and in the nursery
were John, Eleanor and little Henry. Edward had been deeply
touched when she had stood before him and shown a firmness
she had never displayed before.

"Nothing should separate those whom God hath joined together," she had said, "and the way to heaven is as near, if
not nearer from Syria as from England or from Spain."

She remembered the blank amazement in Edward's face
when she had said that. He had laughed aloud and held her
firmly in his arms while he explained the discomforts and
dangers of the expedition.

"All these things," she had replied, "I know full well. They have been the subjects of our songs for more than a hundred years. I know of your great-uncle, Richard Coeur de Lion, who was a prisoner until he was rescued by the faithful Blondel. I am aware of the dangers which you will have to face and I, as your wife, would share them with you."

He had shaken his head and told her that while he loved her for making the suggestion he must forbid her to carry it out.

Edward then learned that the seemingly weak can sometimes be strong and that it is as though they give way on the smaller issues reserving the full force of their strength for the larger ones.

She was determined to accompany him and she did. For he said he would not stand in the way of such love as that and her father-in-law—good, kind, King Henry—had listened with tears in his eyes and her mother-in-law had said that had she been in her place she would have insisted in the same way. Moreover the children would be in the good hands of their grandparents.

And so they had set out.

Of course she had suffered hardship and there had been times when she had thought longingly of the cool rains of England and the comforts of the royal palaces, for it was often uncomfortable—wretchedly so—sleeping in tents, pestered by flies and other obnoxious insects. And then she had become pregnant. Perhaps when she lost her little daughter a few days after her birth she had wondered whether she had been wise; but as soon as her depression over the loss had passed she knew she could never have stayed behind because it would have meant losing Edward and to share his life was of greater importance than being with her children.

And as though there was a sign from Heaven she had almost immediately conceived and this time a healthy child was born. She called this daughter Joanna after her mother, and Joanna had the dark looks of Castile rather than those of the fair Plantagenets; and from the first she was lively and wilful and a daughter to delight in.

People began to call her Joanna of Acre because of the place of her birth, and Edward said that the child would always remind him and the world of the wonderful wife he had who had accompanied him on his crusade and borne him a child during it.

There was another reason why she knew she had been right. That was when Edward had been wounded in his tent. If she had not been there would Edward have survived? He said not. His doctors claimed the credit, of course, while admitting that some was due to him for submitting to the painful surgery. But Edward always said it was her action which had saved his life, and was Providence telling them that God liked well a brave wife who would follow her husband no matter where his duty took him.

She would never think of that occasion without living again the dreadful moment when she thought she had lost him.

Of course they were surrounded by danger and Edward was notoriously reckless. These bold knights believed it was part of the bravery expected of them to shrug aside danger or refuse to see it. Oh, how relieved she was to see those white cliffs, that impregnable fortress defiant on the cliff. Danger could come to them in England. A King could never lie easy in his bed. Her brother had told her that and again and again it had been shown to be true. But in a Holy War, when they were surrounded by the Saracens, danger was not just a possibility, it was a certainty.

For as long as she would live she would have memories of the time she had spent in an alien land. Those still, hot nights, when a sudden noise could set her starting from her bed, would never be forgotten. Constantly they had been on the alert, for how could they know what fearful fate might overtake them at any moment, when there were a thousand dangers lurking waiting to spring. Often she had longed for home, and she knew that if she had asked Edward to let her go he would have arranged to send her back. But she had known she could never leave him. What would her life have been without him? She had once come close to discovering the answer to that question. In her nightmares now she would see the dead man lying on the floor of Edward's tent, and Edward near to death stretched out on the bed. One glance had told her what had happened. The assassin had attempted to kill Edward and Edward had killed him. But in those first moments she had thought that Edward himself had been mortally wounded in the struggle.

There was evil in that land and rumors were always circulating about the Old Man of the Mountains—a fabled creature who might have existed. Who could be sure? It was said that the Old Man lived in the mountains where he had created a paradise on earth. His palace there was made of calcedony and marble, and in its gardens luscious fruits and colorful flowers grew in abundance. Men were lured to it, as mermaids were said to lure sailors to disaster. These victims lived in the Old Man's paradise for many months with beautiful women to wait on them and supply their needs. Then one day the Old Man would send for them and tell them they were banished and must go back to the world. To have experienced this life for so long had affected these men so deeply that they could not contemplate living any differently. The Old Man would tell them that they could win their way back by carrying out his orders, and these dangerous assignments usually involved the murder of someone whom the Old Man wished destroyed. Thus the Old Man created a band of assassins who killed at his will which meant that he was a power throughout the world.

Many people believed that it was the Old Man of the Mountains who had wanted Edward removed, although ostensibly his attacker came from the Emir of Joppa to whose employ he had recently come. The Emir was negotiating peace terms with Edward at that time and his messengers came frequently and freely to the camp. Thus it was that he aroused no suspicion and was allowed into Edward's tent where he was lying on his bed without his armor and vulnerable to an assassin who could easily have plunged the knife into his heart, which was of course what had been intended. But Edward was alert, and his quick eye had detected the dagger which was slipped from the sleeve and raised to strike him, and with great presence of mind he had lifted his legs and kicked aside the raised arm. The action saved his life but he had not escaped entirely and the poison blade went deep into his arm.

She shivered and Edward, standing beside her, noticed.

"You are cold?" he asked in surprise.

She shook her head. "Nay. I was thinking of the assassin."

Edward laughed softly. How often had he found her lost in thought and discovered that she was thinking of the assassin.

"It is all over, my dear. Thanks to your action my life was saved."

She shook her head. "It was the doctors who saved you. They performed that difficult operation . . ."

He winced at the memory. He had never experienced such pain. She had wanted to stay in the tent while the operation was performed but they had insisted on her leaving. Once more she had shown that sternness in her nature and they had had to carry her protesting away.

"I shall never forget how you put your mouth to that ugly wound and drained away the poison with your sweet lips," he said. "Eleanor, my Queen, if ever I forget what you did for me I deserve to lose my kingdom."

"Do not talk of losing your kingdom. It could be unlucky."

He took her hand and kissed it. "My grandfather lost his kingdom and all his possessions besides, even the crown jewels he lost in the Wash. My father came very near to losing his crown. What sort of King shall I be?"

"The best the country has ever known."

"A rash pronouncement."

"Nevertheless a true one."

"You look fierce and stern. I believe, my little Queen, that all this gentleness is a disguise. Beneath is a woman of iron strength."

"I can be strong . . . for you and our children."

He bent and kissed her. She touched his arm . . . that arm which was scarred with the wound and would never be quite well again.

"You still feel it, don't you, Edward?"

"'Tis nothing. Only a twinge."

But she knew it was not so. There were times when his face was grey with pain. She feared that all his life he would be reminded of that fearful moment in the tent when he had come face to face with death.

"God means you to rule and be a great king," she said. "I know it. You see how you are protected. Do you remember that night in Bordeaux when we were seated on the couch talking of home and the children and suddenly lightning struck. The two men who were standing close to us were both killed but we were unharmed."

"They were in the direct path of the lightning."

"Yes, but we were saved. I believe Providence diverted it so that you should live to rule your country."

He smiled at her. "You really believe that, Eleanor?"

"I am sure of it," she said fervently.

He could see that she was comforted by the thought and he reminded her of another occasion when he was playing chess and had suddenly risen from the board without any reason—and afterwards could not say why he had done so. Almost immediately part of the roof had collapsed killing his opponent at the board.

They both turned their faces to the shore and now his thoughts were going back to attempts to recover his strength after that poison had entered his body. He remembered the throbbing pain of his lacerated arm and the agony of the knife which had cut away the gangrenous flesh and the looks on the faces of those about him which showed clearly that they believed they would leave him behind in the Holy Land.

But he had survived. By God, he thought now, there had been so much to survive for. There was England which would be his. There were his wife and his children . . . his father and mother . . . the sacred family which he had been brought up to believe was the most important thing a man could possess. But there was something more important if that man was a king. He had known it for a long time. The blood of his ancestors was in him and sometimes in his dreams it was as if those great men of the past came to him. William the Conqueror, Henry the Lion of Justice, his great grandfather Henry II—those men who had cared for England, who had made it great. It was as though they said to him, "It is your turn now. You have the qualities we need. You, Edward Plantagenet, with the blood of the Normans in your veins. England—our England—has suffered through the weakness of your forebears. Rufus, Stephen, Richard—that brave man who deserted his country for a dream of glory in the Holy Land—disastrous and devilish John, and lastly—oh, yes, we know you do not like this—Henry, the father whom you loved, and who all but destroyed his country because he was so busy loving his family and pleasing an extravagant wife, who was always begging for luxury and draining away the life blood of the nation's trade. You know this, Edward. It is for you, who are one of us, to save England."

"I will," he murmured. "God help me, I will."

He had of late realized his great responsibilities. After the affair of the poisoned dagger, it occurred to him that he did wrong to place himself in danger. His father was aging and though he, Edward, had two sons in the nursery, John and Henry were but babies. His strength had been impaired; he needed the temperate climate of his own country. He had seen that there was no hope of conquering the Saracen. Others before him had failed in that endeavor. Even the great Coeur de Lion had not succeeded in capturing Jerusalem.

When an opportunity had arisen to come to terms with the great Sultan Bibars he had taken it. A truce...it was all he had achieved but that could mean a few years respite. All that blood, all that danger to achieve that! His arm was painful; it had affected his health, he believed. He ought to go home, for who knew what the barons would be plotting. They were always suspicious of his father and they hated his mother, whose extravagance Edward knew in his heart should be curbed. A nation's wealth should not be spent in banquets and fine jewels, indulging an extravagant wife and bestowing gifts and pensions on her impecunious relations. Much as he loved his father he could see clearly his shortcomings as a king.

So he had left the Holy Land and in Sicily the heart-rending news was brought to him. First the death of his eldest son John. Poor Eleanor had been stricken with grief. She had asked herself whether she had been wrong to go and leave her children, and could not stop contemplating what a bitter choice a wife had to make when it was a question of leaving her children to be with her husband.

There had followed the news of his father's death. That had prostrated him indeed. He shut himself away from everyone, even Eleanor, and brooded on the loss of the kind parent who had loved him so dearly. He remembered how in the days of his childhood they had played together; when he had been ill— and oddly enough he had not been a strong child—the King with the Queen had been at his bedside. Matters of state could be neglected; important ministers made to wait in order that a sick child might be comforted. Never to see his father again! Never to talk with him! Never to stroll arm in arm with him in the palace gardens! Never to find comfort in that bond between them which only death had been able to break.

The Sicilians had marvelled at him. He had such a short

time earlier heard of the death of his eldest son but it had not affected him as deeply as the death of his father.

"The loss of children can be repaired by the same God that gave them," he had said. "But when a man has lost a good father it is not in the course of nature for God to send him another."

And he knew of course that he must go home. He must comfort his sorrowing mother, for he guessed how she would take this bereavement. The death of his father had aged him, sobered him, set him looking back and thinking of the death of his great-grandfather, Henry II, who would be judged one of England's most worthy kings and he thought of how he had died, deserted by his sons, sadly aware of it, and hated by his wife—in fact a lonely old man, friendless, and with few to wait at his bedside and offer him comfort. Yet he was a King who had done much for England. And that other Henry, Edward's beloved father, who had brought the crown into danger and indeed had come near to losing it through men such as Simon de Montfort, had died mourned and regretted to such an extent that his children and his wife would be prostrate with grief and would keep his memory green for ever. Ironic, thought Edward, and wondered what his own fate would be. But it was not a matter of choice. Why should not a man be a good king and a good father? He knew that his Eleanor would stand beside him; she would not attempt to rule him as his mother had ruled his father. He loved his mother dearly but that did not mean to say that he did not realize her faults. Now that he was King he would have to curb her extravagance. He was not going to run into trouble with the barons as his father had done.

In a sudden rush of affection he took his wife's hand and pressed it as they stood on the boat deck watching the white cliffs come closer.

From the moment of his father's death he had become the King, but he had not after all hastened home. He had better work to do on the Continent. This was not a time to indulge his grief but to consolidate his position. He visited the all-important Pope to ensure good relations with Rome; then he and Eleanor stayed awhile with her family in Castile, and then they came to Paris where he was entertained by the French King, Philip III, and Philip's mother who was Edward's Aunt Marguerite; he had even met the Count of Flanders at Montreuil and settled a dispute which had stopped the export of English wool to Flanders.

He had made good use of his time and behaved he believed in a kingly manner by setting matters of state before his inclinations.

Now the Queen had turned to him and she said, "Soon we must embark."

"It is a new life beginning for us," he replied. "When we step on to English soil again it will be as King and Queen."

"I wonder if the children will be there. Oh, Edward, our own babies and we may not recognize them."

There were tears in her eyes and he knew that she was thinking of Baby Joanna. He said gently, "You must not fret. It is not for long. She will come back to us."

"I should never have begged you to allow it," she said.

"Think of your mother's delight."

"I try to. Oh I must not be selfish. I have my two darlings waiting for me. It should have been three."

"You must not brood on that. Children die. But they can be replaced. We'll have more. I promise you a round dozen."

"I pray to God that it may be so. But I cannot forget Joanna."

It was natural that her mother should have doted on the child. Joanna had been bright and lively from her very youngest days. It was strange how people were particularly drawn to their namesakes. So it had been with Eleanor's mother. She had adored the baby from the moment she had seen her. She had carried her off to her own apartments and would not relinquish her to her nurses or to her mother; and when it had been time for Edward and Eleanor to leave the Castilian Court, she had become so desolate declaring that when they had gone, taking the baby with them, she would have nothing to live for. What could a loving daughter do? Poor Eleanor, her tender heart had been deeply touched by her mother's lonely state. "We owe her something," she had said to Edward. "Your father made her waste her youth when he was pretending he would marry her. And afterwards he jilted her for the sake of your mother, and no one asked for her hand until my father came along. I was the only child there was time for then, and I am married and gone far away from her."

Edward understood. Poor Eleanor, she was called upon once more to make one of those decisions which fall to people such as she was. A selfish woman would have had no difficulty. She would simply have done what she wanted. But Eleanor must always do what was right for others before she considered herself.

So they had left baby Joanna with Eleanor's mother who seized the child hungrily and had all but hidden her away lest her parents should change their minds.

And now here they were—home in England, baby Joanna left behind in Castile.

But on the shore the children whom they had left in England were waiting for them.

There was a shout of joy as the King stepped ashore, quickly followed by his Queen.

"Long live the King." The loyal cries went up.

Edward stood for a moment, his wife beside him, listening to their cheers.

Then he saw his mother, erect, her outstanding beauty scarcely impaired at all by the years and her grief. She was holding two children by the hand and the Queen's eyes went immediately to them. She gave a little cry and held out her arms.

They were running to her—Princess Eleanor, the daughter who had been named after her, and the little boy, Prince Henry, pale and breathless.

"My darlings." The Queen had knelt down, her arms about them, tears in her eyes.

"My lady," cried the Princess, "you are home at last. It is years and years ago that you went away..."

She could only hold them to her.

"Henry, my darling..." Oh God, she thought. How pale he is! He is too small, too frail...

Then Edward had picked up his son. He set him on his shoulder. He held his daughter close to him and stood there.

A touching sight. This great King who towered above his subjects, dismissing ceremony, in that profound emotion engendered by his reunion with his family.

The Queen—more beautiful than they remembered—standing there beside him. A happy omen. A King come home. Old Henry was gone; his extravagant wife was relegated to the background. King Edward had come into his own.

"Long live the King."

Everyone who witnessed that affecting scene was sure that it was a good augury for England.

Edward was proud as he rode up the steep hill to the castle keep. The road was lined with cheering subjects who were determined to let him know how pleased they were that he had returned, and in their cheers was the hope that in him they had a strong king who would set right all that had gone wrong during the mismanagement of the previous reigns.

Dover had been aptly named by the early Britons Dvfyrrha, meaning the steep place. And what an inspiring sight it was to look down on that magnificent harbor and out to sea where he knew that on fine days the coast of France could be seen. Part of the castle was the work of the Romans and beside it was the ancient Pharos to remind people of their occupation. The castle was three hundred feet above sea level—perfectly placed for defense. No wonder it was called the Key to England.

Here his ancestors had lived. The Conqueror had taken possession of it immediately after the Battle of Hastings and Edward's great grandfather, Henry II, had rebuilt the keep. Oh yes, it was undoubtedly a great moment when he passed into the castle.

The Queen was beside him but she had eyes only for her children, and was longing to discuss the state of Henry's health with her mother-in-law.

There was a chill in the castle in spite of the fact that it was August. She, who had spent so long in warmer climates, noticed it, and her first reaction was to wonder whether Henry suffered from this cold.

In their apartments Edward turned to her.

"Home at last, my love," he said. "I trust it will be long before we have to go on our travels again."

She nodded. A forlorn hope. When had any King of England been allowed to live peacefully in England?

The Queen Mother came to them. Instinctively the Queen knew that her mother-in-law was eager to assert her power and to let them know that she was as important now as she had been when her husband was alive.

"What joy it is to have you home," she cried. "The loyalty of the people was heart-warming."

Edward looked at his mother a little cynically. There had

been no cheers for her and their absence had been rather noticeable at times.

"They are so happy to have you home and so they should
be." Her eyes glistened. She was proud of having produced
such a kingly son. "Why, Edward," she went on, "had I not
seen you before, I should have known that you were the King.
You stand out among all men."

His wife nodded in agreement.

"We must celebrate your return," went on the Queen Mother.
"There must be a banquet in Westminster and then we shall
have to prepare for the coronation."

"We will dispense with the banquet, my lady," said the
King. "The coronation will be costly enough."

"Dear Edward, you must not forget you are now the King.
You must act in a kingly fashion."

"That I intend to do. That is why I do not propose to squander
the exchequer."

The Queen Mother laughed aloud. "Your father would have
given a most splendid feast," she said reproachfully.

"I have no doubt. But I must go my own way. The coronation will be grand. The people expect that, and will be ready
to pay for it. But there is no need to involve them in more
expense than is necessary."

The Queen Mother was sober. "Why, my son, what has
happened to you during your travels? Your father..."

"It distresses me to hear his name mentioned," said Edward.
"I was never so unhappy as when I heard the news, but I tell
you this, my lady: there will be no wasting of money on feasts.
We shall concentrate at once on the coronation."

His wife was proud of him. He was indeed kingly. He could
even subdue his formidable mother. The Queen Mother lifted
her shoulders helplessly.

"The London merchants are rich. The Jews still flourish.
They could easily be taxed..."

"New taxes so early in a reign could tend to make a king
very unpopular," said Edward. "I want to keep the people with
me."

He bowed to his wife and his mother and left the chamber.
The Queen Mother smiled lightly at the Queen.

"He is anxious to show us he is the King," was her comment.
The Queen, who could be bold where her loved ones and

her duty were concerned, retorted, "He *is* the King, Madam, and determined to rule well."

"His father never denied me anything. He always saw from my point of view."

"Edward will see from his own point of view."

"Of course he has been away so long. Perhaps it will be different when he has grown used to us all again."

The Queen was silent for a few moments and then she said, "I am concerned about Henry."

The Queen Mother's face was immediately grave.

"He is not strong," she admitted.

"I was frightened when I saw him. I thought of little John . . ."

"I have watched him constantly. I have seen that he eats when he should. My dear daughter, when he has been ill I have been at his bedside night and day."

The Queen took the Queen Mother's hand and pressed it warmly. "I know well how much you love him."

"The dear, *dear* child. He has been the center of my life since the King went."

"I know it. But he is too thin. Too frail. I could have wept when I saw him."

"I feared it. The journey to Dover tired him."

"Perhaps he should not have made it."

"I feared to leave him behind. I do not think it is good for him to be aware of his weakness. It worries him and he tries to keep up with others."

"Was it so with little John?"

The Queen Mother nodded.

"Oh, I could not bear it if . . ."

The Queen Mother said, "We must do everything that we can without calling attention to his weakness. I have had wax images of him burned at the shrines."

"And no good came of it?" asked the Queen.

"Sometimes he seemed to be stronger for a few days and then he was ill again."

"Perhaps we should hire some poor widows to perform vigils for his health."

"I fear that would call attention to his state."

The Queen nodded. And the Queen Mother, all softness because the welfare of the family was in question, said gently, "Let us hope that now his mother is home he will grow out of his weakness. You know I had my anxious moments with Edward. I remember a time when we went to Beaulieu Abbey for the dedication of a church. He had a cough which worried me and during the ceremony he developed a fever. I insisted on keeping him at the Abbey and staying to nurse him. Oh what a pother there was! A woman sleeping in the Abbey! It was unheard of. It was offending the laws of God they said. I was ready to set aside the laws of God for my son I tell you. And stay I did and nurse him I did. I tell you this, my daughter, because you have only to look at Edward today. Can you ever believe that he was anything but a healthy child?"

"You comfort me," said the Queen.

"Let us hope that Henry will grow out of his delicacy as his father grew out of his."

"I intend to do everything possible to bring that about."

"You can depend on me to stand beside you."

The Queen felt drawn towards her mother-in-law. It was true that the latter was extravagant and she understood through Edward that she had been responsible for much of King Henry's unpopularity; but she was a woman whose unswerving loyalty to her family never wavered.

Whatever else she was, Eleanor of Provence gave the utmost devotion to her family.

The royal party must not linger at Dover. They must make their way to London or the Londoners would be displeased. As Edward remarked to the Queen, he could not afford to be unpopular in the capital. He had seen what that had done to his parents. There was a little tightening of his lips and the Queen was proud and pleased that he was determined not to allow his mother to rule him. She had been a little afraid that this might be the case, for she had seen the power of that determined woman and she knew full well that a strong bond of affection existed between them. But no, Edward was not going to forget he was the King and he would be the sole ruler of his country.

It was a joyful procession all along the route. Edward knew he must not pass too hurriedly. All his loyal subjects wished to see him and a great deal depended on first impressions. He must show them all—even the humblest—that he had their welfare at heart. At this time their loyalty was his and he must keep it so; he must remember that though he was the undoubted son and heir of the late King, the best of all claims to the throne came through the will of the people. That was a lesson he had learned through his father, whose example had taught him how a king should not behave towards his subjects. It seemed strange to him that loving his parents as he did he could see their faults so clearly.

It was a good plan to have the children riding with them. There was nothing that appealed to humble people like children. He could see too that they liked the Queen. It was to her advantage that they had so disliked the previous one that they were inclined to think any predecessor was preferable; but there was something about Eleanor's gentle demeanor and her obvious care of her children which entirely won their hearts.

The scene was set fair. He was sure of it. And it was for them to keep it thus.

Everywhere there were cheers and flowers strewn in their paths.

"Long live the King! Long live the Queen." It was music in his ears.

He could not suppress a sly smile when his mother passed in the procession and an almost sullen silence fell on the crowd. Dear lady, he thought indulgently, she could never see that the people blamed her for everything that had gone wrong because she would bring her poor relations into the country. She could so easily have won their approval. But she simply had not bothered to do so. He loved her tenderly. He remembered her maternal care for him and her passionate devotion to her family; yet at the same time his reason had always told him that she had brought her unpopularity on herself. He remembered that time when the Londoners had pelted the barge, in which she was trying to escape, with refuse and heavy stones in the hope of drowning her. None of the family had ever forgiven the Londoners for that; and yet he understood their reasons. Beloved mother, she was so clever in so many ways, but she could never understand that kings and queens must have the approval of their subjects if they are going to stay safe on the throne.

They halted at the Castle of Tonbridge where Gilbert de Clare, called the Red on account of the color of his hair, was waiting to receive the royal party and declare his fealty to the King.

Edward welcomed this, for Gilbert the Red was a good man to have on his side. A forthright man, Gilbert had never been afraid to make his opinion known, and therefore to be welcomed by him added to that sense of security which the greetings of the people had given Edward.

The Queen Mother was less pleased. She had thought they should not have stayed at Tonbridge. "There is a man who cannot be trusted," she had said to Edward. "He was not a good friend to your father. Now is the time to show men like Gilbert de Clare that it will go ill with them if they are disloyal to their King."

"My lady mother," said Edward courteously, "I know this man's mind. He will be on whatever side he wishes and nothing would change that. If he dislikes my deeds he will be against me as he was against my father. He has now sworn fealty to me, which means that he is ready to support me."

"Providing he gets his way."

"'Tis not his way or my way, it is a matter of how the country is governed."

"And you will let him have a say in that and tell you what to do?"

"Certainly he and the other barons must have a say. That is the way the people wish it to be. But rest assured, dear lady, that it shall be my will that is done—though it may be I have to persuade my subjects to accept it."

"They should obey unquestioningly."

"That is something they have never done. A king cannot prevent the humblest peasant from questioning if only in his mind."

"Peasants, dear son, do not possess minds."

"Ah, dear mother, let us not make the mistake of underestimating the people. We have seen what disastrous effects that can have."

"Your father never considered the people."

"There is truth in that and let us face it—he came near to losing his crown."

"Oh, how can you speak of your father thus!"

He put his arm about her. "We loved him dearly," he said, "but our love did not prevent the disasters of civil war. I am determined that that shall never happen in my reign. This is as strong an arm as ever wielded a sword, dear mother, but my heart and my brain will tell me when it must sheath that sword."

The Queen Mother looked at her son with trepidation. She felt that her rule was coming to an end.

There was feasting fitting for the occasion in the great hall at Tonbridge. Gilbert de Clare sat beside the King and expressed his pleasure in his return. This was an honest expression of his feelings, for Gilbert was not a man for pretense. Like all sensible men, he wanted to see the country at peace with itself, for only then could prosperity come. He was three or four years younger than Edward and had become the most powerful of the barons. There had been a time when he had supported Simon de Montfort against the royal party, but he was a man who would not hesitate to change sides.

He would always prefer to support the King. Moreover there was a family connection. Twenty years before when the King's half-brothers and sisters had invaded the country to see what advantages they could get, Henry had decided that he would be a good husband for his kinswoman, Alice of Angoulême. Gilbert had been not quite ten years old at the time and had had no say in the matter. The marriage had been quite unsatisfactory.

Now as they drank wine together and listened to the minstrels who sang for the pleasure of the company Gilbert contemplated the happiness of the King and his Queen and his eyes grew a little wistful—a fact which was not lost on the King.

"I trust we shall now enjoy a period of peace," said Gilbert. "The barons are hopeful."

"I shall do my best to see that their hopes are fulfilled, for I believe they want the prosperity of the country as much as I do myself."

"It is what the barons have always wished for, my lord."

A reminder of Gilbert's honesty. He was not going to pretend to please the King and pander to some mistaken notion that the dead must be praised and that Henry was a saint. Henry had brought his troubles on himself and as he was King those were the country's troubles. Gilbert implied that the barons would be behind the new King while the new King acted wisely and for the good of his country.

As that was exactly what Edward intended to do he did not resent Gilbert's attitude.

"This is indeed a happy augury," went on Gilbert. "You have your crusade behind you. The people like a crusader king as long as his crusade is in the past and they cannot be taxed to pay for it while their king goes off and leaves his country in hands other than his own. So they like a crusader king who has proved himself in advance to be a great warrior and if that king has a loving wife and a family it pleases them. That is a great boon to a man."

"Forgive me, my friend," said the King, "but do I sense that you are not happy on that score?"

"I will tell you this, my lord: if I could rid myself of Alice and take another wife, gladly would I do so. She comes from an overbearing family. Your grandmother was a wild woman, sire, and when she was Queen of England had power even over King John for long after their marriage, but when she married Hugh de Lusignan she bred a race of harpies."

Edward smiled faintly. Gilbert's wife, Alice of Angoulême, was the niece of Alice of Lusignan who was Henry III's half-sister.

"You speak of my family, sir."

"And my own since I married into it. But truth is truth, and you, my lord, will be the first to recognize it as such."

"So you would divorce your wife and the Pope is proving intransigent, I'll swear."

"You have guessed it. How easy it is to be trapped into marriage. I was a boy of ten. What can a boy of that age do but obey the wishes of his elders, and there he is saddled with a wife for the rest of his life."

Edward laughed. His wife had been chosen for him, and yet had he had a chance to choose from the whole world he would have picked her.

He was lucky. He must be sympathetic with poor Gilbert.

"Best of good fortune," he said, "and when you are free, Gilbert, we'll find a good wife for you."

"With my lord's permission I will find my own," was the reply.

It was a very pleasant sojourn at Tonbridge. Gilbert, Earl of Gloucester, and the most powerful man in the country under the King, was with him.

Edward expressed his gratitude for the hospitality which had been given him; he implied his pleasure in the Earl's support, while he was determined to keep a watch lest it should be diverted.

After Tonbridge, Reigate, where John de Warenne was waiting to receive the party.

Grandson of the great William Marshal and therefore belonging to one of the richest families in the country, as a boy John de Warenne had been one of the marriage bargains of the day; and Henry III had arranged a marriage for him with his half-sister, Alice de Lusignan, who was the aunt of Gilbert Clare's wife. To the King it had seemed an ideal arrangement for, family man that he was, he was eager to settle his impecunious relations as comfortably as he could. Edward had never had any reason to doubt the loyalty of this man who was so close to him through his family ties.

It was a very pleasant stay therefore at Reigate, marred only by the increasing fears of the Queen for young Henry.

"It breaks my heart to see how he tries to hide his weakness," she told Edward when, after the long day's meeting and festivities, they were alone together. "I know the child is far from well. He is so easily fatigued. Your mother said that little John was the same."

"Henry is young yet, my love. He will grow out of it."

"But we lost little John."

"We were not here then."

"Your mother would stand over him like a watch dog. She is devoted to the children, however..." The Queen stopped short, but Edward laid a hand gently on her shoulder and smiled at her.

"I think we understand my mother," he said. "There was never one more devoted to her family. Being clever and beautiful and delighting my father she has grown used to having her own way. She will unlearn..."

But the Queen was uneasy and she had passed on that anxiety to Edward. Their daughter Eleanor was in fine good health. So had Joanna been when they left her in Castile; and Joanna could have been said to have made a rather difficult entry into the world. Acre was not the most temperate place to make one's appearance and there had been a considerable lack of comfort. Yet she had bloomed from the start. The other little one had died, but that may have been due to the hardships her mother had suffered before her birth. No, they could get healthy children. Eleanor was unduly disturbed because of John's death and her conscience continued to trouble her, because she had been torn between leaving her children and her husband.

The next day the Queen continued downcast although she tried to hide her feelings for she knew how her fears disturbed her husband.

But the King was aware of this, and he took her into the chapel at Reigate and summoning the priest told him of the Queen's anxiety.

"There is a shrine close by I believe," said the King. "Let a wax image be made of my son and there burned in oil before the image of the saint. It may be that he will petition God and the Holy Virgin for his safety."

The priest bowed and said it should be done, for it was a much practiced custom to burn in oil a wax figure representing someone who needed special intercession with Heaven.

"Now," said Edward firmly, "it is in the hands of the saints and do you doubt, my love, that they will turn deaf ears to the prayers of a mother as loving as yourself."

He was so good to her, said the Queen. And she could almost believe that she had been foolishly concerned, but her little Henry was such a dear child and she did so long to see him as full of health as his sister was.

"That will come, I promise you," said Edward.

And soon after they left Reigate for London.

Exit Henry
Enter Alfonso

The whole country seemed to be converging on London for the coronation and Edward was sure that this was one of those occasions when it would be unwise to spare expense. The Queen Mother was in her element. She would have liked to take over all the arrangements and order what was to be done as she had during her husband's lifetime.

Instead she must content herself with gathering together her family. It was wonderful to know that her daughter Margaret was on her way from Scotland and Beatrice, her other daughter, with her husband, John of Bretagne, would also be present. Then there was her son, Edmund, Earl of Lancaster, who would be with them. In fact every one of her living children would be there. If only her husband were alive she would need nothing more to make her completely happy.

Margaret was her very favorite daughter. Perhaps because when she was young she had suffered such anxieties about her and her strong motherly instincts had been called forth in all their fury because her darling daughter was being ill-treated by

those barbarous Scots. Often now she thought of how the child
had gone to Scotland, and how she had wept at the parting and
clung to her mother and implored to be allowed to stay with
her for ever. But they had had to send her and she and Henry
had wept together and suffered for their child. And when they
had heard that she was being kept a prisoner in that grim
Edinburgh Castle and given nothing to eat but their loathesome
oaten cakes and a messy mixture they called porridge, Henry,
incited by his wife, had been ready to go to war even if it
meant defying the barons and tearing up Magna Carta and
throwing it in their faces, which, thought the Queen, was the
best thing that could happen to that horrible document. They
had gone to Scotland; they had rescued their daughter, and she
was now reunited with her husband, Alexander, who at that
time had been little more than a child himself. And mercy of
mercies Margaret was now happy. Yes, she and Alexander
were devoted to each other and they had three beautiful children
to bless their union. The Queen Mother hoped they would be
as happy as she and Henry had been. Margaret was of a gentler
temperament than her mother and like the entire family she
was indulgent of that overbearing maternal figure. She had a
daughter who was very dear to the Queen Mother because the
child had been born at Windsor, during that period when Margaret had visited her family and contrived to stay until it was
difficult for her in her condition to go back to Scotland. The
Scots were not too pleased that their Queen's eldest child should
be born out of Scotland. That it was but a daughter perhaps
placated them a little. That child, Margaret after her mother,
was now thirteen years old and she had inherited her mother's
beauty. Moreover Margaret had given birth to a son Alexander
three years after Margaret's birth—a beautiful boy and heir to
the Scottish throne—and four years ago little David had been
born.

How wonderful it would be to have all the grandchildren
around so that she could pamper them a little and make sure
that they loved their grandmother and at the same time assure
herself that their parents were bringing them up in a manner
of which she would approve. She loved to admonish them
tenderly and they all listened to her and accepted her superior
wisdom. Happy days were ahead in spite of her great bereavement.

Then there was Beatrice, her second daughter, who was greatly loved, the wife of John, Earl of Bretagne, a husband who adored her, and they had five beautiful children; Beatrice had accompanied her husband on the crusade and had been with Queen Eleanor at Acre when Joanna had been born so the two had become as sisters having shared the discomforts of the nomad life while at the same time they had condoled with each other over the terrible choice they had had to make whether to leave their children or their husbands. Now they would all be united; and there would be more grandchildren for the Queen Mother to take under her wing.

Edmund would also be there—her dear son, the Earl of Lancaster. He was not as popular with the people as his brother Edward was. Naturally Edward was the King and he had those spectacular good looks. Edward was all Plantagenet—the golden young man with the long limbs of the Normans. People only had to look at him to realize that he was descended from the Conqueror. The English liked strong kings, or they did when they were dead. They had groaned under the harsh laws of the Conqueror, his son, Henry I, and his great grandson, Henry II, while these kings lived, but when they were dead harshness was called justice, and they were revered. Even so early it seemed apparent that Edward would be a strong king. The Queen Mother's lips turned out at the corners when she considered that. Edward had shown clearly that he was not going to take her advice. True he listened to it gravely and sometimes implied that he would follow it; then he went away and did exactly what he wanted to.

Edmund was less tall, less blond, more Provençal than Norman. He suffered from a slight curvature of the spine which it had been impossible to disguise and it had in due course given his enemies the opportunity to call him Crouchback. How angry she had been about that, especially so since there was nothing she could do about it. She found frustration more maddening than anything else.

It had been a matter for congratulation when he had married Aveline de Fortibus, heiress of the Earl of Albemarle, because the marriage should have brought great wealth into the family and shortage of money was a constant complaint. Alas, Aveline had died before she could inherit the fortune and soon afterwards Edmund had taken the cross and gone with his brother to Palestine.

"We must find a new wife for Edmund," she thought; and her energetic mind scoured the ranks of the wealthy.

The greatest joy of all was being with Margaret, and what a pleasure it had been to see her ride into the capital with her husband and her children, for Margaret's entourage was grander than any. A lesson to Edward, thought the Queen Mother. Was he going to allow the King of Scots to outshine him?

She could not wait to carry Margaret off somewhere where they could be alone. There she embraced this most loved of her children—perhaps in the past she had been inclined to favor Edward. That was natural because he was the eldest and the son, but a mother could be closer to a daughter, and ever since Margaret's experiences in Scotland when she had been a child bride, the young Queen of Scotland had had the notion that her parents were omnipotent and nothing could be more delightful than such a notion to Eleanor of Provence.

She took her daughter into her arms and examined her closely. Margaret looked a little too delicate for her mother's comfort.

"My dearest," said the Queen Mother, "do you still find the climate harsh?"

"I grow accustomed to it. The children enjoy it."

"Your father was constantly worrying about you. Whenever he saw the snow he would say, 'I wonder what is happening north of the Border and if our darling child is suffering from the cold.'"

"My dear lady mother, you always worried too much about us."

"I could never be completely happy unless I knew you were all well and safe, and I shall never forget that dreadful time."

"It is all in the past. Alexander is indeed the King now. None would dare cross him."

"And he is a good husband to you, my darling."

"None could be better. He is as near to my dearest father as anyone could be."

"He was incomparable. Margaret, I cannot describe to you how I suffer."

"I know, I know. But he would not wish us to brood. He would be happy that Edward is such a fine man and that the people are with him as they never were . . ."

"With your father? Oh they were wicked to him. They have been so mean . . . so parsimonious . . ."

"Let us rejoice, Mother, that they seem to have forgotten their grievances. Let us hope that there will be no more uprising of the barons. People will always be ready to remember Simon de Montfort."

"That traitor!"

"He opposed our father, my lady, but I do not think he ever meant to be a traitor. And his death at Evesham was . . . terrible. I must tell you of something strange that happened. Not long before I received tidings of Edward's return and that we were to come south for the coronation, we were at Kinchleven on the banks of the Tay. We were in the banqueting hall, the company talking, as such companies do, of their deeds and adventures, but I was melancholy as I have been since news of my father's death and I had the wish to escape from their laughter and light chatter.

"Then the name of Simon de Montfort was mentioned and one of my knights who had sometime since come from England talked of the battle of Evesham at which he had fought, and he boasted that he had struck the first blow which had killed de Montfort. I was weary of all the talk and I rose from the table and said that I would take a walk along by the river. My attendants came with me and among them was this knight. They saw that I was depressed for this talk of Simon de Montfort had reminded me of my father, and I kept thinking of that dreadful day when the news had come to me of his death. I fell into such melancholy that one of my women said they should play games to raise my spirits. So they did. The men wrestled together and there were contests of leaping and jumping and climbing the trees. Their antics were funny and I found myself laughing. The knight who had brought up the subject of Simon de Montfort was the winner of most of the sports, and one of my women said that I should bestow on him a mark of approval so I said I would give him my glove. They wanted a ceremony. He was to come and take it from me. As he stood beside me he looked down at his hands which were mudstained and he bowed low and said, 'Gracious lady, I could not touch your hand in this state. Give me permission to go to the river and wash my hands.' I granted that permission. It was a sort of mock ceremony, you see. And when he bent over to wash his hands I signed to one of my women to push him into the river. This she did and there was much laughter. The Knight turned to smile with us. 'What care I?' he cried. 'I can swim.' Then he began to show us all that he could be as skilled in the water as on land, and he cut all sorts of graceful figures as he moved away from the bank. We applauded and I called out that he was asking for further trophies. Then suddenly something happened. It was as though the waters were stirred by some invisible hand to form a whirlpool. He gave a wild cry and disappeared. His little page must have thought his master was calling for him and he ran down to the river and went in, swimming towards the spot where his master had disappeared. In a moment he too was out of sight.

"It is a game, I said. Our clever knight is trying to show us how clever he is.

"We waited, half laughing, expecting every second to see him rise and swim for the shore with his little page. It took us some time to realize that we should never see them again and to realize that our innocent frolic had ended in tragedy. We never discovered the body of the knight nor that of his page."

"My dear child, what a dreadful story! What was this whirlpool which suddenly appeared in the river?"

"That we did not know, my lady. But I tell you this to let you know how the people—even of Scotland—remember Simon de Montfort. They said that Heaven was angry. That de Montfort was a saint and this was Heaven's revenge on this knight because he had boasted of his part in the murder."

"There will always be those to attach significance in these matters. De Montfort was no saint. He was a traitor who rose against your father. That is something for which I shall never forgive him."

"I was always fond of my Aunt Eleanor. I think she loved him dearly."

"I remember that marriage well. Conducted in secrecy. Your father was furious when he discovered that Simon de Montfort had married his sister."

"But he knew of the wedding. He attended it."

"Only because Simon had seduced your aunt and he thought it best in the circumstances."

Margaret looked at her mother. That was not true, of course. King Henry had consented to the marriage because his sister had persuaded him into it, and afterwards; when he saw what a storm it aroused, he had pretended it was because Simon had seduced her first.

But her mother had always believed what she wanted to and contradiction on such matters displeased her.

"I wonder where they are now?" she asked.

"Who? The de Montforts? In exile in France, I believe. They had better not try to come back here."

"You mean Simon's wife and daughter? What of her sons?"

"Young Simon is dead. He deserved to die the traitor's death but God took him instead. He was guilty of murder with his brother Guy who is the worst of them all. You know how they most brutally murdered your cousin, Henry of Cornwall, in a church at Viterbo. Oh, that was wicked. It broke your uncle Richard's heart. He adored Henry and Henry was a good man, faithful and loyal to your father and to your brother Edward."

"I know, my lady. He and Edward were brought up together—with the de Montfort boys. I remember seeing them together in the days before my marriage."

"There has been much tragedy in our family, Margaret."

"I know, my lady. But now Edward is home and the people love him. Perhaps we shall live peacefully."

"There is perpetual trouble. I shall not feel happy while these de Montforts live."

"I am sorry to have reminded you of them."

"Saints indeed! There was never one less saintly than Simon de Montfort."

"It is a pity he was killed so brutally."

"It was in battle. His side would have done the same to your father or Edward had they been the victors."

"I suppose Guy and the young Simon thought they were avenging him. It is understandable. It would be best if it could all be forgotten."

"My dearest Margaret, you were always the peacemaker. I should like to hear that the de Montforts were all dead. I like not to remember that Guy still lives and his brother Almeric too. *He* is with his mother, I believe, and the girl Eleanor. They call her the Demoiselle. It is a good idea. There are too many Eleanors in our family."

"'Tis true, lady. There is yourself and now Edward's wife and Edward's daughter and our aunt who married de Montfort and de Montfort's daughter . . . I am so pleased I called *my* daughter Margaret."

"Which, my love, means that she can so easily be confused with her mother."

"I know, but Alexander wanted the name."

The Queen Mother took her daughter's face in her hands and kissed it. "I know. He loves you so well, and would have your daughter named for you. I'll warrant he tells himself she is growing up exactly like you."

"How did you guess?"

The Queen Mother laughed happily. Her anger, aroused by the deference to the de Montforts, had evaporated.

"Because, my dearest, he has the look of a happy husband. Now tell me how did you think Beatrice was looking?"

"Very well."

"She has given me five little grandchildren. I am very proud of her."

"I am sorry, dear mother, that I have fallen short of that number."

"My dearest child, all I ask of you is that you are happy. You have my three little darlings and that contents me well. I'll warrant Beatrice is with Edward's wife. I hear they became great friends in Acre."

"Edward is fortunate in his Queen, my lady, She seems so gentle and devoted to him."

"She is a good wife. She thinks he is the most wonderful being on earth. She does exactly as he says all the time. I was never like that."

"I am sure Edward appreciates it."

"Your father appreciated me and yet I always had my own opinions."

"Dearest lady mother, you cannot expect everyone to be like you."

The Queen Mother laughed.

She felt she was nearer happiness than she had been since Henry's death.

"Let us go and find Beatrice," she said. "There is so much I want to say to her. I have you so rarely to myself that I grudge every moment that is spent away from me."

Dear mother, thought Margaret, she cannot bear any of us to care for anyone more than we care for her.

There was excitement throughout the capital which extended to the whole of the country. A king was about to be crowned and soothsayers declared that a new age of prosperity was coming to the country.

The last two reigns had been uneasy ones—the first disastrous and the second slightly less so. Two weak kings had governed the country, now a strong man had come, a man who looked like a king, who acted like a king and having just returned from a campaign to the Holy Land would have the seal of God's approval on him.

Great days were in store for England.

Stories were told throughout the countryside of his strength and prowess. His Queen was a good and virtuous woman. The account of how she had sucked the poison from his wound was repeated. They forgot that she came from a foreign land and that they had laughed at her followers when she had first arrived in the country. Little dark people whom they said resembled monkeys. Now she had grown into a beautiful woman. She had cast away her foreign manners. She was English and a fitting wife for the great King.

Edward had said that there should be hospitality for all at his coronation. He wanted the people to know that he was going to introduce just laws, that he was determined to make his country prosperous. Already he had settled that irritating matter of the wool with the foreign traders. He believed that the people should be allowed to carry on their peaceful trades and only be asked for money when the country needed it.

For once though there should be a lavish spectacle. The London merchants were willing to pay to see their King ceremoniously crowned. It was right that there should be celebrations for this was the beginning of a new era.

Wooden buildings were erected in the palace yards. On these food was going to be cooked, for none should go empty on this great day. There were no roofs on these buildings; they were open to the sky that the smoke of the fires should escape. Here, announced Edward, food would be served to all those who came to the city—no matter who. Men of the country would eat with London merchants, and apprentices and anyone could eat as the King's guest—rich and poor alike, wealthy tradesmen and beggars. For fourteen days there should be this feasting. And on the day of the coronation the conduits and the fountains should flow with red and white wine.

Everyone must be aware that this was a time for rejoicing.

There was no murmur from the people. This was a different sort of celebration from those arranged by the new King's father. Henry had given lavish banquets it was true, but they had always been for his friends and relations. But at King Edward's table there would be just the good plain food which was served to his people. He wanted them to know that he was not a man to set great store by feasting and drinking and the wearing of fine clothes. His pleasure would be in a prosperous land and a happy people.

Perhaps he was subtly saying that they would find him different from his father. If he was, this was just what his people wanted to hear.

The Archbishop of Canterbury, Robert Kilwardby, had arrived at Westminster to officiate at the coronation. Edward considered that he was fortunate in his premier archbishop. It was not that he had any great affection for him. Far from it. They had nothing in common. But Kilwardby, unlike many of his predecessors, was not a man to attempt to interfere in state matters. Something of a pedant and a scholar, he was more likely to be concerned with points of grammar than the country's policies. A scholar who had taught for many years in Paris as a master of arts, one time prior of the Dominicans, he was not a man who saw himself as rival ruler to the king.

"Let us thank God for our Archbishop," said Edward to his Queen.

And so, side by side, Edward and Eleanor his Queen were crowned to the acclamation of the people, and after the ceremony they made their way to the great hall of Westminster where the feast had been prepared.

The royal pair wore the crowns which had so recently been placed on their heads, and Edward whispered to his Queen that he wondered how she was managing to support hers and trusting it was not too uncomfortable. She assured him that she could endure it, and she was overcome with emotion to think how fortunate she was, and she did not mean in becoming the crowned queen of such a country but in being given such a husband.

"I vow," Edward whispered to her, "that once I can take it off my head I shall not wear it again in a hurry."

"You are still a king, Edward, and seen to be such, without your crown."

He pressed her hand and amid the acclamation of the spectators took his place in the chair of state on the dais.

Now was the time for his subjects to do homage to him.

First came the King of Scotland—Alexander, husband to his sister Margaret. A fine figure of a man, this Alexander, a man of courage and pride. He had made it clear that he was not here to do homage to Edward as King of Scotland for one king did not bow the knee to another—but merely to recognize that Edward was his liege lord in relation to the land he, Alexander, held in England. Fair enough, Edward had said; and he was glad to have the King of Scots as an ally.

Alexander, whose kingdom was smaller than that of England, had by the very nature of kings, to make a brave show of his power and riches and there was no one in the entire company more splendidly accoutred than he was. Edward had smiled to see his mother's eyes sparkle at the contemplation of her son-in-law of Scotland. Any show of extravagance delighted her. She would have liked to see this occasion far more splendid. She would have to be cured, thought Edward. As for Alexander, he would doubtless have to face lean times to pay for the show he had made at the King of England's coronation.

So Alexander rode into the hall accompanied by one hundred of his knights only slightly less splendidly garbed than himself, and when he came to the dais on which Edward was seated, he dismounted, throwing the reins on the neck of his horse so that it was loose to wander where it would. His knights did the same so that one hundred and one horses made their way out of the hall to where the people were crowding to see the ceremony.

The King of Scotland had it proclaimed that any who could catch the horses which would be discarded by his company might keep them. There were shouts of joy as the horses came out and were seized by the lucky ones who could catch them.

Not to be outdone in this lavish gesture and determined that the Scots might not have all the credit for such unparalleled generosity, the King's brother, Edmund, Duke of Lancaster, who was also followed into the hall by one hundred knights, did the same. Then the Earls of Gloucester, Pembroke and Warenne let their horses free so that the most memorable event of that coronation day for the people was that five hundred valuable horses were let loose to become the property of any who could catch them.

But there was one other event which was of greater importance and Edward was deeply conscious of it.

One by one the great Dukes, Earls and Barons came to swear their allegiance to the King but there was one notable absentee.

Edward caught the eye of Gilbert Clare, Earl of Gloucester, who murmured, "I see not Llewellyn of Wales, my lord."

"And for a good reason, sir Earl. He is not here. What means this, think you?"

"Defiance of the royal command, my lord."

"Trouble to come, Gilbert."

"It would seem so, my lord. But it is but a little chieftain of Wales."

Edward nodded. All very well to refer to him as that. It was true up to a point but Wales like Scotland had long been a source of irritation—and worse—to Edward's predecessors, and he had hoped that if he showed himself willing to be friendly, he might win the confidence of these people. And now Llewellyn had openly disobeyed the summons to come to the coronation. Edward could be sure that he was not the only one who had noted this—and many present would be aware of its significance.

A curse on Llewellyn!

But this was his coronation and he must feign to be merry and full of hope for the future. He must not allow it to be seen that the absence of a pert Welsh chieftain disturbed him.

But it was on his mind during the feasting which followed the allegiance ceremony. Very merry were those in the hall, and equally so those outside who danced and sang in the streets and grew intoxicated on the King's free-flowing wine. Those who had acquired valuable horses were ready to die for the King . . . at least on coronation day.

The people happy; the future bright. What more could a King ask?

His Queen beside him—happy in his triumph, his mother pleased but comparing this with her own coronation which had been far more lavish, his family gathered about him—he should be content.

But he was too much of a King to be able to brush aside the fact that trouble could be brewing on the Welsh border.

When the company was getting drowsy through the wine, the heat and the merry-making, Edward was alert, still thinking of the Welsh defaulter. Gloucester, Pembroke and Warenne were aware of this.

"Even had he come to the coronation we could not have been sure that he would not have gone back and made trouble," commented Warenne.

"He could scarcely have done that after giving his oath," Edward reminded him. "At least not yet."

"'Tis better we know where we stand with him."

"How can we ever know where we stand with the Welsh?" demanded Edward. "Give them opportunity and they are ready to go to war. Hasn't it always been so?"

"Since the days of the Conqueror," agreed Warenne.

"And before," added Edward. "They can swoop on our lands, attack and then scuttle back into their mountains. You mentioned the Conqueror. He tried to stop it. He even ventured into Wales with an army. Then—great warrior that he was— he realized that because of its mountainous nature, to conquer that land would cost more in lives and wealth and time than it was worth. So he contented himself with forays and little wars which have been going on ever since. I see no reason to go against his judgment. He was a wise man, that ancestor of mine. He had a genius for strategy. He decided to make that strip of land through which all armies had to pass—the English or the Welsh to reach each other—a no man's land. Then he set up those Barons who have become known as the Marcher Barons, and in exchange for the lands he bestowed upon them they must guard the country and be responsible for keeping the Welsh in order. This state of affairs has been going on for two hundred years. I see no reason why it should be changed."

"And what has happened?" asked Gilbert. "The Marcher Barons control the land and they, like the Welsh, have become a law unto themselves. They see themselves as apart from allegiance to any, even to you, my lord."

"That's true," said Edward. "And since Llewellyn sees fit to flout me thus it occurs to me that it may be necessary for me to settle this question of the Welsh once and for all."

"Ah, if that could be done, my lord, I doubt not it would be good for England and for Wales," said Pembroke. "But is it possible?"

"My lord," replied Edward, "nothing is possible to those who think it impossible. The first rule when undertaking a difficult task is to stop saying 'I can't' and say 'I will'."

The lords nodded agreement and Warenne said, "Llewellyn has become very friendly with the de Montforts."

"I know that and I like it not," replied Edward. "The de Montforts caused enough trouble to my father. I am determined they shall not cause it to me."

"There are two of his sons left and one daughter," commented Warenne.

Edward nodded. "Henry died with his father at Evesham as we know, and Simon died in Italy soon after the murder of my cousin. By God, I shall never forgive them for what they did to Henry. They are cursed and doomed for that for ever. To murder him, so vilely while he knelt at his prayers . . . my cousin Henry! You know my feelings for him. He was my companion . . . come to that we were all companions in the royal nursery—Henry of Cornwall, the cousin I loved the best, and those others . . . cousins also . . . the de Montfort children. Henry of Cornwall was a man of outstanding nobility. I learned much from him, for he was those few years older than I which are so important when one is young. I looked up to him. There was a time when I was wild and foolish, when I was capable of senseless cruelty. Thank God my cousin Henry showed me the folly of that. I owe him much, and when I think of him as he must have been kneeling at the altar and those wicked men creeping up on him . . . when I think of the foul and obscene things they did to his corpse after they had murdered him, I cry vengeance on those who carried out this wicked crime. I say a curse on de Montfort."

"As those who saw the same done to the bodies of Simon de Montfort and *his* son Henry cried on you and yours," said Gilbert, who could never resist making a logical comment even if he put his life in danger through making it.

But Edward was a logical man himself. "True," he said shortly. "True. But I had no hand in the murder of Simon de Montfort. He died in battle. That he was mutilated afterwards was the fortune of war. But to take this good and noble man as he knelt in prayer! No, Gilbert, I'll not have it. A curse on the de Montforts... the whole family... even my aunt who became one through her secret marriage."

"Your feelings are easy to understand, my lord," said Warenne. "And it is the de Montforts we have to guard against."

"Guy is a murderer and despised as such," said the King. "He will not prosper. But my cousins Almeric and Eleanor live in exile with my aunt and there is a rumor that Llewellyn is enamored of my cousin Eleanor."

"It is so!" said Gilbert. "She is royal, for her mother is King Henry's sister, and Llewellyn and she it is said fell deeply in love."

"She was a beautiful girl when I last saw her," said Edward.

"Nurtured as she must have been, how would she feel towards the rough mountain chieftain?" wondered Pembroke.

"I heard that she was as taken with Llewellyn as he with her and that pledges were made between them. Of course she is in exile and cannot come here and he—rebel chieftain that he is—is in no position to bring her. Thus are true lovers kept apart." Edward's mouth was firm. "And shall remain so."

"Unless of course..." began Gilbert.

"Unless my lord?" Edward interrupted. "I guess what you will say. Unless we can use my cousin, the Demoiselle Eleanor, as a bargaining counter to bring Llewellyn to heel."

"If that were possible it would be a good plan."

"It would indeed," said Edward. "I think we are noticed. Our serious conversation gives an impression that we are holding a council of war."

"Which in a way we are, my lord," added Gilbert.

"And that is no way in which to conduct a coronation. Let us ask the minstrels to sing."

The coronation festivities continued. There was no more popular man in the city of London than the King. He was strong, said the people. He would not be a man to be ruled by his wife; nor was she a woman to seek to rule.

All knew that the late King had been ruled by his wife and she had been the one they hated; though they despised the King. But this was a new era.

This King was just. The matter of the bridge confirmed their belief in him.

A party of London citizens had asked leave to see the King during that period of coronation celebrations and he, knowing full well the importance of his capital, agreed to receive their leaders and hear what they had to say.

The head of the party bowed low before the King and when asked what troubled him he explained that it was the state of London Bridge.

"My lord King," said the man. "it has fallen into such a state of decay that it is scarcely safe."

"Then this must be rectified without delay," cried the King. "Why has it not been done?"

"My lord, repairs are made from the revenue received from the custody of the bridge and have previously been done regularly that the bridge may be kept in good order."

"Then why has it not been done now?"

There was silence and the King urged them to continue.

"My lord, the King your father, gave the custody of the bridge to the Queen your mother that she might enjoy the revenues therefrom. Since then the lady Queen has collected the dues and careth nothing for the state of the bridge."

Edward felt a surge of anger against his mother. He knew that he need not verify the statement. Was this not exactly what his mother had been doing since she had come to the country? Was this not the reason for her unpopularity and that of his father and would she never understand that it was deeds such as this which had brought them within sight of losing their crowns.

He restrained the outburst which rose to his lips and replied, "My friends, you may leave this matter to me. I can tell you this. The bridge shall be repaired and its upkeep shall in future be looked after from the dues received."

Exultant by his quick grasp of the situation and believing in his promise, for he was already gaining a reputation of being a man of his word, the deputation left and among their friends sang the praise of the new King who would undoubtedly bring a return of just rule to the country.

The Queen Mother was with her daughter and she had just heard the joyous news from Beatrice that she was pregnant again.

As Edward entered she cried, "Dear Edward, do come and join us. I have such good news."

Edward found it difficult to curb his temper. He had a share of that defect of the Plantagenents, but he had told himself that he must learn to keep it under control. It needed all his will power to do this now.

"Your sister Beatrice is going to have another child."

He took Beatrice's hand and kissed it. "Congratulations, sister," he said. "I'll warrant John is pleased."

"Oh yes, but he always gets anxious. He says we have five and should be content."

The Queen Mother laughed indulgently. Nothing pleased her more than to hear of the devotion of her daughters' husbands.

"I wish I could keep you here, Beatrice, until the child is born."

She looked at Margaret and they smiled, recalling the time when they had deluded the Scottish nobles and Margaret had stayed in England to be with her mother when her daughter was born.

"If it is a girl," said Beatrice, "I shall call her Eleanor after you, dearest mother."

The Queen Mother laughed. "Not another Eleanor in the family! My dearest love, it is confusing enough now."

"Still, there is no one whose name I would rather my child had than yours."

"It was a good thing I named my girl Margaret," said the Queen of Scotland. "But I threaten that if I should ever have another daughter she will be an Eleanor too."

The Queen Mother was gratified but anxious immediately. "My darling, I hope there will be no more. You suffered too much when David was born. If you girls only knew what I go through when you have your children you would vow never to have any more. I wait for the messengers . . . and they are always so tardy."

"Oh, my dearest mother," cried Margaret, "you must remember that we are no longer children."

Edward was drawn into this family circle in spite of himself. They had all had a wonderful childhood, so different from royal children. He must always remember—however exasperated he became by his mother's fecklessness—that they had enjoyed a happy family circle.

Edward whispered to Margaret, "I have something of importance to discuss with our mother."

"I will take Beatrice with me to your lady wife," said Margaret. "She will want to hear about the baby."

"Yes, do," said Edward.

When he was alone with his mother he assumed a grave manner.

"I have had a complaint, my lady," he told her, "from the citizens of London."

"Those tiresome people! How dare they complain at the time of your coronation! Have they not been given so much . . . free wine, banquets . . ."

"Free wine and banquets will not repair London Bridge, my lady."

"London Bridge! What has that to do with the coronation?"

"If it were to collapse it would be remembered as the outstanding event of this coronation for years to come."

"Collapse! Why should it?"

"Because it is in need of repairs and the dues collected partly for that purpose have been used for other things."

"What things?"

"You know that better than I for you have had them and misspent this money."

"I never heard such nonsense. In your father's day . . ."

"My lady, this is not my father's day. It is mine, and I would have you know that I will not have money which is meant to repair my bridge spent on other things."

"Your father gave me the custody of the bridge for six years."

"And since that time the bridge has become a danger to the public. Will you never learn? Did the rising of the barons mean nothing to you?"

"The barons have been defeated."

"The barons will never be defeated, my lady, while they represent the will of the people, and only when that is in his favor can a king rule."

"Your father did very well without it."

"That is not the verdict of the world, alas. My father tried to rule without it, and because of this only the greatest good luck kept him his crown and you will remember well, my mother, that he came within a very short distance of losing it.

Have you forgotten those days when he and I were the prisoners of Simon de Montfort and you went to France as a beggar to your sister's court and tried to raise money for an army to free us."

The Queen Mother wiped her eyes. "Do you think I shall ever forget the saddest time of my life when I and your father were separated."

"I trust you never will and that you will remember how easily it came about. The people would not brook your extravagance, your spending of money raised in taxation on yourself and your friends and relations."

"Edward! How dare you! And you my son! Whose side are you on? That of the crown or the rebel barons?"

"There must be no sides, my lady. I am on the side of justice. I am going to see wrong put right. I am going to bring this country back to prosperity and belief in its sovereign. And I am going to begin by repairing London Bridge and taking the custody of it out of your hands."

"Edward . . . how can you do this to me!"

He went to her and laid his hands on her shoulders, for he loved her dearly and there were so many memories that stayed with him of childhood days when she had been his comfort and his solace and to be with her and his father had been the greatest treat of his childhood. "I can because I must. Dear mother, you know of my love for you, but I am first a king and I mean to rule. I love you now as I ever did and never shall I forget your devotion to me and my dear father. But I cannot allow you to place my crown in jeopardy as you did that of my father. For that reason I act as I must and as I see it that is the right and just way to act."

"So you would humiliate me in the eyes of these rapacious Londoners."

"You will win only honor by discontinuing with this custody. All these Londoners are now rapacious because they wish to see their bridge repaired."

"If they want it repaired let them pay for it."

"It is exactly what they are doing. You know that part of the dues paid are for the upkeep of the bridge."

"I am disappointed in you, Edward."

"I am sorry for that but, if in pleasing you I must disappoint my subjects and deny them justice then, dear lady, I must perforce displease you."

She looked at him—so handsome, so noble, and she suddenly forgot everything but her pride in him. She leaned against him and he put his arms about her.

He kissed her hair.

"Dear mother," he said softly, "I could not bear that we should be bad friends."

"You are a stubborn fellow, Edward," she said fondly. "Strange it is that I would not have you other than you are. But I miss your father so much, my son. I shall never cease to mourn."

"I know," said Edward. "I mourn him too."

"You are not like him. He was so fond..."

Fondness, thought the King, often went with foolishness and that was something a king could not afford.

Leaving his mother he went to his wife. He thanked God for Eleanor. How different she was from her mother-in-law. He could never have borne a domineering wife, but it was clear that a weak man needed a strong woman beside him. And he was now admitting to himself that his father was one of the weakest men he had ever known. A king must face up to the truth. He must learn his lessons and the first lesson of all was that until truth was looked straight in the face and admitted— however disagreeable—no progress would be made.

"Edward," said the Queen anxiously, "you look a little distraught."

"An unpleasant matter." He told her of the bridge and how his mother had been using the funds for the wrong purposes.

"I had to do what I did."

"Indeed you had."

"She was hurt. I think at first she thought I was some sort of traitor to the family."

"You, a traitor! That's quite impossible. You are so wise... so strong. You always do the right thing."

He smiled at her fondly. "I know that whatever I do I shall have the support of my wife."

"But that is only right and natural."

He took her hand and kissed it.

"I have something to tell you," she said.

"Eleanor. You are with child?"

She nodded and he took her into his arms. "This time," he said, "let us pray for a boy. I'll have prayers said throughout the churches."

"Not yet, I beg of you. It is too early. I am always afraid when I speak of it too soon that something will go wrong."

"My dearest, why should it?"

"There was John and the little one at Acre."

"My dear lady, many children die. John was delicate. Some children are born that way. As for the little one at Acre, that was not to be wondered at after all the hardships. And what of young Joanna, eh? She was always lively enough though Acre was her birthplace."

"I wish she were with us."

"Your mother will not willingly part with her. And you will have this new one. We have our darling Eleanor. What a handsome girl she is becoming! And little Henry . . ."

The Queen was grave. "I worry about him a great deal."

"I thought he seemed better."

She shook her head.

"Oh come, my love, he is a bright little fellow."

"He is so breathless and he always seems to have a cough. Edward, I don't care for the Tower of London. It's so cold and drafty and there is an atmosphere of gloom about the place."

"It was built as a fortress of course," said Edward. "And it seems like it."

"The Palace of the Tower depresses me, Edward. I do not think that Henry will thrive while he is there. I want to find a place which is more healthy for the children and with the new baby I want to be especially careful. I keep thinking of little John and wondering whether if I had been here . . ."

"Pray do not let my mother hear you say that. She dotes on the children and as you know will scarcely let them out of her sight. She is half elated, half apprehensive, about Beatrice's news. She would love to have them all here under her care."

"I know of course that she did everything possible for young John and I don't suppose there was anything I could have done to save him. But I do want to choose a home for the children and I want it to be a healthy place. Somewhere in the country."

"I will tell you what we must do," said Edward. "When all

the coronation ceremonies are over we shall go down to Windsor. I have a fancy that that will be the place you will choose."

"Oh Edward, you are so good to me."

Edward again took her into his arms and stroked her beautiful long dark hair. He compared her as he often had with his mother and thanked God for giving him such a wife.

The excitement of the coronation had not improved little Henry's condition. Or it might have been that the disease which was robbing him of his strength was moving towards its climax. In any case there was an obvious decline in his health.

The Queen Mother was thrown into a state of great anxiety—even more so than the Queen, whose pregnancy seemed to have endowed her with a certain serenity. But the Queen Mother had now convinced herself that Margaret had not looked as well as she should, and she confided in the Queen that she had had a talk with Alexander who shared her anxiety.

The treatment Margaret had received when she had first gone to Scotland as a child bride had had an effect on her health from which she had never fully recovered. And now that little Henry showed signs of growing weaker the Queen Mother feared that God had turned his face from the royal family.

Death did not come singly, she said. Little John had been followed very quickly by her dear husband and ever since then she had been fearful for her darlings.

Edward ordered that several sheep should be freshly slaughtered so that the little boy could be wrapped in their skins. This was considered to be good for those who suffered from shivering fits because the animal heat was calculated to supply the warmth a sick person lacked.

More wax images of his body were made and taken to various shrines to be placed there and burned in oil. A hundred poor widows were engaged that they might perform vigils in the churches praying for his recovery. The physicians were on constant attention and either the Queen or the Queen Mother kept vigil at his bedside.

They talked of what it could be that ailed him. Little John had suffered in the same way. The child seemed to shrink and grow more and more listless every day.

"Why does this happen to the boys?" demanded the Queen.

"It is almost like a curse," the Queen Mother said. "I wonder sometimes whether it has anything to do with the de Montforts."

"Why be so cruel to a little boy?"

"Because that little boy could one day be King perhaps."

"I hate the Tower," said the Queen. "It fills me with dread. I cannot bear to think of my children living there. Edward has said I may choose where I like and we shall have our home there, but of course the King must move around and I believe it is well that we should all be together. I think I shall choose Windsor. Do you think that would be healthier for Henry?"

"I am sure of it, my dear. Have you visited Windsor recently?"

"No, but I mean to. It has been so necessary for us to be here in Westminster for the celebrations."

The Queen Mother's eyes were momentarily glazed as she recalled her own coronation. She had been brought to the Palace of the Tower and she had not noticed that it was gloomy; perhaps that was because her coronation had been more splendid than any and she had been well aware of the shining approval in her husband's eyes. Oh, to be young again, to go back to all that glory, with the knowledge that she was clever and above all so beautiful that her husband adored her! This mild little creature—good as she was—could know nothing of the happiness which had come to Eleanor of Provence.

And now anxieties beset her. Edward was her dear son but he was stern with her, reprimanding her for spending a little money. Edward had no idea how to live graciously. She did hope he was not going to develop parsimonious ways. And she was worried about little Henry who was going exactly as young John had gone, wasting away, and she knew that wherever they moved would make no difference. And what of Margaret who had never fully regained her strength, and Beatrice was pregnant, and she was always afraid when they had children. She was growing sick with worry.

She let the Queen talk about the advantages of Windsor over Westminster. There was no harm in frightening the poor girl with her own fears.

She herself talked of Windsor and how her husband had loved it.

"He strengthened the defenses," she said, "and rebuilt the western wall. You must see the curfew tower, my dear. He had that built. He had a genius for architecture and how he loved it. If the people had not been so foolish and made such a nuisance of themselves whenever he wanted to spend a little money in beautifying castles, he would have done so much more."

"I like Windsor," said the Queen. "I like the river and I think the air will be fresh and good for Henry."

"I doubt it not. My husband always said it was. I think it was his favorite place. How we talked and grew excited about the changes he made there! He insisted on murals and they were always of a religious nature. He was a very pious man. Oh so good he was! He loved the color green. He liked blue and purple too. You soon realize that when you go into those rooms. It was just after our marriage that he made such changes to the castle. 'For you, my dear,' he said, 'and if there is something you do not like you must tell me.' He made chambers overlooking the cloisters and he had a herb garden made for me . . . Oh yes, my dear, you will be happy at Windsor."

"I feel that I shall be. As soon as I feel that Henry is strong enough for the journey I shall take him there."

Alas, each day the child seemed to grow weaker and the Queen was in a quandary. Should she take him away to the country or would it be wiser to leave him where he was? In the meantime she engaged more widows for the vigils and more images were burned in oil.

The journey to Windsor would be so long but the Queen felt the need to take the child away from London so she arranged to go with him to Merton Priory and there prayers could be offered up for his recovery. "It might be," she pointed out to Edward, "that if they are in a holy place God might listen to us."

So she took the little boy to Merton Priory, which being not far from Westminster, meant that the journey was not too strenuous. As for the child, he was quite happy to go as long as she was with him.

"There," she told him, "you are going to get well. You are going to grow into a big strong boy."

"Like my father?" he asked.

"Exactly like him," she assured him.

But she wished that she had taken him to Windsor. How pleasant for the little boy to have been in those rooms made beautiful by his grandfather. She could have told him the stories of the pictures which adorned the walls. A Priory was by its very nature a quiet place.

"As soon as you are well," she told him, "we are going to Windsor."

"All of us?" asked the little boy.

She nodded. "Your father, your grandmother, your sister and myself... we shall all be there and soon there will be another little brother or sister to join us. You will like that, Henry."

Henry thought he would and he was clearly happy to be with his mother. He had never forgotten the long time she had been away from him.

"When you are well..." She was constantly using that phrase to him but each day when she rose, and even during the night, she would go to his little bed and assure herself that he had not already left them.

As the days passed she knew that Merton had nothing to offer him.

Perhaps, she thought, we should go back to Westminster.

But Henry never went back. One morning when she went to his bed she realized that the vigils of widows, the images in oil and the skins of the freshly killed sheep had been of no avail.

The little Prince had gone as his brother John had before him.

Her spirits were buoyed up by the child she was carrying.

Edward said, "It will be a boy, you see. God has taken Henry but he will give us another boy. I am sure of it, my love."

Edward was upset but not as deeply as she and the Queen Mother were. A deep depression settled on the latter.

"Nothing goes right for me since the King died," she complained.

Those about her might have said that nothing had gone right for others while he lived, but they dared not to her.

It was almost as though she had had a premonition of disaster for, shortly after the death of the little Prince, a messenger came from Scotland with the news which she had been dreading.

Alexander had sent him to tell her that Margaret was very ill indeed, and that when they had returned to Scotland after the coronation her health had taken a turn for the worse.

The Queen Mother, frantic with grief, was ready to start immediately to her daughter, but Edward restrained her.

"Nay, Mother," he said, "you must not go. Stay awhile. There will be more news later."

"Not go. When my own daughter is ill and needs me. You know that when Margaret was a prisoner in that miserable castle of Edinburgh I urged your father to leave at once that we might go to her. Do you think *he* tried to detain me."

"No, dear mother, I know he did not. But this . . . this is different."

"Different! How different? If a child of mine needs me that is where I shall be."

He looked at her sadly and the horrible truth dawned on her.

"There is something else," she said slowly. "They have not told me the truth . . ." She went to him and laid her hands on his chest. "Edward," she said quietly, "tell me."

He drew her to him and held her fast in his arms.

"There is something else. I know it," she cried.

She heard him say what she dreaded to hear. "Yes, dear mother, it is true that there is something else. I wanted it to be broken gently."

"So . . . she is gone . . . my Margaret . . . gone."

"Alexander is heart-broken. He had summoned the best physicians, the most noble prelates to her bedside. There was nothing that could be done. She went peacefully—our dear Margaret. She is at rest now."

"But she was so young . . . my little girl . . . just a child."

"She was thirty-four years old, my lady."

"It is too young to die . . . too young . . . too young . . . They are all dying . . . yet *I* am left."

"And will be with us for many years to come, praise God," said Edward. "I understand your grief. I share it. Pray let me take you to your chambers. Shall I send the Queen to you? She has a rare gentleness for times like this."

"First tell me."

"I know only that she had been ailing for some weeks. She was never really strong."

"I know that well. They undermined her health, those wicked men up there. I shall never forgive the Scots for this. She should have stayed with me. We should never have let her go."

"She had her life to live. She had her husband and her children. She loved Alexander dearly and he her. She was happy in Scotland once they grew up and were together. Let us thank God that she did not suffer. Alexander says her death was peaceful in the castle of Cupar. They had gone to Fife for a short sojourn, and there she had to take to her bed. Alexander says that she was buried with great ceremony in Dumfermline and that the whole of Scotland weeps for her."

"My daughter . . . my child . . ." mourned the Queen. "I loved her so much, Edward. She was my favorite child after she went to Scotland. I shall never forget the anguish we suffered when we heard of her plight. And now she is dead . . . Her poor children! How they will miss her . . . And Alexander . . . He loved her I know. Who could help loving Margaret . . ."

"I will take you to my wife," said Edward gently. "She will know how to comfort you better than I."

While the Court was mourning the death of Queen Margaret of Scotland Beatrice gave birth to a daughter.

It was a difficult confinement and the physicians thought that the shock of her sister's death had affected Beatrice adversely, and for this reason her own health began to fail.

Fortunately for the Queen Mother she could be with this daughter, but this brought little comfort to her because she realized that Beatrice seemed to be in the same kind of failing health from which Margaret had suffered.

Beatrice coughed a great deal; she was easily fatigued and a terrible premonition seized the Queen Mother.

"Has God truly deserted me?" she asked her daughter-in-law.

The Queen replied that she must not despair. Beatrice had her dear little daughter whom she had named Eleanor as she said she would and very soon she would recover. She had had five children before the new baby and had come satisfactorily through the ordeals.

But Beatrice's health did not improve and her husband grew more and more concerned.

The Queen Mother warmed to him when he talked to her

of his fears. He truly loved her. That much was obvious and she knew then that that was something for which she should be grateful. All her children had made happy marriages, and they were rare enough, particularly in royal circles, and she believed it was due to the example she and their father had set to them. "One thing we taught them," she told lady Mortimer, one of her closest friends, "was the joy of family life and how when it is ideal there is nothing on this earth to compare with the happiness it brought."

But what John of Brittany had to say to her gave her no comfort.

"My lady," he said, "Beatrice's health was impaired in the Holy Land. She should never have gone, but she insisted and maybe she will be blessed for it, but I am deeply concerned for her. The dampness of the climate here aggravates her chest. I want to take her back to her home in Brittany and that without delay."

The Queen Mother was silent. Her heart cried out against this. Beatrice was her great comfort now that she had lost Margaret. In looking after this daughter she could find some solace. But if she went away, how lonely she would be! And yet, she had seen her daughter's health deteriorate, and it might well be that John was right. Certainly he was looking at her now with such poignant pleading that she found it impossible to protest.

"She longs to be with her children," said John. "She is torn between you and them. She often reproaches herself for having left them to accompany me on the crusade. I believe that if I took her to our home she might recover."

Whatever the Queen Mother's faults she had never failed to do what was best for her children.

Sorrowing, she took her farewell of her remaining daughter.

She tried not to worry about Beatrice. John had assured her that he would send frequent messengers to her with news of her daughter's health. She would let herself believe that a rest in her own home would be good for Beatrice although she believed in her heart that if Margaret had stayed in her care instead of going back to that bleak Scotland she would have nursed her back to health.

She turned her attention to her grand-daughter Eleanor who

had to be comforted for the loss of her little brother Henry. Young as she was they would soon have to consider her be- trothal in some quarter from which good could come to En- gland. Then there was the Queen who was growing larger every week and must soon give birth—pray God a son this time. If she had a boy that would lift the spirits of them all. It would show that Heaven had not completely turned against them. For with so many cruel deaths one began to wonder. "Oh God, send us a boy," prayed the Queen Mother; and being herself she could not help adding: "You owe that to us."

Edward was deeply involved in matters of state. He was concerned about possible trouble on the Welsh border and these matters occupied him so much that he seemed to feel the family bereavement less than the Queen Mother expected.

"He is not like his father," she mourned. But then who could be like that beloved man? Henry would have forgotten every- thing in his grief for his daughter. He never allowed state matters to come before his love of his family.

Her son Edmund, Duke of Lancaster, was preparing to leave for France. When he came to say goodbye to her she could scarcely restrain her emotion.

"It seems as though you are all going away," she mourned.

Edmund was of a merry nature. Light-hearted and popular with his friends—perhaps he was notoriously generous—he lacked his brother's seriousness. Of course he had not the responsibilities.

"I shall be back ere long, dear lady," he assured her. "Back with my bride."

"Oh Edmund, I trust she will be a good wife to you."

"I am sure of it," he said with characteristic optimism.

She looked at him with affection—the slightly stooping shoulders which had earned him unfairly the name of Crouch- back endeared him to her. He was so much more vulnerable than Edward, and she was beginning to feel a certain resentment towards Edward because he showed so clearly that he did not need her and was not going to listen to her advice. That affair of the bridge had made a rift between them. He would always be her beloved son, of course, her first-born, the most hand- some young man she had ever seen—but he was showing clearly that he did not need her and she had always been at the very heart of her family. It is well for him, she thought, that he has a meek wife without a thought in her head but to say "yes, yes, yes" to everything he wants. That suits him well. He would not tolerate a woman of spirit.

She smiled, thinking of her husband's pride in her, how he would never have thought of acting without her. Oh Henry, Henry, if only you were with me now!

"My dear son," she now said to Edmund, "be wary of the French. My sister married the French King and I have received help from them—mainly through her—but I would say be wary of them."

"Never fear. I shall be able to look after myself and my interests."

"She is a beautiful woman, I hear, and has already proved she can bear children."

"She has a daughter of her first marriage—Jeanne. I trust she and I will have sons and daughters."

"There is nothing that can bring more comfort to the family. Tell me of Blanche, your wife to be, this daughter of Robert of Artois."

"And through him royal. As you know, her first husband was Henri Count of Champagne, and King of Navarre."

The Queen Mother nodded. "I remember Robert well. I was in France when my sister married the French King. That made a bond between France and England when I became your father's bride. But although they said that my sister's husband was a saint and indeed called him Saint Louis, I never trusted them. Your father was to learn many a bitter lesson through them."

"This will be a good marriage, dear mother. Through Blanche, Champagne will come to me until Jeanne, her daughter, is of an age to inherit or to marry."

"And you will live there . . . away from us all?"

"I shall travel back and forth. Do not imagine I shall be content to live in exile. I am going to bring my wife to England as soon as they have celebrated our marriage there. Rest assured you will be seeing me soon."

"I shall keep you to that promise, my son."

"If Edward needs me, you can be sure I shall be at his side."

"Remember that, my dear son. It is well for families to hold together."

It was a sad day for her when he left. But she knew that it was good for him to go. He needed a wife. Perhaps it would have been better if Aveline de Fortibus had lived and inherited, but once again fate had been cruel to them.

She travelled down to Windsor with the Queen who was certain that that would be the ideal place to make their chief residence. It was not so very far from Westminster where the King would have to be so often and the air was good. Perhaps she would have the new baby there.

"The late King was so fond of Windsor," said the Queen Mother as they rode side by side. She was thinking that soon the Queen would not be in a condition to ride and she had taken the precaution of ordering that there should be a litter so that if the journey became too much for the Queen she should ride in it.

"I will say if I am tired of course," said the Queen, "or if I feel the strain."

"No, my dear," said the Queen Mother, "*I* shall say when you are to ride for I am sure you may well be less careful of your health than I."

It was typical of the Queen that she obeyed her mother-in-law and rode in the litter even when she had no inclination to do so.

"Yes," went on the Queen Mother, "Henry was very fond of Windsor, though of course it was there that his father stayed when the barons behaved so badly and made him sign Magna Carta. Henry always said any reminder of *that* would be repugnant to him. All the same he made some wonderful additions. He enlarged the Lower Ward and added a most beautiful chapel. One would have thought that with all he did he and I would have been more fortunate. He was such a religious man."

The Queen was silent. She was too tactful to point out what Edward had told her, which was that his father—good and beloved by his family as he was—had had little idea of the best way to rule.

The Queen marvelled at the beauty of the countryside—the green fields, the rich forest lands and the winding river Thames which flowed close by. This was the place she would choose for her children, and she fell to wondering if she might have saved little Henry had she brought him here.

At Windsor the Queen Mother was stricken yet again. She knew as soon as the messengers arrived from Brittany. The Queen came hurriedly to her and found her prostrate with grief.

It was as she had feared. Beatrice was dead. Weakened by the birth of a child from which she had never recovered and shattered by the news of her sister's death, Beatrice had gone into a similar decline to that which had killed her sister, and in spite of her husband's tireless efforts to make her well she had grown weaker every day.

Every known remedy had been used; the best of the physicians had been at her bedside—all to no avail.

Her body was being sent to England because that had been her wish. She had always wanted to be buried in the arch on the north wall of the choir in front of the altar in Christ Church in New Gate, that church which she herself had founded before her marriage.

It should be done, said John her husband, and her body was sent to England, but her heart had been removed and was to be placed in the Abbey of Fontevraud where her great-grandfather and great-grandmother, Henry II and Eleanor of Aquitaine, lay together with the remains of her great-uncle, Richard Coeur de Lion.

The Queen Mother was dazed with shock. She could not believe this had happened. So many deaths . . . such senseless deaths . . . in such a short time. It really did seem as though the hand of God was turned against her.

She shut herself in her apartments and stormed against the Almighty. Then she remembered her beloved husband who had been a deeply religious man and she knew how distressed he would be if he could hear her. That sobered her. "If this is my cross," she said, "then must I bear it. But when You took him You took away the best part of my life, and now You seem intent on taking what is left to me."

It seemed as though God had taken heed of her railings and was indeed sorry for what He had done, for shortly after the funeral of Beatrice the Queen was brought to bed and to the joy of all she gave birth to a healthy son.

There was great rejoicing throughout the court. It was a good omen. Little John and Henry had gone but the Queen was young and bore children without difficulty. And here was the boy they all wanted.

The Queen Mother came out of her mournful lethargy and began making plans for the child.

Edward was so delighted that, when the Queen, who rarely

expressed a desire which was not Edward's, said she would like to call him Alfonso after her father, he agreed.

The Queen Mother was astounded. "He should have been Edward. Is he not the heir to the throne? Alfonso! Do you think the English will ever welcome a King Alfonso?"

"When he comes to the throne," said the King, "we shall have to give him a new name. In the meantime his mother particularly wants Alfonso and Alfonso it shall be."

And as Alfonso thrived so did the hopes of the family. They had ridden out the storm of ill luck which had brought death to so many of them; they were now set fair and the journey ahead looked full of promise.

The Welsh Prince and
the Demoiselle

TROUBLE, *as might have been expected, came from the Welsh* border.

Gilbert of Gloucester came riding in all haste to the King at Westminster to tell him the news. The King received Gilbert in one of the lavishly painted chambers in the palace which his father had restored.

Edward knew at once that the news was bad.

"Llewellyn?" he said even before Gilbert had begun.

"It was certain to happen, my lord. The Marcher Barons have been reporting trouble there. It seems that the Welsh have discovered some prophecy of Merlin's which says that a man named Llewellyn shall reign not only over Wales but over England as well."

The King turned a shade paler. He was more afraid of prophecies than armies for he knew how deeply the people could be affected by them.

"And this is *the* chosen Llewellyn are they saying?"

"My lord, that is so."

"By God I will show this Llewellyn that he shall never be King of England while the true King lives."

"I thought you would say that, my lord."

"How dare he? What right has he? Is he descended from the Conqueror?"

"He intends to ally himself with the Conqueror's line, my lord."

"It is deeds not intentions he will need if he is to make fact of his dreams. How pray does he think he will become a member of our family?"

"Through his wife."

"His wife! He is unmarried."

"But intends to marry ere long. You will remember that he was at one time betrothed to Eleanor de Montfort, she whom they call the Demoiselle."

"Her father agreed to the betrothal when he was raising the Welsh to fight against my father."

Gilbert nodded. "It is said that the pair became enamored of each other then. It must be nearly ten years ago and the Demoiselle was a very young girl at that time, but her youth did not prevent her falling deeply in love."

Edward shrugged his shoulders.

"My lord," said Gilbert, "this matter is not lightly to be dismissed. Forget not that the Demoiselle is royal through her mother—your father's sister. She is your cousin and if he marries her Llewellyn will feel that he is not without a claim to the English throne."

"Then he must be mad."

"He is mad with his dream of glory. He says he is going to make Merlin's prophecy come true."

"And how will he do that?"

"He will try to win England by conquest."

"And you think I shall idly stand by and let him?"

"By God and all his angels, no. You will fight. You will show him who is master here. Poor Llewellyn, I could feel it in my heart to be sorry for him when I think of what you will do to him when he ventures out from the shelter of his Welsh mountains. But he intends to establish his link with the throne through marriage with the Demoiselle."

"Who is in exile with her mother and her evil brothers."

"This is the news, my lord. He has sent for the Demoiselle. They are to be married when she arrives in Wales."

"From France?"

"He has sent a ship for her. She will soon be on her way. Then when he is married to her, he will do more than harry the Marcher country. The Welsh are with him to a man—and maybe others. Since it was put about that Merlin prophesied that a Llewellyn should be King of England people begin to believe it may be so."

Edward's eyes were narrowed. He stood for a few seconds, long legs apart, staring into the distance. Then he smiled slowly.

"You say the Demoiselle is to come out of exile to marry him, eh?"

"That is so, my lord."

"Do you think she will ever reach him? I do not. The first thing we do, Gilbert, is to send out ships to intercept her. We are going to make sure that Llewellyn does not get his bride."

In a small château in the town of Melun which stands on the river Seine, Eleanor de Montfort, Countess of Leicester, lay dying. Beside her sat her daughter—a beautiful young woman of some twenty-three years—who was known even in her family as Demoiselle.

The dying countess was easier in her mind since the message had come to her a few days earlier, for she had been deeply concerned as to what would happen to her daughter if she should die. Now there was a chance that she would be happy. Llewellyn, the Prince of Wales, wanted to marry her. He had, explained the message, thought of her constantly through the years. He had never married because of his attachment to her and because he considered they were betrothed. What he longed for more than anything was for her to be his bride.

Any day now the news of the ship's arrival would come. The Countess knew that her daughter would not leave her while she lived, but was fully aware that there were not too many days left to her.

She was ready to go. Hers had been a stormy life, and there had been plenty of opportunity to contemplate the past as she lay here on her sick bed. It was strange how well she remembered the days of her youth, and how much more vivid they seemed than what was happening around her now!

But when she was gone her son Almeric would take his sister to Wales, and there her dear Demoiselle would become the wife of a man who loved her and would cherish her.

So many terrible things had happened to her family that she feared the worst. Perhaps she should have expected violent happenings when she married the great Simon de Montfort. But she would never regret that. How often had she said to herself, looking back on all the tragedies which had followed that reckless marriage: And I would do it all over again.

Simon de Montfort was a name which would be remembered with respect for ever. A strange man, a good man, a man of ideals, he had had her support even though he had stood against her own brother, King Henry. Poor Henry, she had loved him too. He had always been so kind, so eager for them all to love him, but he had ruled badly; his extravagance and that of his Queen had almost brought back the dreadful days of King John; and Simon had had to do what he did even though he believed that civil war was one of the greatest disasters which could befall a country; and when a woman's husband was fighting against her brother that was indeed a tragedy. She recalled that time when her brother Henry and her nephew Edward had been brought to Kenilworth as her husband's prisoners and put in her care. She had treated them with respect; she had wanted to shake her brother and say: "Why cannot you see what you are doing? Simon is right." Simon would have ruled wisely. It was Simon who had inaugurated the first parliament. Simon wanted a peaceful prosperous country. Henry might say he wanted this too and so he did, but Henry also wanted money . . . money and lands so that he could satisfy the demands of his rapacious wife. Yet she had loved them both—Henry, her brother, Eleanor of Provence, her sister-in-law. They had ruled badly; they had been her husband's deadly enemies; yet she had loved them all.

What a difficult problem life set, with war in the country and war in the family! Violence had bred violence. What they did to her husband and her son Henry at Evesham would haunt her for as long as she lived. She had nightmares about Evesham. That beloved body to be so treated! It was no wonder that her sons Guy and Henry had done what they did. They had revered their father. They had wanted revenge.

And it had ended thus with the proud de Montforts in exile.

Guy, a fugitive wanted for the murder of Henry of Cornwall which he with his brother Simon had committed in a church at Viterbo. It was a murder which had shocked the world because Henry of Cornwall had been killed while in prayer before an altar, and after he had been stabbed to death his body had been obscenely treated as Simon de Montfort's had after Evesham. It was meant to be a grand revenge for what had happened to their father. Poor Guy! Poor Simon! They had chosen the wrong victim in one noted for his bravery and goodness; they should never have mutilated his dead body, and now young Simon was dead but none would ever forget the murder at Viterbo and she often wondered about what would happen to Guy in the end.

So many promising children and they had come to this! She called to her daughter and took pleasure in looking at her. She was tall, graceful, a Plantagenet. Llewellyn would surely be pleased with his bride.

"My child," she said, "it will not be long now."

The Demoiselle bent over her mother and asked if she would take a cooling beverage.

"I am sinking fast, daughter," she said. "Nay, do not grieve. This is the end of my life—and it has been a rich one—but it is the beginning of yours. You will go happily to Llewellyn."

"Yes, Mother, I shall go happily to him."

"It was long ago when you saw him."

"Yes, but we both knew then . . . I am sure he has not changed and I know that I have not."

"Be happy, my child. When I was very young and scarcely out of the nursery they married me to an old man. When he died I thought I should never marry again. There was talk of going into a convent. Then your father came. To marry in love is the best thing that can happen to a woman."

"You and my father faced terrible odds."

The dying woman smiled. "A mesalliance. A King's daughter and an adventurer, they said. Perhaps they are the best sort of marriages because the people who make them must want desperately to do so to defy everyone about them."

"You and my father wanted to marry very much, I know."

"Ah yes. What days they were! The excitement . . . the intrigue! I suppose I was one to flourish on intrigue. Now I look for peace. That is something we all come to. I want only to

know that you are settled and on your way to Wales. Then I
could die happy."

"I should never leave you, dear Mother."

"Bless you, but I shall not detain you long. When the ship
comes for you you must go. Almeric shall take you. I have
much to say to Almeric."

"Shall I send him to you, Mother?"

"Yes, my child. Tell him to come."

Almeric de Montfort sat by his mother's bedside and asked
himself how long she could live, and wondered what future
there was for him and his sister in Wales.

He loved his mother; he had revered his father. It was a
source of anger that the great man of his times—as he believed
his father to have been—should have died ignobly. It was not
so much that he had been killed in battle. That was an honorable
way for a man to die. But what they had done to his body
afterwards . . . How dared they. So to humiliate the remains of
the great Simon de Montfort! And then they wondered why
his brothers had done the same to Henry of Cornwall.

"Are you there, Almeric, my son?" asked the dying Countess.

"I am here, Mother."

"You must leave for Wales as soon as the ship comes."

"We shall not leave you, Mother."

"'Twould be better for you to leave without delay."

"Do not fret about the matter. Rest assured all will be well."

"Take care of your sister."

"Trust me, dear Mother, to do that."

She closed her eyes as though in relief.

She was right. They should leave as soon as the ship came.
Messengers could be arriving at any moment to tell them they
should set out. His sister would never agree to leave her mother
though—nor would he.

Ever since Evesham the family fortunes had been in decline.
Oh how foolish of Guy and Simon to commit a murder which
shocked the world! Guy had always been violent and he had
hated his cousin Edward; he used to say Edward had everything
in his favor. Perhaps in those days in the royal schoolroom
they had all been a little envious of Edward. The Golden Boy,
the King's son, the heir to the throne. The one who gave himself
airs and tried to rule them all—taller than any of them, the

one who was selected for attention and homage even in those days. Guy had hated him and tried to turn them all against him. Henry of Cornwall had been one of those boys—the eldest— and he had been Edward's staunch ally. Henry the noble boy, who led Edward along the path of virtue. Edward the future King, Henry the saint. It was small wonder that they had made Henry their victim. Almeric could imagine the vicious joy with which Guy had mutilated Henry's body.

Oh it was a foolish thing to have done. It had set the whole world against them. It had brought disrepute on the great de Montfort name. Now when people mentioned it they spoke of the murder rather than the great good which their father Simon de Montfort had brought to England.

Almeric would never forget that time when he had been accused with his brothers of the murder. This was a great trial to him for not only had he been educated in the Church but he was innocent of the crime. It was easy for him to be arrested as he had been working in the university of Padua at the time. Thank God he had been able to prove that he had been nowhere near Viterbo when the murder had been committed and had in fact been desperately ill with a fever.

Now he had been called to his mother's bedside and it occurred to him that if this marriage into Wales could be brought about and Llewellyn became King of England, the fortunes of the de Montforts would be reversed. His sister Queen of England! Proud Edward deposed! What a glorious prospect. And Merlin had prophesied that a Llewellyn should be a King of England. If it were this Llewellyn . . .

His mother's breathing was becoming more difficult. He wondered if he should call the priest.

His sister came in and when she looked at the bed her beautiful eyes were sorrowful.

She knelt by the bed, and her mother sensing her presence stretched out a hand.

Eleanor took it.

"I am here, Mother," she said.

"Go . . . and be happy," said the Countess. "Almeric . . ."

"Yes, my lady."

"Take care of your sister. Promise me. Take her to her bridegroom. Start afresh . . . Do not grieve."

She closed her eyes smiling. Perhaps, thought the young

Eleanor, she was thinking of her own marriage; those days
when she, the bold adventurous princess, widow of an old
man, had met and loved the handsome Simon de Montfort—
the man who was to make his mark on history—the one whom
they called the adventurer.

They had adventured together and the adventure was coming
to an end. She was dying and Simon de Montfort had met his
end long ago on the battlefield of Evesham.

A gentle reminiscent smile was on the lips of the Countess
de Montfort as she slipped away from this life.

There was no reason why they should delay, said Almeric
when news came that Llewellyn, Prince of Wales, had sent
two ships, to escort his bride to her new home.

The Countess was buried in the nunnery of Montargis in
accordance with her wishes and after this had been done the
young Demoiselle with her brother as escort made her way to
the coast where the ships were waiting to take them to Wales.

Those ships were good to look on. Llewellyn had clearly
sent of his best and they were equipped with everything for his
bride's comfort. He had sent a company of knights and men-
at-arms to protect her should the need arise.

And so they set sail. As the coast of France faded from
sight the crew grew apprehensive. It was to be hoped that news
of the journey might not have reached English ears but this
seemed unlikely as there were always spies to betray such news
and the discovery of Merlin's prophecy had naturally been
blazoned throughout the country. It was good from the Welsh
point of view for the English to know this. There was nothing
like a prophecy of this nature to strike terror into the hearts of
enemies. If the English believed that supernatural powers were
working against them they were half way to defeat.

It would be a long journey for the party dared not land in
England or be seen by the English ships. Therefore the passage
through the English Channel would be hazardous indeed.

Fears increased as they caught sight of the coast of England.
The navigator dreaded a strong wind which might blow them
close to the land and worst of all force them to take shelter.
Great was their elation when they saw that the end of the land
was in sight. Once they had rounded the tip known as Land's
End they could sail straight up to Wales.

Alas, as they changed course preparing to sail northwards, four merchant vessels were seen bearing down upon them.

The two Welsh ships had no chance against them.

Proudly the English captain escorted his captives back to Bristol and immediately sent a message to the King that his mission had been successfully accomplished.

Llewellyn ab Gruffyd Prince of Wales was mad with rage when he heard that his bride had been captured by the English.

What of this fine prophecy! Was he always to be beaten by the English? He, Llewellyn ab Gruffyd, the elect—if Merlin's prophecy did indeed point to him—to be foiled once more by the English and just as his Demoiselle was to be brought to him!

He had dreamed of her for many years. He would marry no other. He would never forget her—a beautiful child with eyes that had shone with admiration for him when she had heard that she was to be his wife. That had been years ago when her father Simon de Montfort had been a great power in England and it had appeared that he would depose the King. If only the tide had not turned against Simon, the Demoiselle would long since have been his wife.

The disaster had been due to Edward who had escaped from captivity and beaten the de Montfort army—Edward Longshanks, who looked like a conqueror and was one.

Edward had inspired the faith which leaders demanded—the sort of faith which a prophecy by Merlin could produce. Edward had the looks, the manners, the strength of a king. Only the supernatural could come against him. And Merlin had prophesied . . .

Llewellyn had never believed that Edward could outwit him and take his bride from him, and it had shaken him to realize that the first move in the attempt to make Merlin's prophecy come true had failed.

Life had not been easy for him. When had it ever been for a Prince of Wales? If he was not harried by the English on his borders it was trouble in his own family.

In the first place it had been bad luck to be born the second son of Gruffydd ab Llewellyn; not that he had not overcome that difficulty and Owain, his elder brother, was now in safe custody, his prisoner.

But family conflict was not good and he would have preferred to have had loyal brothers—providing of course he had
been the eldest. A series of adventures had brought him to his
present position.

Wales was a constant anxiety to England but no more so
than England was to Wales. The Celtic Welsh were different
from the English. That mixed race, made up of some of the
greatest warriors in the world, like the adventuring Vikings,
and with the blood of the Angles, Saxons and Romans in their
veins, were born to be rulers and conquerors. The Welsh like
the Celts of the North and those who lived in the extreme south-
west corner of England were of a different breed. They liked
to sing and play the lute or harp, for music meant a great deal
to them; they were poetic and they had vivid imaginations which
bred superstition in them. They were full of fancies; and it had
seemed that they were no match for that hybrid race which
now called itself the English.

To sally forth from the mountains and make war on the
English could be disastrous. Llewellyn thanked God for the
mountains. They had saved his country from being overrun by
the invading English many a time.

William the Conqueror had known he could conquer the
Welsh but even he could not conquer their mountains. He it
was who had established the Marcher Barons—great Normans
headed by lords like the FitzOsborns and Montgomeries. For
two hundred years the Marcher Barons had ruled that no man's
land.

Now there was Merlin's prophecy. Llewellyn believed that
he must be the chosen one. He did wonder why the Llewellyn
in the prophecy had not been his grandfather, a mighty warrior
to whom many had looked for the deliverance of Wales from
the English persecution. He had been known as Llewellyn the
Great because it was said he was the greatest ruler Wales had
known in all her history up to that time.

There must be a greater . . . Merlin's chosen.

Looking back it seemed there had been too much fighting
among themselves. No country could make progress when
brother fought against brother. But that was how it was now
and had been in the days of Llewellyn the Great.

Men of Wales sang of Llewellyn the Great, son of Iorwerth
who in his turn was the only son of Owain Gwynedd who could

call himself legitimate. They were a wild and roving lot those rulers of Wales—loving to sing and make love wherever they went. And as a consequence, boys learned of the exploits of their ancestors through the songs which were sung at their mothers' knees and those mothers were rarely the wives of their fathers.

Llewellyn's own father, Gruffydd, was the result of a liaison between Llewellyn the Great and one of his many mistresses. Llewellyn had had a wife though and she was a daughter of King John of England. Her name was Joan and though illegitimate the King accepted her as his daughter and she, being a woman of character, had tried to bring about peace between Wales and England. After the death of King John she had continued to work for friendly relations between her husband and her half-brother Henry III; in the meantime she produced a son Davydd who naturally thought he had a greater claim to succeed his father than Gruffydd had.

Wales more than most countries had need of a strong man and old Llewellyn was certainly that. He it was who laid the foundations of a great power and showed the English that Wales was a country to be reckoned with. He was also a man who could act forcibly in his domestic relations as he had shown over his wife Joan's love affair with William de Broase. This was still sung of in ballads.

William de Broase had been captured by Llewellyn and held as his prisoner. To obtain his release he offered to pay a ransom and to give his daughter Isabella as wife to Llewellyn's son. This offer had tempted Llewellyn greatly for he saw in de Broase a rich and powerful ally. However, while de Broase was in captivity it had been the habit of Llewellyn's wife Joan to visit him in his prison chamber and they found a great interest in songs and stories of England, for Joan could not forget that although she was the wife of a Welsh ruler she was the daughter of an English King. Broase and Joan fell in love and when these visits of his wife to his prisoner's chamber were brought to Llewellyn's ears he decided to lay a trap for the lovers. This he did and they were caught. Llewellyn's indignation was great but he did not punish his wife, nor did he stop the arranged marriage. He merely brought William de Broase from the prison chamber, announced his crime and hanged him publicly at the town of Crokeen in the presence of many witnesses.

This act was applauded. He had punished the adulterer and at the same time lost none of the advantages which his heir's marriage to de Broase's daughter would bring.

That was the present Llewellyn's grandfather, Llewellyn the Great. Gruffydd, his father, was a man of great girth and equally strong ambition. As the eldest son of Llewellyn he had always believed he had the greatest claim to his father's dominions even though Joan had had that son, Davydd. On the death of their father the trouble between them started, and Davydd, who had the greater power on account of his legitimacy, had very soon seized Gruffydd and had him under lock and key.

But Gruffydd had the support of many Welshmen, and the Bishop of Bangor after excommunicating Davydd went to England to see the King and attempt to interest him in Gruffydd's cause. If the King would help to reinstate him, said the Bishop, Gruffydd's friends would be prepared to pay a tribute to the King. Henry could never resist the offer of money; he invaded Wales and forced Davydd to hand over Gruffydd who was brought to the Tower of London and kept there while the King made a show of judging his case.

Although Gruffydd was not ill-treated still he was a prisoner. He realized that Henry would attempt to extract all sorts of conditions from him before giving him his freedom and one night he made a rope from his linen and attempted to escape through a window. He made a fatal mistake; the rope was too long and he was a very heavy man. He was discovered lying on the ground with his neck broken. And that was the end of Gruffydd.

The death of their father meant that Llewellyn and his brother were heirs to Wales which was now ruled by their uncle Davydd, their grandfather's legitimate son; but two years after Gruffydd's death, their uncle died. The Welsh, who had suspected that Davydd had become too friendly with the English, welcomed the brothers, Owain and Llewellyn, and they divided certain lands between them. It seemed an amicable solution and the people looked forward to peace. Moreover King Henry invited them to Woodstock where he publicly pardoned their rebellion of the past and made an agreement with them to keep the peace; but this involved signing away much of the Welsh lands so that only Snowdon and Anglesey were in the hands of the brothers.

However, peace was maintained—although an uneasy one, for Llewellyn's ambition was great. Owain was less aggressive and would have preferred to shrug aside what they had lost and settle for a quiet existence without perpetual war.

But Llewellyn was not one to remain passive for long and he was soon at loggerheads with Owain who sought the support of their younger brother Davydd. Their forces met in battle and as might have been predicted Llewellyn was victorious; he captured Owain and put him under lock and key; Davydd unfortunately for Llewellyn was able to make his escape to England.

Llewellyn was then bent on bringing back to Wales all that land which had been in the possession of his grandfather, Llewellyn the Great. He had seen his great opportunity when the barons, under Simon de Montfort, rose against the King. He declared for them and what great triumph there had been throughout Wales when it was learned that the King and his son Edward were prisoners of Simon de Montfort!

It was at Hereford that Llewellyn had met Eleanor—the Demoiselle, an enchantingly beautiful girl with a look of the Plantagenets inherited from her mother, the King's sister—Eleanor like herself.

The marriage of Simon de Montfort had been one of the romances of the times. But of course Simon de Montfort was the sort of man who would distinguish himself in whatever he undertook, even marriage. What a man to snatch the King's sister from under his nose! Although in a moment of weakness Henry had agreed to the marriage however much he had tried to deny it afterwards.

The Demoiselle, they called her. He wanted her. No other would do for him. He could imagine his old grandfather looking down from heaven and nodding his head in approval.

A wife who was the niece of the King of England! A prophecy from Merlin!

"What are you waiting for, old Llewellyn would have said. Go in and take what is offered to you."

King of England! That was what the prophecy said. Llewellyn the First. A greater title than that of his grandfather. When they sang their ballads they would sing not of Llewellyn the

Great who had hanged his wife's lover. No, they would sing of Llewellyn the First of England and his beautiful bride the Demoiselle Eleanor.

But he had had bad luck. Edward the King of England was not like his father. He was a man of action. There was no dallying with Edward. The Demoiselle was coming to France to marry Llewellyn and there was a prophecy given by Merlin that a Llewellyn should become King of England. Edward had determined to stop that as soon as he could. So he had captured Llewellyn's bride and made her a prisoner, and the first move to bring about the prediction of Merlin had failed.

But that was but the beginning.

In the meantime the Demoiselle was somewhere in England and Llewellyn was in Wales.

He had always refused to attend the coronation of Edward and swear fealty to him. Was this Edward's revenge?

Llewellyn had to rescue his bride. He had to show the people of Wales that he was that Llewellyn mentioned in Merlin's prophecy.

But how?

The weeks passed and still the Demoiselle remained the prisoner of the English.

Edward was delighted with his Bristol seamen who had intercepted the ships bound for Wales.

He strode into the Queen's chamber, his face shining with delight.

"Merlin's prophecy indeed!" he cried. "Why wasn't Merlin off the Scilly Isles when the ships passed by? Why didn't he raise a storm and sink our craft?"

"God forbid," cried the Queen. She was pregnant once more and was hoping for a boy as they all were—she, Edward and the Queen Mother. They had not mentioned it to each other, but they were all aware that two-year-old Alfonso was not as healthy as they would have liked. He was bright enough, but there was a certain delicacy about him. Thus it had been with John and Henry. The Queen thought: I could not go through that anxiety again.

Now Edward was not thinking of the boy but of this victory at sea which had brought him what was more desirable than a load of treasure.

"They will bring our prisoners to land with all speed," he said.

"Poor Demoiselle!" said the Queen. "She will be most unhappy."

"Poor Demoiselle indeed! If she had reached Llewellyn we should have been hearing that Merlin had come back from wherever he is to help them. Now that, my dearest, is the last thing I want. This Merlin prophecy is nonsense. I have to prove that to the Welsh . . . and perhaps some of the English."

The Queen shuddered. "How can it be true," she said. "But I am sure the Demoiselle is desolate and perhaps a little frightened."

"She shall not be harmed," Edward promised.

"Except that she is taken from her husband."

"He is not her husband. Nor shall he be unless he is ready to bargain for her. By God and all his saints, this is a happy day for us, Eleanor. He has given me the best possible bargaining counter for my dealings with the troublesome Welsh."

"How I wish they would keep within their mountains and we could live at peace."

"We never shall, my love, and till we are all one. If Wales and Scotland were in my hands . . ."

"You have enough to control, Edward."

"That control would be easier with loyal subjects everywhere."

"You think this will ever be so. Alexander is your brother-in-law but he has always been determined not to swear fealty to you."

"And now that Margaret is dead he will doubtless marry again and there will be new loyalties. No, my love, I want to see Wales and Scotland under the English crown. Then we might hope for peace."

"I doubt we should achieve it even then. There will always be rebels."

"You are right. How fares the little one within?"

"Kicking heartily."

"As a boy would kick?"

"How can I know? I can only pray that this time it will be a boy."

"Well we could do with one." He frowned. He was thinking of delicate Alfonso but he would not mention his anxieties to

the Queen at that time. She must not be upset while she was
carrying the child. He had a fine daughter—she was the apple
of his eye, that proud and beautiful daughter of his. His eldest—
eleven years old, strong in body and mind. A Plantagenet
beauty. Nothing of Castile in her. He should not rejoice in
that. It was a slight to his Queen, his dear Eleanor, in whom
he rejoiced because of her gentle looks and her gentle ways
and that quiet strength which was only exerted to bring good
to him. He had Joanna too in Castile. He wished they had never
agreed to let her stay, but they would have her back before
long. And then Alfonso. And Alfonso was not showing the
rude health of his sisters—for there was news from Castile that
Joanna was a spirited and vital child. Why was it that his sons
should be weak? John, Henry and now Alfonso. He might have
had three healthy boys in the nursery. And one little daughter
buried in Acre. Well, it was understandable that born thus in
such surroundings she might not survive. But the Queen was
fruitful. Pray God that this time there was a healthy boy.

The Queen was a little sad, following his thoughts.

"I shall pray for a boy, Edward," she said.

He softened. "My dearest, if it is not then we shall have
our boy later. We have our Alfonso. When he comes to the
throne we shall have to change his name. You know what the
English are. They would think he was not English enough if
he had a Spanish name. What think you of Edward, eh? Edward
the Second."

She frowned. "Please Edward do not speak of that day."

"Ah, you would be sorry to see me replaced."

"Please!"

"I *am* sorry, little Queen. I am not going to die. See how
strong I am." He stood before her in all his glory, his long
legs astride—the most handsome king the country had ever
known. King Stephen had been a good looking man but what
a weak one. Strength and handsome looks and stern, righteous
character, that was what England needed and that was what
she had. But she also needed an heir. There must always be
an heir. For life could only serve a certain span and no kings
however great live for ever. Nor did they know in these days
of continual conflict when their last moment had come.

The Queen must have another boy.

Edward changed the subject. "I had come to speak to you

about the prisoners. Now we have them both—brother and sister."

"You will keep them together."

"Indeed I shall not. How can I know what Almeric de Montfort will plot. Remember who he is, who his father was. Simon de Montfort! That is a name which must have been graven on my father's heart. With my grandfather, King John, it was Magna Carta, with my father, King Henry, it was Simon de Montfort."

"And with you, my king, what will it be?"

"I intend none. I shall be in command I hope and make England a stronger country than she was when I came to the throne. No charters, no reformers...that is what I shall aim for. That is why I shall be very careful with Almeric de Montfort. I have given orders that he shall be taken to Corfe Castle and there he shall remain...my prisoner. He shall live comfortably but I must make sure that he is not allowed his freedom."

"And his sister?"

"I am having her brought to you. You will know how to look after her."

The Queen smiled. "I shall try to console her," she said.

"Never forgetting that she is the daughter of my father's great enemy and strives to be the wife of one of mine."

"I shall remember that and also that she is the daughter of your aunt. She is royal and must be treated as such."

"I know you will do what is best," said the King.

"I shall always do what I think to be best...for you!" she added.

He smiled, knowing she spoke the truth.

Eleanor de Montfort arrived at Windsor in a state of hopelessness. Ever since she had realized that the ship in which she was sailing had been taken by her cousin Edward's subjects she believed that all hope of her marriage was doomed. She was in her twenty-fourth year and but for the fact that her family were in exile she would have been married eight or nine years ago. It had always been Llewellyn for her. She and the Welsh prince had fallen in love on first sight and she remembered still the ecstacy which they had shared when they knew they were to be betrothed. She had often heard of her mother's

stormy passage to marriage, how she and her father had married
in secret and how they had to fly from the country when the
King's wrath was turned against them. That was romantic and
exciting but so much could have gone wrong; and she had been
so glad that her parents were in favor of this marriage she
wanted.

But how quickly life could change and when it was all set
fair like a ship at sea a cruel wind could arise and the ship
which had been sailing calmly onwards could be swept off its
course and sometimes dashed to pieces on the wicked rocks.

So it had seemed with her. All those years ago she was to
have been married and events had turned against her. And now
when she really believed she was on her way to happiness once
more she was frustrated.

And what would Edward do to her when she was handed
over to him like a slave? She had heard that he was strong and
ruthless. She knew that her brother Guy hated him. So had
Almeric. Guy and Simon had murdered Henry of Cornwall.
They would have liked to murder Edward.

Edward would know this. She had heard that when news
had been brought to him of Henry of Cornwall's murder, he
had been stricken with rage and grief and had vowed vengeance. She knew that only recently when he had become King,
before he went to England to claim his crown, he had called
on the Pope to ask for retribution for the murder of his cousin
of Cornwall. Edward hated her family, so what could she and
Almeric expect from him?

She had been terrified when they had taken Almeric from
her. She had clung to him and he had whispered to her: "Don't
break down. Remember you are of royal blood and best of all
a de Montfort. Do not let them have the satisfaction of gloating
over your grief."

But she had been treated with respect as though she, the
King's cousin, were paying a visit to him. Yet he was a ruthless
man and she knew that he would remember how her father had
once succeeded in taking his father from the throne, even if
only for a brief period.

And so they arrived at Windsor.

The Queen, she heard, had given orders that she was to be
taken to her.

The Queen was in the nurseries. The Demoiselle saw a

heavily pregnant woman with a gentle smile, by no means strikingly handsome but pleasant looking.

The Demoiselle approached and sank to her knees.

A hand touched her shoulder. "Rise, cousin," said the Queen. "The King told me you were coming." Kind eyes were studying her face, eyes which clearly showed the sympathy the Queen was feeling for the poor prisoner who had been snatched from her betrothed.

"The King has put you in my charge," she said. "We are cousins and I hope we shall be friends."

The Demoiselle, who so far had held her head high and implied, she hoped, that they could do with her what they wished and she would not beg for their mercy, now felt her eyes filling with tears. Her lips quivered and the Queen said, "Come and sit with me, cousin. As you see I am not far from my time. I want you to meet my son and daughter."

"My lady," said the Demoiselle, "I know I am your prisoner."

"I like not that word," said the Queen. "I am going to make you forget it during your stay with us. Now, cousin, let us sit down and talk."

The Demoiselle awoke each morning to a sense of desolation. She longed to know what was happening in Wales and how Llewellyn had received the news of her capture. She found the Queen sympathetic. Like everyone else she drew comfort from that warm and kindly personality. The Queen would sit at her tapestry, for she loved to work on it. She it was who had started the fashion for hanging tapestries on walls and they certainly gave warmth and color to an apartment. The Queen was growing larger every week and her time would soon come. She did not speak of her coming confinement in the Demoiselle's presence for she feared it might bring home to the poor girl that she herself was being denied the sort of comfort which she herself enjoyed.

The Queen Mother was less tactful. She made it clear that she did not approve of the Demoiselle's being treated as an honored member of the family. She had mentioned this to the Queen, who made one of her rare stands against her mother-in-law as she would occasionally when she thought some matter of kindness or sympathy to a bereaved person was involved.

"My lady," said the Queen, "the Demoiselle is Edward's cousin. You are her aunt by marriage. She *is* therefore a member of our family."

The Queen Mother's eyes narrowed. "She is the daughter of the greatest enemy my husband ever had."

"She is also the daughter of his sister."

"If you could only know what we suffered through Simon de Montfort you would understand. It was her brothers who murdered dear Henry of Cornwall...Edward's cousin and greatest friend."

"But she was not responsible."

"I cannot endure to look at her."

The Queen could only shake her head sadly. If the Queen Mother could not endure the sight of the Demoiselle then she must stay away from where the girl was.

The Queen Mother raged. How different from the days when Henry was alive. Then the Demoiselle would have been sent away from Court. Nothing would have been allowed to offend Henry's beloved Queen.

The Queen was sorry that she had to disappoint her mother-in-law but she felt at this stage that the poor little Demoiselle was in greater need than that domineering lady who would, alas, only see life as it affected herself.

The Queen Mother consoled herself by going to the schoolroom and spending a little time with her dear grand-daughter— such an attractive girl—and darling Alfonso whom she loved, although he gave her such qualms of anxiety.

She was, however, not going to allow the matter to rest, and she thought that it would be better for the Queen if she realized that her soft attitude toward the family's enemies was not a good one and that she would be well advised at times to forget her ever-ready sympathy and listen to sound common sense.

She waylaid Edward. He was not very easy to confront these days. He was very concerned with the Welsh matter. Llewellyn was incensed of course to have lost his intended bride and was out to make trouble. Edward had sent a force up in preparation, but he was very disturbed and it rankled with him that he could not be with his armies there, because affairs kept him for the time in London.

"My dear son," she said, "do you think the Queen is at ease?"

Edward looked startled. "She is well, is she not?" he asked anxiously.

She had aroused him from his Welsh concerns. He really cared about his wife. Such a meek woman! She would have thought he would hardly be aware of her except as a bearer of his children, but she supposed he, being of an overbearing nature, was glad to have a mild creature who could say nothing but yes, yes, yes. Oh for the spirited old days when her word had been law! Henry had had *such* good sense. He always grasped her point of view immediately.

"Oh, the child is well enough I doubt not. I pray it will be a healthy boy. But perhaps she is a little uneasy about our . . . prisoner, which is natural. When you think of what the creature's father did to yours . . ."

Edward's brow cleared. "Oh, the Demoiselle. The Queen is not concerned about her. She tells me she is a charming girl and she grows fonder of her every week."

"I have no doubt this Demoiselle has inherited a little of her father's cunning. One as simple as the Queen . . ." Edward frowned and she added quickly, ". . . and as tender-hearted . . . would see no wrong in anyone . . . not until it was brought home to her. Edward, the girl should be put into confinement. Why not send her to Corfe? Her brother is there . . ."

"Dear Mother, this girl has done no wrong. She was sent for by Llewellyn and I have had the good fortune to intercept her. I have no quarrel with her. It is Llewellyn who is my enemy."

"And not the girl who would be his wife. Edward, surely you cannot mean that you do not *see* . . ."

"I say what I mean," said Edward sternly, very much the King. More than six feet of splendid manhood looking down at her made her not so much quail as decide to change her tactics. In a way she was proud of him, as in a way he loved and admired her. But if it was a battle for power there was no doubt who was going to win. He had everything on his side now. He was the King and she knew him well enough to realize that the Demoiselle's chances of remaining at the palace in the company of the Queen were double those of what they would have been had she not interfered.

She sighed. "Well, perhaps one day you will change your mind when . . ."

He looked at her and that lid which fell over his eyes slightly and reminded her poignantly of his father could have added a sternness to his face but his mouth was tender.

"If I have to change my mind, dear lady, because I am proved wrong, I should be the first to admit it."

He was strong. If only she could have guided him as she had Henry she could have been greatly reconciled to her life.

She wanted to test his love for her.

"Sometimes," she said, "I fancy my days of usefulness are over. Perhaps I should do what ladies of my age so often do . . . go into a convent."

"You would not like that I am sure."

"Would you like it, Edward?"

"Dear lady, you know how I and Eleanor like to have you here. You know how the children adore you. How could we want you to shut yourself away? But if it is your wish."

"Well, I will tell you this," she said. "I have considered taking the veil and have been to Amesbury to look at the place."

The King smiled. He could picture his mother entering the convent, becoming the abbess and setting up her rule there. "And you have decided against it?"

"While they want to take my wealth, yes. I have no fancy to give up my possessions to a convent."

"Nay. You will have to get them to rescind that rule."

"Indeed I should before I entered such a place."

"In the meantime you will continue to bless us with your company."

"For as long as my health is good."

She saw the little lights of alarm in his eyes. She had never been one to complain about her health. She had rather thought that people who professed bad health were in some way to blame for such feebleness.

Edward suddenly thought of his childhood when she had been there—the most important person in his life. She had been love, security . . . everything to him. He would never forget. He loved her deeply and nothing could change that love, and even though he would not brook her interference he could not love her any less for interfering any more than she could love him less for refusing to take her advice.

She had suffered cruelly lately. The death of her two beloved daughters had been a great shock to her. She could be hurt most through her loved ones and whatever her faults she had been the most devoted of wives and mothers.

He was at her side, taking her face in his hands, looking at her anxiously. Joy flooded her heart. Real concern. The Welsh forgotten, the Demoiselle of no importance. Even the Queen's imminent confinement relegated to second place. There was nothing but fear for his mother.

"My mother," he said quietly, "is there something you have to tell me? If you are ill . . . if you are keeping something back . . ."

"My dear, dear son, I am getting old, that is all. Life has been cruel to me of late. Your father's death killed half of me . . . and now God has taken my daughters. Two of them, Edward. How could He! What have I done to deserve that? But I have my sons . . . my most beloved King. If my old physician William were here I would see him. But no other . . . No, it is nothing . . . I am just an old woman who has suffered too much the pain of loss."

"Mother, I am going to send for William."

"Nay son. He is in Provence I believe. It is too far. Let us forget this. I should never have mentioned this."

"I am sending without delay for the physician. He will be here just as soon as it is possible for him to be."

"Edward, my son, you have other matters with which to concern yourself."

"What could be of greater moment than my mother's health?"

Sweet words. Not entirely true but sweet nevertheless.

And he was true to them. It was not long before the Queen Mother's physician arrived from Provence.

September had come and the birth of the Queen's child was imminent.

There was a hush over the palace. Everyone was expectant. It should be a boy. It must be a boy. The Prince Alfonso was a bright boy, but he had that all-too-familiar air of delicacy which had been John's and Henry's. A great deal of care was taken of him and the physicians said that if he could survive the first seven years of his childhood he could grow to a healthy

man. They recalled his father's infancy. It was difficult to
believe now that Edward had ever been a sickly child. Alfonso
was only two. It would be a great comfort if a really healthy
boy were born.

The Queen was a little sad, wondering if some fault lay in
her. It seemed strange. She had had six children—this one
would be the seventh. Three of them only lived. Perhaps one
should not stress too much the little girl who had been born at
Acre. The circumstances of her birth were against her. Joanna
had lived and thrived though, and Eleanor was a fine healthy
child. It was the boys whom it was so difficult to rear. Would
she ever be able to forget little John and Henry? Never! Because
she blamed herself for leaving them. And now Alfonso was
not as strong as he should be. She had moved them from the
Tower and Westminster to Windsor which she believed to be
so much more healthy. But she had to admit that Alfonso had
changed little since he had been at Windsor.

She must pray for a boy—a healthy boy.

In the afternoon her pains started while she stood calmly at
her window looking to the forest where the leaves of the trees
were already turning to bronze, for September had come.

She calmly told one of the attendants to go to the Queen
Mother's apartment and ask her if she would come to her
quickly. The woman departed with all speed and as soon as
the Queen Mother looked into the face of the breathless woman
she knew, and immediately went to the Queen's apartment.

The Queen was serene. The birth of a seventh child is not
like the first. She knew what to expect and she had always
given birth without much discomfort.

The energetic Queen Mother gave orders sharply. Soon there
was great activity in the royal apartments.

As expected the labor was not arduous, but the result was
disappointing.

The Demoiselle chose a moment when the Queen Mother
was absent to come into the Queen's bedchamber to see the
baby.

"What a dear little girl!" she said.

The Queen smiled. "Yes, a dear little girl."

"But you wanted a boy."

"Now I have seen her, she is the one I want."

"The King will love her."

"The King loves all his children."

The Demoiselle nodded, her eyes were misty. Poor child, thought the Queen, she dreams of the children it seems she will never have.

"I have heard she may be called Margaret," said the Demoiselle, noting the pity in the Queen's eyes.

"It is what the Queen Mother wishes," said the Queen. "In memory of the Queen of Scotland."

The Demoiselle nodded and remembered that life was sad for others as well as herself.

She asked if she might hold the baby and the Queen smiling gave her permission. After a while the Queen said, "The children will want to see her. They are being brought in."

The Demoiselle put the baby in the cradle and was prepared for flight in case the Queen Mother came with the children.

She did and the girl slipped away. The Queen Mother frowned but the children were exclaiming loudly.

"Oh, she is only little!" cried Alfonso in a disappointed tone.

"Well," retorted the Queen Mother, "what did you expect her to be? Big like yourself? You are two years old remember. She is but two weeks."

"They said we were to have a brother," said the Princess Eleanor rather reproachfully.

"God sent us a girl instead," the Queen answered.

"Which," commented Eleanor, "was rather unkind of Him when he knew what my father wanted."

"Well, we all have to have what is sent us," said the Queen Mother brightly.

"You don't, my lady," retorted the Princess. "You have what you want."

The Queen Mother loved Eleanor. What a bright child. If the worse came to the worst Edward would have to make her his heir. She would speak to him about it some time . . . perhaps not yet. It was a little tactless while Alfonso lived, but the boy did have an air of delicacy and he was so like little Johnny had been at his age; and very soon Henry had begun to go like it.

Oh what a pity this child was not another boy!

As soon as he could, Edward came to his wife.

She lay in her bed looking at him appealingly.

"Edward, I'm sorry."

He laughed aloud. He was not going to let her know how disappointed he was.

"Why, she is a beautiful child, and Margaret, eh? That was my mother's choice and you agree with it."

"It pleases her so to honor the Queen of Scotland."

"And you, dear good soul that you are, will agree for her sake. God bless you, my Queen."

"I am so glad that you are not angry."

"What sort of man should I be if I were angry with you. By God, we'll have sons yet. You were made to be a mother of them and I a father. Don't fret, sweet wife. We have had seven to this time. There'll be another seven you'll see and if among them there are a stalwart boy or two I'll be satisfied."

She smiled and thought she was indeed blessed with such a husband.

A few weeks after the child's birth there was alarming news from Wales. Ever since the capture of the Demoiselle, as was to be expected, Llewellyn had been making raids into England with some success. Edward had sent an army to deal with him, and had expected news of success. It had been delayed rather longer than he had thought it would.

Then came the news. The English army had been defeated at Kidwelly.

Edward was dismayed. The Queen was anxious. The Queen Mother was furious. And the Demoiselle could not completely hide her satisfaction.

Edward stormed into the Queen's apartment. There was nothing for it. He would have to get together the best of his armies. If a job had to be well done there was only one who should do it and that was oneself.

"Edward," said the Queen, "it is only a skirmish he has won. Need you go into danger? Cannot your soldiers let him know that he must keep the peace?"

"If it were not for this prophecy of Merlin's I might agree with you. He must not win...even a skirmish. His little victories will be sung into big ones. You know the Welsh and their songs. Verses not deeds make their heroes. It may be that this prophecy of Merlin's was made by a poet and sung of until people believed it for truth. Nay, I must teach Llewellyn a lesson. I shall not be long away. I must drive this man back to his mountains. It is the only way."

The King made his preparations to leave and before he went the Queen was able to tell him that she was once more pregnant.

The Demoiselle was white with misery. It was hard for her to keep believing in Merlin's prophecy when she lived close to the power of the great English King.

Edward marched up to Wales and they waited for news. The Queen grew large with child.

"This time," she said, "it *must* be a boy. What wonderful news that would be to send to the King."

The Demoiselle sat with the Princess Eleanor and they worked on their tapestry together.

"You are sad," said the Princess, "because my father is going to kill your lover."

"What if my lover killed your father?" replied the Demoiselle.

"No one could kill my father. He is the King."

"Llewellyn has been promised the crown by Merlin."

"He lived long ago. He does not count now," said the Princess placidly stitching. "Do you like this blue silk?"

"I do," said the Demoiselle.

"Tell me about Llewellyn," said Eleanor. "Is he beautiful?"

"He is the most beautiful man in the world."

"That is my father. So you lie."

"He is beautiful for me as your father is for you."

"But you said the most beautiful." Eleanor cried out. She had pricked her finger. "Do you think my mother will have a boy?" she asked.

"That is in God's hands."

"And God is not very kind, is He? He took my two brothers and my aunts Margaret and Beatrice. My grandmother is very cross with Him." She shivered. Obviously she was sorry for anyone with whom her grandmother was cross. "I'll tell you a secret, Demoiselle, if you promise to tell no one."

The Demoiselle looked eager. She was always hoping to learn something about Llewellyn and she knew that news about him was kept from her.

"I will tell no one."

"I was glad Margaret was a girl. I hope this one will be a girl."

"But why? Don't you know how much they want a boy?"

The Princess nodded gravely. "I heard them talking about
Alfonso. They were saying he was like John and Henry. Then
one of them said: 'It may well be that the king would make
Princess Eleanor'—that is myself—'heir to the throne.' You
see, Demoiselle, if there were no boys and Alfie went the way
of . . . the others . . . I should be the one. *I*, the Princess. Princesses can become queens you know. Real queens—not like
my mother and grandmother who just married kings, but *The*
Queen."

The Demoiselle looked shocked. "You should not say such
things," she said. "They are not . . . becoming."

"I know. That is why they are secret. You don't have to
be . . . becoming . . . in secret."

The Demoiselle studied the ambitious little girl who kept
her ears and eyes open. She supposed there was a possibility
of her realizing her ambition.

Poor child, she had yet to learn the trials of wearing a crown.

As the months passed and the Queen's confinement grew
near there was little news from Wales.

Then less than a year after the birth of little Margaret,
another child was born to the Queen.

There was general despondency. Another girl! They called
her Berengaria because of a fancy the Queen had, and when a
short while afterwards the child grew more and more sickly it
was said that it was an unlucky name to have given a child. It
recalled the sad queen of Richard Coeur de Lion. He had never
loved her; he had neglected her; and she had been an unhappy
woman, a barren woman. Poor soul, said the Queen Mother,
she rarely had an opportunity to be anything else for everyone
knew of the King's preference for fighting crusades and handsome people of his own sex. A man to sing of rather than to
live with.

Berengaria. It was a doomed name.

The Queen was sad, eagerly awaiting news from the Welsh
border, but not more eagerly than the Demoiselle.

But the Princess Eleanor had a light in her eyes which
showed she was not altogether displeased by the turn of events.

Gloom settled over Windsor. The King was on the Welsh
border with his forces but it was not easy to gain the victory

he sought. It was the Welsh mountains which defeated him time after time.

The Demoiselle was like a grey ghost in the palace. She longed for news yet dreaded it. She prayed for Llewellyn; she did not care whether Merlin's prophecy came true or not. It was not a King of England she wanted; she could have been completely happy with a Prince of Wales . . . and peace.

The Queen Mother was so hostile to her that she wondered why she did not force her to leave Windsor. But the gentle Queen would be firm about that. It was after all the King's wish that although she was a prisoner she should not be treated as one. Sometimes she would dream of how different her life would have been if the ship which was taking her to Wales had not been intercepted by the English. She and Llewellyn together with perhaps a little son or daughter. She would not have minded which. Oh how different it would have been from this weary waiting, this never-ending anxiety. Every time a messenger came to the castle she was in terror of what news he would bring. So was the Queen. She feared for Edward as the Demoiselle feared for Llewellyn.

The Queen had discovered how Almeric was faring in Corfe Castle and had assured the Demoiselle that he was being well treated. "In spite of everything," said the Queen, "the King does not forget that you are cousins."

Edward was just, and the Demoiselle did not think he would be unduly cruel unless he found it expedient to do so. He was not like her grandfather King John who had taken pleasure in inflicting pain.

It was circumstances rather than individuals that had decided on her cruel fate.

The Queen Mother had received the Provençal physician William who assured her that her ailments were only those of encroaching age and that as she was usually healthy, there were many years left to her. That made good hearing and she rejoiced that Edward had sent for him. William was to stay in England— those were the King's commands—and he must be given certain privileges which the Queen Mother would decide on.

That was very satisfactory. If Edward could only settle that tiresome business in Wales and they could send the Demoiselle to Corfe to join her brother, and Edward could come home and get his wife with a child who would prove a boy, and if little

Alfonso would show a little more vitality, all would be as well as it could be without the late King.

Meanwhile Edward had begun the Welsh invasion and was at Chester when one of his men at arms came to tell him that a messenger from the Welsh was asking to see him.

"I will see this man," said Edward.

The man hesitated. He was obviously thinking of another occasion when Edward had received a messenger in his tent on the Holy Land.

Edward acknowledged the man's concern and gave him a friendly nod. "Bring him in," he said.

He stood before the King, a tall proud figure.

Edward knew him at once; he had been a prominent member of the Welsh party at a meeting when a truce had been made between the English and the Welsh.

"Davydd ab Gruffydd," he said. "What brings you to me?"

"I have come to offer my services to you."

The King narrowed his eyes. He did not like traitors and that Llewellyn's brother should come to him thus aroused his suspicions. He knew that there was conflict between the brothers. He knew that the elder brother Owain had with Davydd fought against Llewellyn and it was because Llewellyn had been victorious that he was looked upon as the ruler of the principality. It was one matter for Welshman to fight against Welshman but to fight on the side of the English against the Welsh was quite another.

Of course there was a long record of treachery among these people. All the more reason, thought Edward, not to trust him. Still, if he was well watched he could be an asset. It would be good for those who believed in Merlin's prophecy to know that even Llewellyn's brother was fighting with the English against him.

Edward said, "I accept your offer."

"I will show you how to conquer my false brother. I know his weaknesses."

"I know them too," said Edward. "Well, Davydd ab Gruffydd, you shall be my ally. If you work with me, then I shall reward you. If you play the traitor to me I will make it so that you wish you had never been born rather than have to face what I shall inflict on you."

"My lord, I will serve you faithfully, until such time as you see fit to reward me."

Davydd was smiling triumphantly. This would show Llewellyn that brother though he might be he was ready to go to the enemy rather than submit to a minor role in Welsh affairs.

When Llewellyn heard that his brother had gone to the English he was very melancholy. It seemed that he was being persecuted from all sides. He believed that had his Demoiselle been brought safely to him it would have been a sign that Heaven was on his side, and all his followers would have seen it as such. Superstitious as they were they had already begun to doubt Merlin's prophecy and he knew how dangerous that was. He had appealed to the Pope to take the English to task for capturing and imprisoning his bride, but the Pope was not likely to support an unimportant Prince against the growing might of the King of England. He had had his success in those skirmishes but they were not serious war and now great Edward himself had come to march against him. With the King was his brother, Edmund of Lancaster, returned from France with his new bride Blanche, daughter of Robert of Artois, De Lacy, Roger Mortimer, the Earl of Hereford and all the flower of Edward's army. Clearly he had come up this time to conquer.

Llewellyn knew that his real ally was the mountainous country, and but for that he would be a beaten man.

He wondered if she were thinking of him now, if she often remembered that day when they had been betrothed and had believed that before long they would marry. If he failed now, what would become of her? Would they find a new husband for her? After all she was the King's cousin. Dear Demoiselle, so gentle, so beautiful. He knew that she would be thinking of him, praying for him. It must come to pass that they marry. There must be truth in Merlin's prophecy.

Even then news was brought to him of a débâcle in South Wales where Edmund of Lancaster was advancing and there was nothing left for Llewellyn to do but protect what was left to him.

The ships from the Cinque ports were now in the Menai Straits; Anglesey was cut off from Snowdon. It would be a simple matter to starve out the Welsh. That this was Edward's intention became clear for instead of advancing and thereby running the risk of losing some of his men in battle, he set about consolidating his position and strengthening those castles he had captured. With fury Llewellyn learned that he was not only working on the fortifications but beautifying them, as though he already owned them.

Those were dreary months. There was Llewellyn with those of his followers who were faithful and continued to believe in Merlin's prophecies, knowing full well that they would have to give up in time because the King's intentions were to starve them until they surrendered.

Llewellyn spoke to his men.

"Rest assured the prophecy will come true. Llewellyn shall reign over all England and then he will not forget his faithful friends. But it may well be that the time has not yet come. We must perforce suffer long and fight for this great prize."

To fight was well enough. To starve was different.

There came a message from Edward. He would have Llewellyn know that he wished him no ill. All he wanted from him was his loyalty. He must indeed do homage for the lands of Wales, and he would be left to rule over them in peace as long as he did nothing to offend the laws of the King of England. Edward was ready to come to some agreement with Llewellyn. He would restore his bride to him, for he had no wish to hold her against her will and that of Llewellyn. All Llewellyn had to do was swear allegiance to the King of England and accept him as his sovereign lord.

It was a great deal to ask, but there was so much to be gained.

The outcome was that they met at Conway—that great fortress on which Edward had already set his men to work.

Edward was strong, stern, but not without a certain benignity. He had no wish to continue in a war which Llewellyn knew full well he had already lost. Nor did he wish to be unduly harsh. Because of this he had sent for the Demoiselle to come to Worcester and there if Llewellyn agreed to his terms they should all meet to sign the treaty after which the marriage would be solemnized.

From despair Llewellyn was raised to hope. All he had to do was submit to Edward, declare himself his vassal, pay certain monies, give certain concessions and his Demoiselle would be his.

"I will send to you," wrote Edward, "your brother Davydd

who had the good sense you lacked when he joined me. He will lay my terms before you and when all is settled we will proceed to Worcester for the signing and there your marriage shall take place."

Receive Davydd, the traitor brother! How could he! Yet he understood Edward's motive. Edward wanted peace . . . peace between the brothers as well as between England and Wales. Llewellyn had no alternative but to receive Davydd and he did so.

The two brothers regarded each other with reserve.

It was Davydd who spoke first. "I regret nothing that I have done," he said. "I went over to the King because I knew you were fighting a losing battle, and by working with Edward fewer of our castles would be ruined, less of our land desecrated. I have proved that I was right because you now are ready to come to terms with him."

"Perhaps those terms would not have been necessary if we had all stood together," said Llewellyn.

"Perhaps we should have stood together if the land had been fairly divided. We brothers wanted some, Llewellyn, and there was not enough to go around."

"Can we trust Edward?"

"He is a man who prides himself on honoring his word. He can be trusted better than most kings. Already he has fulfilled his promise to me. I have a wife now, you know, Llewellyn."

"Is that so?"

"A rich wife provided by Edward. The daughter of the Earl of Derby is now my wife. She has brought me much joy . . . and riches. You fret for the Demoiselle. Make your terms and marry. A man is meant to get sons not to spend his days in a damp and drafty tent."

"You are a satisfied man, Davydd."

"For the time," said Davydd.

Of course he was right, thought Llewellyn. A man was a fool who did not know when he was beaten. There was a time to stop fighting, to make peace so that he could live to fight another day.

And meanwhile the Demoiselle was beckoning him.

And there he was at Worcester. The King had sent for her and he gazed in delight as she came towards him. She had grown up since he had last seen her, become a graceful, gracious woman. Love shone from her eyes which were appealing, a little apprehensive, as though she feared she might not please him. He wanted to reassure her. It was not for her to falter. Did he please her? He was some ten years older than she was and a soldier led a hard life. Perhaps it left its mark.

He took her hand. He said: "My Demoiselle . . . my beautiful Demoiselle."

"Llewellyn." She spoke his name softly.

It was enough.

The King with the Queen beside him looked on benignly. Happily married themselves, they understood and showed their sympathy. There were tears in the Queen's eyes; she was a good kind woman.

"There need be no delay in the ceremony," said the King briskly. "Once all the terms are agreed to."

All the terms. Edward was a man to drive a hard bargain. But he could be trusted. He had promised the Demoiselle and she was there.

Llewellyn had surrendered all his prisoners to the King of England and they included his eldest brother Owain whom he had held in captivity for more than ten years; he had given up his claims to South Wales and agreed to pay a fine of fifty thousand pounds. Anglesey was restored to him but he must pay a rent for it and if he died without heirs it was to be returned to the King. The barons of Wales would pay homage to Edward instead of to Llewellyn.

Yes, it was a hard bargain that Edward drove. Llewellyn's territory was reduced to that around Snowdon one might say, and the King had freed Owain and rewarded him with lands and done the same for Davydd plus a rich wife. He was showing them how he rewarded those who worked against his enemies.

It was a sorry state of affairs, but Llewellyn was in love. And what mattered most was that he had his Demoiselle.

The Return of Joanna

The reunion of Edward and his Queen resulted in two more pregnancies.

There was a certain anxiety during that bleak March at Windsor as the Queen's time drew near. It was two years since the sad little Berengaria had made her brief appearance, and there was a general feeling that although the Queen was clearly fruitful her children were inclined to be weaklings.

Alfonso's health had not really improved. He was now five years old, approaching the danger period. There were days, however, when he seemed to grow stronger and in the summer he would often appear to be quite a healthy little boy. But during the winter he deteriorated and they had just come through one. Hence this anxiety.

"This one must be a boy," said the Queen Mother somewhat peremptorily as though she were ordering the Queen—or perhaps God—to behave with a little more consideration for them all this time.

Such talk made the Queen uneasy but she knew that the Queen Mother was right. It must be a boy.

"If," went on the Queen Mother, "it should prove to be a girl then she must become a nun."

"That must be a matter for her to choose," said the Queen with a slight touch of firmness.

"No, indeed, my dear," insisted the Queen Mother. "Heaven must know this child is to be dedicated to its service. Then perhaps God will relent and if He has already decided on a girl He might change the child for a boy."

This seemed strange reasoning to the Queen but she did not contradict the Queen Mother. No one did—not even Edward, who usually smiled and listened to her advice and then went away and ignored it.

The Queen's time came. She lay in her bed eagerly waiting, but in due course she heard the disappointing words: "Another girl."

But this time it was a healthy one, quite different from the ill-fated Berengaria.

"There is no doubt," said the Queen Mother, "that this child should become a nun. I have chosen Amesbury, where one day I shall retire myself . . . when the time comes and if the Pope will give me a dispensation which allows me to keep my dowry. I have no intention of giving it up for any convent on earth."

They called the child Mary and the Queen soon forgot her disappointment and knew in her heart that she would not have changed her for all the boys in the land.

The Princess Eleanor was delighted. She had noticed that her father was especially interested in her. He had always shown that she was his favorite and much as he longed for a boy that had never clouded their relationship. She believed that she could read his thoughts.

If the Queen kept producing girls and Alfonso's health did not improve, then the most important child in the royal nurseries was the Princess Eleanor. She loved her little brother, but she liked being important too, and she could not help noticing that as she grew in years so did she in importance.

She was rather pleased, therefore, that little Mary was the new addition to the family and not some bawling boy who would have detracted from her importance and demanded all the attention.

Her thoughts concerning her position were undoubtedly based on fact for she noticed how, on their return from Worcester, her father seemed to spend more time in her company. Like all the family there was a deep bond of love between them but the Princess felt that there was something special between her and her father; she was devoted to her mother of course but she did not find the same thrilling pleasure in her company as she did in that of her father.

She liked to walk in the gardens with him and he, strangely enough, although so many people were wanting to see him, would find a little time for her.

Now that he was back she asked him about the war in Wales and he was quite ready to talk to her, as though she were one of his generals, and he took a great delight in her intelligent questions and comments.

"You are growing out of childhood," he said on this occasion. "Thirteen is it. What a great age!"

She agreed with him solemnly.

"I think it is time you had a household of your own. What think you of that? A complete set of attendants . . . your very own."

"How I should like that!"

"Why not? Are you not my eldest daughter? And so much older than the others. Joanna will have to come home soon."

"It is strange," said the Princess, "that I have never seen my own sister."

"She will come home soon for we will have to contract a marriage for her. There are already negotiations going on with the King of the Romans. His eldest son is Hartman who will himself be King of the Romans one day. I like to see my daughters queens."

"I wonder what Joanna is like."

"Spoilt a little, I imagine. Her grandmother was inclined to pamper her as a baby and no doubt she continued."

"Then," said the Princess with a severity which amused the King, "it is time she came home."

"Oh? So you do not think your parents spoil their children?"

She took his arm and pressed against his side. "Dear Father, your children are treated as children should be treated. Everything you do is . . . perfect."

"What an opinion for a child to have of her father!"

"When you spoke to me so solemnly I was afraid you were going to talk to me about *my* marriage. I could not bear to

leave you, dear Father, and my mother and even my grandmother too."

"It will be some time yet," he murmured soothingly.

Why? she wondered. She had been betrothed to the infant
of Aragon for many years. His grandfather, the King of Aragon,
had recently died and his son Pedro had become King. So
Pedro's son, Alfonso, the Princess's betrothed, was direct heir
to the Aragonese throne. In the circumstances there should be
no delay in getting her married. Panic seized her. Could it be
that this change in her father's attitude towards her meant that
she was to go away from home?

She cried out: "I could not bear to leave you all."

"I promise it will be a long time yet." He took her hand
and held it firmly as though implying he would not let her go.
"I wanted to talk to you about your new household. That is a
much more pleasant subject."

"It *will* be a long time, will it not, my dear lord?"

"Rest assured, my love, it shall be as long as I can make
it."

"But you can do everything you want. If you said I should
never go away, then I never should."

"I can see you are a dutiful daughter who has the right ideas
about her father."

"My father is the King," she said proudly.

He was overwhelmed by his love for her. If I had another
boy, he thought, I should never love him as I do this daughter
of mine.

"Now," he said briskly, "a chamberlain, eh, a keeper of the
hall, a groom of the bedchamber?"

"A cook," she went on, laughing, her fears dispersed, for
if he were giving her a household as he was suggesting he could
not be thinking of letting her leave the country. "A salterer—
yes I must have a salterer."

"Indeed you must! What royal household would be complete
without one. What a grand household you will have!"

"Grand enough for a King," she said. "But then I *am* the
King's daughter . . . his eldest daughter. Poor Alfie could be
jealous . . . if he were of a nature to be. But he will just be
pleased for me."

"Alfonso is a good boy," said the King frowning.

And there was an understanding between them. If Alfonso

should die as his brothers had and there was no other boy then she, the Princess Eleanor, would be in a very important position. She would be the heir to the throne.

They continued their walk and discussed the household she would have.

They were both deeply aware of the significance of that.

The Princess Joanna had sensed that something was wrong. Her grandmother's eyes were red-rimmed which indicated that she had been weeping. An unheard of thing. There had been several occasions when she had snatched up young Joanna and had held her tightly against her in a manner which had been most uncomfortable and had aroused indignant protests from the child.

"Oh my darling!" had been her grandmother's response.

It was very strange. Precocious seven-year-old Joanna had been born with a fiery and imperious nature and it had quickly become apparent to her that she was a very important person at the court of Castile. Her grandmother doted on her, which gave her a sense of her own importance, and since the Dowager Queen was constantly thanking heaven for little Joanna it could not be anything but exhilarating to consider oneself as a gift from heaven for whom everyone had to be grateful.

The little gift from heaven knew herself to be beautiful to look on, that her mental powers were something to be marvelled at, that she only had to show a desire for something and it was hers—providing of course it would not be harmful to her, a concession which, when she grew older, she was ready to grant.

So when she saw that her grandmother was decidedly upset she guessed it was something that concerned her.

It was no use asking the Bishop. Suerus, Bishop of Calixien, was her tutor and like her grandmother he adored her. Indeed Joanna could not believe that she was anything but completely adorable. "Filiola," was his pet name for her. It meant little daughter. "Which I am not," she pointed out to him. "My father is the King of England and my mother the Queen. One day I shall be with them." She liked to say that because when she did they cast down their eyes and murmured a prayer to God which she knew meant they were asking Him not to take their darling away from them. Suerus had replied, "It is true

that you are the daughter of the King and Queen of England
but to me you are as a daughter . . . a very dear child."

The only one who did not show such adulation was her
governess, the Lady Edeline, whom her parents had left with
her when they went on their way to England. Joanna knew that
Edeline loved her just as much as the others but her love showed
itself differently. Edeline could scold and criticize and even
punish. Joanna could not quite understand why it was, but in
spite of all this Edeline was really the one she loved the best.

So of course it was to Edeline from whom she must now
go to discover the truth.

Edeline was mending the lace on a gown of Joanna's, which
had been carelessly torn in play. Edeline had scolded her about
that.

Joanna ran to her and threw herself against her governess's
knee.

"Careful child," said Edeline. "You have made me prick
my finger."

"Oh poor, poor Edeline. It is really bleeding. There I will
kiss it and make it better."

"So you think you have some special power to do that, do
you?" said Edeline. Joanna smiled. Edeline always thought she
must be taken down a little. It was all for her own good. But
she had liked having her finger kissed to be made better.

"Everybody has special powers when they kiss to make
better. But never mind that now. Why is my grandmother sad?"

"Has she told you she is sad?"

"She has crying eyes."

"Perhaps you should ask her."

"I want to ask you, Edeline. You will tell me the truth. Am
I . . . going away?"

Edeline was silent.

"I am then! I am!" cried Joanna.

"It had to come some time, did it not?" said Edeline. "Your
mother left you with your grandmother when you were a baby."

Joanna frowned into her governess's face. "They should
never have left me."

"They didn't want to. Your mother was very, very sad. But
your poor grandmother pleaded so and at last your father said
you might stay for . . . a while."

"And that time is up now? That's it, is it?"

"You are going to England."

For the first time Joanna was afraid. She threw herself at Edeline. "I shall leave Grandmother . . . my uncle the King . . . all the people here I know . . ." She raised her eyes to Edeline's face fearfully and dared not to ask the question which rose to her lips. Edeline answered it. "I shall come with you."

Joanna sighed deeply. It was clear that she had found great comfort.

"When shall we go?"

"It will not be long."

"Oh my poor, poor grandmother!"

The Dowager Queen of Castile could have echoed those words. What would she do without the child on whom she doted? Life had been unfair to Joanna of Castile. She had never been loved as she had longed to be. Henry III had once asked for her hand and then when she had believed herself to be on the verge of marriage he had discarded her for Eleanor of Provence. It had been humiliating beyond endurance. Her mother had been similarly treated in a way and by an English King. Richard whom they called Coeur de Lion had been *her* betrothed and as a young girl she had been sent to England. But she had at least been beloved by Henry II who had seduced her when she was a child in the schoolroom and kept her as his mistress so that it was only natural that Richard should reject her. Then she had been married late to the Earl of Ponthieu who had been Queen Joanna's father and they had produced but the one girl child. This child—rejected by the King of England—had at length been married to the King of Castile, but when he was old and she was almost past child-bearing, so she had had only one daughter—her dear gentle Eleanor who was now the wife of Edward of England. It had been a humiliating life and when her daughter had married and gone out of it she had yearned for someone to replace her.

Then had come Edward and Eleanor on their way home from the crusade with their dear little baby, who had been born in Acre, and when she had seen the child—named after herself, which seemed to make her more especially hers—she had implored them to leave the child with her. Rather to her surprise and to her intense delight they had done so. Of course they had stressed the point that one day little Joanna would have to come home, but she had refused to think of that day. Now it had come.

They had made a match for her. A match, thought the Dowager Queen indignantly. A match for a baby!

And they were going to take her darling away from her. She could not bear it.

There was no one she could discuss it with except the Lady Edeline. Her half-brother the King had his own affairs and that of a child being returned to her parents seemed a very small one to him.

Lady Edeline came to her and told her that the Princess Joanna had guessed that she was going to England.

The Queen opened her eyes very wide and stared at Edeline. "But how . . . could she know?"

"She noticed your melancholy and thought it had something to do with herself and from that she guessed."

"Is she not a very clever child, Edeline? Fancy! So she knew."

"She is bright and sees herself as the center of life. Everything that happens she believes must concern her. That was how she came to her conclusion."

"How can they take her away!"

"She is their daughter, my lady."

"And this match . . . a child."

"It is the custom."

"Do you think they will send her to Germany?"

"I should think that is probably the intention. Her future husband's family will wish her to be brought up in their ways."

The Queen clenched her fists together angrily. "It is a cruel thing to be a royal princess, Edeline."

"Perhaps so, my lady, but there are advantages."

The Queen raised her eyes and studied Edeline. Calm, honest, precise, she would never flatter, always say what she wished. The Queen said fervently: "I thank God that you will be with our child."

"I thank Him too," said Edeline.

It was a long journey from the Court of Castile to that of England, but the Princess Joanna was excited at its prospect.

There was a tearful farewell with her grandmother—but the tears were really on her grandmother's side. Joanna would miss that doting kindness which was more like adoration, but there was so much to look forward to. The Bishop had embraced his Filiola for the last time, and they had left the sunny land of Castile and passed through the rich vineyards of France and in time they came to the coast. How the poor little Spanish attendants chattered in near hysterical fear at the sight of the rough waters they had to cross and how the boat heaved and sighed, and how sick so many of them were and how young Joanna loved the pull of the wind and the protesting groaning of the ship's timbers as she ploughed her way across those frothing waters to the coast of England.

And then . . . home.

She was picked up and smothered with kisses. This was her mother whom she regarded coolly. Why did she leave me? she asked herself. Oh I know my grandmother begged and pleaded, but she left me.

Her father was there—big and splendid. She had never seen such a man. She bowed—very ceremonially as they did in Castile—and he laughed and picked her up.

"Ah, we have a little beauty here," he said, and kissed her rather roughly. She gave him her cool smile. He, too, had abandoned her. "We are pleased to have you home, little one."

Then there was her sister, the Princess Eleanor—fourteen years old, very grown up and beautiful; and very important it seemed by the way everyone treated her.

"Welcome home, Joanna," said this important sister. "And come and meet your brother Alfonso."

Alfonso was five years old—nearly two years younger than she was. He was rather meek too; and a little shy. He looked at her as though he were appealing to her to love him. She liked that.

"And Margaret." A three-year-old who was only just aware of what it was all about, but delighted, as they all were, to have a seven-year-old sister presented to them.

"Mary is in the nursery," said the Princess Eleanor. "She is only a baby."

So now she knew them all—her family. She could reign supreme there as she did in Castile but there was one who might prevent her and that was her important sister the Princess Eleanor.

* * *

The first tussle came over the attendants. The Spanish ones suddenly disappeared.

"Where are they?" she asked her sister.

"They have been sent back to Castile," she was told.

"But *I* do not want them to go back to Castile."

"Our father has sent them."

"I will see him and they will be sent back to me."

The Princess Eleanor laughed aloud. "They went on the King's orders."

"But they were *my* attendants."

"I don't know what happens in Castile, but here when the King gives an order it is obeyed without question. You will have to realize that, Joanna."

"But these attendants came with me."

Her sister shrugged her shoulders.

"I want to go back," said Joanna.

"Don't be silly. You are home with us now and we are your family."

"My grandmother was my family and *she* would never have sent my attendants away if I wanted to keep them."

"This is not your grandmother's court and you have been spoilt there. Someone said it the other day."

"Who?"

"I am not telling."

Joanna seized her sister's wrist and cried, "Tell me. Tell me. Whoever said that shall be punished."

The Princess Eleanor quietly pulled the child's fingers away from her wrists. "You must not be disrespectful to me. I am the eldest and I have my special household. The King talks to me. I will not have this behavior in the nursery."

Joanna was abashed. "I . . . I . . ." she stammered.

But Eleanor waved her aside. "Our mother says we are to be kind to you, to help you to know our ways, so I shall not punish you this time."

"Punish me . . . But . . . *nobody* punishes me."

"Nobody did. They will now."

"Who?"

"Edeline, I suppose. She is your governess."

"Edeline would never dare . . ."

"I think she would. You are with your own family now, Joanna. We want to love you . . . everyone does. We want you to be our dear sister. You have been allowed too much of your own way in Castile where you were alone in the nursery. It will be different here." The Princess Eleanor suddenly knelt down and put her arms about the little girl. "We all want to love you . . . we want you to be our little sister . . . but there are several of us and you cannot be of any more importance than the rest."

Joanna was silent suddenly. Then rather pleased. It would be more fun in England than it had been in Castile, she was beginning to think. And if they had taken her Spanish servants—about whom she cared little—she still had the Lady Edeline about whom she cared a lot.

After that she began to settle in. She was different from her sisters and certainly from little Alfonso. She was more volatile, high-spirited and quick-tempered. Edeline was constantly trying to restrain her but without much result. The Queen said that Joanna, having been born in a torrid climate, was different from the others. The attendants referred to this constantly, making excuses for her behavior. It was characteristic that they should want to, for she was very pretty. She was dark, which seemed appropriate since she had been born in such a land, and she had her mother's Castilian looks rather than those of the Plantagenets. She was referred to as Joanna of Acre and she liked that. It set her apart. She was constantly at the center of some nursery storm and she liked that too. She had to call attention to herself for her sister Eleanor was a very important person indeed and after having reigned supreme in the Castilian nursery she must make her presence felt at home.

There was much that she missed—the warmer climate, the adulation of her grandmother, the feeling that she was at the very center of their lives. Strangely enough she was happier with her family. Her mother loved her dearly and wanted to make up for having left her in Castile; her father was proud of her but instinctively she knew that her elder sister, the important Eleanor, was his favorite; little Alfonso thought her wonderful. She had been warned to be careful of him and not to knock him over or treat him roughly because he was delicate. Margaret was only a child—two years younger even than Alfonso so she did not count for much and as for Mary the baby she was too young to be of any significance whatsoever.

She, Joanna, was old for her years. She had been born with

a certain knowledge, the attendants said. "You may be sure that there will be trouble when that one grows up," they said. She heard them and liked to think it was true. She liked the way they nodded their heads and curled up the corners of their mouths when they said it.

Sometimes the great sister Eleanor condescended to talk to her. They talked about marriage, for they were both betrothed.

Poor Mary the baby would never marry. She was going into a convent. How did they know that? Joanna asked. Mary was a baby as yet. What did she know of convents? The Queen grandmother had said so. It was to please God who had given their mother so many babies who had not lived and two of them boys at that. Alfonso was weak too, and it was Eleanor's opinion that he would never be the King because he wouldn't ever grow up enough.

It was all very interesting.

She, Joanna, was betrothed to Hartman who sounded interesting. She wondered about him. He was a German and would be a king, so she would be Queen Joanna. It was quite a pleasant prospect.

Eleanor told her that she was to have an Alfonso, who would be King of Aragon.

"So you will be a queen too," said Joanna.

"I long to be a queen," replied her sister.

"You are old," said Joanna, "you should be one by now."

"I should have to wait until Alfonso's father died, as you will have to wait for Hartman's to die."

"But they marry people before they are kings and queens don't they. You must be very old."

"I am fifteen," said Eleanor.

Joanna shook her head commiseratingly. "It is very very old."

"What nonsense! It is not old. I shall go to Aragon when . . . I am ready."

"But," persisted Joanna, who would never stop worrying a subject until she had made her point, "you are old enough now. Why don't you get married *now*?"

Eleanor smiled secretly.

"Because, baby sister, I do not think our father wishes it."

Joanna studied her sister with great respect. A secret. Since she had been in England she was now and then beginning to realize that she did not know everything.

It was like a pattern which repeated itself. The Queen lay at Woodstock praying for a boy.

She was fruitful enough. It seemed almost as though one pregnancy was over with its inevitable disappointment and another had begun.

She had wanted to come to Woodstock. She had an idea that it might be lucky to change the place. She had never given birth in Woodstock and she had asked Edward if she might go there for the last weeks of waiting and, indulgent husband that he was, he was ready to give way to her whims.

She had loved the peace of the place. She had walked in the woods with her daughter Eleanor and young Joanna, their attendants following a little way behind them. The trees were so beautiful for it was the month of May—surely the most beautiful of all. She was anxious that Joanna should love the English countryside which was so different from that of Castile and she took a great pleasure in pointing out the buds and blossoms of the hawthorns and the fruit trees which at this time of the year were laden with blossom. She listened to the birdsong and tried to teach Joanna to recognize a bird by its singing.

Joanna liked to be the center of the lessons and to astonish her mother by the quickness with which she could learn.

The child loves praise, thought the Queen a little anxiously. It was true that her own dear mother in the excess of her loneliness had made too much of Joanna and instilled in her a certainty of her own importance.

The Princess Eleanor made a daisy chain and hung it about her mother's neck. How concerned her eldest daughter was. She was always nervous when her mother was expecting a child. In fact she seemed to be aware of the pregnancy before she was told. Dear children, what a comfort they were to her! She could look at those two bright healthy faces and take comfort. If she could not get a healthy boy she could get some fine girls.

So they had walked through the woods and there were always those who would urge her not to tire herself. She did not in the peace of Woodstock. A different place might bring better luck.

The Lady Edeline had said: "You should not fret, my lady. It is better to let matters take their course."

What a wise woman Edeline was. It was a great comfort to know that she was so close to Joanna. When the child went to Germany to marry Hartman she would beg Edward to let Edeline go with her.

Of course she should be going soon. Her future father-in-law wanted her to. But Edward said she was too young. As for Eleanor he was always putting obstacles in the way of her going to Aragon.

"No, no," he often said, "let them grow up first. They are but children."

The truth was he wanted to keep them with him. He was a loving father—and oddly enough although he craved for a son it was his daughters whom he loved.

Oh, if I could but give him a son! she thought.

Lying in her bed she thought of what had happened in this Palace in the years gone by. It had stood here for many many years—in a different form perhaps, for it was natural that places such as this should be added to during the centuries. Here the Saxon kings had held their Wittenagemots. King Alfred had lived here and a more recent ancestor, Henry I, had set up his deer-fold into which he had introduced wild beasts for the amusement of all those who came to watch the behavior of these creatures.

But it was the ghost of the fair Rosamund who haunted Woodstock more than any other. Legends had been created about the fair Rosamund, so beloved of the King, who had incurred the jealous fury of that virago Eleanor of Aquitaine. The Queen was not sure that she believed that that fierce lady had offered Rosamund the choice of a dagger or poison, but that was how the song went.

And in her Bower, which Henry had built for his beautiful mistress, Rosamund had waited for the birth of her child which was the King's also.

Had she too prayed for a boy?

And she *had* given the King boys—two strong ones.

Poor Rosamund who had died in nearby Godstow Nunnery repenting her sins.

The Queen prayed for the soul of the Fair Rosamund.

When her daughters came to sit with her she talked to them

of Woodstock. There were so many stories about the place. She did not wish to discuss that of the Fair Rosamund with her daughters, but they knew that their grandfather Henry III and their grandmother, who was so much a part of their lives, had once stayed at Woodstock and had wandered together from the Palace and into Rosamund's Bower. In this romantic spot they had spent the night. And this had proved to be providential. For that very night a mad priest had gone to the King's bed-chamber and in the darkness had thrust a knife into his bed again and again, thinking the King was there, which he would have been had he not been at Rosamund's Bower.

"Imagine if he had killed your grandparents," said the Queen. "Then your father would never have been born . . . so nor would you."

Joanna was awestruck at the prospect. She could not imagine a world without Joanna of Acre.

The next day the Queen's pains started.

It was, as usual, an easy confinement. It was, as she had thought before, the same pattern. The quick labor, the girl child . . . a weak one this time over whom the women shook their heads.

The children came to see their mother. Eleanor alert-eyed, Joanna curious, Alfonso frightened, Margaret bewildered.

"Dear lady," said Eleanor, "how fare you? It is a girl they tell us."

"Another girl," said the Queen. "She is very small."

"I want to see her," said Joanna.

They were taken to the cradle where she lay and stood silently looking down with amazement and dismay at the wizened little creature who was their new sister.

The Princess Eleanor came back to the bed.

"Dearest Mother, you are not ill, are you?"

"No my child, I am well. Your father will be disappointed but the next one will be a boy."

The Princess was worried. Her mother looked wan, and the thought had occurred to her that if the Queen died her father would marry again. He was a young, virile man. Suppose he married a young woman who could get *boys*?

Her mother misconstrued her looks of alarm.

"You must not fret, child. A woman is exhausted after an ordeal like this. I shall be well in a few days."

The Princess knelt by the bed holding her mother's hand.

"Oh, dear lady, get well, get well."

The Queen touched her daughter's hair and smiled at the others who had come back to the bed.

Edeline came in to lead them away.

"The Queen needs rest," she said.

The Queen needed comfort too for within three days the puny baby was dead—and the long ordeal, the vigil of hope and prayer was proved to be once again in vain.

The Sicilian Vespers

Llewellyn had discovered peace and happiness in the strong-hold of Snowdonia. His Demoiselle was all he had dreamed her to be. Loving, gentle and clever, she was his entirely. His welfare was her greatest concern. She watched over him, cared for him, and was capable of advising him. She taught him the delights of disinterested love. There had always been conflict in his family, brother against brother, and never being sure when the next piece of treachery would arise. Here at last was someone whom he could trust completely. It was a wonderful revelation. It had bemused him a little at first; he had not quite believed it to be true. But now that he had proved again and again that it was so, he settled into a sense of security which was near exaltation.

He had never dreamed such happiness was possible.

The Demoiselle, too, found contentment. Her only sadness came from her anxieties concerning her brothers. Almeric was still Edward's prisoner in Corfe Castle and Guy was still in exile, wanted for the murder of Henry of Cornwall. If only they could be free; if they could be given the opportunity to start again, she could cease to worry about them and give herself completely up to the peace and contentment of her new life.

It was more than a year since Edward had given his permission for them to marry and each day when she awoke she thanked God for bringing her at last to peace.

She loved the mountains—rugged and beautiful, a menace to the enemy, security to themselves.

"Our beloved mountains," she called them.

There were times when she fancied Llewellyn fretted over his loss of power. Then they would talk together and she would try to make him see how unworthily temporal glory compared with what they had discovered. She would feel delirious with happiness when she fancied he was realizing this.

Then that for which they had longed came at last. The Demoiselle was with child.

This was the crowning of their love. Llewellyn was overcome by emotion. He liked to lie at her feet and make plans for the boy.

She laughed at him. "The boy. Always 'the boy'! What if it should be a girl?"

"If she is like her mother I ask nothing more."

"Welsh insincerity," she chided. "You are asking for a boy who looks like yourself."

"Well, which do you want?"

"I shall want whatever I get."

"Oh, there speaks my wise Demoiselle."

"Since we have been together I have known so much happiness that I am content."

"If it is a boy we will call him Llewellyn. Why, he must be the one Merlin spoke of."

She shook her head. "Nay. I do not want a warrior. I want my son to be the head of a happy family. I want him to have children who love and revere him—not subjects who fear him."

"Wise Demoiselle!" he said, kissing her hand.

She was looking beyond him into the past, thinking, he knew, of her father—one of the greatest men of his age, they were beginning to say now. A man who had believed in the right and had for a time subdued a king. In time to come people would remember Simon de Montfort because he had lived and died violently. They would not remember the Demoiselle who had longed for peace and had brought happiness to a wild man of the mountains.

So they planned for the child to come.

One day Llewellyn's brother Davydd called on them. Davydd had in truth come more satisfactorily out of the agreement with England than Llewellyn had. Because Davydd had gone over to Edward, the King had regarded him as an ally. Llewellyn had been the enemy.

Edward did not know Davydd. Davydd was a man who would fight on whichever side was the stronger.

There had been peace on the borders now for some time and Davydd was restless. He wanted to talk to his brother about the possibilities of regaining what had been lost.

The Demoiselle was uneasy when she greeted Davydd. She was sure his coming meant trouble. She did not want even the thought of war to be brought into their happy home.

Davydd sat long, talking with his brother.

"Are you content then," he demanded, "to be the vassal of the English king? Where is your pride, Llewellyn?"

"I have not been so happy before in the whole of my life."

Davydd was sceptical. "A new husband. A new father-to-be. By the holy saints, Llewellyn, what will your son think of a father who was content to pass over his heritage to the English?"

Llewellyn was silent. When he was not with the Demoiselle he did sometimes think with shame of the peace he had made. What would his old grandfather have said? What of his father?

"I was not strong enough against the English," he said. He frowned at Davydd. "I was surrounded by traitors."

Davydd shrugged that aside. "If I had not gone to the English there would be nothing of Wales left to us."

"If you had stood beside me...."

"It was not in me to be any man's vassal ... even my brother's."

"Except of course the King of England's."

"Not for long," said Davydd.

"What mean you?"

"I mean this: We should gather a force together and reclaim that which has been taken from us."

Llewellyn thinking of the Demoiselle shook his head.

"Have you forgotten the prophecy?"

"It was clearly not meant for me."

"Certainly it was not for one who thrusts aside his oppor-

tunity of greatness. Llewellyn, you were meant to rule Wales
. . . and it may well be England. Merlin may have meant that
England was yours if you were bold enough to take it."

There was a deep silence. That thought had more than once
occurred to Llewellyn.

He said slowly: "I have never known such happiness as I
have of late."

Davydd was scornful. "You are newly married. You waited
overlong. Your bride was snatched from you. Oh, it was so
romantic. Dreams, dreams . . . and you are still in a dream.
Think, Llewellyn. When you are an old man your children will
say to you 'And what of Wales? What of your heritage? You
threw it away for your romantic dreams.'"

"It will be for them to go their ways, to learn life's lessons
for themselves, to ask what they would have—happiness such
as I now enjoy, peace . . . joy . . . oh, I cannot explain to you.
Davydd . . . that or war, bloodshed, misery, heartbreak."

"And the glory of Wales? Wales for the Welsh!"

"You waste your time with me, Davydd."

And at last Davydd saw that this was true.

He was thoughtful after Davydd had ridden away. The Demoiselle comforted him.

"He thinks me a fool," he told her.

"A wise fool," she answered. Then they talked of the baby
to come and the beauty of the Welsh mountains.

Our mountains, she called them, and they with his happy
marriage and his child to come were enough for him.

So they lived in their peaceful haven and the time grew near
when the Demoiselle should be brought to her bed. The women
came and shut her in away from him.

He sat outside her bedchamber and waited.

They had not reached the peak of their happiness yet. It
would be different when the child came. She longed for the
child, so did he.

A little boy. Llewellyn. That Llewellyn who was going to
make Merlin's prophecy come true. No, she would not want
that. It would mean going out against Edward's might. Perhaps
Edward would be dead by the time this child grew up. Perhaps
it would be Edward's son whom the child would have to face.

Llewellyn smiled. That must be the answer. No man could
stand against great Edward. It was something people knew

instinctively. Even Merlin's prophecy wilted and faded away in face of Edward.

The labor was long. The day faded. No sign yet. Is she suffering? That was more than he could bear. I should be with her. Oh no, my lord, they said. Better not. It would not be long now.

Oh, my Demoiselle, daughter of a great man and royal princess, what joy you have brought me. This cannot last. There must be no more children. You will say it is natural for a woman to bear children but I cannot endure this . . . torment.

He laughed at himself. His was the mental torment, hers the physical. The women were bustling back and forth. Grave faces and the perpetual cry: It will not be long now.

Then he heard the cry of a child.

He was at the door. "A girl, my lord. A lovely healthy little girl."

He did not look at the child. He could only go to where the Demoiselle lay on her bed weak and exhausted.

He knelt by the bed and the tears flowed from his eyes. He could not stop them. He did not care that the women saw.

"How he loves her!" said the old midwife and she shook her head. There was infinite sorrow in her eyes.

"A little girl," whispered the Demoiselle.

"A beautiful child, my love," he answered.

"You do not mind . . ."

"I want only my Demoiselle. I care for nothing else . . ."

"You must care for the child."

They told him she must sleep now.

"She is worn out with bearing your child," said the midwife.

So he went away and left her and he went to his room and prayed. He had forgotten to look at the child.

They were rapping on his door.

"My lord, come quickly. My lady wishes to see you."

He ran. He was at her bedside. She was looking at him with glazed eyes.

"Llewellyn," she whispered his name. He knelt by the bed.

"My Demoiselle, I am here."

She said: "Take care . . . of the child . . ."

Then she closed her eyes.

One of the women came and stood beside him.

"She has gone, my lord," she said.

"Gone!" he cried. "How dare you. Gone. She is here . . . She is here . . ."

He lifted her in his arms. He stood holding her lifeless body daring God to take her from him.

He was mad with grief. He had no wish to live.

"There is the child," they told him.

He cared nothing for the child. He hated the child. Her coming had taken away the Demoiselle . . . a poor exchange. A tragic exchange. I should never have had a child. Oh God, how I wish I had never had a child. What do I want with a child . . . without her.

He was in a dream . . . a dream of despair. He cared for nothing. He shut himself in his chamber. He would not eat. He would see no one. He had lost everything he cared for.

They begged him to think of the child.

"My lady said that she liked the name of Gwenllian. She said if the child is a girl I will call her that. My lord, shall she be given that name?"

They could give her any name they cared to. It was of no moment to him.

So the little girl who had cost her mother her life was named Gwenllian; and she was content with the wet nurse they had found for her, oblivious of what her coming had cost.

Llewellyn wandered in the mountains—as dark and dour as they could be when the sun was not there. And the sun had gone in on his life for ever. He cared not what became of him.

The Princess Eleanor was in her eighteenth year and it was generally wondered why she was not married. Her betrothed, Alfonso of Aragon, was now the Infant; he would one day be King of Aragon, but every time the matter of the marriage was broached the King was too busy to discuss it, or he found the project of sending his daughter away inconvenient for the time.

The Princess was delighted. She had no wish to go to Aragon. Why should she? She was perfectly happy in England. She had her dear family and the status of an heir to the throne.

Poor little Alfonso was now eight years old and people shook their heads over him. "He will never make old bones," they said.

As for the King, he loved all his children but he could not

help being a little impatient with a boy who was so unlike himself. Alfonso was not going to have that fine physique inherited from the Normans; in fact he was very much a Castilian, dark-haired, soft-eyed and gentle. Admirable qualities in the Queen but hardly suitable for the heir of England. Moreover the King adored his eldest daughter. They rode together and talked together and he could not bear her out of his sight. She was a strong woman; she resembled her grandmother; and for this reason the Queen Mother's love for the girl was almost as strong as that of the King.

She loved to have the Princess visit her. She had gone to Amesbury but only for brief visits. She was trying the place out before she finally settled there, and she certainly would not do that until that tiresome matter of the dowry had been sorted out. She was certainly not losing any of her wealth. She loved her money and possessions almost as much as she loved her family and she was not parting with one penny.

Moreover she loved life too much to shut herself away completely. Perhaps Heaven would be satisfied for the time being with a few brief sojourns in sanctity. After all she was in good health still so there were some years left in which to pay up in full.

Not that she believed she had a great deal to atone for. She had been a faithful wife to Henry; he and she had been as one; she had helped him govern his kingdom. No, she could not see that a great deal of recompense would be demanded from her.

She was fond of her daughter-in-law the Queen, but she found her a feeble creature. She was, however, what Edward wanted because he was an overbearing man—not like his dear father who would listen to counsel . . . from his wife. Edward would listen to no one—not even his mother. Edward believed he knew best.

Fortunately he was a great general. Men feared him; he was just, and as was to be expected from a son of hers and Henry's, he was a faithful husband with a respect for family life. This was good for the nation, for subjects followed the fashions set by their King.

Now she welcomed her grand-daughter Eleanor with the greatest pleasure. She took an enormous interest in all her grandchildren, but Eleanor chiefly, and Mary of course, whom she had determined should go into a convent—Amesbury very likely, if it came up to her expectations.

"My dear, dear child," she said and embraced the Princess. "How it delights me to see you! I have just come from Amesbury and the rest has done me good."

"You look well, my lady."

"I am, my dear. I should never have thought I could have been so well after your dear, dear grandfather died."

"Something in you died with him," said the Princess quickly before her grandmother said it.

"How well you understand! I thank God for you, my child. You are such a comfort to your parents."

Then they talked of the Queen. "I doubt not," said the Queen Mother, "that she will be pregnant again soon."

"Dear Mother! I think she should not bear so many children. It weakens her."

"It is too much. Edward should realize that it is hardly likely he will get a son now. His boys are never strong. I thought Alfonso looked very frail when I last saw him. He is such a darling boy. I have the widows doing vigil for him but what good does it do!"

"It did nothing for the others," said the Princess.

"It is my belief," said the Queen Mother conspiratorially, "That Alfonso will never come to manhood."

The Princess nodded solemnly.

"Well, we have you, my love."

"My lady, suppose poor Alfie . . ."

"Dies?" said the Queen Mother. "Alas, I think that very likely."

"And the Queen only has girls . . ."

"I think that equally likely."

"And I . . ."

"My blessed child, you are the eldest daughter. I'll swear you are every bit as good as a man. It has always maddened me . . . this desire for boys. As though they are cleverer than we are. Have you noticed that? Why, your grandfather used to say I was worth ten of his ministers."

"And so it proved."

"Your grandfather used to say I could have governed the country as well as he could."

It would not have been politic to say: "And his was not very good government," and the Princess was excited because she saw that she had her grandmother's support and everyone would agree that that was well worth having.

"Then, my lady, if all this should happen, do you think that I could years and years hence become the Queen of England?"

"It could come to pass, my child, and I believe that would not be such a bad thing for this country."

"But if I go to Aragon to marry this man . . ."

"Ah, then my dear it would not be so. Your husband would want the crown and that is something the people would never have. No, you would have to be here . . . and you will have to show the people that you are strong and able. Secretly I believe the King thinks so. Look how he has honored you."

"But this is what I want to talk to you about. There is news from Aragon. They want me to leave England at once. Oh, my lady, what am I going to do?"

"It must be stopped," said the Queen Mother. "I will speak to your mother and the King."

"I could not bear it if I were sent away. Not to see you, my lady . . . and the others."

The Princess was watching her grandmother closely. The old woman pressed her lips firmly together.

"Certainly you must not go . . . yet. You are far too young."

The absurdity of this did not matter to either of them. When the Queen Mother made a statement it must be true, however much the facts disagreed.

The King was quite ready to be persuaded that his daughter was too young to leave her home. Though he did cover himself by writing to the King of Aragon that it was "The Queen, her mother and our dearest mother who are unwilling to grant that she may pass over earlier on account of her tender age." He did, however, add that he agreed with this.

The Aragonese were suspicious. To speak of the tender age of a bride-to-be who was in her eighteenth year when so many girls were sent to their bridegrooms at the ages of twelve and thirteen did seem rather strange.

A coolness sprang up between the ambassador of Aragon and the King's court which disturbed Edward and as conditions abroad necessitated the friendship of Aragon, he would have to be careful and not let them think that he wished to break off the contract.

Meanwhile the Queen had become pregnant once more.

Llewellyn continued to mourn. The baby was left to the care of nurses and he never wanted to see her. He would ride out into the mountains because he wanted to be alone with his wretchedness.

They said of him: "If he goes on like this he will die of melancholy."

His brother Davydd, hearing of his state, came to see him again.

"Do you not see how misguided it is to set store of such ephemeral joys?" he asked.

"Who would have thought she would have died," mourned Llewellyn. "We had so little time together. How could God have been so cruel?"

"God is sometimes cruel to a man in order that he may fulfill his destiny."

"Destiny! What is my destiny without her!"

"There was a prophecy by Merlin."

"A false prophet."

"Take care, Llewellyn. It is small wonder that Heaven strikes you such blows if you blaspheme in this way."

"Heaven can strike as many blows as it wishes. I cannot feel any more. I care nothing of what happens to me."

"You are not finished yet, Llewellyn. The future is before you."

"I care not for it. I shall never know happiness again."

"There is happiness to be found outside family life. Give yourself a chance to find compensation."

"You do not understand, Davydd."

"I understand full well. If you stay here brooding you will die of melancholy. Let me tell you, brother, I could raise an army. We could go against the English . . . together. Edward is lulled to a feeling of security. He thinks he has beaten us. Llewellyn, why do we not show him his mistake?"

Llewellyn was half listening. He was thinking: Edward kept us apart. Edward captured her and kept her from me. We could have had more life together. I hate Edward. I hate the world. I hate God.

"We could . . . together . . . defeat him. We could bring Wales back to the Welsh. Llewellyn, don't you see it is your opportunity. It is God showing you a way out of your misery. Llewellyn, you are stunned with grief now, but if you would give yourself a chance you would grow away from it. Oh, I know you will never forget her. I know what you have lost. But you have still to live. You have to go on living. You cannot for her, but you can for Wales."

For Wales! For the magnificent mountains, the valleys and the hills. The honor of Wales. Wales for the Welsh. And perhaps one day Merlin's prophecy would come true. Davydd was earnest. He could not trust Davydd. He had deceived him once.

He was astounded. For a few minutes he had stopped thinking of the Demoiselle.

Now he was listening to Davydd.

He did not care what became of him. Perhaps that was the best way to go into desperate battle.

The Aragonese were determined. They would wait no longer. The Infant wanted his bride. If she did not come to him it was likely that he would look elsewhere; and he would certainly not regard as an ally one who had treated him as the English King had in withholding his daughter.

Tight-lipped Edward explained to his daughter. He saw the stony despair in her face. Then he broke down and embraced her.

"My darling child, what can I do? You are promised to Aragon."

There was nothing she could do. There was nothing the Queen Mother could do. The Princess was promised to Aragon and there was no real reason why she should not go to her bridegroom.

The Princess was on her knees praying. God must *do* something that would prevent her going. She *could* not go. All her plans would have foundered if she did. She did not want to be the Queen of Aragon, she wanted to be the Queen of England. Her mother was pregnant again. If God sent her a son this time she would take it as a sign that he had deserted her.

Something will happen, she kept telling herself. Something *must* happen.

Then came the startling news from Wales. Llewellyn and his brother Davydd had risen against the King. Edward was furious. He had believed the Welsh problem was settled. He had given Llewellyn his Demoiselle and looked forward to years of peace on that border. Now the brothers were in revolt.

He would trust no one to subdue them. He would go himself.

He told his daughter that he was going to Wales. She clung to him and said, "You are going and I shall have to go away. It may be that we shall not see each other again."

"That must not be," he said. "You shall come with me to Wales. You and your mother and your brother and sisters shall be lodged in a safe place, but where I can see you between battles. My dearest child, it seems you must go to Aragon, but not yet . . . not yet. I can hold them off for a bit."

"It sounds as though they are an enemy," she said half tearfully half joyously because he betrayed his love for her so blatantly.

"Anyone who takes my dearest daughter from me is an enemy," he said.

"For a while then, I shall forget," she said. "I shall try to be happy. I shall not think that soon I have to go away. For the moment I can be with my beloved father."

The Queen was also eager to go to Wales. The superstitious belief clung to her that if she bore a child in a different place, she might have a healthy boy.

Thus it was that they traveled north and the King put his family in Rhudlan Castle while he went on with his armies to subdue Llewellyn and his brother Davydd.

Edward had made Rhudlan his *place d'armes* and there he also kept the provisions for the army. It was a great comfort to him to have his family with him. How much less exacting war could be if, somewhere—as safely away from the fighting as possible—he could have them installed. It meant that when there was a lull in the battle and circumstances warranted his taking a little respite, he could be with them.

The Queen was in a state of expectancy. She was optimistic by nature and at every pregnancy she was buoyed up by the thought that this time they would have their son; and even when she was disappointed she would say to herself, "It will be the next time." She was thankful that she could bear children easily—a gift some women had, but which was not always bestowed on queens. Edward always agreed with her that one day the longed-for boy would come. "And if not," he had said not long before, "we have our daughter." He was very upset at this time at the prospect of losing her. She really should have gone to Aragon years before. But it was a comfort to know that Edward so loved his daughters that he could not bear to part with them.

Joanna would have to go too. She was afraid that would come to pass very soon for, although Joanna was eight years younger than her sister Eleanor, she was now ten years old, and this was an age when future brides were expected to be with their bridegroom's families that they might grow up in their ways. How sad it would be when Eleanor went to Aragon and Joanna to Germany. But there seemed no help for it. Princesses were born to leave their homes and go to those of their husbands. She had had to do it; even the dominating Queen Mother had had to do it—although from what she had heard she had believed it was *her* choice.

It was wonderful to be near Edward so that she could have news quickly about the progress of the war. Edward did not expect this one to last long. Welsh chieftains rising in their hills should soon be put in their places and this time, said Edward, they shall feel my wrath. They made a treaty with me. I shall have no mercy on those who break faith with me.

And he meant it. Soft as he was with his family he was becoming a stern King. It was right of course. People only obeyed those who showed the strong arm.

"Let it be a boy," she prayed. If it were, Rhudlan would be remembered as the birthplace of her son. There was Alfonso of course. They were inclined to forget that he was a boy and the eldest. Poor little fellow, did he know that there were whispers about him? He'll not make old bones, they said. Edward was kind to him but he had no pride in him, and sometimes she thought the little boy knew it and lost the will to live. Because John and Henry had died they were expecting Alfonso to do the same. He was nine years old now and had lived longer than either John or Henry. It could really be that like his father he would grow out of his delicacy.

She prayed that he would but even so it would be advisable

to have another brother—a strong boy who would be there to take the throne if need be.

She liked Rhudlan. She immediately felt at home in a castle because as soon as she arrived she ordered her servants to hang up the tapestries she had brought with her. Then of course there were certain items of furniture which were carried from place to place—her bed, her cupboard, her chairs. So one castle was very like another.

She was glad that the custom of hanging tapestries on the walls—a fashion she had brought with her from Castile—was appreciated here. More and more people were doing it.

But Rhudlan was different, of course. The castle stood on a steep bank commanding a good view of the surrounding country. It was washed by the river Clweyd and was impressive with its red sandstone which had come from the neighboring rocks. Her spirit had lifted when she saw its six massive towers flanking the high curtain walls of the King's Tower above them. Edward had done a certain amount of rebuilding when he had been here. Edward could never resist improving his castles whenever he rested. He had his father's talent for the love of architecture, only where Henry had beautified regardless of cost for the sheer joy of improving on the building, Edward was practical, never spent more than was necessary and was mainly concerned with strengthening the fortifications.

Here she waited as she had waited so many times before. This would be her eleventh confinement. Out of them there had been only three boys and two of them dead and the other sickly. Surely God would be good to her now. Surely he would listen to her prayers.

Her daughters came to see her for they were all here—even four-year-old Mary—although the Queen Mother had wanted to keep the child with her. She was determined that Mary should go into a convent. The Queen thought her daughter should be allowed to make up her own mind as to what she would do with her life. Everything would depend, the Queen Mother insisted, on how the child was brought up. She should be made aware from the first what was intended for her. It was necessary for one daughter to lead the secluded life and the Queen Mother had chosen Mary.

The Queen was inclined to leave unpleasant matters until they had to be decided, and Edward had other affairs with which to concern himself, so Mary was left a great deal to the Queen Mother who had even on one occasion taken the child to Amesbury and, no doubt, implied to her that her future would be there.

Her time was upon her. She felt the familiar signs. She was calmer than her women. She had after all gone through it so often.

She called them to her and said, "We should now prepare."

A few hours later her child was born. It was what everyone had come to expect. A daughter. But, she thanked God that this one appeared to be a healthy child.

Edward would not come to her immediately but news was sent to him.

She recovered quickly as she always did. She sent for the children that she might show them the new baby; eighteen-year-old Eleanor, ten-year-old Joanna, nine-year-old Alfonso, seven-year-old Margaret, and four-year-old Mary.

They examined the new baby in its cot.

"She is going to be called Elizabeth," the Queen told them.

The Princess Eleanor's eyes were shining with an emotion her mother did not understand. Her sister Joanna did though. She smiled secretly, and when they left their mother's apartment Joanna followed her sister to theirs.

"Another girl," said Joanna. "Is it not strange that they who so urgently need a boy can get only girls. It is as though God is playing a trick on them. Eleanor, do you think God plays tricks?"

"I think," said Eleanor, "that God has His reasons."

"We all have those," Joanna reminded her.

"I mean He lets things happen in a certain way because it is all part of his plan. I used to think . . ."

"I know what you used to think. Alfie would die and you would be the Queen."

The Princess Eleanor was about to deny this but when she looked at her sister's knowledgeable eyes she changed her mind. No one would have believed Joanna was so young. She was too clever for her age; she listened at doors; she questioned the attendants in a sly quick way, which meant that they betrayed more than they intended. Joanna thus knew a great deal.

Eleanor shrugged her shoulders. "I am to go to Aragon."

"And I to Germany."

"I don't want to go to Aragon. If I do . . ."

"Nothing will be as you want it. You will in time be the Queen of Aragon when you want to be the Queen of England. Queen Consort of Aragon or Queen in her own right of England. It is easy to understand."

Eleanor said angrily, "If God is going to send me to Aragon why does He give the Queen another girl? It would seem as though He is on my side . . . all those girls . . . and then He lets them send me to Aragon."

"And me to Germany," sighed Joanna. "Though I see that is not quite the same, for I could never hope to be Queen of England. You are the one our father wants, sister, but if God does not want it that is no good."

"We could pray for a miracle."

"What sort of miracle? That Alfie would die?"

Eleanor cried out in dismay, "Don't say it. It would bring bad luck. Of course I don't want Alfie to die. I just want him to be too delicate to govern . . . so that they have a Queen . . ."

"Queen Eleanor," said Joanna, with mock respect.

The Princess clasped her hands together. "I *must* not go to Aragon," she said.

"No," repeated Joanna, "you must not go to Aragon. How shall we prevent it?"

"Do you believe if you pray hard enough you *will* something to happen?"

"It has never been thus for me."

"Try it. It is all that is left to us. Pray with me that I shall not go to Aragon . . ." She added as an afterthought, ". . . and you to Germany."

Joanna loved experimenting.

"We'll try it! Special prayers! We'll really mean it. We'll give our whole minds to it. To tell the truth, sister, I do not want to go to Germany any more than you want to go to Aragon."

The Princess Eleanor gripped her sister's hand, her eyes shining with a fanaticism which Joanna found very interesting.

The Princess Eleanor and her sister Joanna were jubilant. Eleanor said she had never doubted her miracle would come to pass and it was for this reason that it had. It was what was called "Faith."

Joanna was impressed. Eleanor must be very important in God's eyes if He could kill so many people just to gratify her ambitions, and that it had all happened so far away over a matter which was really no concern of theirs made it doubly interesting.

It had taken place in Sicily, in that sunny island where people had loved to sing and dance before they were conquered by the French. The freedom-loving Sicilians, restive under the French yoke, had plotted in secret and earlier that year—on Easter Day to be precise—they had risen against their enemies. The signal to rise had been the first stroke of the vesper bell and the Sicilians had slaughtered all the French on the island— eight thousand of them in all.

It was some time after it had happened that the news of the massacre reached England, and it never occurred to Eleanor at the time that this could be so important to her. It had far-reaching effects, however, and the Sicilians, having taken part in what had become known as the Sicilian Vespers, were almost immediately afterwards in terror of the powerful French. They had sought the help of Pedro of Aragon—the father of Eleanor's husband-to-be.

The reason they had turned to Aragon was because Pedro's wife was Constance, the daughter of the old King of Sicily, and they thought that if the crown of Sicily were offered to Aragon that country would not hesitate to come to their relief. They were right and Pedro was received in Sicily with great rejoicing.

It was hardly likely that the French would allow this state of affairs to continue. Charles of Anjou who had been the King of Sicily was very close to the English royal family because he had married Beatrice, the sister of the Queen Mother. Constance had been very anxious for the Princess Eleanor to come to Aragon, that she might forge a link with England which would be stronger than that already existing between England and France, on account of the relationship between Beatrice and the Queen Mother. Naturally the French were now extremely anxious that this betrothal should not take place.

Charles of Anjou very quickly regained his lost possession and the Pope was induced to reconsider the dispensation regarding marriages of royal people, and among these was that

of Eleanor and Alfonso of Aragon who on the very recent death
of Pedro had become King.

The Pope therefore sent his envoys to the King of England
with injunctions that the dispensation which had been granted
for a marriage between England and Aragon was no longer
valid; and the Pope added that he hoped the King of England
would give up all intentions of forming an alliance with enemies
of the Holy See who had joined with those who had used the
bells of vespers as a signal for their uprising.

The King had returned briefly to Rhudlan, and even before
he saw his new daughter Elizabeth he sent for Eleanor.

He embraced her fiercely.

"Oh, my darling child," he said, "this is good news. There
will be no Aragonese marriage. You are not to go to Aragon.
You are staying here . . . with me."

The color flooded her face; her eyes were brilliant with joy.
She had always been the most beautiful of his children. He
could not take his eyes from her lovely face.

"It seems you are made happy by this news," he said.

"Nothing could have made me happier. It is the miracle I
have prayed for."

How they exulted! How they laughed together! "We must
be serious," said the King. "We will pretend to be put out.
How dare the Pope dictate to the King of England, eh? But
the King of England is at war with the Welsh rebels and he
would not risk a threat of excommunication at such a time,
could he? Therefore we must do as the Pope wishes. This must
be one of the few times a Pope's orders have pleased a King
of England."

She clung to him. She would not let him go.

He stroked her hair and murmured endearments. There were
many who would have been surprised if they could have seen
the stern King's expression of tenderness towards his eldest
daughter.

At length he left her and went to his wife's bedchamber.

He kissed her fondly. Dear Queen, who had given him the
children he loved—and in particular her namesake, his eldest
daughter.

"Edward, another girl, I fear."

"Nay, my love, you should not grieve. I love my girls. And
we have Alfonso. We must change his name e'er long. Alfonso

is no name for a King of England. Shall we rename him Edward?"

"No, Edward, no please..."

"You do not like the name?"

"I like it too well," she said earnestly. "I fear it might be unlucky."

"Then he shall stay Alfonso," and he thought, That boy will never mount the throne. And there is nothing wrong with a Queen of England.

By a strange coincidence the arrangements for Joanna's marriage were brought to an abrupt termination.

When earlier that year Prince Hartman, Earl of Hapsburg and Kyburg, Landgrave of Alsace and son of the King of the Romans, had announced his intention of coming to England to see his bride, and if he had come that would have meant a betrothal and Joanna's returning to his country with him, his visit was delayed. His father had been at that time engaged in a struggle of his own and he could not consider sending his son to England without an adequate bodyguard of his best soldiers. The plain fact was that he needed those men to fight his battles and so the visit was postponed. It was of no great matter, wrote Prince Hartman; he would come as soon as he and his men could be spared and then the Princess Joanna should leave with him and would continue her education in the royal house of Hapsburg.

There had been something ominous in that letter. He was determined to come and it was only a temporary postponement. Joanna did not see how she could escape her destiny. It was true that having been brought up in Castile and then sent to England she was not so averse to a change as her sister Eleanor had been. Joanna had the belief that wherever she was people would love and admire her. All the same she wanted to stay in England.

It was at Rhudlan that the news was brought to her father.

He sent for her, embraced her and told her that he had bad news for her.

"There has been an accident," he said. "Prince Hartman was staying at the castle of Brisac on the Rhine and decided to visit his father. He set out and suddenly fog arose. His sailors did not know where they were for it was so dense they could not see their hands when they held them before their faces. Their boat foundered on a rock. My dear child, Prince Hartman, your bridegroom to be, has been drowned. They have recovered his body from the river so there can be no doubt."

"Then there will be no marriage," said Joanna solemnly.

"Well, you are but a child. We will find a husband for you as important, never fear."

"I have no fear, my lord, and I had no wish to go away."

The King smiled fondly. What delightful daughters he had! Joanna was almost as beautiful as her sister Eleanor.

He said: "To tell you the truth, my child, I can feel no great sorrow in this for it means we are not going to lose you . . . yet."

"Perhaps when I marry it will be someone here . . . at home," said Joanna. "I know my sister hopes that she will."

He smiled at her, well pleased.

"Who knows," he said, "such good fortune may well be ours."

Joanna lost no time going to her sister.

They stared at each other wide-eyed.

"So miracles do happen," said Eleanor.

"If you will them to," replied Joanna.

They smiled secretly, believing they had made a great discovery.

The Prince
of Wales

Davydd had been right, Llewellyn told himself. *He felt alive* again. Only the prospect of regaining what he had lost could give him such an interest in life.

About the same time as the Sicilians were rising against the French and awaiting the signal of the vesper bell, he had aroused the whole of that part of Wales which remained in Welsh hands.

They were going to march against the English. The enthusiasm with which he was greeted amazed him. He was greatly admired. He was a man whom they could trust which was more than they could his brother Davydd. Davydd had been for the English at one time and then had done a quick change about to the Welsh. He might be a good general but he was not a man to be trusted. It was different with Llewellyn. Llewellyn's love story was recorded in song; the sad death of his wife had turned the idyll into a tragedy. Llewellyn was a popular romantic figure; and then there was Merlin's prophecy.

In the beginning there were a few victories for Llewellyn. He even took Rhudlan castle and held it briefly. But when

Edward began his march north Llewellyn knew he could not hold the castle and wisely retreated. But the initial success was inspiring.

Edward's wrath he guessed to be great, and he knew that it would be a powerful army which would be marching upon him, and the fact that it was led by the King himself would strike terror into all those who seemed to have endowed Edward with some supernatural power.

All through the summer the war continued. Edward was gaining on his enemies but it was no easy victory. There was an occasional success which greatly heartened the Welsh as when a large force of the English had crossed the Menai bridge and encamped there awaiting the rest of the army to join them. In the night the flood tide broke the bridge over the Straits and the English were cut off. It was an easy matter for the superior Welsh forces—who would have been easily defeated if the entire English army had been able to cross the bridge—to wipe out the stranded English.

"A great victory," cried the Welsh bards. This was God's will. It was like Moses dividing the seas, only this time God had sent the flood tide to smash the bridge. It was Merlin's prophecy coming true.

But alas this was soon seen to be the little victory it was, and it was realized that it could have no effect on the outcome of the war when every day it was becoming more and more clear that Llewellyn and the Welsh were losing.

Once more Llewellyn was forced to retire to Snowdon. Here he brooded on his ill fortune, recalling the happy days with the Demoiselle and he cursed afresh the fate which had taken her from him.

If she had but lived, she would never have let him go to war. She would have kept him a prince of his small country and they would have been content.

What was there left to him now? He could not regain his power. He was no match for mighty Edward. He had lost everything that had made life worth while to him and he longed for death.

There in his mountain stronghold he was visited by John Peckham, who had taken the place of Robert Kilwardby as Archbishop of Canterbury and who had come to discuss the terms on which Edward would make a peaceful settlement.

These terms, said John Peckham, were reasonable and Llewellyn should accept them.

"Reasonable!" cried Llewellyn. "I see no reason in them. They will rob me of my country."

And indeed they would, for Edward had set down that Llewellyn must abandon the Principality of Wales and give it to Edward in exchange for which he would place in Llewellyn's possessions lands to the value of one thousand pounds a year. These would be in an English county as yet to be decided on. The King of England would take charge of Llewellyn's young daughter and would seriously consider the possibility of allowing any male heirs she might have to succeed to Snowdon.

"Reasonable terms to offer a prince!" cried Llewellyn. "My lord Archbishop I do not understand you."

"You are a ruined man," replied the Archbishop. "And there have been abuses in the Welsh churches which have not pleased me."

Llewellyn knew that he was defeated. "My Lord Archbishop," he said, "I know that I must throw myself on the bounty of the King of England but I could not submit to such harsh terms. If the King of England will reconsider his demands it might be possible for us to come to some agreement."

The Archbishop left and later Edward's messengers came with the information that the King would accept nothing but unconditional surrender. He had made terms previously. He had kept his bargain. He had released the Demoiselle and seen her married to Llewellyn. And what had happened? Llewellyn had broken his part of the contract. The King could not trust him again and he—and all men—must see what happened to those who broke faith with the King of England.

There was only one thing to do. To retreat into the mountains, to call together faithful Welshmen, to remind them once more of the prophecy of Merlin and to defend the passes.

To return to the mountains! It was November. Winter was coming. He and his followers would be starved into submission. He must move *from* the mountains. He must join up with friends in the South. He must make his way down to Llandeilo where the English were scoring great victories.

He knew his mountains well and found his way through unfrequented passes, thus escaping the English besiegers, but the Marcher Barons were on the alert. It was true that some of their tenants came over to Llewellyn, but they were useless against the trained forces of the Barons. When the fierce Mortimer brothers heard that Llewellyn was in their district they determined to capture him.

The name of Roger Mortimer was spoken of with dread. Though he was the third son he had already made a name for himself. A violent man, audacious and strong, a lecher into the bargain, who had been reproved by John Peckham for frequently committing the sin of adultery with numerous women. Roger Mortimer snapped his fingers at the Archbishop and was at this time eager to win the approval of the King.

The coming of Llewellyn seemed a heaven-sent opportunity.

There were some who said that Llewellyn had the death wish on him. He had nothing to live for. He lost his land and more tragic than ever his wife. He cared for nothing. He welcomed death, they said afterwards.

It was a strange way for a great Prince to die.

There on Mortimer land he was in his camp when he saw a party of his followers attacked by a troop of Mortimer's men. It was folly, for they had not a chance, and he could have remained in hiding but he rode out to join them, like a man, they said afterwards, going joyfully to meet his God.

He was immediately slain.

When Roger Mortimer heard and came to view the body he was exultant.

"Cut off his head," he said. "I will present it to the King."

Edward received it solemnly.

"The head of my enemy," he said. "Thus perish all who seek to betray me."

"My lord, what shall be done with this man?" asked Mortimer.

Edward was silent for a few moments; then he said: "Let his body be buried in consecrated ground at Cwmhir. I would not have it said that I did not honor a brave man, for brave he was though foolish."

"And his head, my lord?"

"Ah, his head. My lord Mortimer, I want everyone to know what happens to those who are false to me. He thought he would be a King of England. There was some prophecy of Merlin's. I want men to see what happens to those who believe they will drive the true King of England from his throne with talk of prophecies."

The King then ordered that the head should be taken and placed on a pole. It should be set up on the Tower of London and, to remind those who looked at it that this was a man who had believed he might be King of England, a crown of ivy was to be placed on his head.

And so the decaying head of Llewellyn looked down on London's river, and the Queen, when her barge sailed beneath it, looked up and thought of the beautiful Demoiselle who had loved that head, and she shuddered that such a fate could befall two who had loved so truly.

There remained Davydd.

"I want him, dead or alive," said the King, "for although I have defeated the Welsh, there will be trouble while he lives."

When Davydd heard of the death of his brother his feelings were mixed. The prophecy of Merlin concerning a Llewellyn clearly did not refer to that one and that had been a great incentive to men to fight for them. On the other hand with Llewellyn out of the way he was the undisputed leader.

He retreated into the mountains with a few of his followers—a pitiful few. He wondered how it would be possible to attract more men to his banner. He was not Llewellyn. He had once gone over to the English; true he had come back to stand beside his brother when he had thought he had a chance, but now his brother was dead and Wales was in the hands of the English—all but the inaccessible mountains. He talked to those of his followers who remained; he tried to inspire them with promises of what would be theirs when the hated English were driven from the land. Lacking the sincerity of Llewellyn he lacked his fire. No one really believed in Davydd. They guessed that if it should prove to be to his advantage he would sell them all to the enemy.

There was one castle left to him—that of Bere, and when he heard that the Earl of Pembroke had stormed and taken it, he had no place of refuge. He had become a wanderer in the mountains and every morning when he awoke it was to find that his band of followers had dwindled still further.

There came a time when all but three had gone. Thus was Davydd, a Prince of Wales, wandering in the mountains like an outlaw, which he supposed he was. Wales was Edward's now. "By God," he cried, "it shall not remain so. I will show him that Welshmen will not remain vassals for ever."

He was forced to take shelter where he could—in any lowly cottage he could find. He did not always say who he was for fear of betrayal, for even those who would offer him succour were afraid to because the King of England—who was their master now—had said that he was a wanted man.

One night exhausted and hungry he came to a cottage and begged for food and shelter. He was given a dish of meat and a flagon of ale which he devoured while the man and his wife questioned him as to his purpose in being in the mountains.

He said he was a soldier who had escaped when the Welsh army was in retreat and he was trying to get back to his wife and family.

They listened sympathetically and agreed to help him.

"But you need a night's rest first," said the cottager. "Make yourself comfortable and in the morning I will help you on your way."

He sank into a grateful sleep.

When he awoke it was to find soldiers standing over him.

The cottager and his wife were peering into the room.

"Davydd ap Gruffydd," said one of the soldiers, "you are our prisoner. Get up. We are leaving at once."

"It is so then," said the cottager's wife. "We made no mistake."

"Mistake," replied the cottager. "Of course not. I told you did I not? I served with him before he went over to the English."

"He'll go back to the English now," said the cottager's wife with a certain grim humor.

They took him to Rhudlan and there he was put in fetters. He sent a messenger to Edward begging for an interview, reminding him that they had once worked together.

Edward's reply was that he did not parley with traitors, and Davydd realized that the fact that he had once worked with Edward would not be a point in his favor. Edward had had a respect for Llewellyn who had always stood firm in his cause, but for a man like Davydd who changed sides according to the way the wind blew, he had nothing but contempt.

Edward's orders were that Davydd should be taken to

Shrewsbury and there the trial of this traitor (as Edward called him) should take place.

At Shrewsbury were gathered together the earls, barons, judges and knights to assist at the trial and the King made it clear that he was determined to have justice. This man on trial was a murderer, sacrilegious and a traitor to the King. He must be made to suffer the full penalty.

He was quickly found guilty and sentenced to death. The method of his killing was to be one which had never been carried out before. It was called "hung, drawn and quartered." It was the most barbaric form of killing which had ever been devised and Davydd would be remembered as the first man on whom it was carried out.

Davydd's suffering was intense on the last day of his life.

He was dragged through the streets of Shrewsbury at a slow pace to the gallows and there in the view of a great crowd he was hanged. Before he was dead he was taken down and his entrails were torn from him and burned. Mercifully for him he was then beheaded and his body quartered that parts of his body might be displayed in five towns. There was a dispute between York and Winchester for his right shoulder which Winchester won. York had to put up with another presumably less desirable part, and Bristol and Northampton shared the other grim honors. The head was preserved for London and it was placed beside that now unrecognizable one of his brother.

Edward could survey them with satisfaction. He had conquered Wales.

But of course it was not easy to subdue such a proud people. They resented the conqueror, and there continued to be small pockets of rebellion throughout the country. All were aware though of the strength of the English King. He was as unlike his father as it was possible for one man to be from another; he swept through the castles of the land and brought builders with him in order to improve them. Where there had been stone fortresses, magnificent castles were beginning to appear. Being a man of great energy Edward allowed no slackness in those about him. No sooner had he decided that a castle should be improved than the workmen were busy obeying his orders.

Many Welshmen realized that if they would accept him as their King they could grow prosperous, but there were always the rebels. For this reason it was necessary for Edward to keep a strong force on the borders and as he was still unsure of his newly acquired territory he wished to be close at hand himself.

Rhudlan remained the headquarters and there he kept his family, spending as much time as he could with them. He was struck by the coincidences which had allowed him to keep his beloved daughter with him, although he guessed it was but a temporary respite. Still he enjoyed it. She was now nearly twenty years of age, in the prime of her beauty. Of course she should have been married long ago, but he preferred to forget that.

It was a happy family atmosphere at Rhudlan. The conquest of Wales was virtually complete. Everywhere Edward was accepted as the strong man England had lacked since the reign of Henry II, for Richard, strong as he was, had not been a good King for England and had squandered his strength elsewhere. No, Richard was a legend, not a King. Who wanted a King, however brave, however popular a hero in legend who was so fond of his own sex that he failed to get an heir? They preferred Henry II who scattered his seeds all over the land. Better still great Edward—victorious general, strong King determined to bring justice to the land and a good family man. There had never been any scandal about extra-marital relations in which he indulged for there was none. That was rare in a man of power. He had been a faithful husband and a devoted father. He was a rare King.

The only drawback was that he could not get a healthy son. Alfonso was growing more and more weedy every day. Pale of face, feeble of body, he was not the King to follow on such a father.

But glory be! The Queen was pregnant once more.

Would it be the old familiar pattern? The easy confinement, and then . . . another girl.

The King loved his girls dearly and some said that he did not greatly want a boy because he was so enamoured of his eldest daughter that he would like to see her on the throne. That could not be true. Much as he loved her and admired her he would rejoice in a boy. It was only because he looked on her as a substitute that he made so much of her.

In the early April of the year 1284 he was at Caernarvon Castle, a place of which he was immensely proud because he had recently completed the building of it. The structure which had been there before he had raised his impressive castle had been by comparison nothing more than a fortress. And what a spot on which to build. The castle stood on a rock projecting into the Menai Straits. On one side was the sea, on another the river Seiont. Its castellated architecture filled the King with pride. It gave an immediate impression of beauty allied with strength. It was both a delightful dwelling place and an impregnable fortress. Of all his castles in Wales this was his favorite. Turreted towers rose above the embattled parapets. There were thirteen of them and he had ordered that there should not be one exactly like another. He had said there shall not be another castle like Caernarvon and there was not. The towers were pentagonal, hexagonal and octagonal.

Before the entrance tower he had had a statue made of himself—with a sword half drawn from its scabbard in his hands. This would remind the Welsh that he was the conqueror and that all Wales was now under his rule.

As he stood at one of the windows of the state apartments he felt a great longing to be with his family. The birth of his child could not be far off. It was expected somewhere around the twentieth of the month. His family were at Rhudlan and he thought it would be nice to have them with him.

He sent a messenger to Rhudlan. Let the Queen and the rest of his family join him at Caernarvon. He had a notion that his next child should be born at the castle which he had so recently completed and which was the finest in Wales.

In a very short time they arrived. The Queen was very heavy but she assured him that the journey had been easy. She was so accustomed to child-bearing that it caused her little inconvenience. What a pleasure he derived from showing them his castle.

"There is of course much to be done yet, but work progresses."

How he wished he could spend more time with them but they had scarcely settled in when news came that after the family had left Rhudlan trouble had sprung up there and it was felt that the King's presence was needed at once.

"So it goes on," said Edward. "I am of an opinion that we

shall have trouble here for years ahead unless I can find some way of placating these people."

He said a fond farewell to his family.

And the Queen's last words to him were: "This time it must be a son."

"Send me news of him to Rhudlan as soon as he comes," was his answer.

At Rhudlan he went into conference with his generals. There was trouble in the mountains. Certain chieftains were raising their banners and trying to rally men to the case of a free Wales.

"They should be taken to London and shown the rotting heads of those who attempted to defy me," was the King's grim rejoinder.

"They are talking about a Prince who should be appointed. They want a Welshman. They want someone who does not even speak the English language."

"It is not what they want but what I want which will come to pass. They forget they are a conquered nation."

"There are some men, my lord, who will never admit to defeat. The Welsh are of this kind."

"We shall see," said Edward.

He was a little melancholy. He wanted to return south. He was finding that too many problems beset him and they came from all sides. He wanted to be at Windsor or Westminster. That was the center of his government. How could he know what was happening there while he was concerned with the Welsh matter?

"By God," he cried, "these are a defeated people. They shall do as I say or feel my wrath."

And while he was musing this messengers arrived from Caernarvon.

The Queen had given birth to a boy. A healthy boy.

He stared at the messenger. He could not at first believe it. Then he cried out in joy.

"Is this indeed true then?"

"My lord, it is so. The Queen is overjoyed."

"As I am. As I am. And a healthy boy you say."

"They say they have never seen a healthier. If his lungs are any indication, my lord, he gives good evidence of strength."

"Blessings be on you. You shall be rewarded for bringing this news. A grant of land and this day a knighthood is yours."

"May the lord preserve you and the baby Prince, my lord."

The man was grovelling on his knees but Edward had stepped past him.

He would keep his promise to the man and then . . . all speed for Caernarvon.

It was true. The Queen lay in her chamber which she had made beautiful and comfortable after her fashion by hanging up her Spanish tapestries. Beside her was the wooden cradle which hung on rings attached by two upright posts.

"My love," he cried and knelt by the bed kissing her hands.

She smiled at him triumphantly. "The child," she said.

And there he was, lying there, only a few days old but with a look of health on him—so different from the other boys who had all been puny from birth.

"Let us call him Edward," said the Queen.

"Edward he shall be."

"I shall pray that he will grow up to be exactly like his father."

The Princesses greeted their father with their usual devotion, but the Princess Eleanor was subdued. She did not want to speak to anyone, not even Joanna. Eleanor was now twenty years old, Joanna herself was twelve. There would be no more delay, Eleanor thought. How could there be? The child in the cradle had ousted her from her position. Alfonso could not live long. Everyone was saying that. And just as her ambition was about to be realized this boy had to be born.

Joanna was a little mischievous. "I wonder why God sent the Sicilian Vespers?" she said. "It all seems of no moment, does it not? You might as well be in Aragon as here in England."

Eleanor could not speak. She could not shut herself away so she must try to compose herself, so that her father might not see how bitterly disappointed she was.

She could not shut out the memory of Joanna's mocking comment. Whatever was God thinking of!

It was unwise to share one's secret thoughts with anyone— even one's sister.

* * *

Edward received the Welsh chieftains who had come to Caernarvon to pay homage to him.

He received them with respect and after they had made admission of their fealty to him they asked leave to speak to him. This he readily gave.

"My lord," said their leader, "there will be no peace in this land until we have a prince of our own—a prince who is beyond reproach, one who can speak neither French nor English."

Edward was silent. If he could speak neither French nor English that meant that he must be Welsh.

"A prince," he repeated, "who has never offended you, a prince who has never fought against you on the side of the English, you mean." He looked thoughtful. "A prince who can speak no English nor French. I see what you mean. I think I can agree to this. And if I do will you promise me peace in Wales?"

"My lord, we promise it."

"No more rising. No more rebelling. You will accept the prince I shall appoint and make him your Prince of Wales."

"We should do that, my lord."

"Wait here awhile. I shall not be long."

The chieftains looked at each other in astonishment. It was victory beyond their expectations. The King was agreeing to their request. A Welsh Prince for Wales!

The King returned. They stared at him in astonishment for in his arms he carried a baby.

"You asked me for a Prince of Wales," he cried. "Here he is. I give him to you. He has been born in your country. His character is beyond reproach. He cannot speak either French or English and if you wish it the first words he shall speak shall be in Welsh."

The chieftains were astounded. They had been tricked they knew. But something in the King's gesture appealed to them. There was a man of great resource. He was one whom it would be in the interests of Wales to follow.

They conferred together. Then their spokesman said: "My lord, we accept your son as our Prince of Wales."

The King was overcome with delight, as one by one the chieftains kissed the baby's hand and swore fealty to him.

He believed he had completed the conquest of Wales.

Joanna's Marriage

The shining star of the family was now young Edward. He was watched over, crooned over and marveled at. He had a Welsh nurse—for Edward was determined to keep his word to the chieftains—and Mary of Caernarvon guarded him like a dragon.

Eleven-year-old Alfonso loved his brother dearly. Alfonso had always been aware of the sorrow his health had caused. It was disconcerting to know that images of himself were constantly being burned in oil at shrines while widows were paid by his mother and grandmother to keep vigil in those churches, that their piety might induce the saints and those who had some influence in Heaven to do something about his health.

It had been a great responsibility, and the burden of kingship to come was too much for his frail shoulders; and now this new baby who cried a great deal and demanded the undivided attention of Mary of Caernarvon had taken it from him. Everyone marveled at Edward's health. "Another such as his father!" they said. "Look at his long legs. He is going to be another Longshanks, the angel." Whereas poor Alfonso had been short for his age.

They were all delighted with Edward except his sister Eleanor

and even she shrugged her shoulders and realized the hopelessness of a wild dream which had once come to her.

They had Edward. There might be more sons. Her mother
had a natural aptitude for putting children into the nursery.

They had remained in Caernarvon because, said their father,
that was Edward's birthplace and he was the Prince of Wales
and it was good for the Welsh to know that he meant it when
he had said his son's first words should be in Welsh. Moreover
the Welsh must be kept under surveillance for a while, and it
was necessary to wait and see whether they honored their promises.

The Queen thought the castle beautiful, but that perhaps it
might be cold when the winter came. She was anxious about
Alfie's cough which seemed to have grown worse in the last
weeks. However, she was glad to have her family with her; it
was pleasant, too, that the Queen Mother should be staying at
Amesbury, though she had not retired there permanently, for
she was still waiting for the Pope's dispensation which would
allow her to enter the convent without losing her money. It
was, the Queen only admitted in her secret heart, rather a relief
not to have the Queen Mother with them. She smiled a little,
contemplating the advice she would have attempted to give her
son on the way he should treat the Welsh. She would have
wanted heavy fines and great celebrations. Poor defeated people, they had not the means to pay fines. Edward realized that
and that the best way to get their peaceful cooperation was to
treat them kindly. Oh, Edward was so wise.

The physician who was never very far from Alfonso's side
came to her in some dismay.

"He is asking for you, my lady."

She went to Alfonso. He seemed to have shrunk and the
little hand which reached for hers was hot and feverish.

"Dear lady," said the little boy, "I think I am going to die
now."

"No, my love," she said, kissing his hand. "We are going
to make you well again."

"Not this time, dear lady. And it matters little now, does
it? There is my brother now."

"My dearest," said the Queen, "it matters so much . . . to
me, to your father . . ."

He smiled wanly. "Nay, it is all right now. I can go. I have always caused you such anxiety."

"My little son, I love you so."

"You were always my very good mother. But I can go now . . . I want to, dear mother. The time has come."

She sat by his bed, but she knew he was dying. He had been dying slowly for years. She thought of her half-brother after whom she had named him. What a clever man he was, but more wrapped up in his mathematical studies than his kingdom. His son Sancho was getting restive, and she had heard rumors that he intended to depose his father and take the throne himself. How could there be such strife in families! How could fathers go against their sons! She prayed that the baby Edward would always cherish his father and work with him. She need not pray that Alfonso would support his father. Alas, there would be no growing up for Alfonso.

Alfonso had closed his eyes and she could hear that he was breathing with difficulty.

The King came to the bedside and stood beside her, his hand on hers.

"He is going, our little Alfonso," said the Queen.

The King nodded. "It had to come."

"It is as though when he knew he had a brother he gave up trying to live."

"Thank God we have Edward," said the King.

And they stood side by side looking down on the body of their dead son.

It would seem that the people of Wales had accepted their fate. Edward had impressed on them that if they were loyal to him they should reap their reward and they were beginning to trust him. It was true that the bards sang songs of the valor of Llewellyn and Davydd and of Davydd's cruel death at the hands of the English tyrant. But these were the songs of the mountains. In the valleys, towns and villages people began to see that it was better to be part of England which was becoming increasingly prosperous under the King, than a wretchedly poor independent Principality of Wales. They remembered too that Davydd had been a traitor, a man who acted from self-interest. Brave he was but cruel to his enemies, and it must not be forgotten that he had betrayed them at one time to the English.

When chieftains brought to Edward a gift of a crown which they maintained had belonged to the great King Arthur, Edward was greatly impressed. The Welsh claimed that Wales had been the headquarters of the legendary King and Edward was prepared to give them the benefit of the doubt on this, for he saw a way of forging a link between them which would result in amity.

It was soon after the death of Alfonso that he called his family together and talked to them of what he proposed to do.

The Princess Eleanor's eyes glowed as she listened and it was to her her father addressed himself. He wanted her to know that, although he rejoiced in the birth of young Edward and the arrival of the boy must necessarily impair her status in the realm, she was still his beloved and favorite child. He loved his wife; she was a necessary part of him; he felt that he could always rely on her support in whatever he undertook but there was nothing controversial about her. She agreed with him whole-heartedly, whereas his clever daughter would sometimes raise a point of disagreement and very often it was a good one.

The fact was he was happy in his family and now they actually had a healthy boy he was deeply content. The conquest of Wales was a matter of great satisfaction but his happiness with his family meant more to him than anything else. Sometimes he was a little ashamed of that. But it was true.

"We must celebrate this victory over the Welsh," he said, "and I think I have found a way of doing it in a manner which will please them. You know they set great store on King Arthur and insist that this is where he held his Round Table. Now I am going to make it as though Arthur has returned. I am going to recreate the scene. I shall have a round table constructed and I with my knights shall sit round it and swear with them to uphold chivalry and justice throughout the land. This is going to be an occasion which will be remembered. There shall be jousting, tournaments as of old. The past will be brought back."

The Princess's eyes glowed with pleasure. "My lord," she cried, "it is a most excellent plan. The Welsh will be included. It will be the greatest token of peace and prosperity that you can give them."

She had grasped his intention at once. The Queen agreed with him and his daughter as she always did.

"Now," said the King, "shall I summon the knights and we shall set about planning this great spectacle."

And thus in the August of the year 1284 Edward celebrated his conquest of Wales by setting up his Round Table in Nevin in Caernarvonshire, and to this he invited all the most renowned knights of England and the Continent. The Welsh had never seen such magnificence—and that was what Edward intended. He wanted them to realize that they now belonged to a great and powerful nation ruled over by an invincible King. He had compared himself to the great Arthur, and Arthur himself could not have presented a more noble figure than the tall King who in this romantic gesture was telling them that he intended to uphold justice and chivalry throughout their land.

They were aware of what he was doing for Wales. The great castles of Conway, Caernarvon and Harlech owed their strength and beauty to his skill.

Wales was now part of England and it was said that if good sense prevailed there would be no attempt to change that state of affairs.

The Queen Mother's strength had suddenly started to fail. She, who had enjoyed good health throughout her life, was seriously alarmed and it occurred to her that it was time she took the veil.

By great good fortune the Pope had agreed that if she entered a convent she might retain her worldly goods and this decided her.

She had long made up her mind that her grand-daughter Mary should take the veil and it seemed to her that this would be an appropriate time.

Neither the King nor the Queen were eager to see their daughter immured in a convent and the Queen felt that the child—who was only seven years old—should have a little more time in which to discover whether this was the kind of life she wanted.

But the Queen Mother was adamant. "If you deny me this I shall die unhappy," she declared. "You have had good fortune in Wales. God was on your side. Why, there was Merlin's prophecy. That carried no weight because God was determined to aid you. And why do you think? It was because

Mary was promised to his service. If you disregard His wishes now your good fortune will change, depend upon it."

It did occur to the Queen that so often throughout their lives God's will had coincided with that of the Queen Mother. But Edward half believed her and she knew that if he did not give way to her his mother's doubts would creep into his mind, and it was necessary for his confidence to remain firm.

In her quiet way the Queen understood them both far better than they realized and it was easier to let Mary go as she showed no repugnance for the life chosen for her. Poor child, how could she when she had been told from birth what was awaiting her and had come to accept it? And what did she know, in any case, of what life would be with a husband and children?

"Mary will not be lonely there," said the Queen Mother. "I shall be there to watch over her and her cousin Eleanor is already there."

"Of course Eleanor is much older than Mary."

"True, but she is her cousin and of the same rank. I am sure Mary is going to know such happiness as is denied to so many."

The Queen sighed. The Queen Mother had, on the death of her daughter Beatrice, sent Beatrice's daughter Eleanor to the convent at Amesbury. She had wanted a girl from each family to go there for she had a notion that it gave pleasure in Heaven and she was feeling the need more and more as the days passed to find favor there.

The Queen Mother thought that the Princess Mary should enter the convent at the time of the festival of the assumption of the Virgin Mary—since the child bore the Virgin's name.

This was arranged and the family returned to London there to make the journey to Amesbury in order to be present at the ceremony.

Even baby Edward—now a year old—was taken there.

The Queen Mother was well satisfied. None of them would regret this, she was sure. The King, loving his daughters dearly, was a little unsure, but he had insisted that thirteen girls of noble families and of Mary's age should accompany her as her companions.

The ceremony was most impressive and the Queen wept when the monastic veils were thrown over the heads of the young girls and the spousal ring placed on their fingers.

After that all the members of the royal family placed a rich gift on the altar and the King promised his daughter an annual allowance for the upkeep of her state in the convent. The Princesses Eleanor and Joanna discussed the ceremony afterwards and Joanna commented that it was easy to see why convents and monasteries welcomed royal people and those of great wealth.

"The wealth of those who enter goes to the convent of course," said Eleanor.

"Not always," retorted Joanna. "Our grandmother made sure that she retained hers."

They smiled. They loved their grandmother but they were not sorry to see her take up her new abode. They were always a little afraid of her interference and that she would persuade their parents that something she wanted was good for them.

It was fortunate that she had been so impressed by the Princess Eleanor that she had been in favor of her being recognized as the heiress to England—but now that young Edward had arrived no one could do anything about the matter any more.

"How sad to be old as she is!" said Joanna. "She is always brooding on the past and so many people she loved are dead, even those whom you would have believed would have outlived her."

"I don't think she ever got over the deaths of her daughters. It was so strange that Beatrice should die so soon after Margaret."

"I think she loved Margaret better than any of them. She could never forget that affair of her marriage when they almost starved her and kept her from her husband. Oh Eleanor, do you think we are ever going to get husbands? You are quite old and I am no longer young."

"We did not want to be sent away . . . I to Aragon and you to Germany. We had our wish."

"I know. But now that Edward is here it is different. I think we should marry soon. I should like to marry in England. Would you?"

Eleanor smiled secretively. "I think that is what our father wants."

"Then," added Joanna, "since his mother is no longer here he might have his way."

"That is not fair. He always had his way...and always will."

"But you must admit he took a great deal of notice of his mother. Look at Mary. Do you think *he* wanted her to go into a convent?"

"He did not care very much and he thought it would serve him well in Heaven. Had Mary been unhappy he would not have allowed it."

"Well, sister, you are twenty-two years of age. If you are ever going to marry you will have to do so soon."

"And you are fourteen."

"A babe in arms compared with you."

Eleanor sighed. It was true.

"The gentleman of Aragon is still in his kingdom. It may well be those negotiations will be renewed."

"I don't want to go to Aragon."

"Well, sister, even our father would not prevent it if it was necessary to state affairs."

"It was necessary before, but he prevented it."

"Oh, I thought that was God with the Sicilian Vespers."

"Our father took the opportunity that was offered."

"Oh, he loves you truly. You are his favorite and always will be. But alas, in this world we live in, a boy is a boy and therefore of greater importance than we are."

"Yet our grandmother loved her daughters and so does our father."

"Oh yes, but that is a private loving. But I like it well when a woman comes into her own."

"Oh yes, a woman Queen...Queen in her own right...not simply because she is married to the King!"

It was strange, but very soon after this conversation an event took place which was to have a great effect on the crown of England.

It concerned the Scottish succession. There was one thing the Queen Mother had always been grateful for and that was that her daughter Margaret had been spared the suffering she would have undoubtedly endured had she lived to see the death of her two sons—those little princes David and Alexander on whom she had doted. David had died when he was only eleven years old and Alexander the elder, who had just made a good match with the daughter of the Earl of Flanders, had died a few years ago. That meant that only one of Margaret's children was living and that was the girl, named Margaret after her mother, who had been born in England and for whom the Queen Mother had a very special affection. The Princess Margaret was beautiful and for the Queen Mother heart-breakingly like her mother; she was clever too and King Eric of Norway had asked for her hand in marriage. The Princess herself had been most unhappy at first and had implored her father not to send her to Norway.

Politics, however, decreed that she should go. There had long been a dispute between Scotland and Norway over the sovereignty of the Western Islands and the marriage would be of immense help to both sides. So Margaret set aside her prejudices and went to Norway as the bride of Eric. The marriage turned out better than might have been expected and this was due to the gentle and gracious manner of the young Princess of Scotland. In due course a child was born. She was known as Margaret, the Maid of Norway.

Alexander had been a widower for nine years. He had dearly loved his wife and had felt no desire to replace her, but on the death of his two sons, remarriage became a political necessity. He had, therefore, chosen as his second wife Yolante, daughter of the Earl of Dreux, and they were married.

At the wedding a masque was performed and many declared that, among the masked dancers, there appeared one of an unearthly shape who beckoned to Alexander. Later it was said that this was the angel of death who had come for the King.

It did indeed seem that Alexander was ill-fated. Less than a year after the marriage—and there was no sign of a child so far—he decided to give a banquet at Edinburgh Castle. Rumors had been in circulation that the end of the world was approaching and was, in fact, destined to end on the very night fixed for the banquet. Instead of depressing the company this appeared to make them all the merrier, as though they were determined to eat and drink as much as they could before they came face to face with their Maker.

By a strange coincidence a violent storm arose and the darkness was intense.

Queen Yolante had not attended the banquet but had stayed in the Castle of Kinghorn, where the King had promised to rejoin her that night.

All the members of the company protested when he said his farewells to them. He could not ride out on such a night, they told him. He only had to listen to the wind and the rain to know why.

"I have promised the Queen," replied the King, "and I shall keep my word. If anyone is afraid to ride out tonight then he can stay behind."

One of the knights replied, "My lord, it would ill become me to refuse to die for your father's son."

"The decision is yours," replied the King.

So Alexander left Edinburgh in the company of a small band of his most devoted friends. Safely they crossed Queen's Ferry and reached Inverkeithing.

"See," said the King. "Here we are and what harm has befallen us?"

"My lord," said one of the King's men, "you must see that far from abating the storm grows more fierce. The roads are flooded ahead. Our horses cannot ride on paths such as these and there are danger spots on the coast road to Kinghorn."

"I see you are afraid," replied the King. "Very well I shall go on alone. I will take two men to show me the way and that is all I ask."

"My lord, my lord," cried one who was very near to him in friendship, "this is unwise. The road to Kinghorn is very dangerous. The Queen will not expect you on such a night. You know the precipice close to which you would have to pass. In the most clement weather that path must be trodden with caution."

"Enough," replied the King, and there was a light of fanaticism in his eyes, and afterwards some wondered whether he had deliberately challenged death last night. "I am bent on going."

So he set out. The roads of which they had spoken lay along the top of the rocks from which there was a sheer drop down to the shore of Pettycur. In the darkness and driving rain the King's horse stumbled and he and his rider went hurtling down on to the rocks below.

So the King of Scotland went to his death—willingly some said, for he had wanted to join his first wife Margaret, and the story went that on that steep cliff path the angel of death had appeared again as it had at his wedding feast and this time he had followed it to death.

This was a fanciful legend such as the Celts loved. The King of England was sceptical about the angel of death. What struck him immediately was that the little girl in Norway was now the Queen of Scotland, and he had seen a way of uniting the two kingdoms without the disastrous bloodshed which had been necessary in Wales.

Eric of Norway was delighted that his daughter should be betrothed to the heir to England and young Edward was told by his mother that he was to have a bride.

He was mildly interested, but when he learned that it was not to be just yet, he was ready to forget the matter. "It is a happy state of affairs," said Edward to his Queen. "Fortune is smiling on me. Wales in my hands and if Edward becomes King of Scotland when he comes to the throne the two kingdoms can be united. You see how much more peaceful we shall be when we stand together."

"I do Edward. And the people should be grateful to you. I hope they appreciate what you have done for them."

"They applaud what I have done when all goes well," he answered. "If all did not go well they would be quick to blame me. There is a certain luck required in kingship."

"Good judgment often results in what seems like luck."

"Aye, my Queen, and good luck as often looks like good judgment. By God, if I can be as successful with Scotland as I have with Wales, if I can make us one nation, then I shall achieve that which even the Conqueror failed to do."

"You will do it, Edward. I know."

It seemed that he might. Several of the Scottish lords came to see him and when he realized that they were by no means averse to the marriage between the heiress of Scotland and the heir of England, he was jubilant.

"They are over young yet," he said. "But we shall not wait long. We will have the child sent over from Norway and she shall be brought up here in your nursery, my love. There she will get to know and love Edward long before they can be married."

It was an excellent plan.

So good that Edward felt he could make a long postponed

and very necessary trip to the Continent. There were several matters which demanded his attention. He needed to be in Aquitaine for one thing; he had been away too long from this stronghold. It had been a great disappointment when his brother Edmund's stepdaughter had married the son of the King of France. Edward had hoped that marriage of Edmund's with the Comtesse of Champagne would bring Champagne to England. King Philip of France had been too wise to allow that. It was why he had offered the dazzling prize—his own son and heir— to the heiress of Champagne which made it certain that that rich territory should come to the crown of France.

There was another matter. Edward could no longer shut his eyes to the fact that it was time his daughters married. Eleanor was well into her twenties. The match with Aragon could still be made and it was a good one. He had to overcome his repugnance to her leaving England and take up negotiations once more with Aragon.

He would have to leave his beloved girls and go to France. There was one consolation, he could take his wife with him.

Preparations for the King and Queen to leave for France were set in motion.

Before they left Edward paid a visit to his mother at Amesbury.

He found her peevish. She was not well, she said. She was restive. The monastic life was not for her although she realized the need to undertake it. She spent long hours lying on her bed and thinking about the glorious past. She wanted to talk about it to Edward when he came.

So he was now going to France. How well she remembered when she and his father had gone. And there had been that dreadful time when she had gone alone . . . a fugitive from those wicked men who held Henry a prisoner. "And you too, my son. Forget not that."

He did not forget, Edward assured her. He remembered well how she had worked to raise an army.

"Which you did not need because you escaped and went to rescue your father."

"Ah, but it was a brave effort you made. You are an unusual woman, Mother."

She was pleased. "What days they were! Tragic days . . . but glorious somehow."

"We want no more such tragedy," said Edward.

"Your father was a saint . . . a blessed saint."

Edward could not agree to that so he remained silent.

"There is something I must tell you. A man came to me not long ago. He was blind and one day praying at your father's tomb when his sight was restored to him. Edward, your father was a saint. That proved it. I think we should have a church built for him . . . a monastery . . ."

"My dear Mother, this is nonsense."

"Nonsense! What do you mean? I tell you this man came to me. 'I was blind,' he said, 'and now I can see. Oh glory be to Saint Henry.' Those were his words."

"He has deceived you, my lady. He is looking for rewards, depend upon it. I'll warrant he wants some shrine set up and he will be in charge of it, eh? And many will come and lay offerings at this shrine much of which will find its way into his pocket."

"I am amazed. I tell you your father was a saint. Have not people been cured at the tomb of St. Thomas à Becket."

"My father was not à Becket, Mother."

"You shock me. You disappoint me. *You* . . . his son."

"It is because I am his son that I know this to be false. We loved our father. He was good to his family, but he was not a saint and this man seeks to deceive you."

"So not only will you deny your father's goodness but you insult me too. Please leave me. I wonder you trouble to come visit me . . . since my opinion is so worthless you but waste time in conversing with me."

"My dear lady . . ."

"Pray go," she said.

He shrugged his shoulders and, King though he was, he bowed and left her.

As he strode angrily from her apartment he met the Provincial of the Dominicans whom he knew to be a man of piety and learning and with whom he was on terms of friendship.

"You have heard this tale of a man cured of his blindness at my father's tomb?" he asked.

The Dominican admitted that he had.

"I tell you this: that man is a self-seeking scoundrel. There has been no miracle. As for my father I know enough of his justice to be sure that he would rather have torn out the eyes of this rascal when they were sound than to have given sight to such a scoundrel."

The Dominican agreed with the King.

"He is a man taking advantage of the Queen Mother's piety," he replied.

Edward, however, could not leave the country on bad terms with his mother. He went back to her before he left.

She was delighted to see him, for she could no more bear to quarrel than he could.

"Dear Mother," he said, "I am sorry for my abrupt departure."

She embraced him. "We must not part in anger, my son. That is something which would be intolerable to me. You were in my thoughts all through this night. My little flaxen-haired baby! How proud I was of you. Your father too. Our first-born and a beautiful son. Even the hateful Londoners and the Jews loved us for a while when you came."

"I like it not when any of our family are not on happy terms with each other."

"Dear Edward, I know I am an old woman now. The days have gone when I was listened to. Oh, when your dear father was here how different it was!"

"Life must change for us all, Mother."

"But to have lost him . . . and then your dear sisters . . . Oh, I am a lonely old woman . . . of no account now."

"You will always be of account."

"To you, Edward?"

"Always to me."

He began to tell her of his plans for his daughters' marriages and what he hoped to achieve in France. He had to stop her going over those incidents from the past which he had heard hundreds of times before.

But he was pleased to part on terms of affection. The bond between them was too firm to be broken because he had grown into a strong-minded man who would have his own way and say what he thought to be the truth and because she was a selfish old woman who could not believe that she had had *her* way because she possessed an uxorious husband who could deny her nothing, but thought it was because she was always right.

How did either of them know how long he would be away

and what would happen in the meantime and whether they would ever see each other again?

Now that their parents were out of the country and the Queen Mother was in Amesbury the Princess Eleanor was the undoubted head of the family. She was twenty-four years of age and so a mature woman. There was such a difference between her age and that of the rest of the family for Joanna the next was sixteen and Margaret thirteen; poor ten-year-old Mary was in Amesbury; Elizabeth who had been born in Rhudlan was only six and Edward four.

It was true that Mary of Caernarvon, Edward's Welsh nurse, guarded him like a dragon and put him right outside the Princess's rule. He was a spoiled little boy anyway and thought the whole world had been created for him. Eleanor was angry that so much fuss should be made of him because he was a boy. And she would never forget either that merely by arriving he had ruined her dreams. It was true he was a handsome child—fair and tall for his age, very like his father had been. He was bright enough but already showed signs of indolence. Eleanor wondered what her father had been like when he was young Edward's age. One day she would ask her grandmother, but the Queen Mother was a great romancer and colored all stories from the past so glowingly that one was never sure how far one could believe her.

Elena, Lady de Gorges, who had been their governess for years was with them in the schoolroom still. Not that the Princess Eleanor was in the schoolroom, but now that her parents were absent she was a great deal with her sisters and brothers and in that respect could say she was part of the establishment. She had her own of course and grand it was, for when her father was really looking on her as a possible heir to the throne she had been treated accordingly and he could hardly ask her to relinquish her state when Edward was born. Far from it. He was eager to show his darling that she was still as important to him—if not to the country—as she had ever been.

It was very rare, of course, for the daughter of a King to have reached the age of twenty-four without marriage. She doubted whether she would remain in a single state for ever. She knew that her father would see Alfonso of Aragon while he was away and it was very likely that some agreement would be reached.

She hoped not—fervently she hoped not. She wanted to stay in England, and she knew her father wanted her to.

"I must see the King of Aragon," he had said when they parted. "But it may well be that nothing will come of it. My child, it would be a hard wrench if you ever had to leave us."

She had clung to him and he had told her what a blessing she had always been to him.

How she wished he would come back. It would be terrible if anything should happen to him on the Continent. Then Edward would be King . . . a little boy of four. Oh how stupid people were to set such store by the sex of a King's heirs.

Even when her father went away he did not appoint his daughter as regent of England. She could imagine the protests there would have been if that had been suggested. The task went to her cousin Edmund, Earl of Cornwall, son of her grandfather's brother Richard. She was fond of Cousin Edmund who had ever been mindful of her importance and never treated her with anything but the utmost respect.

Joanna was often rather mischievous in her attitude towards her elder sister, so that Eleanor wished she had not been so frank. Joanna liked to inspire confidences and then tease people about them. Joanna was not in the least like herself or Margaret.

As she had said to Margaret, "It has something to do with being born in a different part of the world." It was something people would never forget. Even now she was often called Joanna of Acre.

Joanna was extravagant. She was constantly overspending the allowance Egis de Audenarde gave her. This man had been appointed by their father as their pursekeeper and had had instructions as to how much was to be given them to spend on their needs; and Joanna could be very short-tempered with him when he admonished her for being more extravagant than the means at his disposal would allow.

It was no use trying to remonstrate with Joanna. She did not grow less self-willed as she grew older.

How different was Margaret, sweet Margaret who was always so subdued by her lively sister. Eleanor had noticed that when they were at the altar in Westminster paying their respects to the shrine of Edward the Confessor they had all presented their offerings, but Margaret had slipped in an extra two shillings.

She had done it unobtrusively and when Eleanor had mentioned it to her had colored in embarrassment and murmured that their grandfather had had a special love for the Confessor and she had really been thinking of dear grandfather when she did it.

"You never knew him," Joanna had said sharply, for she would never have thought of giving extra—rather of holding back a little to be spent on something for her own adornment. "He died three years before you were born."

"But our grandmother has made him live for us," Margaret pointed out.

"Oh, people always become saints when they die. I doubt even the old Confessor was such a saint as he is made out to be." Joanna could be quite irreverent. It was fortunate that she was not the one chosen to go into a convent. Joanna warmed to the subject. "I should think he was a very uncomfortable old man." She lowered her voice. "He never consummated his marriage you know. He was too pure. *I* should not like a husband like that."

"What do you know of husbands?" demanded Eleanor.

"As much as you do, sister, since neither of us have had one yet. Of course you are getting so old that *you* may never have one."

Margaret said, "Well you know how frightened we were when we thought they were going to send her to Aragon."

Eleanor changed the subject and said that she was going through her wardrobe to decide what she would need for the pilgrimage.

"I wish we could stay at Court," said Joanna. "I am so weary of visiting shrines."

"It is the wish of the King and Queen and our grandmother that we do this," Eleanor reminded her sister.

"I could almost wish I were Mary," retorted Joanna. "No, no," she cried, crossing her fingers. "I did not mean that. Poor Mary. What a shame to force her into a convent!"

"She went of her free will," Margaret reminded her.

"Free will. What does a baby know of convents? How can you renounce the world when you don't know what the world has to offer? They would never have made me enter a convent, I do assure you."

"There is no need to assure us, Joanna," replied Eleanor. "We believe it."

Then they were all laughing and Joanna was telling them what festivities she would have at her wedding. There should be a masque—how she adored masques! There should be play-acting and tournaments.

"But you cannot have a wedding without a bridegroom," said Margaret. "And yours is dead."

"Drowned, poor Hartman! We willed it to happen, did we not, Eleanor?"

"What nonsense!" said Eleanor. "Now I am sending for Perrot and I am going to tell him what must be done with these garments. So many of my robes need mending."

"We need new ones," complained Joanna.

Nevertheless Eleanor sent for Perrot the tailor, and she discussed with him how her garments could be repaired while some had gone too far to be renovated and she would need new ones.

Perrot was eager to repair as much as possible for he had been warned by Egis de Audenarde that the Lady Joanna was spending more money than he was authorized to supply.

He examined the surtunics and the girdles which held them in at the waist and the mantles which were trimmed with fur and so long as to sweep the ground. He counted up how many silver buttons would be needed and how many gold.

He rather diffidently suggested that the Lady Joanna's mantle should be repaired and perhaps he could find a little more fur to replace that where it was worn.

"I'll not have a patched-up mantle," cried Joanna. "It will show and people will say that the King's daughters dress like paupers."

"I assure you, my lady, that when repaired, this mantle will be very fine indeed."

"Fine in your eyes it may be, but not in mine. I will have a new one for I will not allow the people to see me in what you will make of that."

"My lady, I fear the funds will not allow me to purchase a new mantle."

"You will not patch that one."

"But, Joanna," said Eleanor, "if Perrot does not, what will you do for a mantle?"

"I shall have a new one."

"But you have just heard..."

Then Joanna flew into one of her rages. "I will not be governed by Perrot the tailor," she cried.

"I do not seek to govern you, my lady. Only to tell you that the money allotted will not run to it."

"How I hate this vulgar talk of money! It is because the King is away that you think you can govern us, Master Perrot."

Poor Perrot was so distressed he was almost in tears.

"Perrot," cried Joanna, "I have finished with you. I shall not discuss any further what I shall have and what I shall not have. I will have what I will."

With that she turned and flounced out of the room, leaving poor Perrot quite bewildered and distressed.

Eleanor comforted him. "The Princess Joanna will understand in time that you cannot spend money which is not there. Please do not fret, Master Perrot. I shall tell my father that this has come about through no fault of yours. Now shall we see what I need for my garments and I promise you I shall not attempt to ask for more than my allowance."

Perrot thanked God for the calm justice of the Princess Eleanor and the gentle kindness of Margaret. He knew of course from other servants that the Princess Joanna was a trial.

When Perrot had gone Eleanor said to Margaret, "Don't fret about it. Forget it. You know Joanna. She will recover from her temper sooner or later. Then she will attempt to make up to Perrot for her unfairness."

"I do hope so," said Margaret. "Poor Perrot is most upset."

Joanna recovered from her rage but she did not send for Perrot. She was determined to have what she wanted, so she sent for merchants and bought extravagantly. She was more richly clad than any of her sisters and refused to wear a garment that Perrot had mended. When Eleanor pointed out that she was accumulating debts which would have to be paid she said, "Yes, I will speak to the King when he returns." She smiled mischievously at Eleanor. "He will be so delighted to return to his family that he will forgive us anything."

Eleanor thought this was probably true but she would never

have run up bills as Joanna was doing, for her sister would be
deeply in debt by the time their father returned.

That December the three Princesses set out for Glastonbury.
The King and Queen had arranged this journey for them before
they had left for the Continent. It was well, said the King, for
the people to realize the piety of the royal family and the three
girls were of an age now to show the country that they were
devout. Money would have to be raised for their marriages
when the King returned to England, for he could not keep all
his daughters in the single state for ever. So let the people see
what good pious girls they were.

Glastonbury was the most important of the abbeys because
it held the bones reputed to be those of King Arthur; and since
that monarch had been much discussed at the time of Llewellyn's uprising he was anxious to remind the people that Arthur
did not belong to the Welsh any more than the English.

The fact that the Princesses travelled in winter made their
pilgrimage more commendable for it was no luxury to make
their way through the countryside during the season of snow
and frost, and even if it was not cold enough for that there was
rain and muddy roads to contend with.

So they set out and they did not ride on horseback but in
chariots and in the midst of a large cavalcade of knights, ladies
and attendants of all ranks.

Wherever they went the people came out to welcome them.
There was no doubt that the reigning King and Queen were
more popular than their predecessors had been.

They were warmly greeted in all the abbeys at which they
called and with good reason for it was the recognized custom
that royal visitors meant royal gifts.

When they had paid their respects to the bones at Glastonbury they started on their homeward journey by calling at the
Abbey of Cerne in Dorsetshire that they might pay homage to
the shrine of St. Ethelwold. They spent Christmas in Exeter
where they stayed until mid-January and it was February by
the time they were back in Westminster.

It was at this time that there was a violent quarrel between
Joanna and Egis de Audenarde when he told her blankly that
he could advance her no more money. She had spent so much

more than her allowance that she must stop it forthwith until what she had bought was paid for.

This was one of the occasions when Joanna's temper would not be controlled. That she, a Princess of England, should be dictated to by one of her father's servants—a clerk nothing more—was intolerable to her.

"I will spend as I will, sir," she cried.

"Not of the King's monies, my lady."

"I think you forget to whom you speak," she flashed.

"My lady, you forget that I am in charge of the King's accounts and it is his orders I must obey."

"Get from my sight," she shouted. "I will have no more of you. From this moment you are no more concerned with my affairs."

De Audenarde bowed low.

"My lady," he said, "I withdraw. You must do as you will and it is for you to answer to the King."

Still fuming with rage Joanna sought out her sisters and told them what had happened.

"He was right," said Eleanor. "He cannot spend our father's money."

"What nonsense. How can we clothe ourselves if we do not spend money?"

"You know we have plenty of clothes. Perrot can mend them."

"I will not be seen in patches. When I want new garments I shall have them."

Eleanor shrugged her shoulders. "Do so, but remember it is you who will have to answer to our father when he returns."

Joanna said she would do that willingly. And she spent even more recklessly than she intended so that she could show her sisters that she did not care.

The Princesses were seated at their embroidery in one of the chambers in Windsor Castle which was light and therefore suitable to work in, and at the same time gave them a view of the forest.

Joanna was in a good mood. Strangely enough for one of her restless nature she loved to embroider. It had a soothing effect on her temper, she often said, and she rather mischievously chose colors to suit those moods of hers. It was said that if her women saw her embroidering in sombre colors they knew it was the time to keep away from her. She had been taught the art by the Lady Edeline and had started to learn in the days when she was in her Castilian nursery. The Castilians did beautiful work. That was why they liked to see it set up on walls that it might be continuously on view.

She had spent lavishly on her silks and now showed them with delight to Eleanor and Margaret who sat with her.

"But you had plenty before," said Eleanor.

"I needed more," she retorted.

She was working with a beautiful blue silk which meant she was in a benign mood. Eleanor shrugged her shoulders. It was Joanna who would have to ask her father to pay her debts. It was no concern of the Princesses Eleanor and Margaret.

"Just look at this lady's dress. Is it not a heavenly color? I shall run some gold thread through the blue and make it even more grand."

"She looks as though she is going to a wedding," said Margaret.

"Ah, weddings. I have been thinking of weddings. When do you think the King and Queen will return, Eleanor?"

"It cannot be long now. They have been away nearly two years."

"Matters on the Continent absorb them, I doubt not," said Margaret.

"I'll wager we are discussed," Joanna was smiling. "Weddings. I'll swear there will be weddings when they come back. A husband for me, a husband for you. Oh, Margaret, sweet sister, we shall soon be leaving you."

"Pray do not speak of it."

"She would miss us," cried Joanna. "Would you miss my teasing?"

"Very much," answered Margaret.

"She loves me in spite of my evil nature," said Joanna. "Yes, you do. People do not always like the good, do they? It is most unfair. I am determined to have my way and I tell you this, if I do not like the husband who is chosen for me I'll not take him."

"You will have to take whoever is given you," said Eleanor.

"I won't! I won't! I will not be governed by..."

"By the King?" said Eleanor.

"Marriage is too important a matter," insisted Joanna. "Is it not strange that Margaret is the only one who is betrothed? Little Margaret who is not yet fifteen. What think you of your Duke, Margaret?"

"If our father has chosen him for me then he must be the best husband I can have."

"Dutiful daughter! Will she be as dutiful a wife, I wonder? Eleanor, what think *you* of the Duke of Brabant."

"I thought him handsome," said Eleanor.

"I thought he was more interested in his horses and falcons than his wife-to-be."

"Margaret was only a child when he came here. How could he be interested in her?"

Margaret felt a little uneasy. She knew that the Duke of Brabant had been chosen for her, but as her sisters' marriages had come to nothing she had thought hers might also.

She tried to remember what she could of John of Brabant who had joined their household on one or two occasions and had stayed very briefly. She remembered a high-spirited boy who was always boasting about his horses and had taken as little interest in her as she had in him.

"It will be a long time before I marry," she said.

"Depend upon it," soothed Eleanor, "our father will never let you go at your age. He is sure to say you are too young."

Joanna said: "I have heard the Duke of Brabant is a lusty young man and that already he keeps several mistresses."

"There are bound to be such rumors," put in Eleanor quickly.

Eleanor was glad that there was an interruption at that moment for she could see that Joanna's comments were making Margaret apprehensive.

A messenger came with letters and packets from the Continent.

"News from the King," cried Eleanor and the girls dropped their work and ran to him.

"He must be coming home," said Joanna. "Oh, when, I wonder!"

There was a letter for Eleanor. It was full of loving sentiments to his dearest daughter and they were about to begin the journey home. In the meantime just to show he had not forgotten them he sent them a few trinkets to remind them of him.

The Princesses cried out with pleasure as they unwrapped the packets. There were jewels and silks for them all.

But for Eleanor there was the best of all the gifts—a gold cup and a coronet decorated with emeralds, sapphires, rubies and pearls. There was awestruck silence as they looked at it. Eleanor solemnly placed it on her head.

"It is quite the most beautiful thing I ever saw," said Joanna.

"Our father says it was given to him by the King of France. He says 'Treasure it. I want you my beloved eldest daughter to have it in memory of me.'"

"You were always his favorite," said Joanna.

Eleanor did not deny it.

"They will be home soon," she said softly. "Oh, how I long to see them again!"

Later she reproved Joanna for speaking of John of Brabant as she had before Margaret.

"Did you not see that you frightened her?"

"I think it is well for her to be prepared. Everyone knows what a rake he is. Poor Margaret, I would not envy her, married to him."

"Perhaps it will not come to that."

"If it does, she should know that she will have a philanderer for a husband! It is right that she should be warned."

Eleanor was unsure whether it was better to know or remain in ignorance of such matters.

What rejoicing there was in the city of London when the King rode through. It was two years since he had been away and the people were glad to see him back. He looked as kingly as ever and he brought with him that air of invincibility which gave them a feeling of security. They felt all was well while the King was in his castle.

A few noticed that the Queen had aged a little. There was a new air of delicacy about her which, seeing her frequently, the King had not been aware of; and her children were so pleased to see her, and she them, that it passed their notice.

They were gratified at their reception; the King was closeted with his ministers; but it was clear that he was longing to be in the intimate circle of his family and to talk of domestic matters. In a royal family those domestic concerns could become entwined with state affairs and they all knew this.

When he had studied all his children, glowed with pleasure at the charm and beauty of his daughter, marvelled at the progress of his son and heard from the Ladies Edeline and de Gorges that all was well with his daughters and from Mary of Caernarvon that Edward's health gave no reason, however small, for anxiety, he sought to be alone with his favorite Eleanor and they walked in the gardens together.

"My lord," she said, "you have been to Aragon."

"I have seen Alfonso," he replied.

"Oh? What news of him?"

"Eleanor, my sweet child, would you be very disappointed if I told you that there was to be no match with Aragon?"

She turned to him and laid her head against him. He kissed her hair.

"Then, my dearest, you are not too disappointed?"

"I could not have borne to go to Aragon."

"Nor could I have borne letting you go. To tell the truth, daughter, I can see no happiness for you there. This Sicilian matter was ill-conceived. He is a man who will have a finger in too many pies and pull little good out of any of them. I have talked with him. A match with Aragon . . . yes, it could bring us good. But I could not give you to him. No I could not."

They walked arm in arm in silence for a few moments.

"So I am not to have a marriage."

"A marriage . . . yes. There must be that. But not to Aragon."

"You have someone else in mind?"

"Not yet . . . not for you. But for the others yes. Margaret must be married to Brabant and Joanna must be married, too. As for you, my love, your time will come. But let us have a little longer together, dear child, before you leave me. You cannot know how much I have missed you."

"I can, for it is as I have missed you."

They walked in silence and he wondered whether to tell her of his plans for Joanna.

Better not, he decided. It would be better for Joanna to hear it first from him. He expected trouble there.

So he continued to walk in contentment with his best loved daughter and for a time at least they could be content that they were not to be parted.

* * *

Delighted as she was to see her parents once more Joanna's apprehension had become great for she knew the time could not be long postponed before Egis de Audenarde reported to her father that she had refused to draw her allowance from him and had run up bills on her own.

She could not bear to look at those bills; she could only guess how far they exceeded that sum which had been set aside for her use.

She found her father alone and knew that this was the time when she must confess what she had done. The sooner the better, for so delighted was he to be back in the heart of his family that he was likely to be lenient.

She came into the room where he was seated at a table and to her horror she saw that the accounts lay before him. He was a man who was haunted by his father's follies and the greatest of those had been extravagance. Edward only spent when it was expedient to do so.

She threw herself on her knees and buried her face in his robe.

"My dear daughter," he cried, "what means this?"

"Oh, my father," she said, "I have to confess to some indiscretions."

His dismay showed on his face. He immediately thought that she had become involved with a man. Joanna was different from the others. She was wild. He had always feared that there would be some trouble with her.

"You must tell me," he said.

"My lord, promise me you will not hate me."

He smiled indulgently. "I cannot imagine that could ever come to pass."

"I have been foolish."

"I can well believe that."

"You see, dear father, they were so *old*. I was weary of them. They had been patched up so many times . . . and as your daughter I owed it to you to look of some substance."

"What are you talking of, my child?"

"I dislike Egis de Audenarde. He is an overbearing, arrogant man. You would have thought it was *his* money he was giving us!"

The King breathed more easily. He was beginning to see

that his vain little daughter had quarrelled with de Audenarde and been spending more extravagantly than she should.

"He was commanded to keep my accounts."

"An arrogant fellow. He reproved me . . . me . . . *your* daughter . . ."

"For wanting to spend more of my money than I had given him charge of?"

Joanna allowed a few tears to escape from her eyes while she watched her father intently.

"I have heard what you have spent, daughter. It is a great deal."

She was silent.

"It would have been wiser if you had allowed Egis to deal with these matters. But," he added, "it is done."

"So you are not angry!"

"I find it hard to be angry with one whom I love as I love you, my child. What is done is done. You have spent a great deal of money. Your grandfather and your grandmother spent recklessly. It brought them no good. You will have to be watchful in the future."

"Oh, my dear father, I will. I will do anything if you will forgive me for this . . . anything you ask of me to show my love and devotion to you . . . ask me and I will do it. I will even let Egis de Audenarde decide what shall be spent on my clothes."

"Anything?" said the King. "I am glad to hear that because I have a husband for you and I want you to marry within the next few months."

"Marry! But whom should I marry?"

"That is what I want you to understand. This marriage would be of the utmost importance to me. I need this marriage. I need this man on my side. He is the most important man in England."

Joanna's heart was beating fast; she was too bemused for a few seconds to reason clearly. The only thought which came to her was: The most important man in England . . . then I should be the most important woman.

"Who . . . is he?" she asked slowly.

The King hesitated as though putting off the uncomfortable moment and Joanna was alarmed. "Pray tell me," she said quickly.

"He is a good deal older than you. But one of your temperament needs an older man. He is deeply enamoured of you."

"Please, Father, who?"

"The Earl of Gloucester—Gilbert de Clare."

"Gloucester? But he is an *old* man."

"Older than you certainly but he is not yet fifty."

"Not yet fifty. But he has a wife. He is married to Alice of Angoulême."

"There has been a divorce. For long he has sought it. That has been no marriage for years. I can tell you he is deeply enamored of you. He likes your spirit, your beauty. He admires you so much that nothing will satisfy him than that you shall be his bride."

She was astounded. The most important man in England. She could see that. She began to weigh up the advantages against the disadvantages. She would not leave England. That was the first and most important. Poor Margaret had to marry that rake John of Brabant and go to a foreign land which she might hate and in which she might be a prisoner. An old man who would adore her youth! The most important man in England!

The King was watching her closely.

"There are many advantages," he said. "He is a man of great influence. I need him, Joanna, I need him to be on my side. The Barons have always presented a danger to the monarchy. You know what they did to your grandfather and your great-grandfather. They ruined one and almost ruined the other."

"They could not harm you, Father."

"Nay, I do not intend that they should. But I should like to know that the most powerful of them was bound to me . . . by family ties."

"Is the Earl of Gloucester likely to turn against you?"

"He has turned his coat once. He was with de Montfort for a time you know. But he has fought for me. He did well in Wales against Llewellyn."

"Yet you do not trust him enough. For this reason you would give him one of your daughters?"

"My dear Joanna, I know him to be a steadfast knight where he gives his loyalty. The prospect of marriage to you would make him my friend for life. He is deeply enamoured of you and has been for some time. You will be so beloved that you cannot fail to be happy. To him you will always be young."

"As he will always be old to me."

"He is rich . . . there is not a richer man in the land. He will be ready to indulge you. You must marry. You are of an age to marry. I cannot have all my daughters single. He has fine estates . . . and one in Clerkenwell. If you marry Gloucester, my love, you need never be so far from your mother and me, we can be together at the smallest inconvenience to ourselves."

"You are making me like this marriage."

"You are making me very happy."

"Dear Father, you have been so good about the accounts. You will settle them then?"

"Could I be so churlish as to refuse my daughter such a request when she is determined to make me happy?"

She kissed him solemnly.

Then she left him. She was longing to tell the news to Eleanor.

Now the preparations for the royal wedding which was to take place on the thirtieth day of April were in full swing.

Joanna was delighted that she would be the first of the Princesses to marry. She felt no apprehension. She was going to live in England; she would be close to her family; her bridegroom was old but he was delighted with her youth which would not have impressed him so much had he been her own age.

She commented to Eleanor that marriage was a tremendous undertaking, if one partner was so old that he could not have so very long to live one had a chance of a second choice and if a Princess had married once to please her family it was only fair that in her second marriage she should please herself.

Eleanor was horrified, but then Joanna, from her superior experience, would know so much more of the world.

She delighted in being the center of attraction. Adam, her father's goldsmith, had made her a magnificent head-dress off-set with rubies and emeralds. A beautiful robe was being made for her. Her bridegroom was by no means distasteful. He was old it was true; but he emanated power and the fact that even her father was wary of him aroused her admiration. She believed that she could rule him though. He gave signs already that this would be so. Yes, an aging bridegroom for a while, and then some man of her own choice, *if* she found marriage sufficiently to her taste that she wanted to embark on it again.

She comforted Margaret who was less happy about her coming marriage. And small wonder. John of Brabant was no doting old Earl of Gloucester. By no means so. What would he want of a child of fifteen when, if rumor was to be believed, he had the most flamboyant mistresses in his own country. Poor little Margaret! How lucky was Joanna!

The wedding day arrived. It was to be a private affair conducted in Westminster Abbey by the King's chaplain, but after that the feasting and the celebrations began. The people cheered and made merry in the streets, drinking the red wine which flowed from the fountains. They were pleased that this was no foreign wedding, and the most astute of them liked to see the most powerful of the barons united with the King through his beautiful daughter.

Joanna had always been attractive and there were some who thought her vitality gave her an advantage in appearance over the more beautiful Eleanor. Now she glowed with a new beauty which startled all who beheld it, and was a source of great delight to her husband.

She was very eager to see his estates and he was anxious to show them to her but the King and Queen wanted her to stay at Court to join in the celebrations for Margaret's wedding.

That was to be in July. "It is only just over a month," said the Queen. "Your father and I so want you to be here."

"A husband and wife should be alone together for the weeks following their marriage," said Joanna demurely.

"My dear daughter, you will have time for that."

The Queen, knowing her daughter's love for horses, gave her five beautiful white steeds for her chariot, in which she could ride through London and enjoy the admiration of all who beheld her.

But she liked to talk of her husband's estates. She longed to see them. Moreover she wanted to test whether he would defy the wishes of the King and Queen to please her.

Gilbert de Clare, the newly married Earl of Gloucester, explained to her that as soon as Margaret's wedding was over she would go wherever she wished.

"But I want to go now."

"So do I, my sweet wife."

"Then, Gilbert, why should we not?" Her eyes sparkled.

"Let us slip away . . . the two of us. Oh we should be alone you know. It is only right that we should."

Gilbert insisted that it would be unwise to disobey the wishes of the King.

This made her all the more determined. She had thought, she said a little sadly, that she was the one he wished to please . . . not the King.

He did. He longed to please her, but the King . . .

"My father will forgive me. He always does."

She had her way as she was determined to. They slipped away early one morning before the Court was awake.

What an adventure riding through the morning with her husband beside her, so besotted with love for her that he was ready to defy the King. Not that there was anything meek about him. It was not the first time he had defied the King. In fact that was the very reason why he had won his Princess.

This gave her a wonderful sense of power and that was what Joanna enjoyed.

The King was angry. He knew this was his daughter's show of defiance and that Gilbert had acted as he had to please her. In a sudden outburst of temper he said that her wedding outfit should be confiscated. He knew how much she loved her clothes and ornaments.

In the stronghold of her husband's castle at Tunbridge Wells Joanna snapped her fingers. She had a rich and doting husband. Whatever she wanted—fine silks, velvets, brocades and jewels and horses for her chariot—she only had to ask for.

Exodus

Now that he was home Edward became energetically involved in state matters. He had married Joanna to the chief of the barons; he must now give his mind to the union of England and Scotland which he planned to do through the marriage of his heir to the little Queen of Scotland who was still with her father in Norway; there was another matter which seemed of the utmost importance to him and that concerned his Jewish subjects.

After the Norman conquest England had become prosperous and this attracted the Jews who were soon settling in large numbers throughout the country. They specialized in banking and usury and as they were shrewd and energetic with a genius for business they soon became very rich. They were in addition infidels, a fact which people claimed to use against them, but in truth it was their wealth which was envied. The traders and citizens of the big cities would have liked to see them turned out of the country; stories were circulated about them; it was easy to work up hatred against them which could result in riots, the main purpose of which was to loot their places of business and rob them of their possessions. There was a favorite rumor which was brought out every now and then which accused them of kidnapping Christian boys and crucifying them as they had once crucified Christ.

This was usually the preliminary to riots. There was a demand that they should be expelled from the country but a good proportion of their money came to the King, usually through fines or bribes, and if they were no longer in England the exchequer would suffer considerably. To Henry III they had been a source of income and his love of money and the need to satisfy his wife's insatiable demands meant that he took little action against the Jews.

Edward was much more strongly opposed to them than his father had been. He did not approve of moneylending with high interest rates which was one of the chief methods of making money. He was zealous in his religion and had a keen dislike of all those who were not Christian. He himself was constantly in financial difficulties and had been forced to borrow heavily and to be obliged to pay back, through the amount of interest demanded, more than he had originally borrowed riled him.

The laws against the Jews had been growing more and more severe during his reign—so much so that quite a number of them had been forced out of business. They were not a people to admit defeat and soon found other means of making money. One of these was known as clipping the coin, which meant that gold and silver were clipped so finely from pieces of money that it was rarely noticeable, but the metal taken from the coins could be sold. This was a crime punishable by hanging, and as the confiscation of goods went with it it was again helpful to the exchequer.

Edward was deeply concerned with the Jewish problem. He knew the people would be pleased to see them expelled from the land. The fines imposed on them would be missed. But he knew that there must be continual trouble between them and the Christian citizens, and at this time the rumors of Jewish atrocities were growing. He did not want trouble in the capital. He was seriously thinking of expelling the Jews.

When he went to see his mother at Amesbury she received him with great pleasure. He was shocked to see that her health was failing, even though mentally she was as energetic as ever and wanted to hear all that had befallen him during his sojourn abroad. She was delighted with Joanna's marriage.

"She will keep Gloucester in order," she said with a chuckle.

Although the eldest princess Eleanor was her favorite she greatly admired the lively Joanna.

"And now it is Margaret's turn," she went on. "A pity she is so young. I heard Brabant is something of a rake."

"Doubtless he will improve on marriage."

"It is to be hoped so."

The Queen Mother was wistful. She hated to be shut away from events. She longed for the return of those days when she had been the center of her family and she would never get over the loss of her doting husband. Edward was a good son but he would go his own way. She wanted to be young again, depended on.

"I have heard rumors that the Jews are up to their tricks again," she said.

"Rumors . . . here in Amesbury?"

"I have visitors and they know that if they will please me they must bring me news of your kingdom. Clipping the coin . . . crucifying Christian boys."

"The first yes—the second . . . why, Mother, you know there is no truth in that."

The Queen Mother's eyes blazed. She was thinking of how she and Henry had borrowed money from the Jewish usurers and the interest they had demanded. She had always maintained that they should have given freely of their wealth to the King and Queen for the privilege of living in this country. She had always hated them.

"You should send them out of the country," she said firmly.

"Send them away! There are so many of them."

"All the more reason why they should go."

"It is a matter which needs a great deal of consideration."

"Meanwhile they are the reason for riots in the cities . . . they are reducing the value of the coinage . . ."

He held up his hand. "I know this," he said. "In fact it is in my mind to be rid of them. I am being coerced from all sides . . . It will bring a certain loss to the exchequer."

"You will prosper Edward. I know it. Rid yourself of these people, God will reward you."

She went on talking in the manner he knew so well. If it was something he had decided against he would listen politely, his mind made up. But with regard to the Jews he was prepared to pay attention to her tirade against them, which showed that he was ready to accept her views.

Only when he spoke to her of his intentions regarding young Edward could he get her off the subject.

"Joanna is married; as Margaret will soon be. It is imperative that Edward is betrothed. I want the Maid of Norway brought over. I want her brought up in my kingdom and as soon as possible the marriage will be celebrated."

The Queen Mother nodded vigorously. She had seen her son bring Wales under the English rule. Now it was the turn of Scotland, and if it could be done by a marriage alliance how much better than years of dreary fighting. Young Edward and the little Maid of Norway must marry.

"You must bring her over without delay," said the Queen Mother emphatically.

But before Edward left she talked more of the need to expel the Jews.

On a hot day at the beginning of July the Princess Margaret was married to John of Brabant.

The bride sparkled in her jewel-studded chaplet and belt which the King had ordered his goldsmith to make for her and which were decorated with leopards in sapphires. The slight young girl weighed down by her heavy dress of samite, jewel encrusted, stood beside her rather plump and florid bridegroom who, although he was but some five years older than she was, already showed signs of dissipation.

Eleanor was her sister's chief attendant and Eleanor's gown was of equal magnificence, for fifty-three beautiful silver ornamental buttons had been sewn on to it and she was a dazzling sight.

The people declared that they had never seen such magnificence, for the King and his attendant knights were in full armor and the Earl of Gloucester and his newly wedded wife were present, and Joanna was determined to shine at least as brightly as the bride and her groom, and this they succeeded in doing for in their train were more than a hundred glittering knights.

Six-year-old Edward was there with a train of eighty knights, and people asked each other when they would be summoned to see his betrothal to the little Maid of Norway.

Margaret's heavy dress and all the jewels she must carry

tired her and she was a little afraid of the handsome bridegroom who looked so elegant in his sleeved surtunic with sleeves which flowed to the elbows and his mantle of vair.

The Queen was uneasy. She had not been well during the end of their stay in France and had promised herself that when she was home in England her health would return. She had felt momentarily better to be reunited with her children but her weariness had come back bringing vague pains and she was conscious of certain bodily discomfort.

She was afraid she might not be able to keep up with the energetic Edward but firmly resolved to say nothing to him about her ailments. Fortunately with all this excitement of the wedding even her closest family failed to notice that there was anything wrong with her.

Now she was uneasy about Margaret. Joanna could take care of herself and the eldest, Eleanor, would be of an age when she could accept with serenity a husband—if they ever found one for her. But Margaret was such a child.

She had prevailed on Edward not to send her away just yet, and being always indulgent where his daughters were concerned he had agreed. So it had been arranged that the married pair should remain a while in England where they might become accustomed to each other before Margaret had to leave her home.

So after the celebrations were over they would accompany the bridegroom's father, the Duke of Brabant, to Dover where they would say farewell to him before he left for his dominions.

That seemed as satisfactory an arrangement as was possible.

Meanwhile they could give themselves up to the banquets and entertainments which they had devised for the marriage of their daughter, and she could only pray that the rumors she had heard concerning the bridegroom's profligate life were unfounded.

Two important events followed on Margaret's marriage.

The first concerned the Jews. Edward had discussed the matter with his barons headed by Gloucester. He had already expelled the Jews from his Continental possessions to the great joy of the people there. He now proposed to do the same in England. The general opinion was that this would be a good move. The unpopularity of the Jews was so great that it seemed

Edward could only win his subjects' approval by dismissing them. The Templars were now financially involved in the affairs of the country, and during the past years many Italian bankers had settled in London where they were taking over the business which had once been entirely in the hands of the Jews.

"We do not need the Jews now," said Gloucester. "And the people will more easily accept the Italians. They are Christians. The Jews crucified Christ, that is something for which they will never be forgiven."

The Queen had pointed out that Christ himself had spoken often of a Christian duty to forgive one's enemies, and Edward explained gently to her that the expulsion of the Jews was political as well as religious. "A matter of state, my love," he said; and she who had always accepted his ruling must not attempt to disagree; in any case she felt too weak to contest anything at that time.

His ministers were in favor of the expulsion. The Jews had made fortunes from England; let them go now, but leave behind a proportion of that which they had gained as some said through exploiting the people of England. The King had not wished to be harsh. It was true, he abhorred their lack of Christian faith, but they had worked hard and he would like to be as fair as possible.

He would take a fifteenth part of their goods; they might take with them a part of their movables and enough money to defray the expenses of their journey. Their houses and land would be the property of the King. They should be given time to arrange their move but all must be out of the country before the feast of All Saints.

The persecuted people proved themselves astute to the last. Having been told they could take what they could carry they procured a great ship which was brought up the Thames and into this they were able to load much treasure.

But the master of the ship was determined that they should not, as he said, cheat the King and the country. He sailed off, as arranged, but as he reached the mouth of the river where it opened into the sea he ran the ship on to a sandbank. There he invited the Jews to walk out with him to exercise themselves before they left England. This they did, and when he saw that the tide was coming in he embarked, but told the Jews they had a little time left to them and he would let them know when they must come aboard.

When the Jews realized how the tide was rising they ran to the ship's side, but the captain still would not allow them to come on the ship.

"We shall be drowned," they cried.

"Nay," said the Captain. "Did not your forebears pass through the Red Sea? Call to Moses to come to your aid that the same may be done for you as was done for your forefathers."

The Jews cried out in supplication, but the tide rose and the ship was able to drift off the sandbank and into the river. It was said that the spot was haunted and that at times it was possible to hear the cries of the drowning Jews.

By the appointed time sixteen thousand Jews had left the country.

The Queen's Crosses

Having married two of his daughters and rid the country of the Jews, Edward's eyes were on Scotland. His hopes were high. If he could marry young Edward to the Scottish Queen, now in Norway, he would have achieved a great deal, for he saw an era of peace throughout the island and peace meant prosperity. He could then turn his eyes to the Continent, protect those possessions which still remained part of the Crown and, who knew, he might regain some of those which his foolish father and wicked grandfather had lost? The augury for the future was promising.

It was fortuitous the way events had fallen into shape to suit him.

Margaret, the Maid of Norway, was but six years old—a few months older than Prince Edward. It was a pity they were so young, but if he could get her to England and bring her up in his Court and the marriage was performed at the earliest possible time, this could work out very well.

There was a good Regency in Scotland which had been set up after the death of Alexander—the grandfather of the little Maid. The child's mother, Margaret, had died giving birth to her; and her father, Eric of Norway, was at that time still in his teens. He had been very willing to promise to send the child to Edward so, with his usual foresight and energy, Edward procured a dispensation for the two cousins to marry, and had commenced his negotiations with Scotland and Norway. In due course the Treaty of Salisbury had been arranged though Edward had had to concede that there should be no contract of marriage between the two children until the Scots had given their consent. Edward foresaw no difficulties about this once he had the child in his hands.

More recently he had had a meeting with the Scottish nobles and they had agreed that in the event of a marriage between the two young people Scotland should remain separate unto itself and divided from England. This was agreeable to Edward. He foresaw the future when young Edward and the Maid from Norway would have a son who would unite the two kingdoms. He was looking far ahead.

The important matter now was to get the Maid of Norway into his possession. That little six-year-old was the pivot on which the entire project turned.

He would send for her. Thank God Eric was willing to let her go, although he warned Edward that his little daughter was of a delicate constitution and they had had difficulty in rearing her. Eric thought that the sea journey might prove tiresome for her, and he thought that perhaps it should be delayed until the spring.

This was impossible. Edward would have no delay. The Maid must be at his Court before All Hallowtide. He was sure that if she were not some of those restive barons of Scotland might attempt to prevent her coming to England. The Maid was the undoubted Queen of Scotland, but if she were not there there would be several other claimants to the throne. He must have her with him as soon as possible.

He himself went to Yarmouth to supervise the fitting out of the vessel which was to go to Bergen, collect the precious child and bring her to England.

He took the Queen with him for he felt that a woman's advice would be useful for the comfort of the child. A cabin had been fitted out for her, which was pretty and would give pleasure to a six-year-old.

"What would she like to eat, think you?" asked Edward.

"Sugar and raisins," said the Queen. "Edward is very fond

of them and she is his age. Ginger too was a favorite with the children . . . and walnuts . . . oh yes they did like walnuts. And children love gingerbread especially if it is made into fancy shapes."

So the King ordered: "Let these things be added to the usual stores."

He himself supervised their being taken aboard and side by side with the Queen he watched the vessel sail off on its route to Bergen.

"When that child is in our hands," he told the Queen jubilantly, "I see a new era of peace beginning for England."

"Do you think all those who have a claim to the Scottish throne will all see that?"

"Baliol? Bruce? They must respect the true succession. Our little Maid is in the direct line of succession from Alexander and William the Lion. When the child arrives we will meet her with worthy ceremony and assurances of our concern for her welfare. She shall have a welcome place in our nurseries. She shall learn her lessons side by side with Edward."

"I am so glad," replied the Queen, "then when they marry they will not be strangers. I hope they will be as happy as you and I."

"That is asking a good deal," replied the King; and he noticed then that she seemed paler than usual and perhaps a little thin.

"I think our travels were too much for you," he said solicitously. "We will now have a quieter time with the family. Our dear daughter Eleanor is such a comfort, and we still have Margaret with us and Joanna is not far away at Clerkenwell."

"What a joy it is to be surrounded by one's family!"

They rode back to London, the King in good spirits and to see him so made the Queen happy for she believed that if there was peace between England and Scotland and the perpetual worry as to what was happening on the borders could be removed, now that Wales was under control, they could stay in Westminster and Windsor and be together at home. This put her in such a state of pleasure that the color glowed again in her cheeks, and her eyes sparkled with happiness so the fact that she had lost some weight was not apparent, and the King's mind was at rest concerning her health.

What pleasure it was to rest at Clerkenwell and to see their

dear Joanna do the honors of châtelaine and hostess. She glowed
with pride in her new state. She was already pregnant and had
assumed a new dignity. She could subdue her doting husband
with a look and Edward was amused to see proud Gilbert
reduced to the state of besotted lover by this imperious and
lovely young daughter of his.

Clerkenwell, where the river Holeburne wound its way
through green meadows and wooded hills, was a delightful
spot; and the fact that the city could be seen in the distance
but added to its charm.

Edward said it was wonderful that they should be in such
a romantic spot and so near to London that he could if the need
arose be there in a very short time.

They had returned to Westminster when the news arrived
that the ship that had been sent to bring the precious child to
England had arrived at Yarmouth.

"Let us to Yarmouth without delay!" cried the King; but he
noticed that the messenger was downcast and he could not meet
the King's eyes.

"What is it?" he demanded, his alarm obvious. A hundred
thoughts flashed into his head, each warning him of disasters.
His first was that the Scottish rebels had waylaid the boat and
were taking the child to Scotland.

But this was not so. This was irrevocable.

"The Maid was very sickly, my lord," said the messenger.
"When she boarded at Bergen we feared for her. The seas were
rough; and she became very sick . . ."

"And what happened?" interrupted the King impatiently.

"My lord . . . the child died during the voyage. The cold . . . the
rough seas . . . they were too much for her. She was so frail . . . so
delicate . . ."

The King turned away, fury in his heart.

This was the end of a dream which had hung on one frail
child's life.

The Queen of Scotland was dead. He could imagine what
would happen in the unruly country when the news was known.

He would have to make plans to march up there with all
speed. Gone was his dream of an easy victory.

Civil war was threatening in Scotland.

There was no longer a direct heir to the throne. David,

brother of William the Lion had had no sons; but he had had three daughters. The eldest and youngest of these had a grandson living and the second daughter had a son.

The grandson of the eldest daughter was John Baliol and he believed he had first claim to the throne. Robert Bruce, however, son of the second daughter, reckoned he had the stronger claim because he was a generation nearer to William the Lion. The grandson of the youngest daughter was John Hastings whom Edward had made a Marcher Baron. Edward favored this Hastings but he knew it would be generally accepted that Baliol and Bruce came before him.

These two were of the Scottish aristocracy but were as English as they were Scottish through their upbringing. They had possessions in England where Baliol owned Barnard Castle in Durham and though Bruce's estates were in Scotland he had served as Sheriff of Cumberland. He was an old man but had a son Robert who would be considered one of the main claimants.

Edward could see that his presence was needed in the north and he prepared to set out without delay.

Since the Queen had accompanied him to the Holy Land she had made it a practice to follow him in battle, and although it was not always possible for her to be on the scene she was never far behind.

When she heard they were to go to Scotland she was very uneasy. It was so disappointing after she had believed she would remain at Windsor to welcome the little newcomer to the royal nursery. It was more than disappointment: it was fear. She had become aware that the strenuous journeys were too much for her and she was becoming exhausted by the least exertion.

To have explained this to Edward now would have added to his anxieties so she went ahead with her preparations to follow him.

Edward took his farewell of her telling her they would soon be together and she set about making her preparations.

In due course she was ready and started the journey north. The dampness of autumn seemed to seep into her bones, increasing their stiffness. She felt too ill to ride, and was carried in a litter which slowed the journey considerably.

Her daughter Eleanor had insisted on accompanying her for she was aware of her mother's growing weakness, and it became apparent as they progressed that she was going to have a bout of that fever which often came to her in the autumn.

"My lady," said the Princess, "I think we should remain awhile at Herdeby until your fever has abated."

"Your father will wonder what has delayed us."

"He would not wish us to travel while you are so sick."

"It is nothing," said the Queen. "I have had this before."

"Nevertheless I think you should rest here awhile."

The Queen shook her head but when the time came for them to move on she found she could not rise from her bed.

The Princess was deeply concerned. She went to one of the couriers and told him to go with all haste to the King and tell him that she feared the Queen was very sick indeed.

He left at once and the Princess went back to her mother for she insisted on nursing her herself.

"Why, my dear child," said the Queen, "would you make an invalid of me?"

"You are sick," replied the Princess, "and I am going to nurse you back to health."

Even as she spoke her voice faltered. She had known for some time that the Queen was growing weaker. She had seen the gradual deterioration which her mother had taken great pains to conceal from her father.

That was why the message she had sent to her father informed him that the Queen was very ill indeed and that his presence might well be needed at Herdeby.

Of course he could not leave Scotland. He was engaged in important matters, the outcome of which could be war with the Scots. How unfortunate that the Maid of Norway had had to die when she had. If she had lived her father would not have had to go to Scotland; he would have been with her mother; she would not have had to start on that long journey. Oh, it would have been so different.

But in her heart the Princess knew that her mother was ailing and had been for some time. That dreadful fever which attacked her periodically had sapped her strength, and even when she recovered from it she had seemed a little weaker afterwards.

She sat by her mother's bed.

"I rejoice that your father does not know . . ." whispered the Queen.

The Princess did not tell her that she had sent word to him how ill she was. That would only worry her. It would worry him too up there in Scotland where this threat of war would have to be evaded if possible.

A few days after the message had been sent the Queen took a turn for the worse. The Princess was shocked when she went into her mother's bedchamber. The once beautiful face was pale, the lovely eyes a little glazed.

"Daughter," whispered the Queen, "is that you?"

"Dear Mother I am here. I shall always be here when I am needed."

"You have been such a good child. He was so proud of you . . . He loves you well . . . better than any of them . . . Sometimes I think better than anyone."

"You were always first with him, dear Mother."

She smiled faintly.

"I was so proud . . . Eleanor . . . proud that he loved me. He is a great man, a great King. There are few like him . . ."

The Princess said: "Please Mother, do not speak so . . . as though . . ."

"As though I am going. I *am* going, my child. I know it. I have known for some time that I was growing weaker. I kept it from him . . . But now . . . I can hide it no longer. My life is ebbing away."

The Princess laid her head on the bed that her mother might not see her tears.

She said in a muffled voice, for pretence was no longer possible: "I should send for a priest."

"In a moment, dear child. Not yet. This will be our last talk. Life has been good . . . so good. I loved him from the moment I saw him. I could not believe my good fortune . . . and then when you were all born . . . I loved you all. My children . . . my dear girls . . . my little Edward. God bless you all. I must go now and face my Maker . . ."

"You have nothing to fear, dear lady. There has been nothing but goodness in your life."

"I have sinned, daughter. There are acts I would rather not have done. The Jews . . ."

"You must not worry about them. They are no concern of yours."

"I trust too many of them did not suffer badly. I fear they did. To be turned away from their homes..."

"It was not your fault, Mother."

"I loved worldly goods too much. I set up treasures on earth. It was because before I married Edward I had so little. I was overwhelmed by all that came to me then. Yes, I thought too much of worldly goods. Some of my estates... you know those which came to me through the Jewish usurers. You know I joined with them to get the estates of Christians who were in difficulties and borrowed money... It was wrong, I wish I could go back over my life..."

"We none of us can. And if you have loved treasures and money, you have loved also your husband and your children. The people have loved you. They never hated you as they did our grandmother. If you worked with the Jews to extract payment from those who had borrowed money, you should not blame yourself now. If they had not borrowed they would never have been in difficulties. You have confessed this sin. Now think of all the goodness you have brought into the world. How you have stood beside your husband... and your children..."

"You comfort me, daughter."

The Princess bent over her mother and kissed her clammy forehead.

She knew it was time she sent for the priest.

Edward was nearing the Scottish border when the messenger arrived.

"From my daughter? From the Queen? What news?"

"My lord," said the messenger, "the Princess would have you know that the Queen is grievously sick and she greatly fears that she will die."

The Queen sick! About to die!

He felt as though everything he had built up was collapsing about him.

Trouble in Scotland... but what was trouble in Scotland when his Queen Eleanor was about to die.

He was silent for a long time, thinking of her. There were so many memories. All dear to him.

One of his knights came into his tent and seeing him as one dazed, said, "My lord, what ails you?"

He answered then. "It is the Queen. She is sick . . . dying may be. We are turning back."

"My lord, the Scots . . ."

"We are going to ride with all speed to Herdeby," said the King firmly.

Through the night . . . the miles passed by slowly. How long it took. He was frantic.

He thought of her. Yes, so many memories . . . The little girl they had brought to him. "She is to be your bride." How meek she was. How pliable! How easy to please! The little Princess from Castile. And when she grew older she was beautiful. The only time she had defied him was when she had said she was coming with him on his crusade. "A wife and a husband should be together," she had said. Thank God she had. He was sure he would have died from the poisoned knife of that murderous assassin if she had not been there. She had sucked the poison from the wound. The doctors had said it was the cutting away of the gangrenous flesh which had saved his life. But in his heart he had always believed this was due to Eleanor's act.

Then the birth of the children. How sad she had been because again it was a girl! So many girls. He loved them all. His beloved daughters . . . his and Eleanor's.

And now she was going to die.

It could not be. His daughter was frightened because her mother was ill. She was not going to die. Eleanor would never leave him. He needed her. He could not imagine his life without her. Always on his travels she had been with him . . . in the thick of the fight she had never been far behind.

He would take her in his arms. He would say: "My Queen, my love. You must be well . . . for me."

So through the night. How far it was!

His daughter met him. Her face was pale, her eyes tragic.

He took her into his arms. His beloved daughter, the best loved of all his children.

"My dearest . . ."

She could not speak. She could only shake her head. So he knew.

He went into the chamber of death. He looked at her lying there white and still . . . and beautiful. She had always been beautiful, in life . . . in death.

He knelt by the bed.

"Too late," he whispered. "Too late to see her alive, to tell her once more what she has meant to me. If I could but bring her back. I would give anything . . . anything . . ."

The conquest of Wales, the coming conflict with Scotland . . . In this moment they meant nothing, because Eleanor was dead.

"My lord," they said, "we should return to Scotland."

He shook his head.

"My place is with her."

"My lord, the Queen is dead."

He turned away. He could not speak. He was mute in his misery.

I should have been with her. I should never have allowed her to slip away without me. I should have told her right at the end how much she has meant to me.

She knew of course. But he wanted her to hear it again. He wanted to beg her not to leave him. To tell her how much she meant to him.

But she was gone and now it was his duty to bury her. He would be with her on her journey to Westminster. Scotland. He did not care what happened in Scotland. Baliol; Bruce; Hastings. Let them come with their claims. He could not think of them because Eleanor, his dear Queen, was dead.

He shut himself in alone with his grief. He would speak to none save his daughter. Those who cared for him were glad that she was there. She alone could comfort him.

"I will honor her," he told his daughter. "The whole country must mourn her. They will know that we have lost a good Queen."

"They do know it, Father. Everyone knows it."

"I shall go with her to Westminster and she shall be at Westminster close to my father. I loved him dearly almost as much as I loved her. It is fitting that they should be together."

He ordered that she be embalmed and when this was done they set out on their slow journey to Westminster.

The King ordered that a cross be set up in Lincoln, and at every place where the procession rested there should a cross be set up to remind people of their beloved Queen.

At Grantham, Stamford, Geddington, Northampton, Stony

Stratford, Woburn, Dunstable, St Albans, Waltham, West Cheap and last of all close to Westminster. This last was the most beautiful of all and people called it the cross of the Chere Reine.

As the procession neared London the chief citizens came out to meet it. They wore black hoods and mourning cloaks, and they droned a doleful dirge as they passed along.

So they buried the Queen and people marvelled at the love the King bore her for he continued to mourn her. He ordered that a statue be made and set upon her tomb. It was cast in bronze and showed the Queen in all her beauty with her lovely hair rippling below the jewelled circlet on her head.

The King endowed the Abbey of Westminster with gifts and had masses said for the Queen's soul. He ordered that the wax lights about her tomb should never be allowed to go out and dedicated a sum of money for this purpose.

People came to see the magnificent tomb carved from grey Petworth marble on which were embossed the towers of Castile and the lions of Leon.

The crosses were a constant memorial to her and that place where the last cross had been set up was called after her. Chere Reine Cross, soon to be known as Charing Cross.

Joanna Defiant

The King was constantly with his eldest daughter. Only she could comfort him. They talked of the Queen, how good she had been and how they had failed to appreciate this to the full while she had lived. She had been so self-effacing, thinking only of the good of her family, and they had accepted her unselfishness as part of their lives and taken it for granted.

Gloucester and Joanna came to Westminster from Clerkenwell, and the four of them talked together of what the loss of the Queen meant to them.

Gloucester told the King that he could subdue his sorrow by throwing himself into his kingly duties. There was the matter of Scotland which had not grown less acute because of the Queen's death.

The King agreed. He must drag himself away from his sorrow. He must continue that journey which had been interrupted.

Joanna, now quite obviously pregnant, was inclined to patronize her sister. As Countess of Gloucester, married to the most important baron in the country, rich, doted on and soon to become a mother, she made Eleanor feel that she was missing something in life.

When they were alone Joanna discussed the blessings of the married state.

"Depend upon it," she said, "our father will soon be looking for a bride."

"Our father! He never would."

"Why ever not?"

"He was devoted to our mother."

"My dear sister, how little you know of the world. Of course he was devoted to our mother. He loved her well. But she is dead. He is not an old man. He will want a wife, I tell you. He will want children."

"He has already had twelve and there are six of us still living. Joanna, do you think bearing so many children was what killed her?"

"She was never worried about child-bearing."

"No, because she would think it her duty and she would die in doing that. She knew how ill she was and she tried to keep it from us. Oh, Joanna, our father could never take another wife."

"Give him time," said the wise Joanna. "I'll wager with you that soon there will be talk and our father will be *persuaded* to marry again. Ah, you like that not. My dear sister, you must not devote yourself so earnestly to our father. You must have a husband of your own. I assure you that if you find the right one there is a good deal to be said for the married state."

Eleanor was beginning to think that too. She was no longer young. Twenty-six years old. Still time to marry and have children. Joanna was right. She must have a husband. But she was affianced to Alfonso of Aragon. She had set her heart against going to Aragon—and so had her father. He did not like Alfonso. But she must face the unfortunate fact that she had been affianced to him and that was tantamount to a betrothal. If she married anyone else she would need first a dispensation from the Pope and that might cause trouble with Aragon which was too important a country to quarrel with.

It seemed that she must either ask for negotiations to be opened with Aragon or make up her mind that marriage was not for her.

She consoled herself in comforting her sister Margaret who was greatly pleased when her bridegroom returned to Brabant without her. He was returning, it was said, to receive the congratulations on his marriage from his father's subjects, but it was clear that he was no more unhappy at leaving his bride than she was to see him go.

As for the King, the connection had been made, so politics had been served. He never wanted to part with any of his daughters, so Margaret would be welcome to stay at his Court for as long as was possible in the interests of propriety.

Contemplating Margaret's marriage Eleanor could be content with her single state. It was only when Joanna came flaunting the advantages which had come to her that she was dubious.

Edward tried to draw himself out of his grief and consider the Scottish question.

He called together his ministers and reminded them that this problem was of the utmost importance to them.

One suggested that perhaps he might reduce Scotland to the same state as he had Wales.

He shook his head. "Not so easy, my friend. Llewellyn and Davydd rose against me. They were captured and met their just deserts. With their departure went the claimants to the throne. In Scotland see how many there are. There are the three leading contenders and if these were removed we can be sure there would be others. We should be involved in costly wars lasting years and years. You know how difficult it is to fight in these mountainous lands, and how fiercely men will do battle on what they consider to be their own territory. Nay. What I aim at is to get them to select their ruler, but that he shall reign under me."

He would therefore continue with that journey which was broken by the death of his wife. He would call together a conference and he would let the Scots know that they owed fealty to him as their superior lord. If they acknowledged this they would then be free to select their own king from those claimants who now clamored for the crown.

But first he must have their acknowledgment of him as their superior lord.

His grief over the loss of the Queen was somewhat alleviated by this action and as he rode northwards he gave his mind to the Scottish matter with such complete concentration that he found it was only at odd moments that he had time to remember.

He had summoned the lords of Scotland to meet him at Norham and there the proceedings commenced.

Edward was anxious to prove to the Scots that through the past years Scotland owed homage to the Kings of England.

The Scottish lords, however, rejected this, at which Edward rose and standing before them towering above them all, with his stern countenance and voice to match, he cried, "By St. Edward I will have the due right of my kingdom and the crown of which I am the guardian or I will die in the prosecution of it."

There was an awe-inspiring quality about the English King. It seemed to the watching Scots that he was endowed with some supernatural power. There was a magic about him which had come to him through his great ancestor the Conqueror. He was another such. Coeur de Lion had had it. Henry the second had had a touch of it. It never failed to strike fear into the hearts of those who beheld it.

A few days later when the assembly was meeting the Scots acknowledged the King's superiority and that they were ready to do homage to him.

Edward was pleased. They might then choose which of the claimants should be their King.

The matter should be left to them.

Joanna and her husband had travelled to the latter's estates at Wynchecombe near Tewkesbury that their child might be born there.

The Earl was eager that everything that his beautiful young wife wanted she should have and Joanna was in her element. She was certain she was going to have a son. No one could deny Joanna anything . . . not even God.

Petted and adored, she prepared for her lying in. It was nineteen years ago that she herself had been born in the town of Acre. Now she was producing her first child. How different it would be from her own coming into the world. As she lay waiting and feeling the preliminary alarms and discomforts, she did spare a moment to think of her mother lying in that hot and arid land pestered by flies and even more obnoxious insects, missing the comforts she would have had in her English palace.

This was different. The luxurious bed; the anxious husband; countless attendants.

It seemed that fate was determined to be kind to Joanna. Her labor was not long and there, almost before they could hope, was the child. She heard its cry and she whispered, "What is it?"

"A boy, my lady. A lovely, healthy, little baby boy."

Of course. She had known it would be. Nothing should be denied her.

Her husband came and knelt by her bed. She smiled triumphantly. It was as though he was worshipping at a shrine.

"My dearest," he murmured, "what can I say . . ."

"You are pleased?" An unnecessary question but she wanted to hear again his expressions of gratitude; she wanted him to thank Heaven, as he had since their marriage, for his beautiful adorable unsurpassable wife.

She touched his hand lightly.

"Let us call him Gilbert," she said kindly. "After you."

The King must of course come to see his first grandchild. He called on his way back to Westminster from Scotland.

He picked up young Gilbert, walked round the chamber with him, marvelled at his minute perfections and was happier than he had been since Eleanor's death.

It was while he was in Wynchecombe that a messenger came from the convent of Amesbury to tell him that his mother was very ill and she was asking to see him. It was necessary that he go to her with all speed.

This time he was determined not to be too late and when he arrived at Amesbury he went straight to his mother's bedchamber. Her eyes lit up at the sight of him. She was very ill, he saw at once, and his heart sank. It was cruel. He had lost his wife and now was going to lose his mother. True he had been expecting this, for she would never have agreed to shut herself away from the world until she was fairly convinced that her end was near. Even so such foreknowledge could not soften the blow.

"Oh, Edward," she said, "how glad I am that you have come. I am going . . . at last. Do you know, it is nineteen years since I lost your dear father."

"I know it well," said Edward. "I have reigned as long."

"Oh, Edward, my son, what a good life we had together, your father and I! It rarely happens so, and you with your dear wife . . . Now that she has gone . . . oh Edward, I know full well your sorrow. She was a good woman . . . rarely are women so good. You were lucky in your choice, my son, as I was in mine."

"Mother, I beg of you . . ."

The King was so overcome with emotion that he feared he would break down.

She knew this. "Do not be afraid to show your feelings to your family, my son. Your father never was. Oh, he was a great, good man . . . much maligned, never appreciated by his people . . . They appreciate you, Edward. Yes, I think they love you . . . and they loved the Queen. And now you are a great King. Many say that, Edward. You are the King the country needed . . . after your father and your grandfather. You are strong, a little hard perhaps. But that is what they need, they say. I remember when you were born, my son. What rejoicing! Such a sturdy baby . . . long-legged from the first. Longshanks. Your father liked to hear them call you that. How I suffered when you were ill! So strange that *you* should have been a delicate boy. But we cared so much for you. How often have I nursed you myself. I would have no others near you. Edward. Edward, my son."

He knelt by her bed and took her hand. "Dear Mother, you were so wonderful to us all. You made our family what it was. We were so happy and Eleanor and I tried to follow your example, and we did. Our children were always happy in their homes."

She nodded. "It is worth a great deal . . . worth anything . . . I loved good living . . . perhaps too well some will say . . . I loved land and possessions, jewels . . . We were poor in Provence and when I came to England it was as though I had discovered riches beyond my dreams. Perhaps I loved them too well . . . But I always knew that the real treasure was the love of your father and you children. My real happiness was in you. And when your father died . . . I longed to go with him . . . and that is what I shall do now . . . nineteen years after."

"We could not have done without you during those years, dear Mother."

"You comfort me. Edward, there is something I have to say . . . It is this. You will marry again?"

"There could never be any other for me," he said.

"So it seems now, but that will change."

Edward shook his head.

"You will have your duty to the country."

"I have a son."

"But one."

"Edward is a healthy child."

"It is always wise for a King to have more than one. You will see, my son."

But Edward did not agree.

She smiled gently at him. And her thoughts drifted off to the days of his childhood. Henry was beside her. They had loved their beautiful son so dearly. A shared love . . . Oh, Henry, she thought, suddenly transported back to the present. I am coming to you now.

Edward was with her when she died, for he would not leave her bedside.

He was engulfed in his misery for he had in less than a year lost his beloved wife and mother.

He must return to Scotland soon, but she should be embalmed at Amesbury and a grand tomb prepared for her. Her heart he would take with him to London.

There was a great deal to occupy Edward's mind and this helped to take his mind from his loss.

It was hardly to be expected that firebrands would not rise now and then in Wales for there were bound to be those who resented English rule and attempted to throw it off. They were feeble attempts it was true, but he must be watchful of them. John Baliol, King of Scotland, was a weak man and not the unanimous choice of the Scottish people. A measure of his unpopularity was the nicknames which were bestowed on him. To the people he was Old Toom Tabard which meant empty jacket and Tyne Tabard, Lose Coat which was a reference to his lack of possessions and his unworthiness to be the King of Scotland. The Scots resented the fact that their King had been obliged to swear allegiance to the King of England. Undoubtedly Edward needed to keep a watchful eye in every direction.

There was another factor—and perhaps the most dangerous

of all and this threat came from across the channel. It was hardly likely that Philip of France would not seize every opportunity to discountenance him and Philip had long had his envious eyes on Gascony.

So therefore Edward needed to keep his eyes strained in every direction and be ready for immediate action should the need arise.

Almost immediately after the birth of her son, Joanna had become pregnant, and in due course had borne a daughter whom she called Eleanor after the child's grandmother and great-grandmother. Edward was delighted that the marriage was a success for he had had his doubts on account of the disparity in the ages of the pair. But Joanna seemed content to be admired and adored and Gilbert was completely her slave; moreover his character appeared to have changed and his ambition now seemed to dwell in his nursery where he fussed over his children. He had remained at his home on one occasion when the King had expected him to join his council—the reason being that the baby was ill and he feared to leave her. The fact that the baby was merely suffering from one of those minor ailments which affect babies from time to time seemed to him an adequate excuse for his conduct.

Edward shrugged it aside. He was delighted for Joanna's sake that she had such a devoted husband and he did remember how his own father and mother would have defied all the barons of England for the sake of one of their children.

Then there was Eleanor. He worried a great deal about her. It was unfair that she should not be married. She had seen the union of her two sisters, Joanna's so successful, Margaret's less so. Still they married and it seemed wrong that a young woman as beautiful and vital as his eldest daughter should be denied children.

The Princess Eleanor herself was beginning to feel that she had been passed by. Her father was constantly moving from one place to another and it was not always easy for her to be with him; it was true she had a fine establishment—none of the family, even Prince Edward, had had a better—but that was not enough.

It seemed to her that she must either accept her single state or ask her father to open up negotiations again with Aragon. It was possible that this might not be acceptable to the Aragonese for their *amour propre* must have been wounded by the second withdrawal.

Eleanor began to wonder whether there was a man for whom she would be ready to leave her home and soon after her mother's death she discovered that there was.

To her father's Court had come Henry III, Duke of Bar-le-Duc. He was the eldest son of Thibaut II and on his death Henry had inherited vast lands of great importance because they were situated between France and Germany. The Duchy had been formed as long ago as the tenth century and the reigning Dukes claimed descent from Charlemagne and counted themselves more royal than the Capets.

The Duc de Bar-le-Duc was immediately attracted by Eleanor and it was their pleasure to ride ahead of their attendants in the Windsor forest and then when they were free of them to walk their horses and talk together, he of his duchy in France, she of life in England.

Joanna, whom Eleanor saw frequently, was interested in the growing friendship.

"It would be a good match," she commented. "I am sure our father would agree."

Eleanor shook her head. "I should be afraid to suggest it. There is Aragon."

"How you have been cursed by Aragon! And we thought the Sicilian Vespers had taken care of that."

Joanna studied her sister appraisingly. "You are still handsome," she went on. "In fact you were always the most handsome of us all. Though I often deceive people into thinking I am. Gilbert is certainly of that opinion. You should manage your life better, sister, as I do."

"How can I ask the Duke of Bar-le-Duc to marry me?"

"There are ways. Why not marry him in secret and make it a *fait accompli*. Then no one can do anything about it."

"You talk as though we are the daughters of some ordinary household."

"Our lives are what we make of them," said Joanna sagely, "and if you are going to accept what seems to be your fate you don't deserve a better."

"All very well for you. You have a doting husband..."

"Who seemed very old at first...and who *is* very old. Let

us face it. Gilbert won't live for ever and then I shall certainly make my own choice."

"You talk very recklessly, Joanna."

"And some say act so. But look what it has brought me. Two babies and a third on the way, I do declare. Everything I want. It is amusing how Gilbert tries to anticipate my needs before I know them myself. My dear sister, take what you want. If you don't you'll never get it."

It was easy for her to advise, thought Eleanor.

And then suddenly and it was certainly odd, and reminded Eleanor of that other occasion when she and Joanna had prayed for a miracle. Alfonso of Aragon died. She was free.

Her father came down to Windsor from the borders of Wales.

He took her hands and kissed her. She clung to him. The sadness was still in his eyes and she knew he mourned their mother. He was still insisting that the late Queen should be commemorated in Westminster with dirges and masses for her soul.

"My dearest child," he said, "it is time we settled your future. You are neary thirty years of age. If you are going to marry and know the joy of children it must be now."

"I know, dear Father," she said.

"My inclination is to keep you with me but often, my love, I shall go into battle. That is inevitable. There is Wales, Scotland and the French are watchful. I should like to see you happy as your sister Joanna is. Children are a great blessing, my child. I have noticed your growing friendship with the Duke of Bar-le-Duc."

She smiled and when he saw the joy in her face he was immensely relieved.

"He will happily ask for you," he said. "He loves you well and I am sure you have some regard for him."

"He is a great nobleman."

"Royal indeed. He is a good man, a loyal man. That is most important to me. And the strategic position of his lands could be of great importance to me if I were in conflict with the King of France and I know well he has his eyes on Gascony. I would welcome a match between you two . . . if you were not averse to it."

"Dear Father," she answered, "I have long thought of what

I am missing. If I could see you frequently I should be happy to go to Bar."

Edward embraced her and assured her that ere long there would be a wedding for her.

So it came to pass, for when the Duke of Bar-le-Duc realized that his suit was acceptable he was overjoyed.

Edward was determined that his favorite daughter should not marry a stranger and he invited the Duke to stay in England until the wedding could be arranged, and during the whole of that summer Eleanor and the Duc were constantly in each other's company. During September the King summoned the whole of his family, the chief knights of the country and every nobleman in the kingdom to Bristol where the ceremony took place.

There were celebrations of great splendor for although, unlike his father and mother, Edward was not extravagant, he did believe that there were occasions when it was necessary to show the people the importance of what was taking place. Moreover this was the wedding of his best-loved daughter and he wanted her memories of England to be pleasant. The bridegroom too must be made aware of the might of the family he had married into, for the King would assuredly need his help at some time.

After that the party traveled to Mortlake to be entertained in the household of Prince Edward. He was now ten years old—tall, good-looking and bearing a strong resemblance to his father. He was inclined to indolence and his attendants and young friends did not always behave with the decorum necessary to his rank, which had given the King some concern, but he believed that this was just youthful high spirits and that Edward would grow more sober as he advanced in years.

The Princess Eleanor was happy. It was true that she must leave England and that was something she had dreaded doing, but now it seemed different; and her husband had promised that whenever possible they would visit England, and the King would always be welcome in Bar.

He would return there now to make preparations for her arrival, for he wanted to make sure that she received a royal welcome and he trusted no one to arrange that but himself.

In a few weeks she would join him.

How excited she was making her preparations. Joanna contrived to spend a great deal of time with her. "For," said Joanna, "when you go away I shall see you rarely then."

Joanna had given birth to another daughter whom she called Margaret after her sister. So now she had three children. Childbearing seemed to suit Joanna. Like her mother she came through the ordeals with little inconvenience to herself, and as Gilbert's devotion did not diminish she was happy in her motherhood.

"Sister," she said one day, "I do believe you are with child."

Eleanor blushed slightly. She had suspected it and the fact that Joanna had noticed confirmed it.

"It is what I want more than anything," she declared.

"The Duke will be pleased."

"Yes, as soon as I am sure I shall send a message to him."

Joanna laughed. "Life is good, is it not, sister? Was I not right in telling you you should marry? Poor Margaret, I doubt she will find it so blissful. It is strange is it not that her Duke allows her to stay away from him? I have heard it said that he prefers it so. Oh, we are the lucky ones, Eleanor."

Eleanor agreed with this.

She was in fact pregnant, and when her husband heard this he replied that she must leave for Bar without delay. She must make the strenuous journey in the early stages before travelling should be irksome or dangerous. And it was essential that his heir should be born in the Duchy.

A great cavalcade accompanied her to Dover, the King at the head of it.

They took a tender farewell and the King would not leave the shore until he could no longer see the ship which was carrying his daughter away.

In her new home she was welcomed by her husband, who was determined to give her a display to equal that which King Edward had arranged for their pleasure. He had organized a tournament and had invited from all over the Continent, knights renowned for their prowess. Among these was John, Duke of Brabant, the father of Margaret's husband, who had been known all his life as one of the most accomplished of the knights and had so distinguished himself that he had won the titles of "Glory of the World" and "Flower of Chivalry", which meant that when he jousted people came from every corner of the world to watch him.

"My dearest," said the Duke, "you of course must present

the crown to the winner of the jousts for they will all perform in your honor."

She was delighted. She had always been beautiful but seemed to have become more so since her marriage. There was new color in her cheeks, a new shine to her eyes and a luster in her hair, which she wore hanging loose about her shoulders.

The old Duke of Brabant was overcome by her beauty and he told her that he was determined to win the crown for the honor of receiving it from her hands.

She wished that Joanna could see her now. Would she be a little envious? Perhaps. But Joanna was in command of her life to such an extent that she rarely envied anyone. There was a niggling disquiet in the recesses of Eleanor's mind concerning her sister. She had mentioned more than once the possibility of her husband's dying—and without a great deal of concern—when she would have the husband of her choice.

But she could not think of Joanna on this day. How beautiful it was. The sun was shining, lances glittered and the knights were assembled in their armor ready for the mock battle. She was seated high on her bench with her ladies beside her, under a canopy of scarlet and gold, and all eyes were on her. They marvelled at the beauty of her hair and eyes, her fresh smooth skin. She wished that her father could see her now.

The knights were all eager to win the trophy; there was not one there who was not longing for the honor to have the crown placed on his head by those fair hands.

Yes, she thought, I am happy as I never thought to be. Joanna was right. I needed marriage and children. This is the true life. The crown of England for which she had longed seemed of little importance—a bauble. Here she was a happy wife, a mother-to-be, the Queen of a tournament.

The jousting began and went on throughout the day. The old Duke of Brabant had come successfully through several encounters and she hoped he would win. She wanted this to be his crowning endeavor, for he was clearly too old to joust much more.

She watched him. His opponent was a stranger whom she did not know. But he must be a knight of some repute or he would not be here. He was a tall man and he sat his horse as though he and it were one. Her father was like that. They had the long arms and legs of the Normans, and because of this they had the advantage on horseback.

It was the third turn. She heard the gasp in the crowd; there was a second or so of silence and then people were running on to the field where the old Duke of Brabant lay bleeding on the grass.

His opponent was kneeling beside the old man, imploring his pardon, begging him to use the sword against him, to kill him for what he had done.

The old Duke shook his head. "It was a fair fight," he whispered. "I should have known my day was done."

He was carried from the field into the Castle of Le Bar, where he died shortly afterwards. His death had cast a gloom over the celebrations and the Duke and Eleanor agreed that they must put an end to them.

Some said it was not a good augury for the future. Now that the old Duke of Brabant was dead, Margaret's husband was the new Duke.

In due course Eleanor's child was born and to her—and her husband's—great joy, it was a boy. She insisted on calling him Edward as a compliment to her father, and when the news reached England there was great rejoicing there. The King longed to be with his daughter. That was impossible, of course, but although he missed her sadly he was glad that at last she had a husband and child and he prayed for her happiness.

It was not long before she was once more pregnant and this time she produced a girl. She wrote to her sister Joanna telling her how happy she was and that she was going to name her daughter Joanna to remind her of the sister who had been closest to her.

There was no doubt that happiness reigned in the Duchy of Bar-le-Duc and fortunately neither the Duke nor the Duchess knew at that time how short-lived it would prove to be.

Joanna was now the mother of four children—Gilbert, Eleanor, Margaret and Elizabeth. They had all been born within the space of five years and the novelty of being a wife and mother had vanished.

As with her mother, child-bearing had come easily to Joanna and taken little toll of her looks. Her vitality was as strong as ever. She was twenty-three years old and, although when she was first married it seemed interesting to have an elderly husband, she was now beginning to see him as a very old man whose devotion was so constant that it seemed cloying.

She was becoming increasingly aware of one of Gilbert's squires, a certain Ralph de Monthermer—good-looking, sturdy and above all young. When she compared this squire with her husband poor Gilbert seemed very old indeed and she wondered what would have happened if she had met Ralph de Monthermer before her marriage. She convinced herself that she never could have married Gilbert then and imagined what her father would have said if she had suggested Ralph as a bridegroom.

A squire for the King's daughter! He would have thought she was mad. Perhaps she was a little. In any case she certainly felt reckless when she looked at that young man.

It amused her to play little games with him. To look up suddenly and catch his eyes on her and to ask him if he saw aught wrong.

He would become embarrassed, but only slightly, for he was quite a bold young man. "Wrong, my lady? Nay, right . . . far too right for my peace of mind."

A pleasant allusion to her charms which she liked.

She would make sure that he was placed near her, but not too near. When she sang after supper it would be songs of hopeless love and she very much enjoyed the effect this had on him. When she rode out with a riding party he was invariably of it and she would pretend to be surprised to find herself beside him.

Some would say it was a dangerous situation into which she was sinking more deeply every day, but danger was irresistible to Joanna and she became more and more interested in Ralph de Monthermer.

Who could say how this would have ended and when it would have been brought to Gilbert's notice if of late Gilbert had not been so easily tired that he had liked to retire early. That his last campaign had taken some toll of his health was obvious.

Joanna played the anxious wife for a while but it was a role she soon tired of. Fortunately for Gilbert he did not live long enough to see that she was wearying of it, for one morning when his attendants went into his bedchamber to waken him they found that he had died in his sleep.

It was not altogether a surprise for it had been obvious to the discerning that Gilbert had grown weaker every day.

Joanna received the news calmly. She found it hard to express any deep sorrow. The marriage had been satisfactory while it had lasted but it had lasted long enough. She could not have gone on being a dutiful wife much longer so it was better for everyone that Gilbert should pass on before he discovered this.

And there was Ralph de Monthermer.

She sent for him and gave him her hand to kiss in greeting. He did not release it but continued to hold it and drew her towards him.

"What means this, my lord?" she asked, but he saw the sparkle in her eyes.

"I think you know, my lady."

"My husband is dead," she answered.

"I know it."

"And you think that because of this you may with impunity misuse me?"

"I think, my lady, from what I read in your eyes that I may presume a little of your kindness."

"Do you forget that I am the widow of your lord and the daughter of your King, Ralph de Monthermer?"

"I forget all but one thing, lady, when I am close to you."

"You should leave me now. We will talk of this later."

He hesitated and she half wished he would disobey her, seize her, make love to her. That would have been piquant with Gilbert not yet in his tomb. Instead of which he left, which after all was best.

We have the rest of our lives, she thought. We can for a while pay homage to propriety.

In his death chamber, faintly lighted by a wintry sun, for the month was December, Joanna had ordered that candles be lighted and one by one his squires went in to take their last farewell of him—a good master, a man of strong character, who more than once in his life had defied his King. Yet he was a man to be respected, for in spite of the fact that he had once fought against royalty on the side of Simon de Montfort, the King had given him his daughter.

Joanna was watchful during those days in Monmouth Castle to which they had come that Gilbert might guard his Welsh estates, and only now and then she allowed herself to catch the eye of Ralph de Monthermer, and then hers conveyed the message: "Wait awhile. But not for long."

The family burial place of the Clares was Tewkesbury, and with great pomp Gilbert was taken to the Abbey there. Joanna commanded that a statue should be made of him in his chain armor for he had above all been a great warrior; and on his tabard she had engraved the family arms and in the right hand the spear, in the left his sword.

"Alas, poor Gilbert," she said, "he was a good husband to me, but he was old and it was to be expected that he would go before me."

And she smiled to herself. She had always said that if a woman married once for state reasons—which as a princess perhaps duty demanded that she should—the second time she married her husband should be of her own choosing.

It was imperative that she make sure that she lose nothing by her husband's death. His estates were vast for he had been one of the richest barons in England and when her father was in St. Edmundsbury she took the journey there to be with him.

Edward was delighted to see her.

He embraced her warmly and looked eagerly at her, expecting, she supposed, to see the grief of a sorrowing widow.

She could not pretend to such an extent and when he sought to soothe her she replied, "My dear lord, Gilbert was a good husband to me. I married him because it was your command. But he was so much older than I and as the years passed the older he seemed to grow."

The King was a little disconcerted, but he was pleased to see that she was not as unhappy as he had expected her to be.

"I have my children to think to," she said. "I want to be sure that Gilbert's estates come to me. I know that you would not allow them to be withheld from me."

"There is a certain amount owing to the exchequer, I am told," said the King. "I believe it to be ten thousand marks."

"That cannot be so, dear Father."

"Yes, my dear child, it is so. The ten thousand marks cover debts which he incurred as a fine and which was never paid." The King pressed her hand. "The rest of the estate shall be made over to you. I know it to be considerable."

She was pleased; but she wanted to see how far her father would indulge her. He had come determined to make much of her. He greatly missed his eldest daughter the Princess Eleanor and he was now turning to the daughter who remained in England.

"Dear Father," she said, "could you not forget the ten thousand marks? I would have to raise them and that would not be easy. Please, Father, for my sake and that of my children . . ."

She had slipped her arm through his and laid her face against his. She was very attractive—not as beautiful as Eleanor, nor as gentle as Margaret, nor as good as Mary, nor as dependent as Elizabeth . . . but there had always been something very appealing about Joanna.

Moreover he had something on his mind and that was marriage. He had mourned his Queen and had genuinely suffered through her loss, but several years had passed and many of his ministers had suggested that he should marry again. He was not young by any means. He was closer to sixty than fifty; but he was unusually full of vigor and he felt an excitement at the prospect of female company. Except in his extreme youth he had never been a man to sport outside the marriage bed. He could hardly begin now. He did not want to cast a slur on Eleanor's memory, but it seemed only right and natural for a King to take a second wife.

He had heard eulogistic reports about the Princess of France. Her name was Blanche and she was the daughter of King Philip known as le Hardi. Philip was dead and Blanche was under the guardianship of her brother, the new King Philip le Bel. Before the idea of marriage had occurred to him he had heard Blanche praised for her beauty and sprightliness.

It had occurred to him recently that he must therefore marry and the most suitable bride for him was beautiful Blanche. Negotiations were going on at this time.

While Joanna was pleading with him he was wondering how he was going to break the news to his daughters that he was hoping to marry. They had all loved their mother so devotedly and he had declared many times after her death that he would never put another in her place. Times changed and kings had their duties to perform. No, he was too honest for that. He had never seen Blanche, but from the rumors he had heard he was already in love with her and he had discovered that love at fifty-six could be as strong as it was at twenty. Perhaps more so, because at that age a man who still retained his vigor also had the knowledge that there was not much time.

He would need the support of his daughters. He wanted them to understand. Therefore he would not wish there to be any rift between them.

"My dear child," he said. " I would not wish to displease you for the sake of ten thousand marks."

It had been easier than she had thought. She was exultant. This tempted her to take her schemes a little further.

"My lord," she said, "there is another matter."

He said: "I am listening, daughter."

"There is a squire who has served Gilbert well. I believe he should be rewarded. During Gilbert's illness he was always at his side . . . a very faithful man, caring not what he did for his master's comforts."

"What would you have for him?"

"He is but a humble squire."

"Of what family?"

"A most humble one, my lord, but in manners he is a true knight. Would you, out of love for me, grant him the boon of knighthood?"

"I will do this out of my love for you," said the King.

She kissed his hand.

"Dear Father, how good you have always been to us. The only reward I can offer you is my unswerving love."

"It would always be mine, would it not?" said the King.

"Always," she answered.

Joanna said goodbye to her father and with her retinue returned to Gloucester. She was well pleased. She was free and she had proved to herself that whatever she did she would be forgiven.

She sent for Ralph de Monthermer.

"Why, my lord," she said, "you have grown in stature, have you not. A knight, no less!"

"For which I have to thank my gracious lady."

"The King has always been a good father to us. I have a notion that he would deny me nothing."

She was smiling secretly.

She held out a hand to him. Willingly he grasped it.

"My lady," he began.

"I have decided that we might marry," she said.

He caught his breath in amazement.

"Yes," she went on. "I will be frank. There is that about you which pleases me. Do I please you?"

She laughed aloud at his expression.

"Oh come, my lord. Do not be shy."

"My lady, I am afraid..."

"*You* afraid. Then I have been mistaken. I do not like men who are afraid..."

"Of nothing but displeasing you."

"But you do not please me standing there and trembling like a foolish boy."

He came to her. She saw the wild light in his eyes and it matched hers.

He took her and held her, and she laughed exultantly.

"This," she said, "is what I have waited for."

"You... the King's daughter!"

"And mistress of my knight."

"Joanna... My Joanna!"

Of course it was as she had known it would be. Gilbert had been such an old man. Now she was well matched. This sensuous tireless vital man was hers.

As they lay together she said, "We should wait a while before we marry. It is too soon yet."

"You would... go as far as that?"

"Have you not discovered that there are no lengths to which I would not go?"

"I am beginning to learn."

"Ah, you have much to learn, Ralph de Monthermer."

"And when we are married what will the King do, think you?"

"He will rant and rage and threaten to disown me. Perhaps he will put you in a prison. Are you afraid? Will you hold back?"

"I will never hold back."

"That is well. I would never want a coward. I want to live boldly... freely. Never fear, the King loves me dearly. He would never remain angry with me for long. And if you please me and I want my husband taken from his cold damp cell, I shall ask him and he will be given to me."

"What if your husband has ceased to please you by then?"

"He will have to take care that he goes on pleasing me . . . as he does now."

They made love again and again.

This is living, thought Joanna. Of course this is what I always wanted.

After what Joanna considered to be a reasonable time had elapsed she and Ralph de Monthermer were secretly married. She was delighted by her wedding and the intrigue which had been necessary excited her a great deal, but when the deed was done she was anxious as to how she would break the news to her father.

She knew that at this time he was deeply weighed down with troubles of his own. He was thinking of marrying and really was becoming quite besotted about Blanche of France; it was said that when her name was mentioned his eyes lit up with pleasure and his voice took on an unusual warmth. She was young and beautiful and he wanted to marry her. At the same time he thought a great deal about the late Queen to whom he had always said he would be eternally faithful. He was a man who did not like to break his word.

There was another matter which deeply concered him too. He was worried about his eldest daughter—his dear Eleanor, now Duchess of Bar-le-Duc, who had, some thought, been the one he had loved beyond everyone else before this obsession with Blanche.

Things were going badly at the Castle of Le Bar. During Edward's conflict with the King of France, as was to be expected, Eleanor's husband came out in full support of his father-in-law and, owing to his estates being so close to France, this was extremely useful to Edward. Edward had of course supplied him with arms and money and the Duke had attempted to take Champagne, a project with which Edward was in agreement as its capture would have meant the aggrandizement of his grandson.

Champagne, however, belonged in her own right to the Queen of France who held the title Countess of Champagne. She was furious at what she called the Duc of Bar-le-Duc's audacity and she mustered all the strength she could, which was considerable, to come against the Duke.

The result had been disastrous . . . for the Duke.

His army had been defeated and he was taken prisoner. Not content with that the Queen, feeling vindictive against him, had had him fettered and sent to a dungeon in Paris. The King of France, however, had restrained his wife and while he agreed that the Duke should remain a prisoner he thought he should be treated with more dignity, and—perhaps his relationship with the King of England would make this advisable—the Duke was taken to a more comfortable prison at Bourges. But the King of France was determined that the Duke should not be granted his freedom as he would only use it in the service of the King of England against France.

Eleanor was therefore alone in the Castle of Le Bar wondering about the fate of the husband whom she loved, protecting her little Edward, her son, and Joanna, her daughter, and each day wondering what would become of them.

Edward was frantic with anxiety about her and was planning a meeting. He wanted Eleanor to come to Ghent where he could meet her and they could be together and discuss her future.

Joanna was wondering whether, in view of the King's preoccupations it would be a good thing to spring the news of her marriage on him or whether, beset by anxieties, he would be more inclined to fume against her. There was a great deal at stake, she told Ralph. He could confiscate their possessions. He could send Ralph to prison. There was no knowing how he might act. He had been an indulgent father but he did possess the notorious Plantagenet temper, and although he kept it well in check it could be terrifying when aroused.

After a great deal of thought, Joanna decided that it might be a good idea to set into circulation a rumor that she and Ralph were in love and contemplating marriage. They could see what effect this would have on the King and if he took the matter lightly they could come forth and confess. On the other hand if he expressed his fury they could retreat into silence and let him think the affair had come to nothing.

The King was brooding on his own and his eldest daughter's predicaments when the news of the rumor came to him.

"It's a lie!" he shouted. "She would not dare." He was horrified. He had been thinking that Joanna was not the sort of woman who should remain unmarried, and he had for some time been considering an offer from the Earl of Savoy who had been putting out feelers suggesting a match between himself and the King's widowed daughter.

He remembered that she had prevailed on him to bestow a knighthood on Ralph de Monthermer and his fury increased. Of course there was foundation for the rumor. He remembered how she had cajoled him, how she made him forget her late husband's debts, how she had seemed so happy to be with him and glean such comfort from his presence. When all the time she had been planning to deceive him!

Eleanor would never have done this. Nor would Margaret, Mary nor Elizabeth. Joanna was different. Born in a foreign land, spending the first years of her life with her grandmother. Joanna was different . . . a deceiver . . . a siren. But he would teach her a lesson.

He sent for two of his knights and shouted orders to them.

"Go forward," he cried, "and confiscate in my name all the lands and possessions of the Countess of Gloucester."

The very fact that he referred to her as the Countess rather than the Princess Joanna, his beloved daughter, was significant.

They hesitated.

"Go," shouted the King. "Did you not hear me?"

So they went.

Joanna was in despair. So this was how he behaved when he heard a rumor that she was contemplating marriage. What would he say when he knew that the deed was already done?

"We must act with the utmost care," she told Ralph. "Perhaps we should separate for a while."

Ralph said he would face anything rather than that, and their danger seemed to intensify their passion. She was exultant. This was the lover she had been waiting for all her life. He was ready to face death for her sake and he might well do so, for the wrath of the King—though rare—could be terrible. But she doubted he would ever in any circumstances harm his daughter, though he might well vent his wrath on those who shared her sins.

It was fortunate that she had friends, for one of the knights at the King's Court who had always admired her decided that he would risk the King's displeasure if he were ever found out, in order to prepare her for disaster to come.

This knight secretly left Court and rode into Monmouth Castle and asked to be taken to the Countess Joanna without delay.

She received him at once, and before she could tell him how welcome he was he blurted out, "The King is sending his confessor Walter de Winterborn to you. He is to find out the true state of affairs between you and Ralph de Monthermer."

"I see," said Joanna, her mind working quickly.

"He is to report whether there is any truth in the rumor that you are contemplating marriage. And he is to bring news of a match the King is arranging for you."

"Arranging a match for me!"

"Yes, an agreement is being made with Amadeus, Earl of Savoy, and the King declares he is eager for you to be married without delay. It will put a stop to rumor."

There was no way out. She saw that she could not keep her marriage secret much longer, but she could not face Walter de Winterborn now. She could imagine what his probing questions would be like.

She thanked the knight for warning her and went to find Ralph.

"This is disaster," she said. "The King has a husband for me."

"He cannot have you," cried Ralph.

"Of a certainty he will not. But you see how my father can be when his wrath is roused. Already he has left me nothing, taken everything I possess. Never mind, I'll get it back. But I must have time. If Winterborn comes here he will discover at once. He will question the servants in his confessional manner, and they won't be able to stand out against him however loyal they are."

"Then what do you propose, my love?"

"We are going to leave here at once. I must have time. My father will have to know we are married, but I want to tell him myself . . . and in my own time. Be ready. We are leaving immediately for the Countess of Pembroke's castle in Herefordshire. She will help me. She has always been my friend. I want to talk to her of all this. I must be able to think in peace."

"I will prepare at once," said Ralph.

"I shall take the children with me," she went on. "My father dotes on the little girls and he will see that no harm comes to them, which means that he cannot send their mother away from them. I shall win him round eventually, but it will take time."

"You would always win anyone round," replied Ralph admiringly.

She smiled in agreement and in a very short time they were setting out for Goodrich Castle, the home of the Pembrokes, in Herefordshire.

The Countess had always been a friend of Joanna's although considerably older and she had been recently widowed. Joanna had often confided in her and had complete trust in her. The Countess's daughter Isabella, wife of Hastings, who was one of the claimants to the Scottish throne, was now with her mother at the castle, and they endeavored to show Joanna how delighted they were that she should visit them.

Joanna sought an early opportunity to be alone with the Countess. The rumors had already reached the Countess, but she did not know, of course, that the marriage had already taken place. When she was told this she was overcome with horror.

"But, my dear Joanna," she said, "the King will be enraged!"

"I know, and I want to talk over with you what I must do."

"Could you not have asked his permission?"

"No, because it would have been refused."

"And it was so important to you?"

"My dear friend, you have seen Ralph. Is he not a king among men?"

"He is very attractive, I agree."

"I married an old man to please my father. I believe I now have a right to please myself."

"But not to marry without the King's consent."

"I *have* married without his consent, and nothing can change that. What I want to talk about now is not what I should have or should not have done, but what I am going to *do* now. There is something else, which only Ralph knows. I will tell you . . ."

The Countess looked at her incredulously.

"Yes," went on Joanna, "you may stare. It's true. I am with child." Joanna began to laugh. "You see there is nothing he can do now . . . nothing."

"He can imprison your husband and confiscate your lands."

"The latter he has already done. Tell me, Countess, what can I do?"

The Countess was thoughtful. "There is only one thing," she said at length. "Go to him. Ask his pardon. Tell him how much you love your husband. Tell him you are to have a child."

"He will know that before long. He is angry because I persuaded him to give Ralph a knighthood and told him it was in payment of services to my husband."

The Countess shook her head. "I am sure the storm will pass. The King loves his family dearly as we all know, and I am sure he will not allow more than a passing conflict. He will be angry for a while so perhaps it would be better for you to keep away from him until he is calmer."

"I think you are right. But I shall be sent for and I cannot disobey the summons. I think I will send the little girls on ahead of me. He loves them so much as he does all children, and particularly little girls. They will soften his heart. He will never bring himself to be unkind to their mother."

"That," agreed the Countess, "might be a good idea."

She sent the little girls to St. Albans where the King was at that time and news came to her that the King had received them with as much affection as he ever had, that they had been allowed to scramble over him and pull his hair and he had been delighted when they kissed him unasked.

A good augury! thought Joanna.

It was a shock therefore when the King's guards arrived at Goodrich with orders to arrest Ralph de Monthermer and imprison him in Bristol Castle, where he was to be kept as the King's prisoner. Joanna—he referred to her as the Countess of Gloucester—was to pay immediately the outstanding debts of the Earl of Gloucester which previously she had persuaded the King to forgo.

It was a sign that Edward was in an unforgiving mood, and more angry with a member of his family than she had ever known him before.

For a month or so the King refused to see his daughter, and she remained as though in haughty indifference to his coolness towards her. But meanwhile Ralph was imprisoned in Bristol and she could not allow that to go on.

Continually she discussed the matter with the Countess of Pembroke and her daughter Isabella.

"I must do something," she declared. "I cannot let Ralph stay in Bristol. My father knows that this is the greatest revenge he can take on me . . . to rob me of my husband. I am going to see him and plead with him."

The Countess shook her head and Isabella reminded her of the King's great anger against her. He had been made to look foolish because he had been arranging a marriage for her when she was already married. It was difficult for a proud King to stomach that, said the Countess.

"But he always has been soft with his daughters. We have always been able to overcome his annoyance with us."

"That might have been in matters of little significance. This is different."

"I *must* make him understand. He loves his grandchildren. He ought to be delighted that this child will have Ralph as a father. Come, confess, did you ever see a man more handsome?"

The Countess smiled and Isabella said with a certain amount of fervor, "He is indeed handsome. One rarely sees a man so well set up."

"Ah," said Joanna quickly. "I see you have a fancy for him."

"My lady," said the Countess, "Isabella has a husband and is devoted to him."

Joanna laughed. "I know that well. I should have been annoyed if you had not admired Ralph. Well, now you see why I cannot have him languishing in prison. There is only one thing to do and that is to see my father, to talk to him myself."

"Will he see you?" asked Isabella.

"He will if I present myself. I know him well. He loves us all too dearly not to long for a reconciliation. My dear friends, I shall leave tomorrow for the Court. No, do not try to dissuade me."

"We would not attempt to," replied the Countess with a smile. "We have always known that when you have made up your mind it would be useless to ask you to change it."

"I shall plead with him and you will see that he will relent."

"I pray that it may be so," said the Countess.

Joanna rode into St. Albans on a hot July day.

She was received with some dismay for those in attendance

on the King were uncertain. She was in disgrace, but she was
the King's daughter and they dared not offend her; yet on the
other hand how would the King behave if they treated her as
they had before the trouble?

She was not quite noticeably pregnant and she said that she
was weary from the journey. She trusted she would not be
denied a bed.

They were subdued before her imperious manner. No one
would ever doubt Joanna's royalty. There was an implicit demand in her behavior to be treated with respect.

She sent a message to the King.

"Your daughter is here. It is the first time in her life that
she has been forced to crave an audience but she does so now
and she hopes she will be graciously received."

The King had heard that she was pregnant and he could not
help being concerned for her health. He gave orders that she
was to be well looked after and he would see her the following
day.

Joanna was triumphant. He had acted as she had known he
would. A show of affection, a little cajolery and she would
win him over.

But when she stood before him she was a little appalled by
the coolness of his expression. Never before had he looked at
her in that way. It was as though he disliked her. She did not
quail. She was fully confident of her powers.

He was seated on a throne-like chair which called attention
to his royalty. She stood before him.

"My lord father," she said, "I crave permission to sit."

He nodded and she sat on a stool.

"Why do you come here?" he asked coldly.

"Because you are my father though you are also the King."

"I do not forget it. You offend me doubly . . . as a daughter
and as a subject."

"Dear Father, I cannot bear it when you look at me so coldly.
I remember so much when my dear mother was alive. Ah, I
would that she were here this day. She would listen to me . . . she
would plead with you for me. How unhappy she would be to
see you hating me so."

"She would indeed be unhappy to have borne such a rebellious daughter."

"You loved my mother dearly," she said. "So do I love my husband."

"This...nobody...whom you persuaded me to make a knight!"

"No one deserved the honor more...nor that of being son-in-law to the greatest of Kings. Father, remember...the past...the happiness we have known together. My child will be born in due course, the fruit of my love for my husband whom you have cruelly imprisoned."

"It was a mistake," the King said harshly. "He has his just deserts. I could find him a harsher prison which would no doubt better fit his crime."

At the thought of her husband, Joanna's calm tactics broke down. She cried out, "Release him. He has done no harm. I love him, Father. You understand what that means. I persuaded him to this marriage...I forced him to it...through his love for me."

A faint twitch which might have been of amusement showed itself at the corner of the King's lips. He was thinking. Yes, she would have forced him to marry her. She would have selected him and then he would have had no say. That was his daughter Joanna. How could he help but admire such a daughter. She was all fire and energy. And she was not afraid either.

"Tell me this:" she went on. "Why is it not disgraceful for a man of rank to take a poor woman to be his wife, yet when a woman of rank takes a man of none it is considered so?"

"You are a Princess. He is nobody. You must ask my permission to marry. You flouted me...and the whole country. There were many seeking your hand."

"Seeking to better themselves by a royal alliance. My lord, I married once to please you. You gave me to an old man."

"Gilbert was good to you."

"What else could he be? He did well, did he not, to marry the King's daughter? But I married him to please you. I took this aging man because he was important to your schemes. I lived with him, I bore his children, then he died. Now why should I not marry according to my choice?"

"You should never marry except where I say you may."

"How unfair it is. So I am to be denied love, am I, because I am a King's daughter? One marriage for state reasons...I accepted it. But I claim the right the second time to choose for myself."

"You have no right," shouted the King. "You will do as I say."

"You cannot break up our marriage. Ralph is my husband. Nothing you can do to him will alter that."

"He can remain my prisoner. You will be stripped of your possessions. You will have to learn what happens to any who disobey the King."

"I see I am mistaken. I thought I had a loving father. How we loved . . . once. When our mother was there and the girls and little Edward . . . How we trusted you; how secure we felt in your love. But it was tender blossoms was it not, destroyed by the first cold wind . . . like buds in maytime . . . beautiful but delicate."

She put her hand on her body where she could feel the child.

"My lord . . . perhaps my women . . ."

The King was beside her. "What is it?"

She waved him aside. "It is as though the child feels the unkindness of its grandsire."

"You should be taken to your apartments."

She shrugged her shoulders. "Goodbye, Father; you are a hard man. I could not have believed . . ."

The tears welled into her eyes and suddenly she threw herself into his arms.

"I cannot bear it," she said. "Not my dear, dear father . . ."

He put his lips against her hair. How beautiful she was! How fierce in her passion! He would not have had her otherwise. The wild one, his dear daughter. So proud he had always been of her.

She clung to him. She would not let him go. Not that he showed any sign of forcing her to do so.

"Tell me I am forgiven," she murmured almost incoherently. "Then I will go away . . . Perhaps I may join my husband in his prison . . . Your grandchild will be born in captivity but at least I shall be with my husband . . ."

"Have done!" said the King gruffly.

"Oh, Father, I believe you love me a little after all."

"You are my beloved child and you know it," he said.

She put her arms about his neck and her face was radiant.

"Still . . . your beloved child?"

"You will always be that."

"Oh, my dear Father, how happy you have made me."

"My dear child, I have been so grieved that there should be this unhappiness between us."

"It must be no more. Dear Father, let me tell you how I love my husband. You will love him too if you will but see him. You must love someone who loves your daughter so dearly and has brought her such happiness. Father, to make me happy, will you give the order for his release?"

He took her hand and kissed it. "I suppose I must do this as my imperious daughter commands it."

"None commands the King, but in the goodness of his heart and his love for his children he could not let them continue heart-broken. I want to visit all our mother's crosses and give thanks at them because you have forgiven me. I want to take my husband there so that we can both give thanks to her. If you will love me again I can be the happiest woman on earth."

"I never ceased to love you."

It was her turn to punish him. "It seemed you did. Our mother must have wept at your harshness to me and mine."

He winced a little. He was wondering what Eleanor in heaven was thinking of his plans to marry again, of his longings for the beautiful Blanche, the most lovely princess ever seen, they said.

He felt uneasy because his desire for Blanche seemed like infidelity to Eleanor.

"She will rejoice now because we are good friends," Joanna said. "I am sure she is looking down on us now and weeping with joy."

She would understand, he thought. Eleanor had always understood. Had she lived he would have remained her faithful husband until the end of his days. But she had gone and he was alone, and Blanche by all accounts was so beautiful.

He said: "Your husband shall be released, your lands shall be restored."

She clung to him, kissing him, exultant in her triumph. How right she had been. Strength, sternness, Plantagenet temper— none of that could stand out against her wiles. His sentimentality had helped her of course, his family feeling. But it was her skill which had played on that.

He was so happy to see their relationship restored. He admitted that he would rather lose a castle than have an unkind word or deed from his family. He loved them all so much. They had been the crowning glory of his love for the Queen.

He was anxious about her. All this upset was not good for the baby she carried.

"The child is happy now. You may laugh, my lord, but I can tell you it has settled down now. I believe it knows already that it has a King for a grandfather."

"You talk nonsense," he said fondly.

She wanted to remember every word that was spoken, every gesture he made. She would tell Ralph all about it when they were together again. He would realize that he had a clever wife as well as a seductive one.

She took a fond farewell of her father and everyone marvelled at the way in which he had been won over, for in a very short time Ralph de Monthermer was released and as the Court by that time was at Eltham Palace he went there to do homage to the King.

Edward received him kindly and bestowed on him the title of Earl of Gloucester and Hereford. Honor indeed. He and Joanna went then to Marlborough Castle where their child was born. It was a daughter and they called her Mary.

The King's Bride

The King had received a terrible blow. For some years he had been dreaming of Blanche. He had written to her, received answers to his letters, and had instructed his ambassadors at the Court of France to send all the news they could of the Princess Blanche.

Philip, the artful King of France, was well aware of what effect the news of his sister's charms were having on the aging monarch of England. It was a source of amusement. Edward was building up an image in his mind and it was to the advantage of the King of France to let him do so. The more he desired Blanche the higher price he could be asked to pay for her.

The price was indeed high. Gascony to be passed over to the French for ever.

How can I do it? Edward asked himself. Gascony! It was of the utmost strategic importance to him. The French King was well aware of this—and of Edward's passionate desire— and it seemed to him that he might succeed in getting the besotted King to agree.

Edward's nights were haunted by Gascony. It was as though Gascony lay beside him with the desirable Blanche.

How could he give up the province? Yet how could he live

without Blanche? He had been a widower too long. It was more than seven years since Eleanor had died. She would understand that was a long time for a King who, though aging, was still too young in body and mind to be without a wife.

At last he could wait no longer and made his decision. Yes, Philip should have Gascony and he would have Blanche. His brother Edmund was negotiating for him at the Court of France and keeping him well informed of what was happening there.

That Edmund was uneasy was obvious. He did not trust that wily monarch who because of his handsome looks was known as Philip le Bel.

In due course Edward received word from his brother that Gascony had been handed over to the French and a marriage contract was on the way, but alas it was not to be the contract Edward had anticipated. The fact was, wrote Edmund, that the Princess Blanche had been contracted to marry the Duke of Austria, the eldest son of the Emperor. Blanche, however, had a younger sister Marguerite, and the King of France proposed to substitute her name for that of Blanche in the marriage contract.

The King was overcome with rage and grief. For all the years he had dreamed of Blanche and now he was to have her sister! Marguerite was much younger than Blanche, but a handsome girl, wrote Edmund. It was a difficult situation. The French already had Gascony and it would mean hard fighting to get it back. And Blanche was already betrothed so there seemed no alternative—if the King really wanted a wife—but to take Marguerite.

Edward cursed the King of France. He likened himself to Jacob who had served seven years for Rachael and had been deceived by the girl's father and given his elder daughter Leah. The difference being that he was offered the younger daughter.

But there was nothing he could do about it. He must either accept Marguerite or go without a wife until he entered into more lengthy negotiations.

In the meantime he had family worries. Joanna was in favor again and he had accepted her husband, but he was deeply concerned about his elder daughter Eleanor whose husband, the Duke of Bar-le-Duc, was still the prisoner of the French. Poor Eleanor was desolate, but it was impossible for the King to do anything. He worried a great deal about her and was arranging a trip to Ghent where he hoped she would be able to join him. To be reunited with her would give him great joy, he wrote to her, and in her reply she said that nothing short of reunion with her husband could give her greater pleasure.

There were many matters to concern Edward. There were differences with France besides minor outbreaks in Wales. These he had expected for he could not hope that that proud people would quietly accept English domination. Events in Scotland were working towards a climax and John Baliol was proving a very unsatisfactory ruler. And there were family matters. The behavior of Joanna had given him many sleepless nights; he worried continually about Eleanor and there was young Elizabeth's marriage to think of now. Margaret was not very happy with her libertine of a husband; how different it would have been if they had all gone into convents like Mary. Yet he worried about Mary too because it sometimes occurred to him that she had been shut away from life before she had had an opportunity of deciding whether she wanted to be. Young Edward needed watching too. He was nearly fourteen, and although clever enough would not devote himself to his books, and had a habit of gathering about him, and showing too much friendship to, the least desirable companions.

And now there was the young Elizabeth—two years older than Edward and betrothed to John of Holland. John had been in England some time and was therefore not a stranger to Elizabeth. He was a mild boy and he would be a gentle husband, but Elizabeth had often told her father how much she hated the thought of leaving England.

Of course he should have been as other kings. He should have *ordered* his children to obey him, and if they rebelled enforced obedience. But he loved them so tenderly, and to have been harsh with them would have meant as great an unhappiness for him as for them. The fact was that he had been brought up in an atmosphere of family devotion—no one could have had more devoted parents than he had—and he had accepted it as a way of life. There were times when it was rewarding. He and Eleanor had been so happy with their children; but there was the other side of the coin. Love and indulgence often meant anxiety.

It certainly did with him. If he had been a less fond father would he be worrying about his children now?

The Earl of Holland had been killed recently and John, Elizabeth's betrothed, was his heir. There had been a certain mystery about the death of John's father, Florence, Earl of Holland. Edward had been watchful of him since the death of the Maid of Norway, for the Earl of Holland was one of the descendants of the Scottish Princess Ada, a daughter of one of the brothers of William the Lion: and Florence had been disappointed when John Baliol was chosen as the King of Scotland. From that time he had shown himself to be more a friend of France than of England. He had even gone so far as to promise France his help against the English if Philip paid him well for it, which of course would have meant the end of the proposed alliance with Elizabeth.

Edward could snap his fingers at that for Florence's son John, who had been sent to England to be brought up there, was still in the country. John, when informed of the position, told Edward that he considered himself bound to Elizabeth, and as he had received nothing but good at the hands of his future father-in-law, he would stand with Edward against his own father.

Florence had had a number of mistresses and had thereby acquired numerous illegitimate childern, so he had a ready reply.

"Since my legitimate son sees fit to flout me I will disinherit him. I have worthy bastard sons and can put one of them in his place."

Edward was shocked at such a suggestion and he wrote earnestly to Florence pointing out the folly of his behavior. The threat had not pleased some of his subjects either and they began to plot against him. Florence had many enemies, among them one of his ministers, Gherard de Valsen, who had his own very special reason for hating him, because Florence had wished to marry off one of his mistresses and had chosen Valsen as her husband. This questionable honor was indignantly refused by Valsen, first because he was about to marry the woman of his choice and secondly because even if he were not, he had no wish to take one of Florence's cast-offs. Florence was furious and determined to revenge himself on Valsen. A few months after the latter's marriage, Florence set a band of ruffians to kidnap Valsen's wife and carry her off to one of his castles. There he was waiting for her. He raped her and sent her back to Valsen, saying that Valsen was wrong, he had married one of the Earl Florence's mistresses.

This was his death warrant, for Valsen now placed himself at the head of his enemies and determined on revenge. The plan was to kidnap Florence and this was immediately put into action, and when Valsen had Florence in his power he taunted him with what would be done to him and declared that his revenge would be bitter. Before this threat could be carried out, some of Florence's friends tried to rescue him. The attempt was foiled and in desperation Valsen persuaded his fellow conspirators that Florence must die. He was brutally murdered and his body mutilated.

Young John was declared Earl of Holland.

The general opinion was that Edward had been involved in the conspiracy with Valsen. This he denied and invited the Dutch nobles to come to England and discuss the marriage of their Earl with his daughter. They came and the marriage was agreed on. It should, said Edward, take place without delay.

The King summoned the Bishop of London to Ipswich where the marriage was to take place.

Prince Edward came to Ipswich with a magnificent train and his sister Margaret was also present. She was still in England having constantly put obstacles in the way of joining her husband in Brabant, and the King, knowing the character of her husband, had not attempted to persuade her.

This was an important occasion for the town of Ipswich and the people came out in thousands to cluster round the church and see the royal bride and her groom.

There was a great entertainment and the King had summoned the finest minstrels, tabourers, clowns and lute players from all over the country. There was dancing and feasting, with mummers to entertain the company and wine even for the people in the streets.

When the festivities were over it was intended that Elizabeth should leave for Holland, and preparations were made for her departure.

But Elizabeth did not want to go. She refused to leave her chamber and the King, hearing of this, stormed in and demanded to know what was wrong with her.

She threw herself at him and put her arms about his neck.

"My dear lord, I cannot leave you."

"Now, now," said the King, "you are no longer a child. You have a husband and your place is with him."

"Dear father, you will be going to Ghent very soon. I want to wait and go with you. *Please*, Father, let me stay a little longer with you."

"My dear child," replied the King, "everything is arranged. Those who are going with you are ready to leave. You cannot decide at this time that you will not go."

"I cannot bear to leave you."

"Your love gratifies me," said the King, "but you *must* go, my child. Mayhap we shall meet in Ghent. There. How is that?"

She stood back from him. She looked very beautiful with her long fair hair flowing from the jewelled coronet which crowned it.

"I shall not go," she said firmly.

"You are to go," he replied.

"I cannot. I *will* not."

"How dare you disobey me," cried the King.

"Dear Father, I do not wish to disobey you. But how can I leave my home? If our mother were here . . ."

It was too much. There were so many burdens on his shoulders. He was suddenly furiously angry. His daughters defied him all the time. He had been too lenient with them. They thought because they were pretty and he and Eleanor had always made much of them, they could do what they liked with him. In an excess of anger he snatched the coronet from her head and threw it into the fire.

She cried out in dismay. It was her most valuable piece of jewelry.

"My lord," she cried and dashed to the fire.

He held her back. "You will see," he said, "that you owe everything you have to me. All I ask in return is obedience. Oh, God, who would have daughters!"

Elizabeth burst into tears. "You do not love us any more. You do not love me. You have thrown my coronet into the flames. Oh Father, you cannot love me."

Then the thought of the valuable jewels which the coronet contained was too much for her. She rushed to the fire and retrieved the coronet. It was blackened and two of the stones were lost.

She dropped it for it was very hot and it fell to the floor between them. The King kicked it aside and was about to stalk out of the room when she caught his arm.

"Father, it is because I cannot bear to leave *you*."

He felt himself softening. "Have you burned your fingers?" he asked.

"A little perhaps."

"Foolish child."

"It was my finest jewelry," she said and she began to laugh.

He could never resist their laughter. Eleanor had once said that few things made her as happy as to hear their children laugh, and he had agreed with her.

"Oh, dear Father, you are smiling. I think you are no longer displeased with me. If you are not I am so happy . . . and if I can stay with you a little longer . . . just a *little* longer until you go to Ghent . . ."

He frowned. Then he said gruffly: "Very well. You shall remain until then. And when I leave," he went on sternly, "you will have to remain with your husband."

She was disobedient like her sister Joanna, but they loved him and he was pleased that she so hated to leave him.

He longed to be in Ghent where, he trusted, Eleanor, the dearest of all his daughters, would be with him. Dear Eleanor who was herself in such a tragic situation. He would be able to talk to her of his coming marriage. She would understand.

At last he had arrived and she was there waiting for him. He forgot all ceremony at the sight of her, his dearest child.

"My sweet child," he said, embracing her.

"Oh dear Father, how I have longed to see you."

"You are unhappy, I know."

"There is no news of him."

"We *must* bring about his release."

"Oh Father, if only you could. I and the children long for his return."

He would do everything within his power, he told her. He thought that after his marriage he might be able to do something.

"Eleanor, my child," he said, "you do not think I am wrong to marry again?"

"I have often wondered why you did not before," she answered. "You are a man who loves a family life and it has been hard for you since our mother died."

He had known she would understand. Eagerly he told her of his hopes for Blanche and how the King of France had deceived him and was offering Marguerite.

Eleanor shuddered. "The King of France is a ruthless man," she said. "I have reason to know that. They say the first thing that one notices about him is his handsome looks. Then one realizes that he is harsh, cruel, vindictive . . . and ambitious."

"I have learned that he is not to be trusted and I shall remember that."

"Dear Father, it may well be that you will be happier with Marguerite than with this renowned beauty, whose praises have been sung throughout Europe. That could well have made her a little conceited. Marguerite in her shadow may well be the wife for you. You remember how gentle and kind our mother always was. My grandmother had a reputation for great beauty, and although we loved her dearly we all knew how she thought it always right that she should have her own way. I have heard my mother say that she could never compete in looks with her mother-in-law. But we know, dear Father, how sweet was her disposition."

"My comforter," he said fondly. "I knew you would be."

He felt relieved and happy and determined that he would do everything possible to bring her husband out of captivity. It should carry some weight that he was ready to marry the younger sister of the King of France when he had been promised the elder.

How pleasant it was to be with her though the pleasure was marred by the twinges of anxiety he felt about her health. She had aged considerably since she had left England, which was small wonder since she had suffered so much. He had been so happy that she, married late, should have at last made a love match. But how cruel was fate to rob her of her husband so soon. Fortunately she had her dear children. How he loved his grandchildren and Eleanor's in particular, simply because they were hers.

He must make the most of this visit.

She had brought for him as a present a leather case beautifully enamelled and fitted with a comb and mirror, and he had told her that he would treasure it as long as he lived.

That was a happy Christmas at Ghent. Margaret was there with her husband, and although she was scarcely happy in her marriage she seemed to be reconciled to it. He had heard that she had received several of her husband's illegitimate children and treated them with kindness. Poor Margaret, she was in no position to protest he supposed, but he imagined what Joanna would have been like in such circumstances.

Elizabeth was present and he hoped she would make no more scenes about leaving him. Of course he was flattered that his girls loved him so well. It was a pity they had to grow up.

But his main concern was with Eleanor's health. He was sure that she pretended she felt better than she did because she knew he was worried.

He *must* get her husband returned to her. Once he was married he would do it. That brought him back to the thoughts of marriage. Was he wise? He would soon be sixty. He was virile still. Of course he should have married four or five years ago; he should have considered it immediately after Eleanor's death. No, he could not have done that. It would have seemed so disloyal. He needed more sons really. He had his beloved daughters and he would not have changed them for boys . . . but a King should have sons and he had only Edward.

Edward did worry him a little. He was not growing up quite as his father would have wished. He was clever enough but he would not apply himself, and he surrounded himself with companions of questionable reputation. He would grow out of that for he was young yet. He was tall and good-looking. That was an advantage. The people like a handsome king and above all a tall one. It was fitting for a king to tower above his subjects.

All would be well, and it was right that he should marry again and get more sons.

So he threw himself whole-heartedly into the celebrations that Christmas at Ghent. He was going to say goodbye when it was over to three daughters. He wished he had married them into English noble houses. But of course that was not good. Gilbert de Clare had been a man whom it was as necessary to placate as it was the members of royal houses. That was why he had been given Joanna. And now Joanna had married that Monthermer man. At least it left him a daughter at home. He could not count poor Mary.

When it was over he said goodbye to Eleanor with many

fond assurances of his affection. He brooded after she had gone. She seemed so pale and wan, so different from the healthy young woman of whom he had always been so proud.

It was in March when he returned to England, and he had not been there very long when news was brought to him of his daughter Eleanor's death.

He was prostrate with grief. It was true that he had been worried about her pale looks, but this was quite unexpected. He was filled with remorse. He should have insisted on her husband getting his freedom. He should have stopped at nothing . . . nothing . . .

He was weighed down with anxieties.

Trouble in France, trouble in Scotland. He could see that he would have to take drastic action above the border. And Eleanor, best loved of all his beloved daughters, was dead.

It was only in contemplating his coming marriage that he could lift himself out of his despondency.

It was with great consternation that Marguerite, sister of the King of France, heard that she was to marry the old King of England. Her sister, the beautiful Blanche, of whom the poets sang, used to laugh when she received his letters. She would read them aloud to her sister who marvelled that a great King who had never seen Blanche, should have become so enamored of what he had heard of her.

Blanche had said it was understandable. There were so many songs written about her and Marguerite had known that people were amazed when they saw her.

Her brother too, the King, was very handsome. So much so that he was known as Philip le Bel. She, Marguerite, who might have been reckoned quite good-looking in any other family, was so overshadowed by her handsome brother and beautiful sister that she had come to be regarded as insignificant.

"Never mind," her mother Queen Marie had said, "you can be good. You have a look of your grandfather and you know he was a great man and became known even during his lifetime as Saint Louis."

Marguerite had certainly always given way to Blanche, who in any case was six years older than she was, and she could not remember a time when people had not remarked on her beauty.

Blanche had been very amused at the thought of what Edward was prepared to pay for her.

"Our brother is highly amused," she said. "He begins to value me greatly. I am worth Gascony to the King of England. That is a great deal to be worth, little sister."

"The King of England must love you very dearly."

"He loves a woman he has never seen. And why? Because others think her beautiful. Our brother refers to me as our great prize, and he says the King of England is a lecherous old satyr who longs to have his bed warmed by a young woman."

Marguerite shivered. "Poor Blanche . . ." she began.

Blanche hated to be pitied and that her insignificant sister should attempt it angered her.

"Poor indeed! I shall be the Queen of England. Have you thought of that? It is as good as being Queen of France."

"Well, as you are now a princess of France is that such an elevation?"

"Serious little Marguerite. I expect you are right, but I do fancy having this old man—who is King withal—so eager for me that he gives our brother territory which the English had sworn never to relinquish."

"It must be wonderful to be so beautiful," said Marguerite.

And Blanche tweaked her sister's long hair and laughed at her.

So Blanche had often talked of going to England and she was amused that the English King was kept dangling.

Then a strange thing had happened. Edward was not the only one who sought the hand of Blanche. The Duke of Austria wanted her and he was the son of the Emperor.

Their brother had discussed the matter at great length with his ministers. Gascony was in their hands, why should not Blanche go to Rudolph of Austria? There still remained Marguerite for the King of England.

She would never forget the day Philip summoned her to hear her fate.

"You, sister, are to go to England in place of Blanche."

"But . . . sire . . ." she had stammered. "How can I? They are expecting Blanche . . . It is Blanche . . . he wants."

Philip threw back his handsome head and laughed.

"Expecting Blanche he may be, but he is going to have a surprise. He will get Marguerite in exchange."

There was a great deal of conferring for Edward was greatly feared. He was a formidable fighter—very different from his father and his grandfather—and Philip le Bel had no desire to anger him too much.

"A younger girl!" mused Philip. "Youth is adorable. Why should he not be pleased with you? You may not have Blanche's high spirits but such can be uncomfortable at times. You are milder than Blanche and mild women can be very pleasant to live with. I would say old Edward is getting a very good bargain."

Marguerite alone in her bedchamber was frightened. Then she consoled herself. He will never accept me, she assured herself. He will say he will not take me. Nothing will come of it.

But he did not say that. After expressing his fury at the perfidy of the King of France when it was suggested that the King's infant daughter Isabella should be offered to Edward's son, Edward agreed to take Marguerite.

"He will be so disappointed in me," moaned Marguerite. "He will hate me for not being Blanche."

Blanche was inclined to think this might well be, but she was quite content to depart for Austria instead of England, confident that wherever she went her exceptional beauty would be appreciated and bring her its dues.

Meanwhile Marguerite must prepare to leave for England for her future husband had said he would have no more delay.

So Blanche left for Austria and shortly afterwards Marguerite and her train made their way to the coast. It was a strange journey for one who had never been far from home. The sea was grey and rough and terrifying, and she was glad when land came into sight, although it brought her nearer to the bridegroom whom she was beginning to dread meeting.

At Dover many richly clad men and women were waiting for her and after spending a sleepless night in the castle there she set out for Canterbury where the King was waiting for her.

That moment was something she would never forget. He was so tall that he dwarfed other men. He was old . . . yes very old, but she had been prepared for that. Although he had the bearing of the King and the impression he gave was one of stern strength, at the same time there was a kindliness about him which was reassuring.

"So you have come at last," he said, smiling, taking her hand and kissing it.

He thought: How young she is! Little more than a child. Younger than my daughters . . . my wild Joanna, my beautiful Eleanor whom I shall never see again. Poor child. She looks frightened and no wonder. Sent overseas to an old man!

And she was pretty. Yes, she was very pretty. They had overlooked to tell him how pretty. They must have been bemused by the dazzling perfection of Blanche.

When he looked at this trembling child he was filled with tenderness.

He bent his head to hers. "All will be well," he said. "You must not be afraid."

And from that moment she was ready to love him.

They were married at Canterbury by Archbishop Robert de Winchelsea. Marguerite was not yet seventeen and Edward was sixty. The people who had crowded into the streets and about the Cathedral were enchanted by the fresh young bride, and so was Edward. He kept thinking of the wise words of his daughter Eleanor, and it was not difficult to persuade himself that the younger sister was perhaps after all the better choice.

She was so eager to please, so obviously apologetic because she was not Blanche, that he was determined to persuade her that he was not disappointed and in convincing her he convinced himself.

As for her, she admired his power and his regality; his great height would always be impressive and although his hair— once so fair was now white—he emanated vitality. He was a King—a strong King—none could deny that. That he could be ruthless when dealing with his enemies was obvious, but the tenderness of his feelings for his family was in such strong contrast that he was lovable, and human in spite of his great power.

That tenderness was very much in evidence where his young wife was concerned. He had banished most of her fears and convinced her that far from being inadequate she pleased him greatly.

He was a gentle lover; he told her about the virtues of his

first wife and how when she had died he had been desolate.
They had been together for many years; she had accompanied
him to the Holy Land; she had given him many children; and
when she had died he had had crosses erected at every spot
where her coffin rested on its way to London. He was going
to love Marguerite as he had loved Eleanor and he knew that
she would love him too.

"I will," she told him earnestly.

"My dear little Queen," he replied, "how glad I am that you
came to me. Now we shall grow to know each other and our
love for each other will grow likewise."

Alas, this tender period was brought to an abrupt end. The
news from Scotland was alarming. Always he had been aware
of the trouble that could come from that quarter. Baliol had
been deposed. Rarely had a man less capable of being there
sat on a throne. Edward was the overlord and he was determined
to remain so. He was going to govern Scotland because he saw
that until he did there would be trouble there; and if he were
going to keep his place in France he could not have an enemy
waiting to stab him in the back.

If Baliol had been a strong man, yet one ready to work
under his rule, all would have been well. But Baliol was weak;
he had no talent for governing and, worse still, no will for it.

There was one man who had come into prominence who
gave the King great cause for concern. That was William Wallace. This man had some magnetic power. He was the kind of
man of whom a king must be wary. He had a talent, this William
Wallace, for drawing men to his standard. He knew how to
inspire them.

Edward had set English lords over various provinces in
Scotland to keep order for him and to remind the Scots, should
they need reminding, that they owed allegiance to him.

It was natural that there should be constant trouble between
the Scots and their English overlords. Forays had frequently
broken out and several English had been murdered. But this
was inevitable.

What was to be deplored was that the Scots had found a
leader in this man Wallace.

It was not a question of a minor uprising. Wallace had
collected an army.

Moreover he had put the English to flight at Stirling Bridge and had dared cross the Border and had harried the people of Cumberland and Westmorland. It was intolerable that this could go on. He had taken advantage of Edward's absence in France.

Well, now Edward was home. He had made a truce with France. He had married the French King's sister and he could live in peace—temporary perhaps—with his enemies across the Channel. But he must turn his attention to Scotland, where they had wriggled free from the yoke he had set upon them. He was going to march north. He was going to hammer those Scots into obedience. He had vowed to add Scotland to his crown as he had Wales and nothing—not even his new marriage—was going to prevent his going into action without delay.

He explained to his bride of a week that he must leave her.

"So it is with kings, little one. My first wife Eleanor accompanied me on my journeys. It was her wish to do so. Wherever I went she was not far behind. I would not take her into the heat of battle—though she would have accompanied me—God rest her soul! No, she was close to me. She even bore my daughter in Acre. I trust you will want to be close to me at all times."

"Oh, I shall," said Marguerite fervently.

"I know it," he cried. "Now I must go. You will follow me in due course, but with less haste than I must go. I want you now to go to London and stay there awhile in your lodgings at the Tower. There the people will see you. They will wish it. We must always consider the will of the people . . . and the people of London in particular. When the time is right I will send for you. Will you come?"

"With all my heart, my lord."

He kissed her tenderly. "You are a sweet wife," he said, "and I am glad you are mine. I could wish I were forty years younger and even then I should be older than you, sweet child. I tell you what I dearly hope. Perhaps it is too much to wish for. I hope that you may already be with child."

"I hope it too," answered Marguerite.

"If it should be so send a messenger to me with the news. It would mean a great deal to me."

"And to me, my lord. I will send a messenger without delay."

"God grant our wish may become reality. How I curse this man Wallace who takes me from you."

"Is it just one man, my lord?"

"Aye, one man. For without him the Scots would not have arisen in rebellion. Not such rebellion. Small forays we can deal with. It is when a great leader arises, one who catches the imagination of the people, that we must take heed. So, William Wallace, my enemy, I come to take you, and when you are in my hands I promise you you will wish that you had never been born."

"My lord, perhaps he thinks he does right for his country."

She blushed a little. She had not meant to voice an opinion. But the King seemed not to have heard.

His face darkened; she saw his clenched fist, and she was for the first time afraid of him. William Wallace had brought out a side to her husband's nature which she had not seen before.

But almost immediately he was soft again. "Farewell, dear wife. I shall soon be back and I'll tell you this: I'll have the head of William Wallace on a spike to adorn my tower . . . just as I did the rebels of Wales."

The next day the King rode off at the head of his army, and it seemed to the young Queen that the name of William Wallace was on everyone's tongue.

The Adventures of
William Wallace

William Wallace had always hated the English. When he had
sat in the study over his books in the home of his uncle he had
dreamed of glorious battles, of driving the English overlords
out of his country, of forcing Edward to make an ignominious
retreat behind the border and stay there.

So much did he dream of this that it had become an obsession
with him, and his hatred was the biggest force in his life. He
only had to hear the word "English" for the blood to rise to
his temples and a fury would seize him. When he saw an
Englishman he had to restrain the desire to attack him on the
spot; and he did see Englishmen fairly frequently because the
King of England had set them to guard the garrison towns; and
when he rode into Stirling he would encounter them in the
taverns or strolling through the streets, lords and masters of
the place—and letting anyone who offended them know it. It
was not uncommon to see a dead Scotsman hanging from a
gallows. What was his crime? he would ask. There would be
a shrug of the shoulders, a lift of the eyebrows, a tightening

of the lips expressing hatred which dared not be spoken. "Oh, he was a bold laddie. He offended the English."

William was filled with love for his country and hatred for the oppressors. As he wandered through the streets of Stirling he would say to himself, "It shall not always be so. One day . . ." He was waiting for that day. It would be a day of fulfilment for William Wallace.

He would ride back to Dunipace the dream of military glory with him. He would sit over his uncle's table when they had eaten and talk with him. He had been with his uncle since his early boyhood because his father had thought that his brother, the priest of Dunipace, would be a good mentor for his son. William had shown from an early age that he was inclined to be rebellious; he had led his brothers—Malcolm, his senior and John his junior—into trouble now and then. If he thought he had suffered from an injustice he would always have to avenge it and his father, Sir Malcolm Wallace, had decided that his brother who was in the church and a quiet life at Dunipace might have a sobering effect on his son. The priest was also a scholar and could be entrusted with the boy's education.

So William had left his parents and his two brothers and gone to his uncle. He had been attentive to his lessons and done well, but his wild nature had never been tamed and the boy who had gone to Dunipace was very much like the young man of eighteen who in his uncle's study had heard of the plan to marry Edward's son to the Maid of Norway and when the little girl died Edward had made himself a kind of overlord and allowed weak John Baliol to be crowned King of Scotland.

He raved against the state into which his country had fallen. He cursed Edward.

His uncle, a peace-loving man, had warned him. "What is to be will be," he said. "It is no use railing against fate."

"What is to be will be, yes," retorted William. "But there is no reason why those of us who love our country should not help to make it proud again. We are the ones who will make it what it was intended to be."

"Leave well alone," advised his uncle. "You could go into the church . . ."

"Into the church! Uncle, you know me."

"I know you well," replied his uncle sadly. "And I know

this, that if you persist in speaking so freely to all you meet, if you show so clearly your hatred for the English, you will be in trouble."

"I'd welcome it," cried William. "And you will see what trouble I shall make for them."

"Edward is a mighty King. All know that. He is very different from his father. If he were not so concerned in his differences with France it would go ill with us."

"I will never sit happily under the tyrant's heel."

"If you do not provoke them . . ."

"Not provoke them! They occupy our towns! They swagger through our streets pushing us aside when they would pass, taking our women, acting like conquerors. And you say, 'Don't provoke them!' They will learn they have not conquered Scotland . . . and never will."

"Wild talk," said his uncle soberly, "and it will take you to trouble."

But William had never been one to turn away from trouble.

"No," said his uncle, "we live in comparative peace. 'Tis true the English King stands over us. He wants to govern this land. He wants to take us as he has our fellow Celts in Wales. I see his reasoning. He wants to make this island one country."

"To be governed by him."

"He governs the English well."

"By God, uncle, I believe you are on his side."

"Do not take the name of the lord in vain in my house, I pray you, nephew. I am on the side of peace and I see a time when, if our countries were as one with one king, much bloodshed could be saved."

"Indeed it is so, if we would be subdued by this tyrant."

"If we did not revolt, if we were placid under his rule, we should enjoy the good rule which prevails in England. It is because he fears revolt that he is harsh."

"And good reason he has to fear it. He will discover that we too can be harsh."

His uncle shook his head. He would never change William. He was as wild as he was when he had first come to Dunipace.

It was soon after that conversation that William's father, Sir Malcolm Wallace, came in haste to Dunipace, and his eldest son—named Malcolm after him—came with him.

The priest welcomed his brother and nephew with pleasure, but he quickly learned that they brought no good news.

William came hurrying down to greet his father and elder brother, and his father, after embracing him and assuring himself of his good health and that of his brother the priest, said he was in great haste and must talk in secret.

In the study Malcolm Wallace told why he had come.

"We can no longer tolerate the rule of the English in Elderslie," he explained. "I have made that very clear, and I have placed myself and our family in danger through so doing."

"Father, I am proud," cried William.

His father held up his hand. "It may have been folly. But they are after me. I have sent your mother with your brother John to Kilspindie in the Carse of Gowrie and I want you, William, to follow them there with all speed."

"And you, sir?" asked William. "Where will you go?"

"I and your brother Malcolm are going on to the Lennox. There is a plan to form a body of troops to move against the English."

"Father, I shall come with you."

"No, my son. I have a more important mission for you. I want you to go to Kilspindie and protect your mother and young brother."

William hesitated. He longed to go into battle against the English but the task of protecting his family was, he could see, of the utmost importance.

"When shall I set out?"

"At the earliest possible moment. There will soon be a price on my head, depend upon it, and members of my family will not be safe."

"I will go at once, sir," cried William.

The priest shook his head and said that he would tell the servants to serve a meal, and while it was being prepared William could get ready to leave. The priest was sad. He felt in his heart that no good could come of this rebellion, and he would have been happier if they could have worked the matter out in a conference between the Scots and the English.

William arrived in Kilspindie to find his mother and young brother John eagerly awaiting him.

His mother was anxious. "I did not want your father to go off with Malcolm in this way."

"Oh, Mother," cried William, "you are like my uncle. You are ready to pay any price for peace."

"Peace is the most desirable thing on earth to a woman with a husband and sons."

"Nay, Mother," replied William. "Honor is more. I tell you this. One day we are going to drive the English out of Scotland, and I . . ."

He paused. He did not want to talk of his dream. It was too precious and he felt that if he talked of it it might be unlucky. He did not want to say that he saw himself at the head of an army, leading the Scots to victory, crushing the might of Edward. But that was the dream and it grew more vivid as he grew older.

Kilspindie! How dull it was. There was no danger there. John had lessons from a tutor but William was too advanced for that. His mother worried about his interrupted education. She was safe enough in Kilspindie, she said. She wanted him to go to Dundee to a brother of hers who would house him and he could attend the school which was attached to the monastery there.

When he assured her that he was old enough to have done with schooling she shook her head. She was anxious that he should complete his training and she persisted in her efforts to persuade him. He had been sent to her to protect her, he reminded her. There was no need, she had said. In fact she was safer without a son who had a habit of speaking his thoughts about the English aloud. If she lived quietly she would need no protection.

It was a fact that the quiet life of Kilspindie had no great appeal for him. If he could have joined his father he would have done so, but he had not heard where he was, so he finally agreed to leave Kilspindie and go to Dundee to his maternal uncle.

This proved to be a fatal decision. His uncle received him with warmth, and he was soon installed in the school where he worked hard hoping to complete his education as soon as was possible so that he might devote himself to his destiny. He longed to join his father but he knew he should not go out and look for him, but stay where he could easily go to the aid of his mother if she should need him.

He was soon very popular in his uncle's house, particularly with the housekeeper who irritated him mildly at times with her constant attentions, for she would insist that he did not go out into the cold winds without his warm jacket and that he eat every scrap of his porridge. He teased her and she enjoyed his teasing and she was clearly delighted to have a young man in the house.

The castle of Dundee was in the hands of Governor Selby, one of the worst of Edward's deputies, and this man was very unpopular in the town. His punishments for insubordination were exceptionally harsh and being an arrogant man he insisted on the utmost respect from the Scottish inhabitants. When William strolled through the streets of the town he burned with fury. He would sit in the taverns and listen to the tales of injustices and he was ripe for trouble.

It so happened that one day he attired himself in his best cloak and tunic of green, the fashionable color, and setting his dagger and sword in his belt went out to meet his friends in one of the taverns.

In the narrow street he saw a young man coming towards him accompanied by two friends, and it was clear at once that the young man was someone of importance by the sycophantic manner of his attendants. William did not need to be told who he was. He had seen him before, riding with his father, Governor Selby.

The young man expected William to doff his hat and bow low. Instead of which William barred his way and showed clearly that he had no intention even of stepping aside to allow him to pass.

Young Selby looked William up and down with an insolence which set William's Scottish heart beating with rage and excitement. At last he was face to face with one of the enemy.

"And who is this?" asked Selby turning to one of his friends. "He is uncouth enough to be a Scot."

"And you are arrogant enough to be English," retorted William hotly.

"You heard him," cried young Selby. "He insulted the King."

"What, that tyrant!" cried William, his blood up, so that he was in his most reckless mood.

"By God's body," cried young Selby. "You heard him. He speaks thus of great Edward!"

"I would I could do more than *speak* against him."

"Methinks we must teach the Scot a lesson," drawled Selby. "When he is hanging by his neck from the gallows he will not be so bold nor look so pretty in his good green clothes."

Selby had his hand on his dagger, but William was before him. He seized Selby by the neck, shook him and then plucking his dagger from its sheath he thrust it into the young man's breast, withdrew it, and threw the young man to the ground. It was clear from one look at the governor's son stretched out on the cobbles that he was dead.

William had killed his first Englishman and it had all happened in a few seconds. For a moment Selby's attendants were stunned, but not for long. William, however, was quicker to act than they were. The son of the governor killed by his hand! This would be certain death for him—probably torture. If he were caught now he would never live to save Scotland. He turned and mustering all his strength fled from the scene.

He had run back to his uncle's house before he realized the folly of this. He was known. He had been seen. It was the first place they would come to look for him.

He must go. But where?

His uncle's housekeeper seated at her spinning wheel stared at him in horror for his green tunic was spattered with blood.

"I cannot stay," panted William. "They will be after me. This is the first place they will come to. I have to get away . . . quickly."

"You have killed someone!"

"The Governor's son."

"May God preserve us. You were seen?"

He nodded. "Farewell, Goody. I dare not stay."

"Wait! I have a plan."

"They are already on their way here," he said.

"You would meet them if you tried to leave. One moment. Here." She had stripped off her dress. "Put that on . . ."

He protested but she cried angrily, "Do as I say. It is your only chance."

He saw the reason of that and obeyed. The dress was far too small.

"Wait," she said and ran from the room. A few minutes

later having put on a gown, she returned with a shawl and a cap similar to the one she always wore.

"Put these on," she commanded. "The shawl will hide the ill-fit of the dress and the cap will make a woman of you. Then sit at the wheel and spin."

He saw the wisdom of her reasoning and obeyed. He was just in time for as he turned to the wheel Selby's men burst into the house.

"Where is he?" demanded the leader of the men. "Where is young Wallace?"

"Young William..." said the housekeeper. "How should I know? In the town most likely. That's where the lazy young lad spends most of his time. 'Tis lassies and taverns for him and 'tis there you'll find him."

The men looked round the room and scarcely gave a glance to the one they thought was the servant at the spinning wheel.

"He may well be hiding here," said one of them. "Search the place."

They went over the house. They looked in every room, and all the time William went on spinning.

When they came down they said to the housekeeper: "If he comes send to us at once. He is a wanted man."

"I will my lords, I will. Oh sir... my lords, what has he done then?"

"Murder, Goody. That's what he has done. And he'll hang for this. But not before we make him suffer. The governor's son..."

"Oh, no, my lord...oh *no*..." The housekeeper had flung her apron over her face and was rocking to and fro.

"Cut down in his youth. By God, blood will flow for this. Wait till the governor recovers from his grief."

"'Twas murder...'twas murder...the wicked young man," sobbed the housekeeper.

"Aye, 'twas murder. Remember. If that murderer comes here...which it seems he will at some time. Keep him...come to us and let us know. You'll be rewarded, good woman. And you will see justice done."

"How could he? I always knew he was wild. I knew he'd come to no good."

The men went out. She went over to the spinning wheel.

"Go on. Don't stop. Go on for a while. Till I know it will be safe."

William obeyed her, exulting in the manner in which they had deceived the English.

She sat beside him. "We must bide our time. Meanwhile prepare yourself to go. Where will you go?"

"I must go to my mother in Kilspindie. I must assure myself that she is safe."

"You will have to be careful. When you reach her you will not stay there. It would be as well if you took her away. Oh, my laddie, what have you done? Why did you have to kill the Englishman?"

"My task in life is to kill Englishmen and to drive them out of our fair land."

She shook her head. "I would that we could live in peace."

"You talk like my mother."

"Aye, laddie, 'tis women's talk. We see no good in dying but there's much good in living."

"To be humiliated . . . to be insulted . . ."

"Hush. We should be thinking of getting ye away. You must wait till nightfall. Then we must slip out. We will go to the stables where your horse will be ready. Until that time you are my servant Tabbie . . ."

"And my Uncle!"

"I will tell him what you have brought on yourself. He'd never betray you. For what has happened, should we be caught, I'll take the blame."

"You are good to me. You risk your life for me, you know."

"Do ye think I would side with the English?"

"Never. But to risk yourself . . ."

"Tish!" she snapped. He stood up from the wheel and kissed her.

Riding through the night to Kilspindie he was thinking of what lay ahead. He had at last entered the battle. He would be a wanted man. The murder of a governor's son would be regarded as treachery to the King of England. John Baliol, King of Scotland, would be no help to him. He was Edward's man. What Scotland needed was a king worth fighting for. But Edward had allowed them to put old Toom Tabard on the throne because he knew he was a weak man and that suited wily

Edward, for who was the real ruler of Scotland? Edward. Edward was the enemy.

William's coming was received with some dismay at Kilspindie, for when it was learned that he had killed Governor Selby's son, his mother's relations were horrified and feared that his recklessness would bring trouble to them all. He could not stay at Kilspindie, they said. That much was clear for the hue and cry would soon follow them there.

There was an immediate gathering of the family to discuss what could be done and William realized that in coming here he had placed his mother and all of them in danger.

"You must go at once," said his relations, and they added: "It would be unwise to leave your mother behind."

After some discussion it seemed that it might be safe to leave John at his school, but certainly Lady Wallace must go with her son. And immediately at that, because it could not be long before their searchers came to Kilspindie, for they would guess he would come to his family.

"Let there be no delay," said their host, whose great concern seemed to be to get them out of his house and with all speed. It was agreed that they should disguise themselves as pilgrims on the way to the shrine of St. Margaret; and having no desire to stay any longer than they need, where their presence inspired such fear, they set out immediately.

Their disguise was good and they were accepted in the hamlets and villages through which they passed for what they pretended to be and in due course they reached Dunipace.

William's uncle was amazed to see them. He shook his head. He had known William's hot blood and violent hatred of the English would bring trouble to him and his family. However, they must rest and be fed and discuss with him what their next action should be.

When they had eaten he took them to that study where William had worked and dreamed in the past, and there he bade them sit down.

"I have ill news for you," he said gravely, "which I did not want to tell you until you had eaten and rested a little. I fear it will be a great shock to you."

"Pray do not keep us longer in suspense, uncle," begged William, and he went to his mother and took her hand because he guessed that the grave news concerned his father.

"Your father engaged the English at Elderslie," said his uncle. "It was a foolhardy thing to do. He and his retainers were outnumbered."

"They have taken him," cried Lady Wallace in horror.

"Nay. He died in battle and with him . . . Malcolm."

Lady Wallace stared straight ahead of her. William put an arm about her and drew her to him.

"The devils!" he cried. "So they have killed my father and my brother!"

"Your father and Malcolm took some of them too, nephew. They inflicted losses on the English in losing their lives."

"Gone," whispered Lady Wallace. "My husband . . . *and* my son . . ."

"By God," cried William. "They shall pay for this. I will not rest till I have slain twenty English in repayment for those two lives."

"Nothing can repay," said his uncle. "It is a pity your father engaged in such a battle. He was certain to lose."

"I am proud of him," cried William. "I shall avenge him and my brother."

"You must first concern yourself with saving your own life. You are a wanted man . . . and you are Sir William now. You must care for your mother and brother."

William faltered as the implication of what this meant came to him. His father . . . his brother . . . dead in one day. And he the head of the family. He looked at his mother. She seemed frail in her misery.

"Mother," he said, "I must get you to some place of safety. You have done nothing."

His uncle said, "Do that as soon as you can. Take her to her brother, Ronald Crawford. He is a friend of the Governor of Ayr and I doubt not can persuade him that your mother is innocent of what they would call treason. But he cannot save you, William. Nothing can save you. You are a wanted man."

"I know it well," said William.

"Then take your mother from here. Make sure of her safety and then . . . take heed for yourself."

It was sound advice. They left Dunipace that night and in due course they arrived at Lady Wallace's brother's home in Crosbie. When he heard the story he said his sister must stay under his protection, but there was nothing he could do to save

William. So William, feeling his mother was in good hands, rode on. But he did not go far, for he wanted to be close to his mother in case she should need his help, and he came to rest at Auchincruive on the banks of the Ayr, about two miles from the town of that name. Here lived some distant relations and he thought to himself how fortunate he was to have so many family connections who could be relied on to give him a helping hand when he needed it. The owner of the place was Sir Duncan Wallace and of course he could not deny shelter to a relative.

But Wallace was in danger and he must take the utmost care. It might be wise to let it be known that he was merely a weary traveler who had asked for lodging for a few nights before he passed on his way. No one here had seen William so he could disguise himself under another identity, and if he would do this Sir Duncan could offer him shelter.

There was nothing for William to do but accept these terms. He wanted a few days while he could think out his next plan of action. Baliol was very unpopular and Wallace would like to see him replaced. Robert Bruce had at least as good a claim and was Baliol's deadly rival. Bruce was an old man, but he had a son and Robert Bruce the second had married well, for in doing so he had acquired the lands and titles of the Earl of Carrick. He even had a son—another Robert—who was said to be a fine soldier and a man of ambition. Unfortunately the Bruces had made agreements with England; they had sworn allegiance at Carlisle on the host and sword of Thomas à Becket. If the Bruces had not been so ready to comply with Edward's demands, if they had taken up arms against Edward, William would have been ready to place himself in their service.

But it was not so. There was no regular army in Scotland. The only protesters were those who, like William Wallace, acted on their own. It was no good. He should assemble an army. If only he could! Instead of which he must skulk under an assumed name, awaiting the opportunity which it seemed would never come.

Overcome with grief at the loss of his father and brother, frustrated by the fact that he was a fugitive, he fumed and raged and suffered in silence while he wondered what he could do next and where he would go.

So frustrated was he by hiding in Sir Duncan's house that

he found the urge to wander out irresistible and making sure that he did not call attention to himself by his dress he often made expeditions into the town. When he saw the English soldiers there he had great difficulty in restraining himself, but the thought that if he betrayed himself and was caught that would avail Scotland little, he was very careful.

The Governor of Ayr was Lord Percy and he was anxious to remind the Scots that he was the master. His English soldiers were in evidence throughout the town and they took a great delight in showing the Scots how superior they were. They enjoyed challenging them to displays of strength in which it was advisable to let them win.

Strolling into the streets one day William came upon a little group watching a giant of a man, stripped to his waist, displaying brawny arms and big muscles.

He was calling attention to his fine physique. He was an Englishman, he cried. There were many such as he in England. Was there one Scot who could compare with him? If so let him come forward. "Let two of you stand forth and I will show you how I can lift two at a time off the ground. Come forward. Come forward. What, are you afraid?"

He seized two gaping youths and lifting them from the ground threw them so that they fell against the rough wall. The crowd simpered, and the two young men picked themselves up bruised and bleeding and slunk off as quickly as possible.

"Brave Scots!" cried the giant. "You stand and gape. Will none others challenge me? Then see, *I* will challenge you. Here is a great pole. Give me a groat and for that you shall have the privilege of striking me one blow on my bare back. You will see that it will be for me as though a fly has settled there. Come, you . . ."

He selected a young man from the crowd who shamefacedly produced his groat. The giant took it, examined it, nodded and put the pole into the Scotman's trembling hands. The crowd gaped while the Scotsman struck the blow. The giant turned his head. "Did you hit me? Why bless you, my little Scottish laddie, I was not sure. I thought a light wind touched me, nothing more."

The crowd laughed and the discomfited Scot slunk off, the poorer by the loss of his groat and his dignity.

William, watching, felt his palms tingling. He assessed the

giant. A strong man, yes, but he himself was as strong. The giant was tall but William was equally so and less fleshy, which meant more agile. By God it would be worth a groat to give him a blow he would remember for months to come.

He stepped forward.

"Ah," cried the giant. "Here's another brave Scotsman."

"Here is the groat. Give me the pole," replied William.

"Surely, surely, my pretty gentleman. Here is the pole. Come, I am ready."

William lifted the pole; every bit of strength was in his arms as he brought it down across the giant's back. There was a crack; the giant staggered; he fell forward. His back was broken.

There was a shout of dismay. The watching soldiers crowded round their champion. They surrounded William too.

"By God, he is dead," said someone. They rounded on William. "You killed him."

"In just combat," William replied.

"You . . . Scot!"

"You . . . Englishman."

It was the sign. They would have seized William but he was too quick for them. He felled two with the pole he was carrying and then throwing it aside he snatched the dagger from his belt. In a short time five of them were lying on the cobbles . . . dead.

He knew he must get away. He must find his horse, ride like fury and get as far as he could from those enraged men.

But he could not. The crowd was too dense. They surrounded him. They all wanted a glimpse of the man who had killed the giant.

He turned to fight, but there were too many Englishmen against him. He kicked out and one man fell back reeling in pain, but there was another in his place.

He was seized and carried off.

"To the jail," they chanted. "Throw him into the jail."

It was fortunate for him that they did not know who he was or they would have devised a cruel end for him. As it was he was just a Scot who had been challenged and had killed the challenger and then had slain others in the foray. Such bloody fights which ended in death were common enough. But he had killed Englishmen and he was a Scot, and for that he should be thrown into jail until they decided what to do with him.

The old jail in Ayr was a noisome spot. His cell was so small that he could not, being tall, stand up in it. There was no light in it and he who had been accustomed to the fresh air found the lack of it intolerable. He could scarcely move; the smell of the place sickened him; the rats came out and watched him. He could see their yellow eyes in the gloom. He knew they were waiting until he was too feeble to fight them, then they would attack him.

He was in despair. His bright dream had vanished; it had been swept away because of a brawl in the streets of a town. What a fool he was. He should never have challenged the giant; he should never have lost his temper and killed those Englishmen. He should have learned his lesson over Selby's son.

He could never curb his fury. He felt too deeply the humiliation of his countrymen. It was because of this ardor in him that he had sworn to dedicate his life to his country's cause; and because of it he was here . . . in this fearsome prison. And how could he ever escape from it? Once a day his food was pushed through a grating. It was always decaying herring salt from the barrel . . . inedible except to a starving man; and with it came a little water . . . just enough to keep him alive. If it were not for that he would have believed they had forgotten him.

At first he had tried to devise a means of escape. He had pummelled the stone walls with his fists until they had become lacerated; he had tried to prise open the iron bars of the door but even his strength could make no impression. Then on his diet of evil-smelling herring and water his strength began to be sapped away, and despair came to him.

This is the end, he thought. This is all then.

Once as he lay there the door opened and a lantern shone on to his face. He heard two voices. "Can't last much longer," said one.

"Give him another day," said the other.

The light went out. He lay there. He tried to interpret their meaning but he was too tired. Later he roused himself. He was dying then. That was what they meant. They would take him out of this hell . . . when he was dead and he wanted nothing so much but to leave this place.

He was light-headed, unsure of where he was and yet a thought kept hammering in his brain. He would only be taken out of this place if he were dead so he must die . . . and if he were not dead, he must pretend to be. It was imperative that he get out.

The lights were there. He lay still, his eyes half closed.

The voice said, "He's gone this time."

Someone prodded him with a foot. He did not move. Half conscious, one thought kept recurring: I shall only leave here when I am dead . . . I must be dead . . .

"I'll take him by the legs . . . You take the shoulders . . ."

Vaguely he was conscious. He was leaving the cell; he was leaving misery, hell on earth; he had cheated the rats; he would never again taste barrelled herrings.

"Over the wall . . . into the midden . . ." said the voice.

Blessed fresh air. It intoxicated him; he was swooning with the joy of it. He was flying through the wonderful heady sweet clean air . . . then he fell into unconsciousness.

He awoke. It was dusk and he was in a small room lying on a truckle bed. Everything was sweet smelling. That was what struck him first.

He thought, I died then and came to heaven.

Then he closed his eyes.

He heard voices.

"He'll recover."

"He's strong as an ox."

"I never thought he could . . . after the state he was in."

They were talking of him. He opened his eyes to daylight. A young woman was standing near a window and the light shone on her face. He was sure then that he had come to heaven because she had the look of an angel. Her long fair hair hung in two thick plaits, one of which fell over her right shoulder; her overdress with wide sleeves to the elbow was of blue and beneath it was a petticoat of buttercup yellow that almost matched her hair; her eyes were blue, her cheeks rosy.

"He is looking at us," said the young woman. "He is awake."

He heard himself ask: "Who . . . are you?"

She moved towards the bedside. "Mother," she called. "Mother, come here."

There were two of them. A woman and her daughter.

"Where am I . . . ?"

"Safe and well," said the young woman.

She came to the bed and smiled at him.

"You are beautiful," he said.

The elder woman put a cup of warm broth to his lips and he drank it eagerly.

"You see, daughter," she said, "he takes it now."

He looked from one to the other of them.

"You look . . . happy," he said faintly.

"We thought you would die," answered the girl.

They would not let him talk much then but gradually he learned from them.

He owed his life again to his uncle's housekeeper, who had made him sit at her spinning wheel and spin when they came to look for him. She had sent her nephew to find out what had befallen him and when she had heard the description of the young man who had killed the giant in the streets of Ayr she had known it was he. He had been thrown into the prison and she had sent to her sister who lived in Ayr and begged her to find out all she could. Ellen, her daughter, was a beautiful girl who was friendly with many of the men in the town—English and Scottish. She was intrigued by the story of the young man in jail and when she was told in secret that he was William Wallace, who was becoming something of a legend, she was very excited and determined to do all she could to help him.

When she went into the town she lingered by the jail gates. The guards were only too happy to talk to her. Ellen was known as a very desirable young woman who, while she would not bestow her favors on all and sundry, could be very generous to those she liked. She was very much sought after, and she and her mother lived well in their cottage because of the good things which her admirers brought to her. Thus, when she lingered at the jail gates, the guards were only too happy to talk to her, and from them she learned about the giant slayer and how he lay now in his cell from where, they joked, he could kill no more Englishmen. She knew that he was near death. She knew that when he was dead they would throw him into the midden, and when they did so for the sake of her aunt she would retrieve his body and if it were possible give it decent burial.

They were waiting; they knew it was at the hour of dusk when bodies were disposed of and they saw this one thrown out; they rescued it and carried it home and there to their amazement they discovered that there was still life in it. The secret nursing appealed to Ellen's nature. She loved intrigue. Moreover she saw that when he was in health William Wallace must have been a very fine figure of a man indeed.

She and her mother vied with each other for the honor of tending him. First they cleaned off the filth of the prison which was no easy task.

"He is all they say of him," said Ellen, and her mother agreed.

They took a pride in finding nourishing food for him, and gradually they brought him back to health. They were delighted that they had played a small part in preserving the life of the man whom people had said might well be the savior of his country.

Sir William Wallace. When his name was mentioned Scotsmen rejoiced. One day William Wallace was going to lead them against the English.

Once he had turned the corner they knew he would live, for his recovery was rapid, and when he heard what had happened he was deeply moved.

"It is good to have friends," he said. "Ellen, you might have been thrown into prison yourself for what you have done for me."

"Our Ellen would have found a way out," said her mother fondly. "Our Ellen has friends."

Ellen laughed and Wallace wondered about her. As the days passed he wondered a great deal. She would sit beside his bed and tell him how she had fed him, and on more than one occasion when he was distressed she had lain beside him in his bed and soothed him in his delirium.

"It seemed to comfort you," she said.

"I can think of no greater comfort," replied William.

"You were as a child," she told him. "It was difficult to believe this was the great Wallace."

"I was a child," he said, "completely dependent on your goodness."

She nodded and, leaning over him, kissed him.

"Ellen," he said, "I am dependent on you still."

There was something warm about Ellen—warm and generous. It was the very essence of her attraction. Ellen loved easily though not deeply; but when she loved she gave freely.

It was inevitable that as Wallace's health improved they became lovers.

Her mother knew but to her, knowing Ellen, that had been inevitable from the beginning. Ellen had always had lovers from the time she was fifteen. It was a natural way of life with her. She was no prostitute and she generally took one lover at a time. It was part of her generous serene nature. She never said, "What shall I get from this relationship?" but she took what came as generously as she gave.

William was enchanted with her. He was glad that he was too weak yet to leave the cottage and carry on with his mission, for he could dally with a good conscience. It was the first time that there was something he wanted to do rather than fight the English. He was amazed at himself.

Theirs would be a transient relationship. They both knew this and accepted it, but they both wanted it to go on and on, and for each of them the wrench of parting would cause some sorrow. Hearts would not be broken—they both knew that. Ellen's heart was so resilient and William's was given to a cause. But that did not mean that they did not long for this pleasant state of affairs to go on and on.

Between sessions of lovemaking he talked to her of his plans. She could help him, he said. He would trust her. She knew so many people; she knew what was going on in the town; she could draw secrets from the English, for naturally they were as charmed with her as the Scots were. "You will have your share in the plan to set Scotland free," he told her.

She told him that should be her pleasure, but in fact she was more eager to satisfy her lover and herself than concerned with Scotland's plight. Such as Ellen would always find a comfortable way of life whoever ruled.

But she was fond of William Wallace. He was different from any lover she had had before, and while he was with her she was all his. She brought scraps of news from the town. Her friends often let drop items of interest. That was a comfort to William. He did not feel he was wasting so much time after all.

There were some friends with whom he wished to get into

touch. They were two young Irish men—one named Stephen the other Karlé, whom he had known long ago and who had been inspired by his talk of saving Scotland. While he had been lying bodily exhausted in his bed, his mind had been active. What he needed to do was gather men like himself together. It was folly to become involved in brawls with the English, especially when they could result in almost fatal results. What he should do was gather together a strong force and go into battle against them. A small band of friends could become the nucleus of an army. He wanted to talk of this with Stephen and Karlé; and if Ellen could make enquiries as to their whereabouts and bring them to him that would be a beginning.

This might not be the difficult task it appeared to be at first because he was sure that news of his exploits had reached them. They would question his uncle's housekeeper, and as she knew very well that they were his good friends she might send them to him.

Of all this he could talk to Ellen, and with the passing of each day he was growing in strength and they both knew—while rejoicing in his return to health—that this spelt the end of their idyll. It gave a bitter-sweet flavor to their relationship. Ellen knew it could not last. Already her friends in the town were complaining that they saw little of her and asking why it was she stayed at home. It would not be possible to keep the secret much longer, the fact that they harbored a young man in their house. Ellen knew how to live in the present. She had been doing it all her life.

In due course she was able to bring Stephen and Karlé to him and how he rejoiced to see them! They talked together the four of them of the injustices of the English and how Selby still raved about the death of his son and swore to reward any who brought William Wallace to him dead or alive.

"So I am an outlaw," cried William, laughing.

"Do not joke about it," begged Ellen.

"What else is it but a joke?" he demanded.

"It was not a joke when they had you in Ayr jail," Stephen reminded him.

"They did not know that I was Wallace."

"Thank God for that," replied Ellen.

She brought ale and bread for them and they went on talking

of how they would sound out men and build an army. "That is what we need," cried William. "Arms and men!"

There was intense excitement in the little attic room of the cottage, which was approached through a trap door and an ideal place in which to hide a secret guest. There it was agreed that Stephen and Karlé should travel around the garrison town, being careful not to become involved in trouble, and to discover when convoys of supplies were being delivered as they were often.

"Our first plan," said William, "would be to waylay one of these. If we were successful we could capture many of the things we need. That would be a beginning."

"We need more men," said Stephen. "But it should not be difficult to find them. It seems that there are many Scotsmen now looking for a leader."

"Scout round," said Wallace. "Find a company of men but we must be sure that we can trust them. Better to have but a few loyal Scotsmen than an army and one traitor among us. We will capture one of the English convoys, and when that is successful another and another. That will set us up with arms and what we need for battle. The first should be easy for we shall take them unawares."

So they planned carefully.

He took his leave of Ellen.

"You will come back," she said.

"Aye," he answered. "I shall come back. Methinks I shall be in need of your special comfort often. Then—if it be possible—you will find me at your door."

He was strong again and he would never forget he owed his life to Ellen and her mother. They had rescued him from the foul midden and he shivered to contemplate what state he must have been in when they found him. They had nourished him, they had cosseted him and they had been good friends to him, and Ellen had been mistress as well. He owed them a great deal and he meant it when he said he would never forget his debt to them.

The Irishmen, Stephen and Karlé, had been energetic in their efforts and they found fifty who were ready to serve William Wallace, swearing that their dedicated desire was to drive the English from Scotland.

Moreover they had discovered that Captain Fenwick was to lead a convoy through Loudoun to Ayr and in this convoy were horses, food stuffs and arms which were being taken to Lord Percy, the Governor, at Ayr.

If they could capture this it would be a beginning, for with these goods in their possession they could begin to build up their army. If they were successful there would be such a shout about it that men would flock to join Wallace. They would see.

With great exultation Wallace assembled his men in the woods where they camped throughout the night. As dusk was falling he spoke to them. He talked of what the English had done to the Welsh and how they must all stand together to prevent the same humiliation falling on Scotland. They were aware of the arrogant English in the garrison towns. Their King, old Toom Tabard, chosen by Edward of England, was now in English hands, completely subservient to them. William's father and his brother had been killed by Captain Fenwick's company so this looked like a sign from heaven. Captain Fenwick was now being delivered into his hands—along with all the supplies and ammunition they needed to start their campaign.

They were with him to a man—loyal to Scotland, all of them. There was not one who was not ready and willing to give his life for that country.

It was early morning when the convoy appeared. Wallace watched its approach and noted that there were somewhere in the region of two hundred men guarding it. Two hundred against fifty! On Wallace's side, however, was the element of surprise which was always useful. He hoped none of his men quailed at the sight of those well-equipped soldiers on their splendid horses while they had only humble equipment and were on foot.

They emerged from the wood.

He heard Fenwick shout, "On Guard. 'Tis the outlaw."

The outlaw was Wallace and Fenwick was exultant. What glory for him to be able to capture the man and take him to Lord Percy!

Then he saw the men emerging from the wood, and though they were more than he had at first thought, they were a straggly band. What good would they be among trained soldiers?

At their head was one who was unmistakably Wallace—tall, distinguished, handsome, a leader in every way.

Wallace recognized Fenwick and made straight for him.

"Charge!" cried Fenwick and the horses galloped towards Wallace's men.

Wallace drove his spear through the body of a horseman. It broke and he snatched his sword from its scabbard. He turned towards Fenwick shouting: "Murderer! This is for my father!" Before Fenwick could lift his arm Wallace's sword pierced his heart and he fell from his horse. Great exhilaration filled William. His father was avenged. So should Scotland be. He was as one inspired. They said afterwards that Heaven had sent angels to protect the Scots. It was not easy to imagine how it could have happened otherwise.

Many of the Englishmen's horses lay writhing on the ground as the battle ensued. William, shouting encouragement to his followers, hacking right and left, felling the English as he went, miraculously escaped all harm, though sometimes narrowly. Before the battle was over a hundred English bodies lay on the Loudoun field.

Those who had been set to guard the convoys attempted to join in the fight and that gave the Scots the opportunity to seize the booty.

The English lost heart and those who remained, seeing the convoy lost and so many of their companions dead and wounded, seized what horses were left, their great object being to get away.

This was triumph indeed. The saddle horses were led into the wood, their burdens joyously examined.

"It is a sign from Heaven!" cried William. "This day we have begun to turn the English out of Scotland."

They dared not stay in the Loudoun woods for they knew there would be immediate retaliation. They must hide their booty and find headquarters where they could safeguard the spoils of their victory.

"It is of the utmost importance that we keep our secrets," William told them. "Depend upon it they will double their guards after this. And they will come looking for us and in particular myself. Remember though: This is a glorious beginning. We have seen that God is on our side. Let us thank Him now for this victory, and when we have done that we will take our booty to a safe place and I'll swear to you that after this loyal Scotsmen will come flocking to our banner."

They hid in woods during the day and travelled by night, and William decided that the forest was the best place for their headquarters. Now and then some of them went into the towns to listen to the talk, and they came back to report that everywhere the raid on the convoy was discussed and Wallace's name was on every lip.

"There is a glint in the eyes of Scotsmen when your name is mentioned," William was told.

"That is good, but we must beware of traitors. We can be sure the English will set their spies everywhere."

"Lord Percy is furious," was the report. "He has reprimanded the guards at Ayr prison for throwing what they thought was your dead body over the wall. He calls them idiots because first, they did not ascertain who you were and secondly, did not satisfy themselves that you were dead."

William was delighted; his head buzzed with plans.

"A beginning," he cried. "We are on the road."

During the next few weeks they made forays into the town; they attacked bands of Englishmen and took what they could from them. He was beginning to collect a store of ammunition. They had "won" as they called it many fine horses. They had arms of all description. Nor did they need to go hungry.

William did not wish them to stay in one place too long as he considered that dangerous and they moved around constantly, and he trusted his men—in particular Stephen and Karlé who became his closest friends and associates. That was not all. His uncles—and other members of his numerous family who were too old to join him—sent him money and goods for his cause. He was by no means merely the outlaw who could make himself a nuisance to the intruders; he was a name to be reckoned with.

"It may not be long," he told his men, "before we go into real battle."

Moving from forest to forest they came near to Ayr and he immediately thought of Ellen and his desire for her was so strong that he found it difficult to resist. There was no reason why he should not disguise himself and slip into the cottage, after dark. He could leave again before dawn.

He would go. He could not stop thinking of Ellen and until they had been together he would go on doing so. He persuaded himself that it would be folly to allow himself to be obsessed by her. The best thing was to see her and get the longing out of his system.

He must disguise himself and the idea came to him that he would go as a priest. No one would molest a priest and it was the last calling which would be connected with William Wallace. The idea amused him and he decided to put it into practice.

It turned out to be an unfortunate choice. For as he approached the house he was seen by one of Ellen's admirers. This man was coming to visit Ellen, but when he saw a priest going to the house he hung back and waited, not wanting to come face to face with the holy man who, he suspected, might have been going to remonstrate with Ellen on her way of life.

The priest knocked at the door. He was let in. Ellen would surely not keep him long. He would wait until the man came out.

Meanwhile Wallace was received with surprise by Ellen. Then he threw off his habit and she was in his arms and they were laughing at the efficaciousness of his disguise.

"And you came as a priest!" It seemed a great joke to them. "And such a one that I believed you to be of the church."

He told her that his longing to be with her had been so great that he had had to take the risk of coming to her.

She said she had hoped he would some day and whenever he came there would always be a welcome for him.

They went up to the attic where she and her mother had sheltered him all those weeks and they lay together on the truckle bed as they had in the old days.

He told her afterwards that he with his men were in the nearby forest and that they planned to be there for some days.

"So," she said, "it may well be that I shall have another visit from you, sir."

"That could well be," he replied.

"Perhaps tomorrow night?"

"Why should it not be?"

"I shall look for you."

"Are you still my true friend, Ellen?" he asked.

"Until we die," she answered.

So they made love again and again, but he was wary for

the first streak of light was in the sky. He did not want to be seen in or near the town of Ayr by daylight for, good though his disguise might be, there was a price on his head.

Meanwhile the man from the town waited outside Ellen's house for the priest to emerge. He wondered why he did not. A priest . . . to spend the night in the house of a light woman! It was unbelievable!

He had an impulse to knock at the door to discover what was happening but he decided not to. He would wait there until the priest came out and then he would follow him.

He was watching when the door opened and the priest came out. Ellen was with him—beautiful Ellen—with her hair streaming about her shoulders and a loose robe scarcely covering her nakedness. She and the priest embraced in a manner which left no doubt as to their relationship and then the priest lifted his long robes and ran.

He followed him to the edge of the forest. He saw him throw off the robe. There was something familiar about the man who emerged.

Could it be . . . Wallace!

What should he do? There was a price on Wallace's head. What riches, what glory for the man who delivered him into the hands of his enemies!

The night had not turned out as he had fancied it would. He had missed the charms of sweet Ellen. But who knew, perhaps there was a better way in which it could have been spent and this was that.

Ellen opened the door. Two guards stepped into the house. "What do you want?" she asked.

"We want you, mistress."

"What now?" she demanded, thinking they had come to take her by force. That she would fight against with all her might. She liked men; she enjoyed her pleasures with them; but she should never be taken by force if she could help it.

But she was mistaken. They were on another mission.

She was to go with them, they told her, because their masters had something to say to her.

She was taken to stand before Captain Heron and his aide, Butler. They surveyed her coldly with none of that admiration to which she was accustomed.

"You are on good terms with the traitor Wallace," said the Captain.

"Wallace?" she wrinkled her brows. "Who is he?"

"Come, mistress, that will not do. He is your lover. He slept in your bed last night. He came disguised as a priest. We know of this."

"You are mistaken."

One of the guards caught her arm and twisted it backwards. She cried out in pain. "How dare you," she began.

Her face was slapped.

That to Ellen, who had never had anything but the desiring hands of men laid on her, was a violent shock. She knew then that she was in serious trouble.

"Listen to me, woman," said the Captain, "we know that you are a friend of William Wallace. We know that he visits you. Do not deny it. If you hold anything back from us, it will go ill with you. Do you know what we do to women like you? I will tell you. We shall roll you up in a bale of hay and set fire to it."

"You could not," she stammered.

"Could we not? We shall see. Bring in the hay."

It was true. They had it ready. "It would be a waste of such pleasant flesh," said the Captain wryly. "Come, be sensible, girl. Wallace visited you in the guise of a priest last night. When does he come again?"

"He . . . will not come again."

"He came last night did he not?"

She did not speak and he signed for them to bring the hay.

"Yes . . . yes," she said quickly. "He came last night."

"And when does he come again?"

She was silent. They seized her and two of them threw the bale of hay at her feet.

"Tonight," she cried. "He comes tonight."

They released her.

"When he comes," the Captain said, "you will hold him there. Divest him of his clothes . . . That will be no difficult task, I am sure. Then when he is in your bed before you join him put a rush light in your window. It shall be our signal to come and take him."

She stammered, "I cannot do it . . ."

"You will do it," she was told. "And if you do not you

know what awaits you. Do your duty and we shall not forget
you. You will be rich. We shall not forget. There is a high
price on his head. It is time a woman like you had a husband
so that she did not have to rely on any pleasant-looking man
who comes her way. Deliver Wallace to us and Lord Percy
himself will want to thank you. He will find a man who will
marry you. A knight no less, and he shall be a man of your
choice. So you see, mistress, great good can come to you . . .
great good or cruel death. Remember it."

Ellen went thoughtfully back to her home. Marriage with a
goodly knight. A fortune. Never again to wander through the
town returning the glances which came her way . . . looking for
a handsome gentleman. A steady husband, a man who could
give her fine clothes . . . that for the betrayal of Wallace.

She knew what she had to do. They were afraid of him.
They wanted him bereft of his clothes so that they could take
him easily. So had Delilah betrayed Samson.

She waited for him. He came as he said he would. She
opened the door and there stood her priest.

"It was dangerous to come," she said.

"Would I not risk danger for a night with you? 'Tis worth
it, fair Ellen."

She led him to the bedchamber. Her heart was beating fast.
It would soon be over. She thought of him as he had been
when they brought him in from the midden. Her mother had
said: "He is William Wallace, the greatest man in Scotland";
and they had been proud of him. She had been proud of him.
Her mother was now sleeping in her room. She knew of course
that men visited her daughter. It was a way of life and it brought
them comforts. She had not told her mother that Wallace had
come last night. She would have done so, of course, but they
had taken her off to be questioned, and when she came back
she did not want to alarm her mother.

They went to her attic. It would all be so easy. She could
feign ignorance. But he would say, "Why do you put a light
in your window?" and she would answer, "Because I wish to
see you. I see so little of you. I want to feast my eyes on you
while I can."

Then soon they would come to take him . . .

She had loved him in her light and easy way as she had
loved many men, but never one quite like William Wallace.

She did not like to think of men being tortured. Men were not meant for that. Why could they not all live comfortably together? There was so much in life that was good.

He lay naked on her bed. Now was the time. Set the rush light in the window . . . and wait.

They could not be far off now. They were out there looking at her window waiting for the sign.

"I cannot do it," she cried suddenly. She sat on the bed and covered her face with her hands.

"What ails you, Ellen?" he asked.

"They are coming to take you. They have threatened to burn me in a bale of hay if I do not deliver you to them. I am afraid . . . but I cannot do it."

He was off the bed. "They are coming for me! When?"

"Now. There is no time. They are waiting for the signal."

In a second he had grasped the situation. He had the answer as she had known he would. "Strip off your clothes, Ellen," he said.

She did so and he put them on. They were too small of course but he covered their inadequacy with a big cloak as he had once done with a shawl at the spinning wheel. Then he set one of her hats on his head.

"They will kill me," she said.

"No, they will not. I am going to tie you to the bedpost. You must tell them that I had wind of the plot and that I made you strip and give me your clothes. I then put them on and tied you up. So that you could not give the signal. Now I will leave you. There is nothing to fear. I'll see you again before long."

He went out of the cottage. He ran shouting to the guards in a falsetto voice remarkably like that of Ellen.

Two of them came out. He pointed to the cottage. "He is in there. He is naked . . . Go in and take him."

The alarm was given. The two guards were not going alone. They knew Wallace. As speedily as they could they got a band of them together and stormed the cottage.

Ellen told them how she had been following their instructions when Wallace had suddenly seized her and tied her up. So well did she tell her story and so appealing did she look half dressed and in distress that they untied her and reassured her that no harm would come to her, before making off to catch the impudent fugitive. Before they were assembled he had reached his horse, untethered it and was galloping off to join his faithful band in the wood.

It was a warning. He could not go on chancing to luck to extract himself from such situations. It could quite easily have been the end. It would have been easy for Ellen to have put the light in the window and for them to come and take him.

If they had what would be happening to him now? It would be the end of his dream as it had come very near to being when they had thrust him into jail.

He must take care. He must not involve himself in these reckless situations.

Thank God, Ellen had been loyal to him at the end—but Heaven knew how near she had come to betraying him. The devils, to threaten her with burning—and it was a sentence they would have carried out, too.

He discussed the affair with Stephen and Karlé, who were horrified. There would be a bigger hue and cry after him than ever, so he must lie low for a while. They should leave this place at once and find another wood to shelter them.

He agreed and they left the woods with all speed and made their way towards Lanarkshire.

There he with his men remained in obscurity for some time, and the English deceived themselves into thinking that his near capture had subdued him to such an extent that his one desire was to keep out of their way. When no more convoys were robbed for a few weeks a rumor was circulated that he had been drowned while attempting to cross the Forth near Stirling for it was said if he had crossed by the bridge there he could not have failed to have been seen.

He liked to go into the town though, and found it difficult to stay away, and when they were encamped near Lanark he often went in disguised, sometimes as a pilgrim, sometimes as a farmer. He enjoyed sitting in the taverns and listening to the talk.

It was thus he heard of the unpopularity of Sheriff Heselrig who was as harsh a man as would be found throughout the country, he was told. King Edward should have been more careful of the men he sent to guard the garrison towns, for so many of them were such as to breed rebellion wherever they went.

"Tell me of this Heselrig," he said. "Tell me what he has done to make the townsfolk of Lanark hate him so much."

"Hush, be careful what you say," was the answer. "Speak in whispers."

He immediately lowered his voice and his informant went on. "There is a beautiful maiden—the heiress of Lamington—living here. She is renowned for her wealth as well as her beauty."

"Tell me more of her."

"The Sheriff persecutes her. She is a brave lassie and will not agree to his demands."

"And what does he demand?"

"Her hand for his son."

"What a good Scottish lassie to marry an Englishman!"

"Oh, aye, if she is rich enough."

"And she is very rich."

"Heiress to old Hew Bradfute. Hew died three years back and young Hew was to have inherited . . . and would have . . . had he lived."

"Young Hew . . . ?"

"The beauty's brother. He met his death one dark night . . . His body was found lying in an alley. A brawl, they said, but it is whispered . . ."

"Yes, please tell me what is whispered."

"Who are you? You ask too many questions."

"Just a man with a little land to farm who comes into the town now and then and likes a bit of chatter. Come, sir, tell me about young Hew and how you think he met his death."

"Oh, 'tis not for me to say, sir. It's just in the mind—that's all."

"Come tell me more."

"Well, 'tis whispered here that Sheriff Heselrig, wanting the Bradfute money, had the idea that if it belonged to the maiden, his son might marry her and so it would pass to his family. That weren't possible while young Hew lived for he was his father's right and natural heir."

"And how goes this matter?"

"She is a bold brave maid, is Marion Bradfute. She swears she'll have none of the Sheriff's son."

"I should like to see her.",

"Then you should go to the kirk one Sunday. She is always there."

The story of the brave Scots lassie and the importuning English Sheriff appealed to Wallace's imagination. He didn't trust that Sheriff. Sooner or later he would force his son on the lass.

The next Sunday he was in the church. He did not need to ask who was Marion Bradfute. It was obvious. She was richly gowned as became an heiress and indeed she was beautiful. He had never seen such a beautiful girl. Ellen, who had seemed so desirable, was common clay beside her.

She was aware of his scrutiny and blushed a little, but it was clear that he had made some impression on her.

The next Sunday he was in church again; he noticed that she whispered with her maid and he guessed they were talking of him. When they left the church he followed them at a discreet distance. They went through a gate, beyond which lay the fine mansion which had aroused the cupidity of the Sheriff. He knocked boldly on the gate.

It was opened by an old man who demanded his business and he replied that he required to see Mistress Bradfute on an urgent matter. Who was he? was the question. He answered he would tell that to Mistress Bradfute and he believed that she would then know him.

The old man shook his head and went away leaving William outside the gate. In a few moments the maid who had accompanied her mistress to the church came out. She did not seem greatly surprised to see him. They must have known that he had followed them.

She bade him enter and he followed her into the house.

In the hall with its vaulted roof and high table at one end of the dais, Marion Bradfute was waiting for him.

"Who are you?" she asked. "And why do you come here?"

He hesitated only briefly and said: "I am William Wallace."

Her eyes opened wide and he noticed how beautifully blue they were, set off by long dark lashes.

She smiled suddenly. "I think I knew," she said. "You are welcome. I should like to talk to you."

She looked about her. "Let us go to the solarium," she said. And she called to her maid to bring refreshments for them.

She led the way up a ladder-like staircase to the solarium, a sunny room as its name suggested because of the two big windows cut into a bay at either end. It was indeed a grand place such as he had rarely seen in Scotland.

She went to the window and sat down implying that he might sit beside her, which he did.

She said, "You know of me?"

"I know that you are Mistress Bradfute noted for your beauty."

"And my wealth," she answered. "I have come to be afraid of that."

"You are in some trouble, I know that too. I have chatted in taverns and learned what I could."

"What are you, the hero of Scotland, doing in taverns?"

"Biding my time when I can rise up and turn the English from our country."

"You come here in disguise."

"That is necessary, Mistress. There is a price on my head and you are unwise to let me into your house."

"In a way there is a price on mine. Sir William Wallace, I have long admired you along with thousands of Scots."

"I want more from Scots than admiration, Mistress. I want them to join my banner. When I have an army I promise you Scotland's humiliation will be over."

"You will subdue the English, I know it. I am proud to have spoken to you."

"I have never seen a girl as beautiful as you," he replied.

She smiled, well pleased. "It is my fortune the Sheriff wants for his son."

"I have heard that you resist him."

"Yes, but I fear him very much. I believe he killed my brother."

"I had heard this too."

"I wonder what ruse he will employ to trick me."

"You are surrounded by good servants?"

"Yes, they have been with my family for many years. They hate the English oppressors."

"Has he threatened you?"

"No. I have warded him off with crafty talk. I have not said I will not marry his son—but I am determined not to."

"I shall gather together a force and march into the town."

"Have you such a force?"

"I have followers . . . as yet not large enough. But the time will come when I have an army behind me."

She put out her hand; he took it and kissed it.

"How glad I am that you came. I feel less afraid already."

She had risen, implying that it was time he went. She did not wish the servants to gossip—even though she trusted them.

He saw that he must take his leave though he longed to stay.

"I will be back," he said. "May I come tomorrow? We will discuss this matter further and if you should need me urgently send a man you can trust to the Lanark woods. There he will find me."

He was amazed that he had trusted her so deeply. But afterwards he understood, for he could not stop thinking of her.

On the next day he called again and they discussed her affairs at length. He talked glowingly of his plans and recounted his past adventures.

She listened entranced. So these legends she had heard of William Wallace were true.

By the end of the week they were in love.

They walked together in the enclosed garden.

He said, "You know I love you."

She nodded.

"And you?" he asked.

"I love you," she answered.

"What bliss this is . . . to be together! I would we could be together always, but failing that we must make the most of what time there is together."

But she was no Ellen.

"If we were married you could not live as you do now," she reminded him.

Marriage! He had not thought of marriage. How could a man dedicated as he was, settle down to a normal married life with a wife and family?

He was silent and she said, "Ah, I see you do not want to marry me."

He said, "I would I could. But I am a man dedicated to a cause and it would be no good life for the woman who married me."

"Then," she replied firmly, "we must say goodbye, for

though I loved you truly I would never be your leman. If we cannot marry then that is the end for us. We cannot meet like this if our love is to be unfulfilled."

William was plunged into deepest melancholy. "Oh, my God," he cried, "if I had not vowed to drive the English from my country . . . how happy I should be to marry you. But I have vowed solemnly that I shall not rest until I have saved my country."

"I understand well," she said sadly. "Marriage is not for you, William Wallace, and as no other course will do for me, let us say goodbye. Let us make it short. There is no point in lingering."

"I shall never leave you to the Sheriff's son."

She laughed bitterly. "It is strange that he whom I hate should be so eager to marry me and he whom I love reject me for a cause. Goodbye, William."

"Nay," he cried. "It is not goodbye. I shall watch over you. If you are in need you have only to send for me. I am going to avenge your brother. I am going to capture Lanark and drive Sheriff Heselrig out of it. I will be back."

She shook her head in melancholy and he left her and galloped back to the woods.

He was wretched. He was melancholy. He had lost his interest in life.

Stephen and Karlé were worried about him. They begged him to tell them what was on his mind.

Accustomed as he was to letting them share his confidences he told them the whole story, how he had heard of Marion and had gone to the kirk to see her, had spoken to her and fallen in love with her.

"'Tis dangerous to adventure with women," Stephen reminded him. "Remember Ellen."

"Ah, I remember Ellen. Ellen was a wonderful woman. I could never regret my friendship with her."

"And now there is Marion Bradfute. You trifle with danger, William."

"I act as I must. Having heard of a beautiful woman in distress what could I have done? Her brother slain at the instigation of this villain Heselrig. I tell you this: I shall not rest until I have his blood."

"You have said that it is unwise to concern yourself with these small adventures. You have said you will stay in hiding until we can gather a force to work with us. That is coming to pass ... gradually. William Douglas has sent word that he is on his way to join us and he has a considerable force. Sir John Menteith has sent word that he will come to us. We have to be patient, William, and ere long we shall have a strong enough force to go against the English."

"This is no small adventure. I love Marion Bradfute."

"It is but a short time ago that you loved Ellen and most indiscreetly visited her and came within an inch of losing your life."

"Marion is not Ellen. She refuses to be my mistress. She wants marriage ... or nothing."

"How could you marry?"

"That is what I told her. I should be constantly leaving her."

"Perhaps," said Stephen, "she could be made to understand that."

The other two looked at him in amazement.

"Yes," he went on, "suppose William married this woman. It would solve her problem and his. The Sheriff's son then could not have her, and how could he complain because she already had a husband. She knows who William is. She will understand that he has a mission to perform. I am coming to the opinion that it might be good for William to have a wife. She would be a woman he could trust, as he could not trust some leman he might otherwise take up with."

William was wild with joy. Of course it was possible. She would understand that being who he was he could not settle down to a normal married life. It would not be for long. When Scotland was free then they could make plans together, raise a family and return to the quiet life.

They discussed it together and the more they did the more plausible it seemed.

The very next day William rode over to the Bradfute mansion and asked Marion to marry him.

By the end of that week they were married. A priest had been brought into the house and there in the solarium where they had talked together so recently, the ceremony was performed with only a few faithful servants as witnesses.

For several days he stayed in the mansion. He was a proud and happy husband. He had for a bride the most beautiful girl he had ever seen and she adored him. He was the great Wallace, already a hero. She told him that she wanted to join with him in the struggle, she wanted to do everything she could to help. She knew that there would be times when he would have to leave her. She would bear his absence with fortitude; she would do everything she could to help. She was growing as enthusiastic for the cause as he was. And she was proud of him. She was sure he was going to be the general whose name would go down in history as the man who had brought freedom to his country.

He was loath to leave her but he knew he must return to the woods and while he stayed in her house it was important that his presence should be kept as secret as possible. Who knew what would happen if Heselrig discovered that not only was William Wallace in their midst, but he had married the heiress he wanted for his son.

So he went back to the woods. He was delighted to find John Menteith was there with a few men. He was eager to hear all that was happening and said that he had sounded out friends of his and there would soon be an army large enough to make an attack possible.

Sheriff Heselrig came knocking at the gate and it was more than the gatekeeper's life was worth to refuse him entrance.

He went into the house calling to the servants to bring their mistress.

Marion came to him, her heart beating fast with fear and anger at the sight of this man. His smile was pleasant enough. He had so far stopped short of threats and attempted to win her by cajolery.

He was unsure of the people of the place. They were sly, they paid lip service to him but he fancied it would need very little to put them into revolt. If he forced Marion to marry his son that might be the very spark to set the blaze alight. He needed men and arms. That outlaw Wallace had played havoc with the convoys. He was not quite ready to force the girl. But he thought, By God I am getting near it.

He bowed to her and she returned his greeting coldly.

"You look in good health, Mistress Bradfute," he said.

"Thank you, sir, I find myself so."

"Such beauty and to live alone!"

"I live as I prefer to," she answered.

"You need a husband, Mistress. Many have remarked on it."

"Thank you, sir, but I know best my own needs."

"Oh come, Mistress, do not be coy. You know my son is mad for love of you."

She was silent.

"You will take him," he said.

She still did not speak.

He wanted to slap her face, to call his men, to drag her to the priest. He had gone to so much trouble to bring about the marriage he desired. All would be well if she, the silly girl, would but say yes.

"I shall send my son to call on you tomorrow," he said.

"I am not receiving tomorrow. I have other plans."

"The next day then."

"The same applies . . . and to every day when your son decides to call."

"You are uncivil, Mistress."

"I speak as I feel."

"You will change your mind. I have been over-lenient with you."

"I will choose my own husband."

There was something triumphant about her as she said those words and the Sheriff paused. There had been gossip . . . servants always tattled. He had not believed it . . . not of the virtuous Marion. It had been whispered that a man had been coming to the house. Someone had seen him. It must be one of the serving wenches taking a lover. God knows that was common enough.

And yet . . . there was a look about her which set the warning jangling in his mind.

Tomorrow. It should be tomorrow.

He bowed and took his leave. Now she was afraid. She had seen the purpose in his eyes. He was tired of waiting. He was going to do something desperate if she did not take action.

She did so without delay and sent one of her servants riding to the secret hiding place of her husband.

* * *

It was dusk when William rode into the town. This time he did not come in disguise.

There could be no doubt who he was, as he rode at the head of his troops. William Wallace, the hero of Scotland.

People ran into the streets. "Wallace is here," they cried. "He has come at last."

The sentinels saw him. They gave the alarm.

"Good people," cried William. "I come to release you from chains. No more slavery. Rally to my banner and we will drive the English out of Lanarkshire."

But the people were afraid. They knew what had happened to Scottish rebels before. It was death of a terrifying kind. It had been done to Davydd of Wales and it was now the recognized reward of treason. And to fight for Scotland was treason in the eyes of the English.

So they waited and watched and showed no allegiance to either side and if their hearts were with the Scots they made no attempt to join them.

Soon the streets were swarming with English soldiers— trained men, as Wallace's were not, and even faith and their belief in a righteous cause could not stand against such discipline and superior weapons.

It did not take the English long to beat back the Scots. Wallace refused to retreat and he was left with a small body of them and they were close to Marion's house. The others had fled back to the woods. Marion had opened her gates and stood watching, and when she saw the English bearing down on her husband and the few men who remained with him, she shouted to him, "Quick . . . Come in and I'll lock the gates."

It could save their lives.

Wallace saw that. He shouted to his men, "Do as she says." They were only too glad to obey. He followed and Marion hastily bolted the door.

They could break it down, but that would take time and by then the Scots would have had the opportunity to escape.

William embraced her. "You have saved us, my love," he cried, but she pushed him aside.

"There is only a little time. You must be gone. Come. I will show you a way through the garden where you can escape to the woods."

She was right of course. It could not be long before the English had broken down the gate and were swarming in.

They followed her across the grass. She opened a door in the wall and they were gone.

Now the English were battering at the door. She went into the house and up to the solarium. They could come now. William and his men were safely on their way to the woods.

She picked up a piece of needlework and tried to stitch but her hands were shaking. She was alert, listening for the sound of the English coming into the house.

She did not have to wait long. She heard the great shout as the gate stove in and this was followed by the clatter of feet in the courtyard.

Now they were in the house. She could hear their voices. It would be any moment now.

Someone was mounting the stairs. She guessed who it would be and she was right. Heselrig himself.

"Where is he?" he demanded. "Where is the traitor Wallace?"

She leaped to her feet and stood facing him. "Far out of your reach," she cried.

"You have him here."

"Search. You'll never find him."

"By God, you let him through your gate and barred it against us. That's treason."

"I do not see it as such, sir."

"But I do. I would run you through this moment if it were not that my son is to make you his bride."

"That he will never do."

"You fool. Do not anger me now. I could harm you. Be sensible. Marry my son and we will forget your conduct to-night."

"I shall never forget it as long as I live. I am proud of it."

"You are mad."

"Nay, I am not. Happy I am that this night I saved my husband's life."

"Your husband! You are saying..."

She did not care now. She was proud of Wallace, proud of herself. She wanted the whole world to know.

"You are speaking to Lady Wallace, Sheriff. Show due respect, I pray you."

He stared at her disbelievingly.

"You think I would take your son when there is Wallace? I have been his wife two weeks since. You have lost your fortune, Heselrig."

The stunning truth hit him like a sword thrust. He knew she was not lying. There had been gossip. A man had been visiting her. Wallace! The wanted man! And he had let him slip through his fingers. He had let *her* slip through his fingers.

It should not happen again.

He lunged towards her, his sword ready to thrust.

She looked at him in some surprise as the blade pierced her bodice. Then she was falling and her last thoughts were: "I died for William Wallace."

William was roused from his sleep. Karlé was telling him that there was a woman to see him. Karlé was looking distraught. It was trouble he knew.

The woman stood before him, her eyes wide with horror, her mouth twisted with grief. He recognized her as Marion's personal maid.

When she saw him she covered her face with her hands and wept silently.

"What is it?" cried William. "Pray tell me. Your mistress..."

The woman lowered her hands and stared blankly at him. "Dead, my lord."

"Dead!" He would not believe it. He could not. It was too much to bear.

"The men came in... after you had gone. Heselrig was at their head. He went to her room. She told him she was your wife... and he ran her through with his sword."

He could not speak. He could not move. He was too stunned by the grief which overwhelmed him. Reproach was uppermost. He should never have involved her in his affairs. He should have stayed to protect her.

That would have meant capture, said his common sense, and what good could you do to her if you were their prisoner?

But dead! Never to see her again. His wife of a few weeks.

Karlé was at his side. "'Tis grievous news," he said.

"It can't be true. It must be wrong."

There was silence, broken only by the twittering of the birds and the sudden gurgle of a stream as it trickled over the boulders.

"It is true," said Karlé. "We must accept it. Come with me. Talk to me. Let us see what can be done."

He watched the woman as she turned and went sorrowfully away.

"Marion is dead," said William blankly. "I shall never see her again."

"You will recover from your grief," said Karlé soothingly. "Remember there is the cause."

William turned on him angrily. "Do you think I shall ever forget her? My wife . . . Marion . . . She was so beautiful . . . she was all I ever wanted . . ."

"Remember what you want most is the freedom for Scotland."

"I want only her . . . safe and well in my arms."

"That is for today," replied Karlé. "But there is tomorrow. William, it was disastrous from the first. Something like this had to happen. You have chosen the dangerous life and you must live it."

He was silent for a few seconds. Then he turned to Karlé. "There is something left," he said. "Revenge. Yes, that is what I shall live for now. My sword shall not rest happy in its scabbard until I have had his blood. Vengeance," he cried in a voice of thunder. "Vengeance!"

He would not listen. They were a goodly company. They had failed before because they were so few. More had joined them. They were ready now to go into the town.

"Heselrig for me. No man must slay him. His blood is for me." He was living for that moment when he should run his sword through that body, when Heselrig should die.

He planned carefully. They must succeed. He would never have a moment's peace until he had avenged Marion's death. But both Stephen and Karlé had warned him, he must plan with care. This time they must succeed.

They would creep into the town by night. They would go to Heselrig's house. He would be in bed like as not—so much the better.

Wallace would divide his forces. But he with his own picked men should take Heselrig.

It was dark as they came into the town. There was no sign of activity. Only a few guards to give the warning but they were speedily despatched before they could utter a sound.

Into the streets they went. All was quiet. Everything had gone according to plan.

He was standing at Heselrig's door. He knocked on it imperiously. "Open . . . open on the King's business." He laughed exultantly. It was indeed King Edward's business for he was going to find himself a sheriff the less after this night.

The bolts were drawn. The startled face of one of the guards looked at him only briefly before he was felled to the ground.

Wallace started up the stairs shouting: "Sheriff. Come forth. It is an urgent matter."

Heselrig appeared at the top of the stairs, a robe hastily thrown about him.

"Who comes?" he asked in consternation.

Wallace was before him. "Death comes," he answered, and lifting his dagger plunged it into the Sheriff's heart.

For a moment Heselrig looked startled. Then he shouted, "Help me. Assassins . . ." as he fell to the floor the blood gushing from his mouth.

William bent over him and stabbed him several times.

"For Marion," he cried. "For my lost love."

There was a sound above him. He heard a voice.

"Father, what's wrong? Where are you?"

William stood up laughing inwardly. The son! The one who had aspired to become Marion's husband!

Let us have a look at this brave young fellow, he thought.

The young man appeared on the stairs. He looked at the body of his father and screamed.

William caught him by the arm and he saw the terror leap into the young man's eyes.

"What . . . ?" he stammered. "Who . . . ?"

"Wallace," answered William, "husband to Marion Bradfute. She was murdered by your father. He has paid the price and so shall you."

He lifted his dagger.

The lifeless bodies of the Sheriff and his son lay side by side on the stairs.

* * *

There were shouts in the town.

"Heselrig is dead! The tyrant has been slain. Wallace is here."

The people came running into the streets. Some had weapons which they had previously managed to conceal. Now was the time. The Sheriff could harm them no more and Wallace was here.

There was slaughter in the streets of Lanark that night and the English who had been taken by surprise were defeated. By the morning William Wallace had won his first town for Scotland. Those English who were not killed had fled. Wallace had come for revenge and he had won victory as well.

It was unhoped-for success.

They must make the most of it. He garrisoned the town for fear the English should return. The citizens were with him. They would fight with Wallace against the oppressor. Heselrig the tyrant was dead and could no longer harm them.

They rallied round William Wallace, calling him their savior, their deliverer.

It was a beginning. Wallace had killed Heselrig and taken Lanark. Throughout the country there was a call to arms. At last there was a hope of driving out the English. Even Wallace, in his wildest dreams, had not imagined such success.

This was just what he needed to take his mind off his misery; he could throw himself into the fight; it was magnificent. All over the country people talked of Wallace. He had become a legendary figure and it was said that the English shuddered at the mention of his name.

He was acclaimed as commander of the Scottish armies. He declared he was acting on behalf of the King John Baliol whom he called the prisoner of the English, and more and more flocked to his banner.

William Douglas joined him and they took Scone together. They overran the Lennox. Volunteers were joining the victorious army by the thousand.

Within the space of months the whole of Scotland was free and the Scots had even made forays over the Border into Westmorland and Cumberland.

This was the state of affairs when Edward returned from France, free of his commitments there, and married to the sister of the King of France.

He decided at once that he must subdue Scotland for ever.

Betrayal

Queen Marguerite was traveling north from Canterbury where she had paused to make offerings at the shrine of St. Thomas. She was pregnant and delighted with her state. It was an achievement to have conceived so early and she prayed to St. Thomas to give her a healthy boy and at the same time preserve her own life.

Edward was marching North. He had told her that he would like her to be near him as his first wife had always been; and she, who felt that she must try to be as much like that first and well-beloved wife, was eager not to fail in her duty.

If she could give him a son how delighted she would be. Even the sainted Eleanor had only left him one son among all those daughters, although she had had several who had lived for a while and then died.

Poor Edward, she knew that he suffered great anxieties. His son Edward was proving to be too wild for his father's comfort and that of the nation. There had been complaints about the life he led with his chosen companions and the King had confided in her that he dreaded to think of what might happen when he died and his son came to the throne.

He had said that he would like to spend more time with the

younger Edward. But there was always pressing business to engage his attention. He had had the trouble in France and now as soon as he was home it was to hear that this upstart William Wallace was making trouble in Scotland.

The matter was very serious and depressed him greatly. She thought how overjoyed he would be if she could send him news that they had a son.

She was greatly impressed by the grandeur of Canterbury and she listened intently to the Abbot who told her how St. Thomas had been done to death by the King's knights and the spot where it had happened had become a holy one. He told her how miracles had been performed there on the stones where the blood of the martyr had fallen and she had knelt and begged the saint to look down on her and give her a son.

From Canterbury she and her retinue travelled north and crossed the Humber into Yorkshire. She was making for Cawood Castle, a country seat belonging to the Archbishop of York, but because there had been some delays on the journey she realized that it would be unwise to go further, and they came to rest at a little village on the banks of the Wherfe called Brotherton.

It proved that she had been right to call a halt for she had not been there more than a few days when she began to feel her pains.

She took to her bed for it was clear that the child was about to be born.

There was great rejoicing when it was for it was the hoped-for boy.

"I shall call him Thomas," said the Queen, "for I know that it is to St. Thomas that I owe this great joy."

So the child was Thomas and a message was sent to the King to tell him that the Queen was safely delivered of a boy.

Edward received the news with joy. He was at York and ready to march on Scotland. Seven thousand horse and eighty thousand foot under his skilful generalship would soon put Wallace to flight.

It was a good omen, he said, that the child was a boy and healthy. It was Heaven's answer to his doubts whether he should have married again. Eleanor in Heaven was looking down on him with that bland understanding which she had shown him throughout their lives.

As soon as the Queen was well enough to travel he wanted her to take the child to Cawood Castle and there he would be able to see them before he set out for Scotland.

Marguerite quickly recovered from her confinement and was eager to set out, and in a few weeks was on her way to Cawood, that castle which was situated on the south bank of the Ouse which the archbishops of York had used as a residence as far back as the tenth century. Like most castles it had little comfort to offer but as this was high summer they suffered more from the smell of the privies than the cold.

Edward's visit was a hasty one for he had much on his mind. It was depressing to contemplate that after all his efforts Wallace should have managed to rally Scotland and challenge his supremacy.

He was delighted with the boy though and told Marguerite that nothing could have pleased him better and given him more heart for what lay ahead than the sight of her with their baby.

"My lord," she asked timidly, "I have said he shall be Thomas, but if it is your wish..."

"It is yours," he said fondly, "and therefore Thomas shall be his name. As for myself, I think at such a time it is well to honor the saint of Canterbury. I may need his help."

She was anxious at once. "But you are going to subdue the Scots with all speed."

"Subdue them, yes, but with speed who can say? This fellow Wallace has caught the imagination of the people. They have made a hero of him. It is never easy to conquer a national hero as one who is despised. Baliol was easy. A weak man. This Wallace is different. But never fear, by the time our next son is born I shall have subdued the Scots and taught them what it means to flout me."

Then he kissed her fondly and talked to her of his plans as he used to talk to Eleanor; and she listened attentively, so meekly and with such adoration that it might have been his first wife sitting there.

He joined his armies and marched across the Border. There was no resistance. But the Scots had laid waste to the countryside so there were no provisions. Good general that he was he had foreseen this and had ordered ships to sail up the Forth with what his army should need.

These were late in coming and he was fraught with anxiety. So many armies had been beaten through lack of supplies.

He took Edinburgh and waited there, and it was the end of July before the ships began to arrive.

There came also some of his spies who had roamed the country in the guise of beggars and pedlars. They had news for him. The Scots under Wallace were at Falkirk.

"We shall attack without delay," said Edward, and he led his army to Linlithgow Heath, there to await the moment to go into action.

It was evening when he rode round his camp making sure that all was well and to give heart to his men. It had always been so. He knew they looked to him. When they saw his tall figure on its horse some new strength came to them. They had the belief that in battle he was invincible. He knew that that belief must be upheld and with an enemy like Wallace who would have a similar effect on his men, it was more than ever important to maintain it.

These men would follow him wherever he went and if he told them that victory was possible, no matter what odds they faced, they would believe him.

He did not, however, believe he faced fearful odds now, for even though Wallace had built up an aura about himself, that could not stand against a corresponding aura of a King who had proved himself a great warrior for many years and led a well-disciplined army. The Scots must lack the training of Edward's men. They had beaten the troops of the garrison towns but that was not the English army. Wallace was a brave man. He respected Wallace. He understood Wallace. But if he captured him he would show no mercy. It was not good statesmanship to show mercy to the man who was responsible for driving him out of Scotland.

His son should be with him now. He was disappointed in Edward. He was showing himself to be unworthy of the crown. He had thought of this ever since he had held his young son Thomas in his arms. But a baby. It was years before *he* would grow to manhood. And in the meantime there was Edward. Edward had no desire to learn to be King; he preferred to frivol away his time with companions like himself. It had been a mistake to send Gaveston's boy to him. He was getting quite a hold on him, Edward was following him slavishly as though their roles were reversed. He heard bad reports from their guardians.

Edward, soon to be seventeen, was no longer a young boy. He was old enough to show some manhood. Oh yes, he was very worried about Edward. He could not talk to Marguerite about him. It would seem disloyal to Eleanor in some way, but perhaps Marguerite heard tales of her stepson's behavior. If she did she was too tactful to say so.

He must stop brooding on family affairs. There was a battle to think of.

Daybreak. The trumpets were sounding. The men were rising and there was that excitement throughout the camp which must precede a battle. The King's horse was frisky that morning. He was startled by the blare of the trumpets and seemed to resent the bustle and activity about him.

The King's groom was waiting when Edward came out.

There was a grim satisfaction about him. Today was the day when he would begin to bring an end to the legend of William Wallace.

He was about to leap into the saddle when the horse turned abruptly. Edward was thrown to the ground and the horse attempting to move off kicked the King in the ribs.

The pain shot through him and fear with it, for he had heard the crack of bone.

Oh God in Heaven, he thought, on such a day!

It would be considered an omen. They would go into battle telling themselves that God had turned against them. The stories they had heard of the invincible Wallace were true. They would go into battle . . . without the King . . . and Wallace would be triumphant.

Never, Edward told himself. He stood up a little shakily. He put his hand to his side. The pain made him wince. He guessed that his ribs were broken."

His groom said, "My lord, you are hurt."

"Nay," growled the King. "Say not so. 'Twas nothing. Bring back the horse. It was the trumpets that startled him."

The horse was brought. He patted its head. "Nothing to fear, my boy," he murmured. "Nothing to fear." And he was thinking. Oh God, how could You do this to me? First you favor this man Wallace and now you break my ribs just as I must lead my men into battle. But you'll not beat me. It'll need more than broken ribs to do that.

"Help me up," he said. The groom did so.

He sat there for a second and then rode forward.

"Ready!" he cried. "What are you waiting for?"

The Scottish cavalry turned and fled; the archers followed them, but the infantry stood firm. Edward was invincible; seated firmly in the saddle he gave no sign that his broken ribs were causing him to be in agony as he shouted his orders and his men could always see him in the forefront of the battle.

None could stand against him. The Scots were fierce in their patriotism; they believed Wallace could lead them to victory. But this was mighty Edward whose name had filled them with dread even as Wallace's had with pride.

He was there in person—the great King before whom Baliol had bowed, and young Bruce had not raised his hand. Only Wallace had stood against him. But even Wallace was no match for Edward Plantagenet.

It was bitter defeat for the Scots. Twenty thousand of them perished while few English lives were lost in exchange.

They had felt Edward's might and they remembered it from the past. He had conquered Wales and vowed to do the same to Scotland. Even Wallace was no match for him.

The bedraggled Scots fled back to their mountain stronghold and Edward rode on to Stirling.

The Scots had taken the precaution of laying the land waste, but the English decided to rest there for a while. It was necessary for the King to recover from his injury.

He first saw to the defenses of the castle and gave orders for his men to spy out what was happening in the land, attack where necessary and bring back what booty could be found.

Meanwhile he must retire to his bed, his physician in attendance. The neglected broken ribs must heal as quickly as was possible.

Fifteen days passed before he could sit a horse and the incident had aged him considerably, but his splendid vitality which was mental rather than physical was again with him. It was as though he defied fate to harm him while he had work to do.

He had subdued the land below the Forth; and he had no doubt that Wallace was re-forming his armies in the north; but Edward knew that if he advanced the problem of supplies would be acute, and he had no intention of making that error which a lesser general might have been tempted to do.

He marched through Clydesdale to Ayr, his intention being to go into Galloway, but again the spectre of the lack of equipment and food rose before him. He could not be sure that he could be successful. Moreover some of the lords were getting restive. The Earls of Hereford and Norfolk among them. Their men and horses were becoming exhausted; they needed a rest after such a campaign, they said; but the King suspected they were disappointed because they had received no Scottish land or castles as payment for their fidelity to their King. Edward would remember that; but at the same time disgruntled earls could be as much a hazard as lack of supplies. He must satisfy himself that he had crushed Wallace's rebellion, and it must be some time before the Scots could get together an army for their losses had been great.

He garrisoned the towns below the Forth and sent a deputation to certain Scottish lords ordering them to meet him. Wallace was not among them. They parleyed together and Edward promised them a temporary truce until Whitsuntide. This they eagerly accepted needing the time to reorganize. Edward needed time too.

He returned to London.

The Queen was pregnant again. This was promising. Like her predecessor she was fruitful.

Joanna, the Countess of Gloucester, and her husband, Ralph Monthermer, were at Court and the King's daughter and his young wife had something in common, for Joanna also was expecting a child.

There could not have been two women less alike than the gentle young Queen and flamboyant Joanna.

But the King had thought it would be good for them to be together at such a time, and of course even Joanna could not disobey a summons from the King. Besides Ralph wanted to be at Court. He was delighted because he had found favor with the King who had quite forgiven the pair their secret marriage and had bestowed the great favor on Ralph of allowing him to hunt in the royal forests and take away as much game as he chose. This was the greatest of favors for Edward was as devoted to the hunt as so many of his ancestors had been.

Ralph was very pleased with life. Great honors had come his way as husband of the Princess; the King liked him; and Joanna was as obsessed by him at this time as she had been when she had married him.

He was of course one of the handsomest men at Court, and Joanna had never for one moment regretted her hasty marriage. She disliked bearing children and was a little disgruntled at this time because she was expecting one in October and she said it was too soon after Mary.

It was irritating to have one's activities restricted and be expected to sit and talk of babies with the young Queen whom Joanna secretly thought very dull.

As for Marguerite she could talk of little else but the coming baby and the one she already had.

She hoped he would be a boy. She believed the King wanted boys so much, but of course he was so kind he would never show his disappointment if it were a girl.

"Of course he will not be disappointed if it is a girl," said Joanna. "My father loves his girls . . . better than he does his sons. He adored my sister Eleanor and he has been very lenient to me. On the other hand he is continually displeased with Edward."

"Edward I know gives him great cause for sorrow. Joanna, what do you think of Piers Gaveston?"

Joanna smiled secretly. "Very clever," she said.

Her sister Elizabeth was also at Court. She had lost her husband almost two years ago and had, after a suitable interval, come home to England. There had been rumors that the Earl of Holland had been poisoned; he had had so many enemies and as he had died of a dysentery—as so many people did— this could have been a possibility.

However, like all of Edward's daughters she had never wanted to leave England and was delighted to be back. She had confided to Joanna that when she married again it would be in England. "You did," she said. "I shall do the same."

"You may need a certain amount of cunning," replied Joanna.

"Then I shall come to you to help me."

Joanna laughed aloud and said her wits were at her sister's disposal.

Then they talked of their sister Margaret who had been less fortunate than they. From all accounts Margaret had a good deal to endure from Duke John of Brabant.

"He fills his palaces with his bastards," said Joanna. "I'd not endure that."

"It is easy to say you would not when you don't have to."

"Margaret was always too meek. If I were her I should ask our father to use his influence on her husband and make him stop his philanderings."

"Do you think he would?"

"At least he would have to philander in secret which could be undignified for a ruler. But Margaret has the bastards there and treats them with honor."

"She always had a gentle loving nature. And now she has a son, I daresay she is happy enough."

"It would not be enough for me. But our sister Margaret is like the Queen. *She* needs little to satisfy her. She has her young Thomas whom she believes to be the most perfect child ever born, and now there will be this new one. It would not surprise me if young Thomas went the way of our brothers John and Henry. He has a delicate look about him."

"Oh, do you think so?"

"Undoubtedly, and I don't like his French nurse."

"She seemed pleasant enough."

"I think that a Prince of the royal house should have an English nurse. We do not want French customs here."

"The Queen seems happy with her."

"Of course she is. They chatter away in French all the time. It makes her feel at home. But I don't think she is good for the child and he does look delicate."

It was clear, thought Elizabeth, that Joanna had taken a dislike to their half-brother's French nurse, but it was a fact, however, that young Thomas was showing a certain delicacy.

Joanna pointed it out often to Elizabeth. She was irritated by the Queen's fussing over her child. Joanna had little time for hers. Nurses were engaged for children, she said, and if they were good tried English ones all was usually well.

The King came to visit his family. A short respite, he thought, before he had to return to Scotland, which seemed to be in-

evitable at some time in the future. He could not expect peace
to reign much longer; in any case he was determined to subdue
Scotland as he had Wales.

Elizabeth thought he looked older and tired. She had heard
how he had broken his ribs and gone into battle, which was
characteristic of him of course, and although it might have won
a battle it had certainly not improved his health. Because he
was so vital he sometimes forgot how old he was.

Joanna, concerned with her own affairs, did not notice that
the King was looking tired and old.

She inquired of him how he found young Thomas. Did he
not think the child was pale and had he noticed his cough?

The King was horrified. He had noticed these things and
was trying to persuade himself that Thomas was suffering from
the ailments of childhood and would grow out of them. He
said so to Joanna.

"I believe the same thing was said about our brothers John
and Henry," persisted Joanna. "I know what is wrong with
Thomas. It is that French nurse. She coddles him too much;
she over-feeds him. She brings French customs into your Court."

"Do you really think it can be so?" murmured Edward.

"My lord, I am the mother of children."

She was, he thought, but it was said not a very good mother.
She left her children a great deal with their nurses—even more
so than was necessary—that she might be constantly in the
company of her husband.

It was true Eleanor had left the children to follow him into
battle and he had always thought her the best of mothers.
Marguerite might have to do the same if the Scottish war broke
out.

He watched the French nurse. Joanna had sown seeds of
doubt in his heart.

He spoke to Marguerite about it. "My dear," he said, "I do
not think the French nurse is the best for Thomas."

"Oh, but she loves him so."

"Perhaps that is why she over-indulges him."

"Do you wish me to speak to her . . . ?"

"No, my love. I will arrange for an English nurse. Joanna
knows the very one."

"But . . ."

He patted her hand. "The French nurse shall be sent back

to France. I shall reward her well so that she thinks happily of her stay in England."

Marguerite had difficulty in restraining her tears, but she managed to because she knew that Edward did not like them. She wanted to protest. Joanna has done this. But how could she make trouble between the King and his daughters!

What could she do but accept the decision? She was too much in awe of her husband to do otherwise and she did not want to offend Joanna.

By a strange coincidence when the new nurse came Thomas's health began to improve. Joanna was triumphant and commented continually on Master Thomas's rosy cheeks. "He has completely lost his cough," she said. And she reminded the King that she had brought about this happy state of affairs.

Poor Marguerite felt sad and lonely without the nurse, for it had been so comforting to talk of home sometimes.

Then the Court adjourned to Woodstock for it had turned very hot and the air was considered to be good there. On the fifth of August Marguerite gave birth there to another boy. She called this one Edmund.

Two months later on the fourth of October Joanna's son was born. He was named Thomas. Joanna was delighted that the irksome business was over and left Court to return to Gloucester.

The Princess Elizabeth was determined to follow the advice of her sister Joanna. She was so happy to be back in England and had confided in her sister that she was going to find a handsome husband and marry him before her father found some foreign Prince for her.

"You have always said that as we married once for state reasons, the second time we should choose for love."

"I have and always shall," affirmed Joanna.

"You have never regretted it."

"Never," declared Joanna; and Elizabeth thought that Ralph Monthermer must be a very unusual man to have won her wayward sister's affection so whole-heartedly.

Joanna was young and beautiful but there were times when Elizabeth felt that the flush in her cheeks was a little too bright and her beautiful eyes too brilliant. It was almost as though there was so much fire in Joanna that it was burning her up.

But Elizabeth was too concerned with her own affairs just
then to think over-much about her sister. She had found the
man she wanted to marry. He was Humphrey de Bohun, the
Earl of Hereford and Essex and High Constable of England.
He was also a very rich young man, witty and high-spirited.
As soon as Elizabeth saw him she wanted him.

The King was at first not inclined to agree to the marriage
for daughters should be good bargaining counters, but when
she reminded him that he had allowed Joanna her free choice
it was hard to resist. However, if he had retorted that Joanna
had married without his consent, that might be considered an
invitation for her to do the same. Events weighed heavily on
him. He suffered pain in his ribs for he had never fully recovered from that accident. His doctors said that he should not
have ridden into battle in that state and it was not surprising
that he still felt pain.

He was weary of the Scottish troubles which were far from
settled. He deplored the fact that he had been unable to complete
the conquest. He was never sure when Wallace would appear
again and drive the English out of the garrison towns. Then
his brief victory would have been in vain.

He was too old and tired to enter into conflict with his
daughters. He liked to see them happy. It was a marvel to him
that Joanna had made the perfect marriage from her point of
view. It was perhaps better for the Princesses to remain in
England particularly when, as they reminded him, they had
married once for state reasons.

Elizabeth was appealing and beautiful in love. He had his
good Queen Marguerite and was happy with her. He wanted
his daughters to be happy too. In fact he was glad that he had
failed to win the beautiful Blanche. She could not have suited
him as well as Marguerite did. His Queen was docile and
tender. Blanche would doubtless have been more demanding.
How could he, who had been so lucky in both his Queens,
deny his daughters their happiness?

It was a dull November day when the wedding of Elizabeth
and Humphrey de Bohun was celebrated at Westminster.

Elizabeth certainly looked radiant in her golden crown which
was set with rubies and emeralds, and there was great rejoicing
throughout the city. It was clearly a love match and the people

liked to think that their Princesses were not married out of the country.

Joanna and Elizabeth were now both happy; Margaret had her problems, but she was far from home and he believed growing older was now able to look after herself; poor Mary seemed contented in her convent with the consolation that she would not have to consider a period of penitence when she grew older as so many did; if she had missed a happy family life in England, at least she was sure of her place in heaven. Little Thomas was thriving—now he had an English nurse— and young Edmund was doing well. He had a fine family . . . with one exception.

Yes, it was true. That very one who should have given him most pleasure was the one who caused him the most anxiety. His son Edward.

He often said to himself: "Pray God I do not die just yet. God help England if my son were the King."

He had a duty to live, to conquer Scotland, to make England great and to keep young Edward from the throne until he was more mature, more fitted to rule.

Edward was no longer a boy; he was getting on for twenty years of age. A man indeed. Yet how frivolous he was. Rarely had so much talent been wasted, for Edward was by no means unintelligent. He was tall and handsome and had ability. Alas, he was lazy and frivolous and liked to indulge in rough practical jokes which sometimes caused distress to those about him. There had been complaints and these disturbed the King because they were well-founded.

He often thought of the baby he had presented to the Welsh. What a bonny child he had been and how he and Eleanor had gloried in him! But something had gone wrong somewhere. Had Eleanor accompanied her husband on his travels when she should have been giving attention to their children? Had he failed in some way?

He was sorry now that he had given him Piers Gaveston as a playfellow. He had only wanted to honor Gaveston's boy. Gaveston had been a good and loyal knight of Gascony who had served his King well and so, when he had died leaving a young son, Edward had taken him into the royal nurseries and he had been brought up there.

Edward and young Gaveston had become fast friends. They

were inseparable and Edward seemed to care for him more than he did anyone else.

It was not a relationship the King liked to see. He must do something about it.

Young Edward must accompany him when he went to Scotland.

The time had come to make war on Scotland. The King was feeling his age. He was advancing into his sixties and would not admit that he more quickly became exhausted as he never had in the old days.

He was obsessed by his dream of uniting England, Scotland and Wales, and the desire had become fraught with a feverish determination because time was running out.

There was little opposition in the south and he marched through Edinburgh and Perth and as far north as Aberdeen. In Moray the lairds submitted to him and the only town which did not fall easily into his hands was Sterling. As usual the nightmare of the campaign was the fear of running out of supplies—one which must always affect a commander when his army was far from home.

He was going to make a treaty with Scotland and for this purpose he summoned all the lords to St. Andrews but there was one with whom he would not make terms. That man was William Wallace.

Edward had thought a great deal about Wallace. He knew that he was in hiding somewhere. He believed he understood the man well for he was not unlike himself. Wallace was tenacious, a patriot of the first order. Wallace would never make terms and while he lived he was a danger.

He wanted Wallace delivered to him. He wanted to see Wallace in chains. He would never rest until he had Wallace's head on a pike over London Bridge as he had had Llewellyn's and Davydd's. That was the way to subdue a people. Kill their leaders and humiliate them. And what could be more detrimental to a hero than to have his head severed from his body and placed where all could jeer at it?

He had made it very clear that there would be no truce with Wallace. With that man it must be unconditional surrender. He had hinted that he would make it well worth while for one of Wallace's associates to deliver their leader into his hands.

* * *

Wallace had become a spectre which haunted Edward's dreams. Wallace was in hiding somewhere and the mountains of Scotland provided a secure refuge. It was not easy to hunt a man down there. At any moment Wallace would rise and there was evidently a fire in the man, an aura of heroism and leadership which inspired men. Edward wanted inspired men on his side not on the enemy's.

He knew what it meant to men to follow a leader. He himself was an example of that. Would he have won his battle if he had not got on to his horse, ignoring his broken ribs and ridden at the head of his men? He was sure the battle would have been lost if he had given way to the advice of his attendants and called his doctors. Soldiers were superstitious; they looked for omens. Listening to the legend of his ancestor, William the Conqueror, he knew what store that great man had set on superstition. He had never let it work against him, and even when it appeared to he would find some way of assuring those about him that it was in truth a good omen they were witnessing and he would twist the argument to make it so. Victory must be in men's minds if they were going to conquer.

He could subdue Scotland and soon; but not while William Wallace lived.

There were many Scots who were not entirely loyal to the Scottish cause. Some had worked with him if they had thought it would be to their advantage. The Scots would know the hide-outs in the mountains better than he did. Some might even know the whereabouts of Wallace.

He sought in his mind for the man he felt best fitted to the task and after a great deal of thought the name of Sir John Menteith came into his mind.

Menteith was an ambitious man who had been a prisoner in England briefly. Edward had released him on condition that he follow him to France and serve with him against the French. When Menteith had returned to Scotland he had joined Wallace and harried the English. He was a man who found little difficulty in changing sides and he liked to be on that of the winners. Edward despised such men but it would have been foolish not to admit that they had their uses.

It had come to Edward's ears that Wallace was in the Dumbarton area and it was almost certain that he had a mistress there. Women had played a certain part in Wallace's career. He had nearly been captured once at the house of a prostitute; and then the affair at Lanark had come about because the Sheriff Heselrig had killed another of his women.

Perhaps it would be better to seek him through a woman.

When he was in St. Andrews he summoned Menteith and taking him into a private chamber sounded him on the matter of Wallace.

"My Lord Menteith," he said, "I have thought much of that traitor William Wallace and it is my desire to bring him to justice. You know that he is one with whom I will make no terms. I want him . . . dead or alive."

"My lord King," replied Menteith, "Wallace is as slippery as an eel. It would not be easy to apprehend him."

"Nay. If it were we should have done so long ere this. But the man is a fugitive, hiding in the mountains, awaiting the moment when he may strike me in the back. It was hinted to me that he is in hiding somewhere in the Dumbarton area. I believe he does not like to stay too long away from the towns for he is rather fond of women. Would you say that, Menteith?"

"I believe, my lord, that there have been some romantic adventures in his life."

"Then depend upon it, he will not want to cut himself away from the society of that sex. I believe there was an occasion when he was almost caught visiting a leman."

"That was so, my lord."

"I am ready to bestow the post of Sheriff of Dumbarton on one whom I would consider worthy to hold it . . . It is a fine town, Dumbarton, a fine castle."

How Menteith's eyes sparkled! He is my man, thought the King.

"Of course, if the rebel was in an area it would be the duty of one soon to be its Sheriff to deliver him to me."

Menteith nodded. "But a hard task, lord King."

"Hard tasks are meant for those worthy to hold high office. Once they have proved themselves honors come their way."

"My lord, you fill me with the desire to serve you well."

"Forget not, Menteith, that that is your duty."

"I shall not forget my duty, sire."

"Nor the rewards of duty. If you bring me Wallace I shall be grateful to you. But I want him . . . and I want him soon.

While he lives in hiding we can never be sure when and where he will rise with fools to follow him."

Monteith bowed and retired, his head full of plans.

The idea came to him suddenly when he thought of what the King had said. Through a woman, yes. There must be a woman in Wallace's life. It was almost certain that he would come into Dumbarton or some such place at dead of night to visit some woman.

Then he remembered Jack Short, one of his servants, so called because of his small stature—a wiry man with darting ferret eyes. Menteith had employed him now and then for some unsavory task. The man had few scruples and he and his brother—now dead—would do anything if the reward was good enough. Jack Short was a man who knew what was going on. He made it his business to. He could be plausible; he had an oily tongue and oddly enough numerous people could not see through his falseness.

There was one person for whom Jack Short had really cared. That was his brother—another so like himself that the two were often mistaken for each other. The brother had been killed in an affray and his killer had been William Wallace. Jack Short hated William Wallace.

Therefore he was an excellent choice.

Menteith summoned him and explained what he wanted. "Jack," he said, "if I can deliver Wallace to Edward I shall be rewarded and so will those who help me. I believe you could be of service to me in this matter and that would bring great good to you—apart from giving you the satisfaction of revenge."

"He killed my brother," said Jack Short, his eyes glowing in his usually cold face. "He was close to me when he died. Wallace lifted his sword and cut off my brother's head. I was too late to get to him but by God if . . ."

"This is your opportunity. Let us decide how we shall set about this. Vengeance, and reward for it. A good combination, eh Jack?"

William Wallace was in fact living in a disused hut in the mountains close to Glasgow. With him were a few of his friends, Karlé and Stephen, those two faithful stalwarts, among them. Wallace always said that he would rather have twenty men he could trust than a thousand whom he couldn't.

He was saddened by the way things had gone. Edward had changed everything. He might have known that Edward was a formidable enemy. He could have conquered the others: he had succeeded until Edward had arrived, with his armies and his military skills. Edward was a legend. So was Wallace. They were two strong men coming face to face, but Edward was the King of a great country and he had the arms, the men—everything that Wallace had so sadly lacked.

But he would not despair.

One day, he promised himself, he would conquer Edward.

In the meantime there was nothing to do but wait and plan with his good friends. They would talk together of gathering an army again, of marching against Edward. They would learn the lessons of defeat for there were more to be discovered in them than in victory.

Sometimes he was impatient. Then Karlé would soothe him. Karlé, Stephen! What good friends they were and always had been!

But he was in hiding. He hated having to skulk into Glasgow at night; he wanted to disguise himself and go by day. But it was dangerous. He went at night to the house of a woman. She was pretty enough and generous, and although she did not know him as Wallace sometimes he thought she suspected him of being that great warrior.

One night, as he lay with his friends round the fire they had lighted in the hut, they talked of what one of them had heard that day in Glasgow—that Edward was at St. Andrews and many of the Scottish lords were swearing fealty to him. That made Wallace furious. That Scotsmen should so far forget their country as to bow to Edward!

And as they sat there one of the guards came in with a small draggled figure wrapped in a ragged cloak.

"I found him prowling nearby," said the guard. "So I brought him to you for he said he knew you and wanted to offer himself."

"You know me, man," said Wallace. "Come near the fire and let me look at you. By what name are you known?"

"As Jack Short," said the man. "I knew you once, Sir William."

Wallace said, "I remember I never saw men so short as you . . . and was there not a brother?"

"Ay, a brother. You killed him, sir."

"I killed him? Then he was an enemy of Scotland."

"Not so, Sir William. He was a fool of a man, my brother. He wanted to fight for Scotland though. He was there at one of the forays and lost his way in the battle. You believe him to be on their side. 'Twas not so, I swear."

"Why do you come here?"

"I have searched for you, far and wide. I wanted to tell you that my brother was no traitor. I want to make you understand that, sir."

"I killed your brother. Then if he was no traitor you must hate me for that."

"No, sir. He was soft in the head, my brother. You would never have killed him . . . if you had known. He wanted to serve Scotland and he did . . . but his brain was addled and he did not know which way to turn. He wouldn't be sure who was the enemy. So I come to tell you, he was no traitor and to serve you with my life."

William said, "Do you fancy yourself as a fighter then?"

"Nay. I am short as my brother but my brain is not addled as his, poor boy, was. I cannot fight . . . though I might be of some use on a battlefield. But I can fish and cook over a fire and help a gentleman to dress."

"We all look after ourselves here, Jack Short."

"But 'twill be easier for you to give your mind to greater matters, sir, if I do things for you. I was fishing this afternoon and I have good fish with me. Let me cook it for you and you shall taste my skills."

William was amused. "Why not? We should like a tasty meal, eh Karlé."

Karlé was thoughtful. He was too apprehensive about everything, thought William. He looked for danger in every pool and tree.

"Come! The fish, Jack Short, and you shall stay with me and be my servant. How like you that?"

Jack Short knelt and kissed William's hand.

He was good. There was no question of that. Life was easier

with him. He had a talent for catching and cooking fish. He would go into the town and come with provisions they needed.

"It saves our taking risks," even Karlé admitted.

One day Jack Short said to William, "My lord you should never go into Glasgow. Your leman should come to you."

He knew of course why William made his nocturnal visits. Jack Short could be trusted to know everything.

"What," cried William, "would you have us all betrayed?"

"God forbid that that should ever come to pass. I would but make it easier for my lord."

"You do make life easier for me, Jack," said William. "I am sorry for what I did to your brother."

"'Twas his fault. No . . . not his fault . . . his folly. Forget it, my lord. For I have found joy in serving you."

Jack would lie at his master's feet and talk about what news he picked up in Glasgow. He told of the women he saw there. "There is one," he said, "fair of hair and rosy of cheek with sparkling blue eyes and a ready tongue. I noted her specially."

He watched his master. He knew by Sir William's smile that she was the one. He had discovered where she lived. If he could but follow Wallace there one night that would be good but he had to take care, for Karlé was a most suspicious man.

What he had to find out now was when Wallace was visiting the woman and he did not always say. Jack Short asked his questions slyly, obliquely. But he had to find the exact time. There must be no mistake. If anything went wrong and he was betrayed as the spy he was, Menteith would kill him, even if Wallace's men did not, and he would never enjoy that reward which had been promised him.

He went fishing and was late coming in with the catch. The fire was slow in burning.

"Hurry man," said Wallace, "I am going to the town this night."

Jack's heart beat fast. Serve them with fish . . . then take one of the horses and gallop into town. He knew what he had to do, Menteith and his men had been waiting in the town ready for the day.

He slipped away, leading the horse at first lest they should hear him.

In the town Menteith was glad to see him.

"Tonight," cried Jack Short. "He is coming tonight."

Menteith said: "To the woman's? We will take him as he comes in."

Karlé had a sixth sense where his master was concerned.

"I like not these trips in the town," he said.

"I like them," answered William.

"Can you not do without women?"

"No, Karlé. They revive me. They lighten this dreary exile."

"They have been your downfall before."

"Never. I escaped narrowly from Ellen's house I know. And Marion . . . It was because of her that we took Lanark, remember."

"Have a care."

"It's safe enough."

"Don't go tonight."

"I must. I have said I will. She will be waiting."

"Perhaps she can find another friend."

"Tonight is my night. She is faithful to me when I am there."

Karlé laughed and said, "Then I shall come with you."

This was not unusual. Often when he visited the woman Karlé would come. He would sit below and talk to the servant, and usually drink some of her home-brewed ale and perhaps eat a piece of bread and bacon.

So they rode towards town, leaving their horses tethered in the woods. Quietly and swiftly they went to the woman's house.

The door was open but they did not see anything strange in this. William presumed that expecting him she had left it ajar.

He pushed it open. They were surrounded. Karlé reached for his dagger but he was too late. He fell bleeding to the floor. Wallace was seized. They did not want to kill him.

Edward wanted him alive.

It was the complete humiliation to ride in the midst of Menteith's men, his hands shackled—a prisoner.

Jack Short had betrayed them. He had been deceived by that simple ruse. He had always been careless. But the biggest traitor of all was Menteith. He should not rave against Jack Short who was of little account. Menteith was the criminal. He had betrayed Scotland. That was what was important. And Karlé—beloved Karlé—had died because he had insisted on coming with him.

He himself was the prisoner of mighty Edward, who would never let him go.

He fears me, thought Wallace exultantly. He fears me as he fears no other. He knows that he can never be safe in Scotland while I live.

So they brought him to London and he was lodged in a house in Fenchurch Street.

They did not leave him there long and soon there came the day when he was taken to Westminster Hall to answer the charges brought against him.

His trial was brief. He was judged a traitor to King Edward.

"I have never been that," he said, "for I have never acknowledged him as my lord."

He made a brave show. His strength, his vitality, his aura of greatness must impress all who saw him. But he was Edward's prisoner and Edward was determined that he should never again raise an army against him.

There came the day of his sentence. His crimes were enumerated. Sedition, homicide, depredations, fires and felonies. He had attacked the King's officers and slain Sir William Heselrig, Sheriff of Lanark. He had invaded the King's territories of Cumberland and Westmorland.

"Your sentence is that you shall be carried from Westminster to the Tower and from the Tower to Aldgate and so through the City to the Elms at Smithfield, and for your homicides and felonies in England and Scotland you shall be hanged and drawn and as an outlaw beheaded, and afterwards your heart, liver and lungs shall be burned and your head placed on London Bridge in sight of land and water travellers, and your quarters hung on gibbets at Newcastle, Berwick, Stirling and Perth to the terror of all those who pass by."

William listened almost impassively. It was the death accorded traitors to the King and the King would say, "This man was to me one of the greatest traitors who ever lived."

Edward would say he was just and in his own lights doubtless he was.

On the twenty-third day of August the barbarous sentence was carried out with revolting cruelty. Many gathered at the Elms in Smithfield to see it.

No cry escaped from William Wallace. He knew he was not defeated. He knew his fame would live on after him and be an inspiration to all those who cared for the freedom of Scotland.

The Death of
the King

Wallace was dead. None should guess how relieved Edward was. Because a traitor had met his just deserts there should be little said. Edward feared the spirit of Wallace for he knew the Scots would continue to sing of him; he would still be their hero. But he was dead and one did not fear the dead—however death glorified them—as one feared the living.

He would arrange for a tournament. There should be rejoicing. They would have a feast of the Round Table and the great chivalry of the land would be present. Any of those who might remember the gory sight they had witnessed at Smithfield would forget it as they joined the merry party at Westminster.

True the head of the hero looked down on them. But all must know that he was a traitor. In Scotland it would be different. He wondered what people thought in Newcastle, Berwick, Stirling and Perth where parts of the once great Wallace were shown.

But he would not think of it. There was reason for rejoicing. Marguerite was pregnant again. He thanked God for his Queen.

315

She was always so gentle, so sympathetic, so understanding. Last year her beautiful sister, that Blanche on whom he had set his heart, had died and he had commanded that prayers be said in Canterbury for her soul, because she was the sister of his dearly loved consort. How glad he was that fate had been kind and given him Marguerite. He might have been mourning for his Queen now if he had married Blanche.

The tournament delighted all who took part in it and in the following May Marguerite gave birth to another child.

This time it was a girl, and Edward declared himself delighted. They had their two boys and now he wanted a girl, and his dear kind obliging Marguerite had given her to him.

"I have a boon to ask," he said as he sat by her bedside. "Will you grant it, little Queen?"

"It is granted before it is asked," she answered.

"It might not please you."

"If it pleases you, my lord, I am sure it will please me."

How docile she was! How eager to make him happy! Oh happy day which had sent him Marguerite!

He said: "Should you mind if we called this child Eleanor?"

She hesitated and he thought, Ah, I have asked too much.

Then she said, "Would it not sadden you to remember . . . ?"

He took her hand and kissed it. "How could I be sad when I have the best woman in the world?"

A quick prayer to Eleanor. He had not meant it to slight her, only to comfort his living Queen. He would have prayers said for Eleanor's soul and flowers laid at the foot of all the crosses.

He said, "I loved well three, all Eleanors . . . my mother, my daughter and my queen. God took them all but he sent me my Marguerite who has given me nothing but joy since I first saw her face."

That was enough for Marguerite.

Little Eleanor was baptized in the royal chapel of Winchester for the Court was there at this time. After the christening the baby, lying in her state cradle covered with ermine and a counterpane of gold, was shown to the nobles.

Edward was delighted with her. Dearly he loved his daughters. They all enchanted him. His little sons were adorable but in his heart it was the girls he loved best.

That set him thinking of his eldest son. He wondered how he and Eleanor could have had such a boy.

That brought back the nagging thought that very soon he would have to do something about Edward.

In the solarium in her manor of Clare in Gloucester Joanna was sitting with her women while one of her minstrels played for her amusement. She seemed deep in thought as he strummed on his lute and sang those songs which were special favorites of his mistress—usually of love and passion.

As she watched the boy desultorily she was wondering how he had fared at her brother's court whither she had sent him to play some of the newest lays. Edward had liked them and so had his great friend Piers Gaveston. In fact, Gaveston only had to like something and Edward was sure to like it too. He was rather foolish about that young man and Gaveston knew it. He was continually asking favors and being indulged.

The King did not like it and had spoken to her about it. Young Edward simply did not care. He himself would be King one day and Gaveston was constantly reminding him of it.

She shrugged her shoulders. Edward would be very different from his father. She was sure he would not want always to be riding off on these boring wars. Why could not a man be allowed to enjoy life? Why must they always be thinking of this conquest and that?

It was due to her father's war that Ralph was away at this time. She was resentful, thinking of her handsome husband far away in the north, possibly in Scotland. Edward had said that if he was given the glories of knighthood he must honor them. She would join him, for she could not bear to be so long away from him. It was not right that they should be apart. She would be with him now but he had left in such haste on the King's business and she had been rather surprised during the last few days by the lethargy which seemed to have come over her. She wanted to be with Ralph, God knew, but the thought of the journey appalled her. That was strange, for previously she had thought nothing of journeys. She would have gone to the Holy Land with her husband—as women had before—if the need had arisen. Yet for the last few days this tiredness had beset her.

Perhaps she was growing old at last. She was thirty-five.

She was no longer very young. She had been reminded of that last year when her eldest daughter Eleanor had been married to Hugh le Despenser. Eleanor was only thirteen years old it was true, but to have a marriageable daughter made her feel she was really getting old.

It was a sweet song the minstrel was singing. It took her back over the years. She had first heard it when she had been Gilbert's wife. She was smiling. How enamored he had been of her, that old man! There had been nothing he would not do for her, and how glad she had been when he had gone and there was Ralph . . .

"We shall marry," she murmured. "I care not what my father should say . . ."

She was back in the past . . . the excitement of those days . . . her determination to defy the King . . . the first moments of passion with the man she had wanted so fiercely . . . Blissful, invigorating, stimulating, entrancing . . . all she had ever dreamed of.

"Ralph," she whispered. "You should be here now . . . You should have defied him . . . refused to leave me . . ."

One of the women leaned towards her. "You spoke, my lady?"

She did not hear. She did not see the woman. She had slipped forward in her chair, for the scene about her had faded suddenly and she was descending into darkness.

"My lady is ill," said the attendant, looking fearfully at the minstrels.

They dropped their lutes and ran to her. They lifted her head and looked into her strangely remote face.

One of the minstrels said in an awed voice, "My lady is dead."

The King could not believe it. He was sick with grief. Joanna, his beautiful daughter . . . dead! But she was so full of life, the most lively of all his daughters. One never thought of death with Joanna.

He was so old; she was so young. His own daughter. And she had died as her sister Eleanor had died. They were too young to die. Some of the children had died and their deaths had not been unexpected. They had ailed from birth. But Joanna . . .

He was tired and weary and very, very sad.

He must write to the Bishop of London and tell him that his daughter Joanna had departed to God. There must be private masses and orisons for the soul of his daughter. He felt that Joanna would need some intercession in Heaven, for he suspected that she was scarcely free from sin. Nor had she been given the time to repent before she was taken.

He sent letters to every prelate in the kingdom.

"Pray, pray," he commanded, "pray for my daughter Joanna."

He roused himself from his grief. He felt sick and ill. He kept thinking how unnatural it was that Joanna should be dead and he live on.

It could not be long, could it, before he was called?

He looked into the future. Scotland was yet to be won. Who would have thought it would take so long? But Wallace was dead now. Could he complete the conquest before he died? And if he did could young Edward hold it? Oh God, why did You give me such a son? You gave me good daughters and my son . . . my eldest son—the only one of Eleanor's to live—is unfit to wear the crown.

He must speak with him. He must imbue in him a sense of duty. Unworthy kings were a danger to themselves and the nation. Remember, oh remember my grandfather John. What misery he brought to England . . . and himself! And my father—my beloved father—he had not the gifts that make a king!

He himself had them. It would be false to deny it. He had conquered Wales; he had done as well as was possible in France. He would not be afraid to stand beside his ancestors. Great William, Henry the First and Second. No, he would be counted with them.

Death haunted him. Who could say when it would come. It came unexpectedly to some, to his dear daughter Joanna for instance; and to an old man such as himself the call was overdue.

He sent for Edward.

The boy stood before him. Boy! He was a man. It was twenty-two years ago that he had been born in Caernarvon and he had had such bright hopes for him. He was handsome—and very like his father in his youth—the same long limbs, the same flaxen hair, the upright carriage. But what was it he lacked? That virility which had been his father's, that essential masculinity. There was an almost feminine quality about Edward. It shocked his father deeply. Men would not respect him; they would not follow him into battle.

Where to begin? How to explain kingship to such a creature. He had told him often of the need to please his subjects, that he must be just yet stern. He himself had been harsh at times. He had inflicted severe punishment on those who had offended him. Necessary, he had always told himself. A King must be respected through fear.

Young Edward looked elegant. The King wondered whether his clothes had been designed by Piers Gaveston. His long loose coat was of deep blue caught at the neck with a magnificent sapphire brooch. His long wide sleeves trailed gracefully and his shoes had a longer peak than was normally worn. His beautiful fair hair was held back by fillets of gold set with more sapphires.

"Pretty as a girl!" thought the King distastefully.

"Edward," he said, "I would have speech with you. Joanna's death has shocked me deeply."

"As it has us all." The Prince spoke with feeling. Joanna had been his favorite sister and she had been inclined to laugh at his exploits as he had at hers.

"Death comes swiftly in some cases and lingers in others. But in due course it will come to us all. I want you to be ready, Edward."

He began to talk of the need to keep the Welsh under control. They could never feel really safe there. They must always be sure that their defenses were intact.

Scotland was of course the main concern.

"But Wallace is dead now," said the Prince. "He can never worry us again."

"Wallace lives on in the people's memories. They are making songs about him now. He has become a legend. Beware of legends. I shall soon be leaving for the north. I must safeguard what I have won. I don't trust the Scots. Those who have sworn fealty could turn against us."

A slim white hand adorned with jewels touched the Prince's lips as he stifled a yawn. He had heard it all before. When the old man had gone there would not be all this preoccupation with the Scots. Piers and he talked about it often. When the old man was gone . . .

The voice droned on. The need to do this and that. The Prince was not listening and when the King paused he said: "I have a request to make to you, my lord."

The King opened his eyes wider. "What request is this?"

"Ever since you put Piers Gaveston in the household we have become close friends."

"I know that well and perhaps the friendship has become too firm."

"You have always said that one cannot have too many friends, my lord."

"If they are good and loyal one cannot of course."

"Piers *is* good and loyal. He lives for me, Father. All he thinks of is my comfort. I want to reward him."

"He has his reward. He has royal patronage. He has lived in the royal household. What more could a man ask?"

"I should like to show my appreciation and there is one thing he greatly desires. I have promised I will do my best to get it for him."

"And what is this?"

"Ponthieu."

"Ponthieu! What do you mean? Piers Gaveston wants Ponthieu!"

"I have promised him that I will get it for him. Dear Father do not disappoint me."

"Disappoint you! I tell you this, I know little but disappointment from *you*. Ponthieu! Your mother's inheritance to go to this . . . this . . . adventurer!"

"My lord, pray do not talk of Piers in this way."

"I will remind you, sir, that I will speak of my subjects as I will. No! No! No! Gaveston shall never have Ponthieu while I live. And let me tell you this, I like not this man. I have heard that he has a strong and growing hold over you. That it is spoken of in whispers and disgraces our royal name. No, sir. Go and tell him No! And that I regard his pretentions as insolent. He had better take care. As for you, you will leave with me for Scotland, and that will be very soon, I promise you. I am going to take you away from your fancy companions. I am going to make a *man* of you."

The Prince was pale with fear and anger, but he knew his father's rage—though rare—could be terrible. He knew too that he must take his leave before the full fury of the King burst upon him.

When he had gone Edward sank into his chair. He felt sick with rage and apprehension.

What can I do with him? he asked himself. Why did he grow up like this. *My* son ... and Eleanor's. Everything I gave him. The best tutors ... the best governors! He has been schooled in war. If he were foolish and without talent it would be understandable. But he is not. He could have been clever. He could have been a worthy king ...

And now ...

Action was needed.

Piers Gaveston should be banished without delay. That friendship must be severed; and he would get an undertaking from the adventurer—and from the Prince—that they should never meet again without his consent.

Edward was marching up to Scotland accompanied by a sullen Prince. Gaveston had been banished and the Prince was telling himself that he would never forgive his father for robbing him of the one he loved best in the world. There was one comfort for the Prince. The old man was looking more sick every day. He could not last much longer. He was not in a fit state to come marching north. Why couldn't he leave these matters to his generals.

The King was too preoccupied to notice his son's depression.

A new danger had risen in Scotland.

Robert the Bruce, the grandson of the claimant, Earl of Carrick, who for some years had been on terms of friendship with Edward, had left the English Court and gone to Scotland. He had at one time been one of Edward's partisans and Edward had quickly become aware of the man's talents.

Now he was in Scotland and for what purpose Edward had guessed. He had often wondered what would happen to Scotland when his son was King and he had believed that many of the Scots who feigned friendship with England now, would turn when a strong king was replaced by a weak one.

So Bruce was in Scotland. What did it mean? He was soon to learn. Bruce had gone to Scone where he had been crowned King of Scotland by the Bishop of St. Andrews.

It was clear to Edward that Bruce had been waiting for his death believing that it would be easier to defeat Edward the Son than Edward the Father, which was, he feared, a wise conclusion. He had, however, decided to wait no longer.

Bruce would have seen Wallace's head rotting on London Bridge. "By God," said Edward. "I'm not dead yet and before I go I'll have that traitor's head beside Wallace's."

He did not like these heroes. Wallace had been one. He believed Bruce would be another.

"Oh God, give me strength," he prayed. "Let me finish this task before I go."

But God did not listen. Each day he grew weaker. He hated to admit it, but riding exhausted him and when he could only travel four miles a day he had to stop pretending and to accept the litter which those about him advised him to use.

They came to rest at Burgh-on-Sands and all knew—and even the King must agree—that he could go no farther.

He ordered that he should have a room from which he could see the Solway Firth. He knew he would never leave this bed. He would die in England in sight of that water which separated England from Scotland.

The news would reach the Scots that he was on his death bed. That would fill them with rejoicing. Edward would be glad too. Oh, God preserve England with my son Edward as her King.

His dear Queen would mourn him; so would his daughters. There were some who loved him.

But he must think of the future. There was little time left. He had seen the sun rise but it might well be that he would not see it set.

He sent for his son. His sight was failing a little. The priest should come to him; but he had his duty first.

"Edward, my son . . ."

"Father."

He saw him through a haze—handsome, tall. Such a fine King he could have made. Where did we go wrong? Edward asked himself. Where, oh where?

"Edward," he said, "take care of your little half-brothers and sister."

"I will, Father."

"When I am gone I want you to send a party of knights to

the Holy Land. There is much wrong I have done in my life . . ."
His voice trailed off. He thought he was looking up at London
Bridge and seeing Wallace's head . . . or was it Llewellyn's or
Davydd's. He had been harsh in battle. He had slaughtered
many. He had commanded that his enemies be hung drawn
and quartered as Wallace had been. An example to others, he
had said. Others had been tied to the tails of horses and dragged
to the gallows. The deaths of brave men had made spectacles
for the people. He had had a cage built for the Countess of
Buchan, who had worked against him and had the ill fortune
to be captured, and condemned her to remain there like a wild
beast until he gave the order for her release which he had never
given.

These things he remembered as he lay on his bed. They
were enemies of England and he had lived for England. But
he must send those knights to the Holy Land to please God,
that He might forgive him his sins.

"My heart shall be taken from my body and the knights
must carry it with them."

"Yes, Father," said Edward dutifully. "It shall be done."

"Pursue the Scottish war, Edward. Carry on where I have
left off. God sees fit to take me before I have finished my task.
He has left it to you. Take my bones with you into battle.
Always carry them before the army when it marches. I shall
be there. The Scots will know that my bones are with my army
and that will strike terror in their hearts."

"It shall be done," said Edward.

He was thinking, A few days and I shall be King. Piers,
my Gaveston, my first act will be to bring you to me.

As though reading his thoughts the King said, "Never recall
Gaveston without the consent of the nation."

Edward did not answer. One must not make promises to a
dying man.

The King did not notice. The light was fading fast.

He was murmuring something. Edward bent close to listen.

"Let my bones be placed in a hammock . . . carry them before
the army . . . Let the Scots know I am there . . . and I will lead
my army to victory."

That night the end came. Edward the First was dead and
the reign of the second Edward had begun.

BIBLIOGRAPHY

Aubrey, William Hickman Smith	*National and Domestic History of England*
Barlow, F.	*The Feudal Kingdom of England*
Bryant, Arthur	*The Medieval Foundation*
Carrick, John D.	*Life of William Wallace of Elderslie*
Costain, Thomas B.	*The Pageant of England 1272–1377 The Three Edwards*
Davis, H. W. C.	*England Under the Angevins*
Green, Mary Anne Everett	*Lives of the Princesses of England from the Norman Conquest*
Guizot, M., translated by Robert Black	*History of France*
Hume, David	*History of England from the Invasion of Julius Caesar to the Revolution*
Jenks, Edward	*Edward Plantagenet*
Johnstone, Hilda	*Edward of Caernarvon*

Norgate, Kate	*England under the Angevin Kings*
Paterson, James	*Wallace, the Hero of Scotland*
Powicke, Sir Maurice	*The Thirteenth Century, 1216–1307*
Seely, R. B.	*The Life and Reign of Edward I*
Stenton, D. M.	*English Society in the Middle Ages*
Stephen, Sir Leslie and Lee, Sir Sidney	*The Dictionary of National Biography*
Stones, E. L. G.	*Edward I*
Strickland, Agnes	*Lives of the Queens of England*
Tout, Professor T. F.	*Edward the First*
Wade, John	*British History*